JOSÉ LATOUR

José Latour was born in Havana, Cuba, where he won his first literary prize at the age of thirteen. *Outcast* is his seventh novel, and his first written in English. He has travelled extensively in the United States, Eastern and Western Europe, Canada and Mexico, and he is the vice-president of the Latin American division of the International Association of Crime Writers.

He has two sons and a daughter, and lives with his wife and family in Havana.

Outcast

— ✦ —

JOSÉ LATOUR

HarperCollins*Publishers*

This novel is entirely a work of fiction.
The names, characters and incidents portrayed
in it are the work of the author's imagination.
Any resemblance to actual persons, living
or dead, events or localities
is entirely coincidental.

HarperCollins*Publishers*
77–85 Fulham Palace Road,
Hammersmith, London W6 8JB

The Collins Crime website address is:
www.**fire**and**water**.com/crime

First published by Akashic Books, New York 1999

This edition published by Collins Crime 2001
1 3 5 7 9 8 6 4 2

A catalogue record for this book
is available from the British Library

ISBN 0 00 711160 6

Set in Perpetua by
Rowland Phototypesetting Ltd,
Bury St Edmunds, Suffolk

Printed and bound in Great Britain by
Clays Ltd, St Ives plc

To Alex, Alain and Désirée

Part One

1

Elliot Steil sat on a backless bench in the shady public park, rested his left ankle over his right knee, slipped off a well-worn tasseled loafer, and began massaging his foot. A couple of minutes later, he gave the same treatment to his right foot, then finally placed both heels on the cement walkway and wiggled his toes as he held the marble slab on which he sat.

Trying day, Steil reflected. His coffee and sugar reserves had simultaneously given out two days before, and breakfast had consisted of forty grams of stale white bread washed down with a glass of cold water. A few minutes later he found his bike's rear tire punctured. He spent seventy-five minutes waiting for a bus, and at 10.02 a.m. punched his card at the Polytechnic Institute where he taught English, two hours and two minutes late.

Lunch was a meager, poorly seasoned mixture of rice and insufficiently cooked red beans escorted by overripe tomatoes. The teacher had left the building at 5.00 p.m. pondering if he should walk home or waste some more of his free time on the almost nonexistent Havana public transportation system. The scheduled 8.00 to 11.00 p.m. blackout and pending household chores led him to cover the eight kilometers on foot.

When riding the bus or his bicycle, Steil frequently forgot about the problematic metatarsal bones he had inherited from some unknown ancestor. The orthopedic corrections made for the regular shoes he bought at stores became ineffectual after a forty- or fifty-minute walk.

Steil sighed and lifted his gaze from the walkway. Two approaching teenagers cut short their exchange of buzzwords to glance at him, then looked at each other, smiling broadly.

The lanky, blond boy in dirty high-top sneakers and oversized shorts, carrying a basketball under his arm, suddenly raised his head and pressed his nostrils closed with his fingers.

'Whaddaya know? Shoulda brought my gas mask,' quipped the taller, light-skinned black kid as they passed Steil.

Both youngsters bent over in a series of hiccups and moans, meant to be laughter. Six or seven steps further on, their merriment subsided, and they slapped each other's palms – first at shoulder, then thigh level – before returning to their conversation.

Steil didn't resent the comment; in fact, he smiled in amusement, certain that his feet were odorless. After twenty years of high school teaching, he had grown used to teenagers' ways. What troubled him was the regressive Spanish that kids were speaking. How could they effectively learn a second language when they mispronounced and clipped their mother tongue? Every school year the number of students who spoke an appropriate Spanish dwindled; the ones who did were almost exclusively girls. Boys with above-average writing and communication skills swept everything under the mat to avoid being ridiculed unmercifully by their male peers.

The lanky, blond boy dribbled the ball proficiently with his left hand, talking to his companion as they sauntered away. Steil put his loafers back on and resumed his long walk.

One hour later, just after rounding the corner of his block, Steil was spotted and surrounded by kids excitedly babbling something about a gleaming new car and a tourist. Knowing that pain and exhaustion made him lose his temper, he patiently tried to extricate himself from the gang. But the children kept blocking his way, jumping and yelling that the *americano* had given them chewing gum. Steil stopped dead in his tracks and glared at them angrily, imposing silence.

'Okay, Lemar. What's the matter?'

'An *americano* is looking for you. He came in that car,' the boy said, pointing straight ahead. 'He gave us chewing gum.'

4

For a moment Steil was too surprised to react and kept his gaze fixed on the nine-year-old undisputed group leader. 'Fine, thanks a lot. Now get back to whatever you were doing.'

Steil turned and peered at the pearl-gray Toyota Corolla parked at the curb, right in front of his apartment building. It had tourist plates, and behind the steering wheel sat a dim figure. Moving tiredly, the teacher approached the driver's seat, placed his left hand on top of the car, and stooped over. A man in his late sixties looked up, his bushy eyebrows rising for an instant and his lips parting in surprise.

'Looking for someone?' Steil asked.

'Thank God,' the driver said. 'Nobody seems to understand English around here, except for "gimme". Yes, I'm looking for Elliot Steil.'

'That's me.'

Now the blue eyes glinted with excitement. The stranger tilted his head to the side and smiled fleetingly before getting out of the car and extending his hand. The door clicked shut on its own.

'Dan Gastler,' he said. 'Glad to make your acquaintance.'

'Pleased to meet you. Er . . . is there anything I can do for you?'

'The other way around.'

'Pardon?'

'I've been retained to do something for you. Can we talk in private?' His accent sounded familiar to Steil. Georgia maybe?

'Oh . . . sure, sure. This way, please. Just a minute. Roll up the window and lock the car.'

Steil's apartment building had been erected in 1924, and the old red bricks showed where plaster had fallen away. The small Otis elevator was out of order, so the two men took the neglected stairway to the third floor. Steil led the way through the right side of a U-shaped hallway and past three front doors, before inserting a key into the cylinder lock of apartment 314.

The teacher hastily retrieved a soiled shirt draped over an old green armchair, picked up a kerosene lamp with a blackened glass-chimney that stood on a coffee table, and kicked a slipper under another, matching armchair. After switching on a sixty-watt bulb, he deposited the lantern on the kitchenette's drain board and threw the garment into a dark bedroom where disorder reigned. Steil closed the main door, opened a window overlooking the street, and motioned Gastler to a couch.

'Please, sit down, Mr Gastler.'

'Call me Dan.'

'Okay, Dan. Would you . . . ? Can I get you a glass of water?'

'Water will be fine,' Gastler said before plopping down. He wore a tan sport shirt, which matched the color of his baggy khaki pants and deck shoes.

An embarrassed Steil opened his antediluvian Hotpoint refrigerator and poured water into two discarded Classic Coke cans. There were no glasses for sale in Havana stores, and the cans were a present from some bimbo who had accidentally broken his last water tumbler almost a year before.

Poorly hiding his amazement, Gastler accepted the container and sipped from it, while Steil stared at the visitor from his armchair: sandy-colored sparse hair, ruddy complexion, a heavy-set build, a couple of inches under six feet. Their eyes met briefly, and the teacher shifted his gaze, then gurgled his water.

Gastler emptied his can and placed it on the coffee table. He pulled a wallet from his back pocket and produced a Florida driver's license, a credit card, and a business card. 'Check my credentials,' he said, smiling broadly and extending them to Steil.

For the first time in his life, the teacher held a credit card and a foreign driving permit in his hands. Both were issued to a Daniel E. Gastler. The business card said 'Licensed Private Investigator' under the name. Steil nodded in confusion, handing back the IDs.

'I've been told Cubans have some sort of identity card,' Gastler said.

'We do, yeah.'

'Can I see yours?'

From the patch pocket of his light-green, short-sleeved shirt, Steil removed a slim blue notebook and handed it to Gastler. The visitor put on a pair of rimless bifocals, peered attentively at Steil's photograph, and flipped several pages before returning the document. Then he heaved a sigh of relief. Removing his glasses, he leaned back on the couch.

'Elliot, I've got some good news and some bad news.'

'Bad first,' Steil said expectantly.

'Your father died on May 14.'

The teacher leaned back in his seat and stared at the visitor. But he was no longer seeing him. In his mind, a jovial face appeared, towering above him. His small hand was lost in the huge warm one that guided him along a forest trail. He always remembered his father either that day in the Everglades, or reading the *Havana Post* on a rocking chair in their Santa Cruz del Norte home, or teaching him how to throw a forward pass in Sebastian. There were many other memories, but one of those three usually popped up first on his mental screen. Steil felt nostalgia, some self-pity, and a little sadness.

'Hadn't seen him for the last . . . thirty-four years,' he said, shifting his gaze to the floor.

Gastler remained silent.

'How did he die?'

'Lung cancer.'

Steil frowned. 'Did he smoke?'

'Never lit one in his whole life.'

The teacher forced a smile, shook his head, and looked sideways for an instant. Then he stood, entered the kitchenette, opened a cupboard, and returned to the living room brandishing a plain white bottle with no label.

'Would you like a shot of bootlegged rum, Dan? It's called Train Spark.'

'Train Spark? Why?'

'Beats me.'

'Okay.'

Steil poured a small amount in Gastler's can and a stiff one for himself.

Gastler downed his ration. 'For Chrissake!' he gasped.

The teacher swallowed his own without batting an eye.

Gastler cleared his throat. 'We were friends, Bob and I. Last March doctors told him his condition was terminal, and a couple of weeks later he came to my office and we had a pretty long conversation. Mostly about you.'

Steil clicked his tongue and refreshed his drink. Gastler seemed to consider pressing on with his story, but decided against it. The teacher drank.

'What's the good news?' he asked.

Gastler parted his lips. He took a deep breath, thought over what he was about to say, then smiled disarmingly. 'I'll tell you over supper at a restaurant of your choice.'

Steil watched him fixedly and bit his lower lip, pondering the invitation. He hadn't dined out for the last four, perhaps five years. But he was exhausted. He recalled the scant and unappetizing menu he had planned for the evening, stealing a glance at his watch.

'All right. I'll take a shower and change. Meanwhile, Cuban airwave piracy presents Crossfire, live from Washington.'

The teacher turned on a black-and-white, twenty-four-inch Russian TV set and operated one of two dials protruding from a plastic box over the set. To Gastler's surprise, within a few seconds he was watching Pat Buchanan.

'I can't believe this,' the American said.

Steil chuckled and went into the bedroom. Five minutes later, while the teacher showered and Kinsley prodded an arms expert on the Korean nuclear crisis, the electric power was cut. Taken by surprise, Gastler was wondering what was wrong when he heard the Cuban holler from the shower.

'Sit tight, Dan. It's an emergency blackout. Should've started at eight.'

'Okay. No problem.'

The visitor heard angry shouts in Spanish coming from nearby apartments. Several pops followed, and Gastler correctly identified them as glass bottles smashing on the street. He shifted his gaze to a tall bookcase crammed with paperbacks written in English. A minute later Steil emerged from the bathroom, barefoot, a towel wrapped around his waist.

'Each city district has a blackout timetable,' he explained as he moved into the kitchenette and fumbled for a matchbox. 'Sometimes they are brought forward, or there are unannounced emergency blackouts. People get really angry.'

Steil found the matchbox and struck a match. Its tip fell off. The same thing happened with the next two. In a spurt of anger, the teacher let out a cascade of Cuban profanities, and the fourth match burst into flame. He lifted the glass-chimney of the kerosene lamp, lit the wick, and reinserted the glass, then moved the contraption to the coffee table.

'Did you hear bottles crashing on the street?'

'Yeah.'

'That's the newest form of protest.'

'Seems kind of foolish to me,' Gastler scoffed. 'They'll never hit those really to blame for the power cuts.'

'Guess you're right,' Steil admitted. 'I'll get dressed.'

'Take the lamp with you. I don't need it to sit here.'

Shortly after 8.00 p.m., Steil emerged from the bedroom in his Sunday best: a tan linen guayabera, maroon slacks, and brown moccasins. He placed the lamp on the coffee table and closed the window. Dressed up, freshly shaved, and with his hair properly combed, the teacher looked five or six years younger than his forty-four.

'I'm ready,' Steil announced.

'Okay, let's go,' Gastler declared, slapping the palms of his hands on his thighs and standing up. 'Blow out the lamp.'

At that moment, as if by enchantment, the wick sputtered and the flame died. The last drop of Steil's kerosene reserve was exhausted.

*　　*　　*

The Floridita Bar and Restaurant had been renovated in 1991, but since the Cuban government's new financial guidelines decreed that patrons had to pay in freely convertible currencies – meaning US dollars – Steil was no longer able to visit what for many years had been his favorite watering hole. By its sheer contrast to his usual surroundings, this place seemed opulent to Steil, rather than merely nice. Red velvet curtains, pure white table linen, silver-plated cutlery, uniformed waiters, and a maître d' in a dinner jacket were unusual sights for the average Cuban diner. Only three tables were occupied when Gastler ordered drinks.

They sipped two daiquiris each, making small talk. Gastler authenticated his credentials by recalling two of Steil's childhood adventures. The first was a 1956 trip to Silver Springs, when the boy had gaped at fish and divers through the underwater portholes of a semisubmersed boat. Another was a fall he took in Santa Cruz del Norte, while learning to skate. On both occasions he had been alone with his father.

Silence prevailed during the crab soup, shrimp salad, and lobster Thermidor. A bottle of Chilean white wine was emptied. After coffee, Gastler asked for the check, glanced at it, and handed a hundred-dollar bill to the waiter. The American suggested a nightcap at the cocktail lounge, so Steil guided him to his favorite section, the bar's left corner, close to an Ernest Hemingway bust. They perched themselves on stools, agreed on Wild Turkey straight, and Gastler added a beer chaser for himself. Steil glanced reverently at the mural depicting the port of Havana in the eighteenth century. It was flanked by two beautiful bronze lamps over neatly aligned rows of glassware.

'So much for the embargo,' the American said, pointing to the well-stocked eight-door refrigerator, which displayed several brands of US-manufactured liquors and cigarettes.

'The main problem isn't the embargo; it's money,' Steil pointed out. He was quoting from Susana Vila, a divorced economist he had been dating on a more or less permanent basis for the past four years. 'If the government had enough money, it could buy whatever it needs in neighboring countries, paying a surcharge. Or just paying the regular world market price. México could sell Cuba all the oil we need to end the blackouts. But the government doesn't have the dough to pay for it.'

'That's what I figured.'

'Listen, Dan, the cliché "burning with curiosity" fits me snugly right now. How did you find me? You have a message to deliver? Is there something my father wanted me to do for him?'

Gastler nodded and rested his forearms on the well-polished mahogany bartop, interlacing his fingers. He looked straight ahead as he spoke: 'It appears to me you two shared this . . . combustible quality. You're burning with curiosity; Bob was burning with remorse when we talked.'

Steil laughed softly. 'Whaddaya know.'

'In fact, he anticipated you'd be pissed off, consider him a scum bag, a motherfucker.'

'Motherfucker he was,' Steil said bitterly.

Gastler remained silent for a few moments, sliding his forefinger along the rim of his shot glass.

'Is your mother alive?'

Steil shook his head. 'She died ten years ago. Brain hemorrhage. Had a history of severe hypertension.'

The American sipped his liquor. 'Probably his whole attitude changed when he learned he'd die soon. He wanted to make it up to you, but he wasn't rich. All he had in the bank was . . .'

'Just a minute, will you?' snapped Steil, losing his careful professorial enunciation as he swung left to face Gastler. 'You gonna tell me he wanted to buy forgiveness?'

'All he wanted was to get you out of this fucking mess.'

The full implication of Gastler's words left the teacher dumbfounded. He had toyed with the idea of leaving his country, especially in the last few years of economic collapse, but a mixture of pride, fear, and love prevented him from taking any steps in that direction. Pride kept him from ferreting out his runaway father to request an affidavit to apply for an immigrant visa at Havana's US Interests Section. His fear was double-edged. Steil mildly disliked all kinds of ships and boats, and wouldn't even consider surreptitiously crossing the Florida Straits on an insecure raft. The alternative entailed filing a Cuban emigration form, openly taking a stand with serious political repercussions. He would be labeled a disaffected non-person, fired from his teaching position, and possibly harassed by some ultra-revolutionary neighbors. He was a respected member of the community, and many of his former students, now young university graduates, Army officers, mid-level managers, or just plain blue-collar workers, greeted him kindly in the streets and volunteered their good offices whenever he needed them. Having concluded many years before that Cuban would-be immigrants to the US and other Western democracies were helpless pawns in a political chess game, Steil estimated a fifty-fifty chance of being approved, and he feared losing his modest social status. To further complicate the issue, he loved the beautiful, suffering island where he had been born. Immigrants were sold a one-way ticket, and he wasn't sure he could endure living abroad for the rest of his life.

Without uttering a single word, Steil returned to his previous position. Was this a once-in-a-lifetime break? He emptied his glass and motioned to the bartender. The only other customers in the dimly lit lounge were a Cuban hustler and her client, probably a Mexican, cooing quietly at the opposite end of the bar. The barman served generous refills and returned to his glass-polishing out of earshot.

'His last wife cleaned him out,' Gastler explained. 'His pension wasn't big, and all he had in the bank was fifteen grand. He paid in advance for his funeral and deposited nine thousand in my bank account to rent a yacht, cruise down here, find you, and get you out, if you want.'

'You're willing to risk several years in prison for nine thousand bucks?'

Looking at the bartop, Gastler smiled. 'The nine thousand will barely cover expenses, Elliot.'

'Then . . . I don't get it.'

'Your father saved my life. I owe him.'

'Really?'

'Yeah. Germany, December 1944. I had been wounded in my left leg, and Bob put his hide on the line for me, carrying me on his shoulders for almost an hour.'

Steil shook his head in wonder. It was the kind of heroic act he would never have ascribed to a fleeing father. 'I didn't know.'

'He didn't like talking war.'

Childhood recollections surfaced from Steil's memory. 'That's true. Kids like to play soldiers, you know, and somehow one day I learned from Mom that he'd fought in World War II, and I begged him to tell me stories. He kept refusing, and I kept insisting until he grabbed my arms, shook me, and ordered me never to ask him about the war again.'

'That figures,' Gastler said. 'He never joined the Legion, never socialized with Army buddies, never went to parades. I hadn't seen him for fifteen or sixteen years. I reckon he got in touch with me 'cause he thought I could do the job.'

'What makes you so sure you can pull this off?'

Gastler sipped a little whiskey and followed it with a gulp of beer. 'Cuba has several thousand miles of coastline, and no government in the world can effectively patrol that length of shore twenty-four hours a day. It also plays in our favor that Cuban PT boats are short on spare parts and fuel. Coming in, I watched people fishing almost two miles off the coast on truck and tractor inner tubes, and I have a thirty-one-foot yacht. It's moored in the marina named after this dude . . .' Gastler signaled in the general direction of Hemingway's bust. 'So . . . smuggling out one or two people should be a piece of cake. Are you married or something?'

'Something.'

'Meaning?'

'A date now and then. Nothing permanent.'

'You have kids?'

'Nope.'

A silence ensued. Considering something, Gastler straightened his back and grabbed the edge of the bar. He had strong forearms sprinkled with freckles and brown age spots. Steil reflected on the difference between a weather-beaten face and a suntanned one. Up close, Gastler looked like the kind of guy who spends most of his time indoors, but sails, hunts, or plays tennis on the weekends. Probably not an excessively tiring sport, as Gastler's roll of fat around his middle attested. Maybe fishing and beer-drinking from a twenty-foot runabout or powerboat that remained in its boat slip from Monday through Friday.

'Like I said, piece of cake. Can you swim?'

'I float. My best time in the one hundred meter freestyle is nineteen minutes, sixteen seconds.'

Gastler laughed heartily before waving aside Steil's statement. 'Oh, c'mon, nobody's that bad.'

'I'm just trying to convey the idea that, if I accept your offer, you can't depend on an accomplished swimmer you can pick up a mile offshore.'

Gastler's smile froze. 'Listen Elliot, there are some guys in Miami trying to make a buck in this business, among them a friend of mine. I talked to him a few days ago. You can't enter the marina, haul your gear to the dock beside my boat, and hop aboard. The place is swarming with guards, and they'll bust you. But if I declare I'm sailing to Varadero, leave the boat yard alone just like I arrived, cruise close to the shore, and we have agreed beforehand on a pickup time and place, you can climb aboard easily.'

Steil drained his glass. His cheeks and lips felt a little numb. He counted his intake from memory: two stiff ones at home, two daiquiris, three glasses of wine, and two whiskeys. The teacher never made crucial decisions while drinking, but he craved another shot. He motioned the bartender. After serving Steil, the man tried to refill Gastler's glass, but the American raised his hand.

'I have to drive,' he said apologetically.

The barman smiled and glided away. Steil swallowed half of the drink and carefully rested his glass on the bartop. 'How can I climb aboard?'

'Do you know anything about boats?'

'Not a damn thing.'

'Okay. Here's what you need to know: If I sail eastbound, the way it is when I steer a course for Varadero, the right side of the ship looking forward faces the coastline and the left side faces the ocean. I can hang a ladder from the left side, cruise at very low speed, and you can climb aboard without being seen from shore.'

'How close to the coast can you get?' Steil asked, suddenly feeling the liquor hit him hard.

'My draft is five feet.'

'Your what?'

'Depth of water the yacht draws. To play it safe, I shouldn't sail in less than ten feet. Now, if I pick you up at a shallow beach, you might have to swim out two or three hundred yards to reach a ten-foot depth. In other places I could get at you one hundred yards or less from the shore.'

'You have any particular stretch in mind?'

Gastler nodded, checked that the saloonkeeper couldn't overhear, and for the first time nailed his eyes on Steil's. 'West of the Almendares River there's sailing depth very close to the shore, perhaps less than one hundred yards.'

'That's a heavily populated area,' Steil said, a touch of alarm in his voice.

'That is precisely what makes it pretty difficult to watch. Coming in yesterday afternoon, I noticed dozens of swimmers, a few of them pretty far away, a handful throwing lines from truck inner tubes almost half a mile off. There were no PT boats around, no choppers hovering above. Nobody seemed to care. Besides, that's a standard course for boats heading east from the marina.'

Steil shook his head; he was seeing the American's deeply lined face out of focus. 'Sorry, Dan. I'm a little boozy right now. Couldn't we meet again tomorrow? Give me a chance to think it over?'

Gastler unfastened his gaze from the teacher and looked straight ahead, like a man nearing the end of his patience. A split second later his features relaxed. 'The less we see each other, the better. Here's what I want you to do. I want you to explore several spots on that particular stretch tomorrow, the day after, and on Friday, always in the late afternoon. We'll meet at some other place next Saturday at noon, and over lunch you'll let me know your decision. If it's no, I'll sail back home with a clear conscience; if it's yes, you just have to tell me the exact spot where you'll be swimming at dusk that same day, and some big landmark I can easily identify. Are you with me?'

'I'm just a little dizzy, not sloshed.'

'Glad to hear that. Now, maybe neighbors or friends will ask you who I am, why I came. If you leak a single word of this conversation, I won't give a cent for our freedom. Got that?'

Steil tried to nod energetically, and two blurry faces jumped up and down.

'Fine. Cook up the best story you can. I don't know, make up an American you met at a party. Don't mention Bob, nothing about his death. I flew over, don't mention the boat. Got it?'

'Got it.'

'Don't try to contact me under any circumstances. Don't phone the marina. And, please, survey the shore carefully where I told you to.'

'Yessir.'

'Where can we get together next Saturday at noon?'

Steil thought it over for several moments, blinking slowly. The unexpected turn of events, plus too many drinks, had overwhelmed his usually quick brain. 'There's a new place called Morambón at the corner of Fifth Avenue and 32nd. Never been there, but since it caters to the tourist trade it should be good.'

'Allright. We ought to leave now. Do as I told you and tell me your decision next Saturday at the Moram . . . whatever. Fifth and 32nd. Ready?'

'Sure.'

'Bartender? Check, please.'

*   *   *

Elliot Steil woke at 5.23 the following morning. Remembering Dan Gastler immediately sent waves of joy rolling inside him. He stayed in bed to nurture the almost forgotten sensation and realized that even a dubious hope fueled his spirit to soaring heights.

It's what happens to outcasts, he thought, and Anita Robles came to his mind. Sometimes he wished he hadn't bumped into her at a store two years back. For as long as he could remember, the teacher had felt like a second-class citizen, but after the Anita experience he had downgraded himself another notch.

In the late seventies, Anita had been an unobtrusive student of Steil's who excelled in English. Fourteen years later, in a casual encounter, she had embraced him warmly and kissed his cheek. The usual it's-been-ages and how're-you-doings? let Steil know that Anita was now assistant manager in a travel agency. He also learned her marriage was one made in heaven and that her seven-year-old daughter was an angel. She wanted to know how he was getting along.

'Same as always,' the teacher said with a resigned smile.

'Do you want a change?' Anita asked.

Steil shrugged, pulling down the corners of his mouth.

'Why don't you drop by my office next Monday?' Anita suggested as she fished out a business card from her purse. 'I might have something for you.'

The mildly curious teacher figured the least he could do was see it through. That Monday, Anita explained to him how tourism was growing at an incredible 30 percent annual rate, and English-speaking Cubans were in great demand. Her firm operated thirty air-conditioned buses, and she needed five guides in a hurry. Would Steil like to become one? He would get free clothing, nice meals, and earn almost the same salary he made as a teacher. She also mentioned that the best guides made as much as forty or fifty dollars a month in tips. Steil jumped at the opportunity and filled out the application form.

Five weeks later, looking embarrassed and avoiding his eyes, Anita told her ex-teacher that his 'verification' had not been favorable. The report stated that several 'trustworthy people' shared the opinion that the teacher was not revolutionary enough to interact with foreigners. Anita also made it clear that she might face serious trouble if he filed a complaint. Steil wanted to know who had blackballed him. Anita swore she didn't know. The one-paragraph report didn't name names.

'I'm sorry, teacher,' she said, concluding the interview. 'I know you're a nice person, but it's the way things are. There's nothing I can do.'

*

Even after swallowing that bitter pill, Steil hadn't seriously considered moving to the US. The possibility lurked in the back of his mind, but when he examined the matter it became obvious that what he truly wished was to end forever a state of affairs in which unknown persons behind closed doors could make, on an essentially political basis and with full impunity, irrevocable decisions on absent human beings. They could decide who got the promotion, the apartment, the new car, or the post-graduate course abroad. Who worked with foreigners and who did not. Who was good and who was bad. There was no middle ground, no such thing as a 90 percent revolutionary. Those who didn't approve of every single political or governmental measure were considered potential enemies.

But this had nothing to do with his homeland and memories. Having lived most of his life in Cuba, he felt deeply rooted in its soil. The kindness inherent in most people was baffling; race relations were harmonious, the lifestyle easygoing and romantic, the women beautiful, the climate great. But how much unfair punishment could a man take? Enough was enough. He wouldn't refuse an offer that millions of his fellow countrymen would risk their lives for. The decision was made. He was trying to relate his marketable skills to job opportunities in the States when his bladder demanded relief. The teacher rose, walked to the bathroom, and turned on the light.

Steil had never experienced a hangover and, after lengthy consideration over the years, had come to believe his body stored some sort of rare chemical that neutralized alcohol and freed him from headaches, heartburn, and bloodshot eyes. But for some strange reason the mysterious chemical didn't work at all during consumption, and he got as loopy as any common guzzler with an average number of drinks. Only when he crawled into bed did the unknown element kick in.

Lathering his whiskers, Steil became annoyed at himself for having drunk too much. Gastler had had to hail a hard currency cab and slip him a twenty to pay for the ride. The teacher simultaneously cursed the worn-out razor blade and the Cuban peso, a worthless paper with no purchasing power outside of state-owned stores, where the ration card reigned and quotas could not be exceeded at any price. The official exchange rate was at par, yet one dollar bought 140 pesos in the black market in May, 1994. His monthly wage equaled $2.25, when at special, dollars-only stores a soda cost 80 or 90 cents, and a decent pair of shoes 40 or 50 bucks. Steil finished shaving, brushed his teeth with water, returned to the main bedroom, and hit the light switch.

He searched his pants pockets and was relieved to find $14.55 along with his own fat roll of 500 pesos. Staring at the American bills, Steil shook his head sadly. Gastler's change amounted to almost seven months of a teacher's income. He spent a few seconds on his hands and knees looking for the missing slipper before recalling he had kicked it under a living room armchair. Once shod, he donned a pair of cutoff jeans and an old, short-sleeved white shirt, then entered the second bedroom and turned his bicycle upside down to remove its rear tire. A neighbor who made a living vulcanizing punctured inner tubes opened shop around 6.00 a.m.

Steil had almost finished when he heard three knocks at the front door. He opened it to a white-haired, slightly overweight black woman holding a cardboard box and beaming at him.

'Congratulations, Daddy,' she said happily.

'Is that it?' Steil asked in surprise.

The black woman nodded.

'Come in. I'm starving.'

Sobeida supplemented her 108-peso pension buying groceries for seven households. For 30 pesos a month per family, she visited the block's ruined store on a daily basis, presented the ration cards to clerks, and purchased whatever was for sale. Once a year, on Mother's Day, bakeries supplied one cake to each household. Since that required baking half a million cakes in Havana, production and sales began in mid-April. A five-person family or a lone wolf each got one standardized cake of the same weight, price, and flavor. Children under thirteen were sold a cake on their birthday; girls on their fifteenth birthday and couples getting married were also included in the state plan. After Mother's Day, those who could afford it bought cakes on the black market.

Steil rinsed his hands in the kitchenette's sink, shook off the drops, and found a knife, two teaspoons, and two saucers in a cupboard. He lifted the box's lid and cut two large slices that made his mouth water; both the icing and the cake were made of rich, dark chocolate. The teacher returned to the living room and presented a serving to Sobeida, who had made herself comfortable on the sofa. He eased himself into an armchair. Munching on his first piece, Steil praised the cake humming admiringly.

'Good, isn't it?' Sobeida exclaimed.

'Best I've had in years,' the teacher mumbled.

They ate in silence. Sobeida refused a second helping, but Steil cut an even bigger piece for himself, then returned to the armchair. He was carefully scraping the saucer with the teaspoon when the woman made her second pitch.

'I got a two-ounce packet of ground coffee, Elio.'

Neighbors, as well as most of his sex partners who had never read Steil's full name in official papers, would have sworn it was Elio Esteil, an understandable distortion. On his block he was called Elio or Tícher. For some reason, Sobeida considered Tícher a little disrespectful.

'How much?'

'Thirty.'

'Okay.'

Sobeida produced a sealed cellophane envelope from her ample skirt and handed it to Steil. The teacher rose, marched to the main bedroom, and returned with 230 pesos − 200 for the under-the-counter cake, 30 for the coffee − which the woman folded and inserted between her breasts.

'Gotta run, Elio. Thanks for the slice.'

'You're welcome.'

Sobeida crossed the doorway, stopped as if suddenly remembering something, turned around, and addressed Steil from the hallway: 'Heard the latest one?'

He shook his head. The woman looked around and drew closer to Steil, adopting a conspiratorial tone. 'This fifth-grade teacher lectures her pupils while showing them a photo of Clinton: "Because of this man, we lack food and medicine; because of this man, we don't have enough oil for our power plants, trains, and buses; because of this man, we experience shortages of almost everything." After peering closely at the photo, Pepito raises his hand. "Yes, Pepito," she says. "Know something, Miss? When he's clean-shaven, he looks like an altogether different man!"'

Steil laughed briefly and admonished Sobeida, shaking his forefinger in her face and eyeing her knowingly.

The teacher brewed and sipped two cups of espresso before having his inner tube fixed. Back at the apartment, he mounted the tire. After changing into the same clothing he had worn to the Institute the day before, he dropped his swimming trunks and an old towel into a plastic bag and pedaled to work. He felt certain he was in the midst of a very lucky streak when he was served rice, one poached egg, and grated cabbage for lunch. During the English department meeting held between 1.30 and 2.47, he remained silent, absorbed in his own thoughts. His aloofness unsettled Oscar Gayol, a nice enough young man who had become embittered by his own opportunism.

Three years earlier, Gayol had accepted the position of department head in the aftershock of learning that Steil's nomination had been rejected by 'higher levels'. Disregarding a Southern American drawl far removed from what academics considered proper pronunciation, Gayol rated Steil one of the best language teachers in Cuba. He had met only three people

– a Havana University professor, a literary translator, and a State Council interpreter – whose mastery of English surpassed Steil's. Gayol couldn't understand why such a top-notch expert remained as a lowly teacher in an obscure institution.

The man had also been won over by the way Steil shared new terms learned by systematically monitoring American radio and television stations; how he readily served as a substitute for absent colleagues; and his knack for doing all this in an inconspicuous and unassuming way. Steil's substantial private library, mostly paperbacks, was open twenty-four hours a day to English students, although it was generally understood that after 10 p.m. only extremely good-looking females could quench their thirst for knowledge at the divorced teacher's apartment.

For these reasons, the day Gayol learned that Steil's nomination had been rejected, he took the stairs to the administrative floor two at a time, and explained his misgivings to the principal. His boss admitted that, yes, comrade Steil was a fine teacher. However, serious personal shortcomings blocked his appointment. For instance, the routine investigation had unearthed that comrade Steil, besides watching and listening to American stations all the time, had the nerve to give private lessons and translate documents at his home, an unacceptable deviation from official educational policy by a man who had obtained his Bachelor of English Literature degree free of charge. His wavering response to political rallies was neutralized by his commendable behavior during the Institute's month of agricultural work every school year, but comrade Steil drank too much, had a rather promiscuous sex life, and bought food on the black market. Comrade Steil hadn't volunteered to fulfill an internationalist mission in Nicaragua back in the eighties. And perhaps comrade Gayol didn't know that comrade Steil was the son of an American citizen and any day might fly the coop. So, the principal concluded, the municipal Board of Education had decided that instead of appointing

23

comrade Steil to the post, it was wiser to designate comrade Gayol, a trusted Party member, a veteran of the war in Angola, and also a good English teacher. Of course, comrade Gayol was aware that what he had just learned shouldn't be told to comrade Steil. He would probably resent it, and anyway, the man was too old to change.

That Steil had never charged a cent for private lessons or translations was lost among the other true and damaging facts. Gayol experienced conflicting feelings for a couple of months, but self-interest prevailed. At the department meeting in which the new chief was introduced, Steil limited his reaction to what over the years had become his usual resigned expression when confronted with incomprehensible human behavior: a click of the tongue, a forced smile, a sad shake of the head, and a sideways glance.

Gayol had a guilty conscience. He had searched in vain for a way to talk things over candidly and stave off the growth of what he suspected was a hidden, permanently nurtured hostility. He hated being subsumed into the category of opportunistic political bastards, but at the same time realized his accepting the position had lessened the credibility of any avowal of innocence he might make.

Nevertheless, that afternoon Gayol made another of his half-hearted attempts at patching things up. Other teachers had bolted out at the end of the meeting, and he was thrusting papers into his briefcase as Steil slipped on his loafers and grabbed his plastic bag.

'Got something on your mind, Elliot?'

Steil was caught off guard, and to deflect suspicion over-emphasized what was intended to be an innocent reply: 'Who, me? Certainly not. Why? Should I?'

Gayol took this as an expression of Steil's grievance. Regretting the initiative, he clicked his flat, fake-leather case shut. 'No, of course not. Have a nice day.'

Six minutes later, Steil was pedaling through the unusually

24

wide Santa Catalina Avenue, a biker's dream on its downhill stretches, but a nightmare on its uphill kilometer. Close to its end, as the teacher coasted past the green lawns of a huge sports complex, a tractor hauling a big trailer roared by ten inches from his side, and for the next five minutes Steil concentrated on the heavy afternoon traffic around the Luminous Fountain. Feeling like a sardine among sharks, he abandoned his regular route and headed for the coastline.

Sweating profusely under a brilliant spring sun, he climbed 26th Street, looking at the nice houses and small apartment buildings that urgently needed fresh coats of paint. At the outskirts of Vedado, the poor dwellers of El Fanguito could be seen returning to their nearby shacks after work. Three blocks further on, across the iron mesh roadbed that transversed a river, the panting teacher filled his lungs with the fumes from an industrial pollution that had turned the once limpid Almendares into a dark, murky stream devoid of life.

Just before 4.00, Steil reached the stretch of shoreline Gastler had indicated. The scent of the sea brought in by a soft breeze enthralled him. He pedaled slowly along First Avenue, and after 10th Street peered curiously at the huge mansions that had been fully renovated or were undergoing repairs. Senior citizens told anyone willing to listen that truly rich people had forsaken Miramar in the late '40s and early '50s for the greener pastures of the new and highly exclusive Biltmore development, but the real estate they had left to the emerging middle class looked quite impressive.

The teacher hadn't been around this section of the city for the last three or four years and was surprised at its transformation. The contrast between dilapidated residences and those already refurbished was striking. New facings, fresh paint, chain-link fences, sliding gates, well-tended gardens, casement-mounted air conditioners, metallic drapes or mini-blinds on windows, dish antennas on rooftops – all bespoke a frenzied renewal to accommodate the headquarters of foreign companies

25

doing business in Cuba and bringing in much-needed hard currency.

The few cars driving past were mostly recent imports with foreigner's plates. Some deeply suntanned young women in French-cut bikinis and flip-flops paced the sidewalk hunting for clients packing 'foolas', recent slang for greenbacks. Since bikers were considered paupers, the hookers paid no attention to the ogling teacher. Steil suspected the recent entrepreneurial upsurge might have spurred some residents into renting bedrooms to the girls as trick pads.

On the corner of 20th Street, he found a bicycle parking lot behind the squash courts of a rundown beach club for Cubans. A lone security guard told him the locker room was under repair. Steil clicked his tongue, forced a smile, shook his head sadly, and gave a sideways glance. He'd been given the same excuse the last time he was here.

He undressed in the men's restroom and, barefoot, crossed a huge open-air dance hall to reach the club's U-shaped jetty. The clear water was calm, and tame waves blandly slapped the concrete structure. The teacher passed a few kids diving off the jetty then climbing back on, and took a right turn on the eight-foot-wide slippery surface. He stopped five or six yards away from two elderly couples engaged in pleasant conversation, prolonging another quiet day in the afterglow of their lives. The curious glances of beach bums had followed the too-pale outsider, and Steil felt a little befuddled and out of place.

'Would you please keep an eye on this for me?' he asked the couples as he placed the bundle of clothing on the moss-covered surface. They nodded courteously, and he dived in.

Bob Steil had been so firmly convinced that swimming was the perfect exercise that his son had unwittingly developed an aversion to the sport. But for a number of reasons – of which concealing fear and pleasing Daddy were at the top of the list – Steil had learned the essentials of the sidestroke and breaststroke, the two styles that allowed his face to remain at or near the surface of the water. Frog-kicking and with somewhat jerky arm motions, the teacher distanced himself twenty-odd yards from the jetty. He relieved himself when the familiar anxiety gripped him. It was his standard reaction since he'd read in a magazine article that human urine might scare away sharks. The way he saw it, man-eating beasts lurked beneath the surface of the sea if the distance to the bottom exceeded five feet. To divert his mind from *Jaws* and its sequels, he looked west.

Three or four miles away, the coastline jutted out in some sort of promontory; this was probably where Gastler's yacht was moored. Steil surmised that if someone really wanted to sail a boat to Varadero from the marina, the logical course would be half a mile, perhaps even a mile offshore. The teacher spat out the taste of brine and slid his glance over the sea front. It was densely packed with adjoining one- and two-story houses, none of which had a feature remarkable enough to become a sailor's landmark. But about a mile away from where he swam, an outlandish modern tower could be used to orient a stranger cruising by. He decided to investigate the spot the next afternoon.

Steil turned his head left, noticing that the long shore current had made him drift a little to the east. With a few strokes he returned to his initial position, facing the two couples. He braced himself for the really tough part of the scouting, then filled his lungs to capacity and dived down. He managed a six- or seven-foot descent before his eardrums started hurting. He estimated the bottom was still ten feet away and returned to the surface. His heart beat wildly, and he felt drained and exhausted. After recovering his breath, he swam back to the jetty, climbed up the nickel-plated ladder, thanked his apparel custodians, and lay prone on the hard surface.

For the first time he considered the rafters. People fleeing Cuba furtively by sea did it by different means. A few somehow got into perfectly sound motor yachts manned by skilled sailors and safely negotiated the distance between any point on the Cuban coast and neighboring countries. Rafters were at the other end of the scale. Collecting discarded lumber, huge polyurethane boxes, oil drums, tractor or truck inner tubes, ropes, wires, and any other piece of junk that could conceivably aid their endeavor, they built rafts and sailed at night.

Rafters battled bad weather, adverse currents, blistering sun, thirst, hunger, seasickness, and sharks. Havana gossip periodically included tales of rafters who had been sitting on the edge, legs dangling into the water, when . . . Steil shook his head at the thought and rolled over. The lucky ones were picked up by freighters, US Coast Guard cutters, or pleasure boats, but the number of those who vanished was anybody's guess.

Steil accepted the fact that certain people had good reasons for risking their lives: escaped prisoners, men who feared long prison sentences, even folks who had been denied immigrant visas and were desperate to rejoin close relatives living abroad. Nevertheless, the cases he'd heard about involved mostly young, nonpartisan guys who were fed up with scarcity and Communist rhetoric and didn't see any better prospects ahead. They also shared another distinctive trait: nine out of ten had trouble distinguishing a pocket compass from a watch.

Looking at a snow-white cloud bank, Steil concluded that his own risk was minimal. Belated love had made his old man indulge in one last paternal act, which could turn out to be the most important act of all. His father had chosen the right man to carry it out, and all Steil had to do was overcome his seafaring aversion, swim a little, and follow Gastler's instructions to a tee. No futzzing around, no lollygagging. He would inspect the modern tower that afternoon.

With one swift motion, the teacher sat up, grabbed his

clothes, smiled at the elderly foursome, and, slipping occasionally on the jetty, headed for the men's restroom.

* * *

On Thursday evening, Steil had just sprinkled salt into the water that was boiling in a saucepan when somebody knocked on his front door. Shirtless, he wiped his fingers on his cutoffs and went to see who it was.

He was met by big black eyes and a knowing smile. The teacher chuckled. The white lettering on the woman's dark blue sweatshirt read JUST DO ME! in English.

'Am I interrupting something?' Susana asked mischievously.

'A plate of spaghetti.'

'Ugh.'

'Come in.'

In addition to the sweatshirt, she wore a denim skirt and worn-out pumps. Her hair was neatly trimmed, and not a dash of makeup spoiled her creamy, unlined face. Susana dropped her canvas handbag on the couch before giving Steil a peck on the cheek. She had a clean smell.

'Be with you in a minute,' he said and returned to the kitchenette. Susana followed him and leaned in the doorway. The teacher opened a cupboard, produced a brown paper bag with his pasta ration for June, and dropped the full half-pound into the water before addressing her.

'How're you doing?' he asked, shooting a glance at her.

Susana rolled her eyes and sighed. He watched the spaghetti slowly soften.

'Let's go to the movies,' she suggested.

Steil shook his head. 'I'm beat, Susy. Had six groups today. And then I went to the beach.'

'Alone?'

Steil nodded. 'I must have pedaled thirty kilometers.'

Susana peered at his bare back. 'Yeah, I see the light tan. For God's sake, Elio, you're a bag of bones.'

The teacher raised his arms and inspected his torso. 'I'm okay.'

'How many pounds have you lost in the Special Period?'

'Last time I got on a scale, forty,' Steil said, looking at the steamy saucepan.

Susana's knowing smile returned. Within two steps she was at his side. 'Now you can be played like a big upright bass,' she said, fingernails running along his rib cage, her full, wet lips brushing his shoulder. 'Mmm, you're still salty.'

Steil picked up a ladle and stirred the spaghetti. 'I showered,' he moaned. 'Had to go easy on the soap.'

'I'm not complaining,' the woman whispered, then stood on her toes and nibbled at the lobe of his ear. 'Are you planning to watch that horrible man with the funny suspenders tonight?'

Steil smiled; it was one of the television programs he had considered for the evening. TNT first, to see if the movie was to his taste; Larry King if it wasn't. 'It depends on the blackout,' he said teasingly. They both knew the TV set wouldn't be turned on that evening. Her hands were making circular motions on his chest, fingers gently raising hairs. He felt her breasts against his back.

'I got it from a friend who works at the power company,' she said in a suggestive voice, then paused before kissing his neck. 'There's serious trouble at five power plants; nine to six blackout tonight.' The tip of her tongue explored the back of his ear. 'Best thing a tired man can do is go to bed early, have a full night's rest.' After gliding over his midriff, her fingers slid beneath his cutoffs. 'Especially underfed men who need to conserve their strength. Specifically underfed men who go swimming in the afternoon. Oh, my goodness, what have I found here? A member of the Rapid Response Group, ready to go into the cave where the enemy hides and open fire?'

Steil roared with laughter and lost his hard-on. A smiling Susana retreated back to the doorway. In the right mood and chuckling frequently, Steil turned off the gas, strained the pasta, and poured it into a soup dish. Moving into the living room, he asked, 'You want some?'

Susana stared at him, wide-eyed. 'Are you gonna eat it like that?'

'What's the matter with it?'

'What do you mean, "what's the matter with it"? For God's sake, Elio, plain spaghetti?'

'Oh, excuse me, ma'am,' Steil scoffed as he picked up a fork. 'I forgot you just flew in from Miami. See, because of the blockade . . .'

'Cut the crap,' Susana interrupted. 'I know there're no toppings available, cheese can't be found at any price, but no tomato sauce? No oil? No onion, or garlic, or . . . something?'

'Susy. I . . . just . . . don't . . . have . . . any.'

Susana shook her head in disbelief and led the way to the living room, where they sat in the armchairs. 'I guess you turned me down flat,' he said with a smile.

Sounding a little sad. 'Yeah. Thanks anyway, Elio. I already had supper.'

Steil started eating hungrily. In an awkward silence, she watched him rotate the fork and gobble and slurp and masticate and gulp.

Susana Vila was a thirty-five-year-old supermarket cashier in what would have been called a submarket anywhere outside of Cuba. An economist by profession, she had resigned from the Central Planning Board in protest against what in the late eighties was officially designated the 'process of rectifying errors and negative tendencies'. At the time, her husband had sided with the Party, and the already-crumbling marriage collapsed a few months later. Having been unable to swap their three-bedroom apartment for two smaller units, the divorced couple was forced to share the bathroom and the kitchen in what had come to be a very stressful living situation. Their fourteen-year-old son, at a boarding school thirty miles away, had a three-day leave every two weeks.

When Steil met Susana in 1990, he was immediately attracted to the fiercely unsubmissive brunette. Early in the morning, riding his bike to the Institute, he frequently saw her jogging at a nearby park. Her white shorts exposed nice thighs and a solid, slightly oversized behind. She had a flat stomach, and medium-sized breasts bobbed freely under her T-shirt.

They met by chance on a Saturday, when Steil visited the supermarket to buy a bottle of non-rationed rum. After that, they waved at each other for a couple of weeks as the teacher pedaled to work and Susana trotted off. Then she disappeared for a few days, and Steil returned to the store.

'I never see you anymore,' he said. 'Overtrained?'

She smiled bitterly. 'Too much jogging and forced dieting don't mix.'

'Right. Problem is, how am I gonna brighten up my mornings from now on?'

Her next smile was coquettish.

'How about a movie on Saturday night?'

It had been going on for almost four years, in a very independent way. At the beginning they had seen each other frequently, made love once or twice a week, talked a lot. At some point Susana had concluded the teacher needed a fully committed, strongly motivated, very-much-in-love woman who might steer him clear of alcohol and womanizing, his remedies for an empty, unsuccessful life.

She was not that person. Susana refused to consider remarrying, had no vocation for nursing losers, and decided to focus the relationship on its sexual aspects alone. She gave up lecturing on the Cuban economy, stopped complaining about having to live under the same roof with her ex-husband, and almost never mentioned her son and parents, the three people she truly adored. Instead, Susana behaved like a nymphomaniac, a role the teacher seemed to enjoy enormously. If she arrived unexpectedly and an embarrassed Steil told her he had a visitor, she would pretend to be furious and whisper from the hallway that he'd better save something for her, 'cause she'd be back the next evening. Of course, she had never carried out the threat. She'd wait for him at the store, and within a week, a smiling Steil playing the part of the wounded lover would drop by to ask if she had dumped him. Steil never would have guessed he was the only man Susana had gone to bed with since her divorce five years earlier.

'Now, the dessert,' the teacher said, beaming, when his plate was empty.

She accepted a slice of cake, and later he made espresso. While Steil brushed his teeth and changed the bed linens, Susana did the dishes. She was drying her hands when the teacher let out his familiar mating howl from the bedroom. In the bathroom she undressed, washed up, and hung her clothes, before turning off the lights and entering his bedroom.

Reclining on the headboard, in the soft glow of the night lamp's forty-watt bulb, Steil stared as she approached the bed. Susana was one of the few women he'd come across who looked her best in the raw, and he couldn't take his eyes off her. Absolutely marvelous, he thought as she kicked off her pumps and lay next to him. She propped herself on her elbows, and abstractedly studied the headboard, swinging a leg in the air. Steil turned a little and slid his hand lightly over her back, before feeling the solid muscles of her splendid rump. On the radio, a jazz quartet was playing Billy Joel's 'I Love You Just The Way You Are'.

It suddenly struck him that it was the first time he felt certain he'd make love to a woman for the last time. Almost always, split-ups were unpredictable and feelings waned in a gradual fashion. Running away forever provided the certainty no other situation offered. It made him feel lousy having to keep from her what he would soon do. And then it got worse.

'Elio?'

'Yeah?' he replied, kissing her back.

'I've been thinking.'

'About what?'

'You can't go on like this.'

His tongue left a wet, zigzagging path down her spine, from between her shoulder blades to the crack of her buttocks. His right hand caressed her calf. 'Go on like what?'

'Starving.'

'I'm not starving. Turn over.'

Susana complied. The tip of his nose circled her left nipple.

'Listen, I know the store manager sells a few things on the side. Rice, oil, green peas, beans.' Susana was silent for a few moments. 'I'll make the introduction. Say I know you personally, you're okay, won't squeal on him. Elio, pay attention!'

Supported by his left forearm, Steil moved his right hand up the inner part of her thigh as he kissed her navel. 'I swear I'm giving you my full attention.'

'It'll cost, you know. Prices are incredible, twenty pesos a pound of rice, fifteen a pound of red beans, fifty a pound of cooking oil. But you'll survive. The essential thing is to survive.' Involuntarily, Susana spread her legs apart. 'Can you afford it?'

There was no response. His tongue was exploring her pubic hair.

Susana bent her knee, so the sole of her foot rested on the mattress. 'Elio, can you afford it?' She breathed deeply.

Steil knew that, as a rule, asking something and not getting an answer made Susana pretty mad.

But almost a minute later: 'Elio, honey, just a little lower, please? Honey?'

The exception proves the rule, the teacher concluded.

*   *   *

At 11.55 a.m. on June 4, 1994, a hot, humid, and overcast Saturday morning, Elliot Steil confidently entered the Morambón's deserted bar, sat on a stool, and ordered a beer.

Speaking English, wearing baggy white cotton shorts, an

34

aloha shirt, leather sandals, and a plain white cap, the teacher could have been mistaken for a tourist. Yet close observation would have shown that the slightly suntanned patron didn't behave with the debonair detachment of insouciant foreigners. Under his armpits, huge sweat stains suggested recent physical exertion or anxiety. His smile looked forced, and his eyes reflected a sheen of alarm.

Steil had only two dollars and a five-peso note on him. At his apartment were his identity card, key ring, and drowned watch. The bicycle was six blocks away, on the front lawn of a private home whose owner found bike parking highly profitable.

The teacher sipped from his crystal mug and concluded that if for some reason Gastler didn't show up, he would have to leave the two bucks on the bartop, get the hell out of the place . . . and do what? Longingly, Steil eyed several Havana Club rum bottles resting over a silvery refrigerated cabinet behind the bar. He felt like quickly downing six ounces in two slugs.

On the previous evening, Steil had had a visitor. Virgilio Toca was in his late fifties and lived in the same building as the teacher. He managed a small branch office of the state-owned savings bank, smoked three packs a day, loved to play dominoes, and shared his two-bedroom apartment with his wife, two married daughters, their husbands, and five grand-children. Toca was also a Party member and in charge of surveillance at the block's Committee for the Defense of the Revolution. He had the courtesy of devoting five minutes to three topics – weather, blackouts, and the coming soccer World Cup – before directly addressing the true reason for his visit.

'Hey, my grandson said you had a visitor the other night, an American driving a rented car. How come?'

Smiling, evading the man's probing eyes, and trying to subtract significance from the visit with a mocking tone, Steil told

Toca that last Saturday night he had met an American at a party and, since the tourist didn't know a single word of Spanish, had been forced to interpret for him. Addresses were exchanged and, surprisingly, the grateful foreigner had taken him out to dinner on Tuesday night. Toca wanted to know the American's name; Steil hesitated before saying it was Ralph something, and changed the subject, offering a shot of Train Spark to his visitor.

The bank manager left a few minutes later, and Steil cursed his own stupidity. No doubt some snitch had jotted down the rented car's license plate, and it would be easy to find out the American's name was not Ralph. What if the whistle blower had witnessed the first brief exchange with Gastler? Guys who had partied together wouldn't be so cool toward each other. Worried, he tossed and turned in bed before falling asleep a few minutes before 2.00 a.m.

When Steil left the building the next morning, he suspected that eyes behind windows followed his every move. After an hour and a half of aimless biking across the almost-deserted streets of Vedado, the teacher felt certain he wasn't being tailed, so he headed for Miramar.

Through a slightly frosted windowpane, Steil saw the pearl-gray Toyota Corolla entering the restaurant's parking lot. Heaving a deep sigh of relief, he slid off the stool and hotfooted to the door.

'Hey, mister,' the bartender yelled after him in English.

'Be right back,' Steil replied without breaking his stride.

He pushed the bar's plate-glass door and held it open. Gastler got out of the car, waved at him, and stooped over to lock the door. He wore a white polo shirt, bell-bottom dungarees, and the same pair of deck shoes. As the aged American came closer, Steil felt his affection for the man expand. He could have pocketed the money and forgotten his moral debt to a dead pal, and no one would have been the wiser. And yet here he was, courting danger for a perfect stranger.

'Hi, Dan.'

'Hey, pretty sharp threads,' Gastler said approvingly, eyeing Steil's loud shirt.

'C'mon in.'

They approached the long bar, and Gastler ordered a beer as he sat to the right of Steil. The bartender pulled the tab off a Hatuey, poured its contents into a mug, and moved away. Gastler gulped half of it, rested the mug on the bartop, wiped his lips with the back of his left hand, and turned to Steil.

'Well?'

'Let's do it.'

'Congratulations. Life here isn't worth shit,' Gastler said, then polished off the remainder of his beer. 'What are you waiting for?' he asked, glancing at Steil's almost-full mug as he placed his own on the Formica. 'Let's have lunch.'

Twice the American cut Steil short – over mango slices and while they sipped the second course, a chicken consommé. Choking on his discoveries, the teacher left half of a well-done, eight-ounce tenderloin steak untouched, which under normal circumstances he would have wolfed down in sixty seconds. At last, over vanilla ice cream, Gastler uttered the anticipated words.

'Okay, let's have it.'

Steil deposited his teaspoon on the saucer, pushed away his cup, wiped his lips with the napkin, and informed Gastler that one of the last Soviet undertakings in Cuba had been the erection of a rather huge building complex at a choice lot flanked by Fifth Avenue, Third Avenue, 64th Street, and 66th Street, Miramar, to serve as embassy, consulate, and living quarters for the staff. Gastler nodded, excused himself, marched to the parking lot, and returned with his bifocals, a Havana tourist map, and a cheap ball-point pen.

'Mark it,' he ordered.

Steil amateurishly unfolded and refolded the thick paper before complying. Between sips of espresso, the teacher indicated that the office building was topped by an unmistakable eight-story limestone tower of which he made a rough sketch on the map's margin. Sliding his forefinger over the chart, Steil added that many people used to swim fifty or sixty yards into the sea – where the depth reached between fifteen and twenty feet – from the deserted stretch of coastline two hundred yards away from the diplomatic mission. Finally, the teacher pointed out that the two black dots to the left of the chosen site, identified with small beds as the Neptuno and Tritón hotels, were twin twenty-story towers, which could serve as supplementary landmarks.

Nodding repeatedly, Gastler kept his eyes on the map for a few moments and then consulted his wristwatch. Steil noticed it looked costly. Gastler removed his glasses, placed them in a metallic sheath, closed it with a click, and slipped it into the left pocket of his dungarees.

'Now, Elliot, for our mutual sake, I want you to come clean with me.'

'About what?'

'Did you tell anyone about me or . . . your decision?'

'Absolutely not.'

'Did you say good-bye to anyone? Some broad, maybe?'

'No.'

'Fine. Now, sundown will be at seven fifty-five, but according to the weather forecast, the day will remain cloudy, and after seven thirty a lonely swimmer might attract attention, so I'll try to sail past this place around seven twenty-five, give or take a few minutes.'

Gastler finished his third beer, repressed a belch, and began instructing Steil. 'The moment you see a white yacht approaching, get ready. You're a slow swimmer, so hit the water when I'm here, right by the . . .' He squinted at the map, and with his forefinger tapped one of the black dots.

'Neptuno Hotel?' volunteered Steil.

'The one farthest from you.'

38

'That's the Neptuno.'

'Okay. Swim out as far as you can. Fifty yards minimum, sixty would be excellent, seventy would be perfect. The farther the better, to reduce the chances of your bobbing head being seen from the shore. In a little while I'll give you a yellow swimming cap I have in the car. Stick it under your shorts before going in. When I'm less than fifty yards away, put it on. A rope ladder will be suspended astern. Hold on to it and remain in the water. Let the boat pull you ahead for a while, a minute or two, and keep clear of the propellers. Take off the cap and drop it; it'll sink. Then climb aboard. Got that?'

'Yeah.'

'I'll be at the wheel. Don't talk to me, don't stand up. Move on your hands and knees below the deck. You'll find the main cabin, a dinette, and on its table, a towel and some clothing. Get dressed and help yourself to the icebox. Don't come up before I ask you to a couple of hours later. If by any chance a Cuban PT boat stops us, our story is you had a cramp as I happened to sail by. I invited you to come to Varadero with me, as a guide. Later you'd ride back to Havana on a bus. I offered to radio your rescue to the marina, and you told me not to bother because you live alone and no relatives will panic if you do the vanishing trick. You saw this as an opportunity to practice your English, visit a fine beach resort, and maybe earn some mazuma taking me to the hot spots in town.'

Gastler stopped talking and looked Steil straight in the eye with the coldest ice-blue irises the teacher had ever seen. They reminded him of his father's, save for temperature: Bob's had been flame-blue.

'Any questions?' Gastler asked.

'My watch drowned yesterday. It wasn't waterproof, and I forgot to take it off before swimming.'

'Take this one,' Gastler said as he unfastened the leather strap of his own watch. 'I'll buy a cheap one at the marina, and we'll swap them later on.'

Steil was fastening it on his wrist when Gastler spoke again. 'You have six hours to kill. What's your plan?'

Steil cleared his throat. 'I'll be reading at the National Library.'

'You aren't returning home.'

'No.'

'And you aren't going to a bar.'

'Of course not,' Steil said, a dash of annoyance in his voice.

'Don't get mad, don't get bagged, and drive your bike carefully,' Gastler said a little didactically. 'I'm too old to give it another try if you botch it today.'

Considering his mood, Steil asked for Shakespeare's *The Tempest*, and was told he had to wait twenty minutes. He sat alone at a rectangular reading table, letting his gaze glide over a section of the city. Gastler could never imagine the cockamamie stories he had been forced to concoct just to masquerade as an American. He had rented the shirt and borrowed the sandals from people who would curse him for the rest of their lives. Only the cap had been legally bought at a dollars-only, state-owned store.

Steil admitted his lack of preparedness for the unusual. He had never before been involved in unlawful activities. Even his sexual exploits had been confined to unmarried or divorced women. Thinking about women in general made him recall his last conversation with Natasha three days before. It had been a bad idea. His ex-wife had sensed something was radically different, something ominous or dangerous or sleazy, and kept asking what was the matter. But Natasha was no longer the red-blooded, happy-go-lucky girl he had married in 1979. She was still mentally unstable, and her reactions were unpredictable, so he couldn't do what he really wanted to: take off his shoes and shirt, plop down on her couch, and talk over the whole thing with the only woman he had ever met who could keep a secret and figure out what was best for him.

Steil's memory moved to Sobeida. On Friday night, over coffee, he patronizingly explained to his regular black-market supplier that he had to make a week-long trip to Santiago de Cuba, and it didn't seem safe to leave the 5300 pesos he had saved at home. Would she please keep them for him? Sobeida tilted her head, eyed him suspiciously, and replied with a baffling statement: 'You know a lotta folks drown, don't you?' He felt compelled to play the part of a misunderstood man by rolling his eyes, lifting his arms in mock exasperation, and accusing Sobeida of being insane. Sobeida disregarded his protestations of innocence. When she was ready to leave, money stashed in a shoe box, she made the sign of the cross over his forehead and lips as two big tears rolled down her cheeks.

He picked up the book and a Webster's dictionary, then returned to the reading table. In Act One, Scene One, Gonzalo soothed Steil's spirit when, referring to the boatswain, he quips, *'Methinks he hath no drowning mark upon him; his complexion is perfect gallows.'* Since first reading the play as an undergraduate, Steil had enjoyed this kind old soul, whose character combined merriment and wisdom. Now, lines he had initially liked for literary reasons assumed new undertones. In the middle of the storm Gonzalo wails, *'Now would I give a thousand furlongs of sea for an acre of barren ground; long heath, brown furze, any thing.'* When the passengers arrived on the island safely, the teacher became engrossed in the immortal play.

At 5.45, a courteous attendant told him it was closing time. He pedaled back to Miramar, parked his bike close to the Tritón, and sat on a park bench on the corner of 60th Street and 3rd Avenue. At 6.28 Steil examined Gastler's gold watch. It had Roman numerals, the three usual hands, a moon phase dial, a calendar, and a half dial for a second time zone. Tension started tying a knot in his stomach. His crotch, overheated by the swimming cap, itched. He interrupted a discreet scratching when a beautiful young brunette in a power bob approached him, smiling. Her tight black miniskirt disclosed all the voluptuousness of perfect thighs. She wore a transparent green tank top, cut off about an inch below her breasts, and spike heels. Steil forgot his tribulations and appraised the hooker the way a cattle buyer examines the herd. She didn't show signs of malnutrition, oozed self-confidence, and was in the prime of her life. The woman stopped two feet away and, still smiling, inserted a cigarette between her lips. From his sitting position, the teacher could see the soft curve of her breasts.

'*¿Me das candela?*'

'Sorry, no Spanish,' Steil said.

'Gotta light?'

Steil shook his head. 'Smoking is hazardous.'

Her English probably didn't include hazardous; she looked confused. Steil noticed the cheap rings on her fingers and the quarter-pound copper earrings she wore.

'No light?' The tip of her cigarette jumped up and down.

'No light.'

'How 'bout drink?'

Steil shook his head again. 'I can't.'

The girl gave him a knowing look, removed the cigarette from her lips, and leered at the prospective customer. 'Maybe with me you can.'

Steil laughed softly. 'Maybe. How much?'

'Fity dollar.'

'Fifteen?'

'No. Fity,' the girl repeated.

Steil concluded the income gap between Cuban and American chippies was narrower than he thought. 'Where did you learn English?' he asked.

'In school.'

'High school?'

'Yeah. Yu wanna fuck or yu wanna talk?'

'Neither.'

'For yu forty dollar.'

'No. Thanks anyway.'

'Okay. Only 'cause yar so cute. Thirty.'

Gap widens, Steil thought, before glancing at Gastler's watch and standing up. The woman smiled openly, believing she had closed the deal.

'Sorry. Gotta go. Bye.' Steil turned and walked away.

The young hooker knitted her brow. 'You gay?' she called after him.

Steil nodded slowly without looking back.

* * *

Two and a half hours later, in a strange mood that kept full exhilaration in check as he waited for the other shoe to drop, Elliot Steil sat on the foam-rubber, vinyl-covered cushion of a dinette seat in the main cabin of a power cruiser built in 1960.

On the table were a bottle of Cuban rum, two-thirds full; a plate with the remains of two ham-and-cheese sandwiches; one empty and one full bottle of Canadian mineral water; and two discarded paper napkins. The teacher's hands were closed around a water tumbler filled almost to the brim with equal portions of the Cuban-Canadian mixture.

Steil faced the five steps that led to the deck, and shelves that contained a radio-telephone unit, a small TV set, a VCR, a CD player, and several books. To his right, under a curtained window, were a tape deck, a black metal box, and what looked like a stereo speaker. Across the anti-skid floor to his left were a galley with a two-burner gas range, an aluminum sink, kitchenware shelves, an icebox under a chart table, and a toilet behind a closed door.

The gasoline-powered engine hummed reassuringly in the bilge, and the sea was so calm that liquids remained motionless in their receptacles. Steil figured if this was typical sailing, he would be forced to reconsider nautical sports.

The teacher sipped from his glass, then slid off the seat and reached the toilet with three strides. He wore a light-gray

43

pullover with multi-colored waves printed on its front, navy-blue cotton shorts, and rubber thongs. Gastler's watch remained on his wrist. When he returned to the cabin, he was seized by curiosity. He stared at sea rails and hand grips, wondering about their purpose. Moving fore, Steil opened the stateroom door and stole a look at a double berth thwartship. He closed the door and devoted a minute to inspecting empty lockers, fire extinguishers, and charts, before going back to the dinette. He was skimming a book when he heard Gastler's booming voice.

'You can come up now, Elliot.'

The teacher dropped the book on the table, grabbed his drink, and climbed the steps to the deck, carefully ducking to avoid bumping his head. He joined Gastler at a small cockpit protected by a windshield and lateral glass triangles, and glanced at the switches, levers, and illuminated dials behind the helm.

'Welcome aboard,' Gastler said, smiling broadly before tripping two switches. Three white pilot lights that were burning astern, in the prow and over the cockpit, went off.

'I don't know what to say. Thanks is too small a word,' Steil commented, while noticing that the cabin was also in darkness. Gastler shrugged off the remark and turned the wheel to port. The yacht veered from NWW to NWN as he pushed the throttle forward and the engine revved. Steil inhaled deeply and raised his eyes to a starless, charcoal-gray sky. A soft breeze disheveled his hair.

'Been celebrating, uh?' Gastler observed, looking at Steil's glass.

Steil pondered his reply. 'It is as . . .'

'Mind if I join you?'

'On the contrary,' Steil said, extending his drink to the skipper.

'Think you can find the bottle in the dark?' the American asked, grabbing the glass.

'Sure.'

A few moments later, Steil returned to the cockpit and found Gastler taking a sip. 'I'll take swigs. Couldn't find another glass with the lights off,' the Cuban said.

'Fine. To freedom.'

'To freedom,' concurred Steil before rising to the occasion by gulping down a long one. 'Are we in international waters?'

'We will be soon.'

'Why did you turn off the lights?'

Gastler sipped from the glass before replying: 'Just a precaution. I don't want to call the attention of US patrol boats. If they stop us, we'll say you left Cuba on a raft two days ago. I was cruising by at dusk when you spotted me, asked for help, and I obliged. We'll feed the same story to immigration officials in Miami, okay?'

'Okay.'

'We'd never met before. No prior connections between us. Got it?'

'Yeah.'

'Let's have one in memory of Bob.'

Ashamedly, Steil realized that in the last twenty-four hours he hadn't devoted a moment of reflection to the man who had made his escape possible. He saw a huge hand gripping a football. *Thanks, you sonafabitch*, Steil said to himself. His eyes watered, and he gulped down two mouthfuls to put his conscience at ease. The recollection of his Friday evening visit to the Colón cemetery entered his mind. Nearby flower shops had nothing to offer, and he couldn't leave a last bouquet on his mother's grave.

'I told you at the Floridita that I'm an English teacher,' he said in an effort to shake off unpleasant memories. 'How can I make a living in the States?'

'Certainly not by carrying coals to Newcastle,' Gastler replied.

For close to an hour, conversation and rum flowed smoothly. Scanning the horizon over the prow and sporadically glancing at the dials, Gastler did almost all the talking. He ridiculed teachers' wages in America, and suggested a two-pronged approach to planning Steil's future. Considering that Cuban illegal immigrants were immediately presented with green cards, he said, the teacher should shun Miami's Hispanic community and accept the first available low-paying job at a small American company – where his knowledge of both Spanish and English would be useful – then work his way up to some mid-level managerial position. After two or three years burning the midnight oil, saving money, and acquiring resident status, perhaps Gastler might help him secure an SBA or bank loan to open his own small business. A deli, a gas station, a second-hand store, a diner, or a laundromat – it didn't matter what. Its essential asset would be his having learned all the tricks of a trade working for someone else.

Both men had long ones in honor of the future entrepreneur. Somewhat abruptly, Gastler changed the topic to sailboats. Half-dizzy and partially dumbfounded by a combination of the liquor, exhaustion from the swim to the yacht, and the slight plunging of the cruiser, Steil listened to a long tirade about sloops and ketches, furling and dropping sails, how self-steering vanes made possible long voyages for solitary sailors, and the questionable joy of confronting the elements in a gale. The teacher felt his eyelids closing, and had to make a very conscious effort to reopen them. Fifty minutes standing in thongs had hurt his feet, and he imagined the comfortable-looking bunks below deck. But Steil refused to be impolite with the man doing so much for him. A minute later, the near-empty rum bottle fell from his hand.

'Hey, are you falling asleep?' Gastler asked, smiling amusedly. 'Want to go below deck?'

'It's just that . . .'

'Oh, c'mon. Let me help you. C'mon. Let's go.'

Steil felt strong hands gripping him by the biceps. His legs weren't responding appropriately. He wondered how the yacht

46

would stay on course. Perhaps there was some sort of automatic pilot, like in planes.

'I'm okay,' he mumbled, looking for the steps to go below deck.

'Sure.'

'I'll just lie down for a little while.'

'Sure.'

And suddenly he was pushed overboard.

2

After surfacing, Steil managed an embarrassed smile. Had he stumbled? Was it a joke? Anyway, Gastler would pick him up. For about ten seconds, he waited confidently as the yacht sailed away, then for another two or three agonizing minutes, he hollered frantically. *Any moment now*, he mumbled to himself between shouts. *A rudder breakdown? Why doesn't the old fart cut off the fucking engine?* But the notion that something was very wrong became suddenly apparent. He began puking violently, and the bitter outflow of half-digested food, alcohol, and bile cut short his wild cries. By the time his stomach calmed, the power cruiser had disappeared into the night, the receding sound of its engine still audible. Steil urinated, and watched in stupefaction how the upchucked sandwiches swayed gently on the water's surface.

He braced himself for mutilation. The dozens of sharks circling in would begin their unexpected feast, first on his calves, then his thighs, balls, dick . . . Elliot Steil wept for a long time. Gonzalo's words popped into his mind: *'Now I would give a thousand furlongs of sea for an acre of barren ground.'* He laughed hysterically before throwing up a second time. Shivering and exhausted, he abandoned hope and floated flabbily, gazing at the overcast sky.

Is this the way I go? Did I fall overboard? I think he pushed me. Yeah, he pushed me. Why? What did I do? I didn't antagonize the man. You don't drown a man 'cause he dozes off, dammit! And this . . . this murderer owed my father? I should've checked up on him. But how the hell could I have? Asked State Security? Made a phone call to Dad's grave? You sent him, Dad; it's your fault. It's always

been your fault. I am your fault. Know something, Dad? I always
wanted to have a heart-to-heart talk with you. Mom brought me in;
you're greasing my way out. Why did it take you so long? I mean,
there were condoms in your time, and contraceptive gels. I've looked
it up. Abortions were possible in case you got carried away. So why
did you accept a responsibility you weren't going to live up to? The
constant supplier of hard-and-fast rules bunked off when we needed
you most. You fucking fled, you sonafabitch. Why? I mean, what the
hell did I do to you?

From his mother's stories, he knew that Bob Steil had been
born on April 20, 1926, in a small railroad station five miles
north of the Georgia–Florida border, along the tracks con-
necting Valdosta to Jacksonville. He was also fairly certain that
the station's name had been Fruitland and that the stream
running southeast fifty yards to its left had the melodious
nomenclature Suwanooche.

His knowledge of the rest of his father's childhood was
minimal. He knew that the next station to the east was Head-
light, but he couldn't recall the name of the westward depot.
Was it Harlow? Harwell? Harvey? Had the family moved to
Sebastian in the thirties or forties? Was Bob a high school
dropout? As a boy Steil had visited these places, heard their
names, listened to the stories, but certain details had slipped
his mind.

And there was his own inextricable mixture of fact with
fantasy. Bob had been six feet one tall, had knocked out a
Golden Gloves heavyweight champion in Palm Beach, capped
seven Krauts with his bare hands. Or had he? Bob could out-
brag, outdrink, outspeak, and outstare any man. Or could he?
Until 1957 he had been the merriest and most affectionate of
fathers this side of Pat Boone. Or had he?

The indisputable facts were that Elliot Steil's grandfather
moved his wife and two sons to Florida, lured by the Fellsmere
Sugar Producers' Association. The company operated a factory

twelve miles to the west of Sebastian, a small community on the eastern coast, and employed seasonal workers migrating from the cotton fields of Georgia and South Carolina. In the late thirties Ebenezer Steil made forty cents an hour as a cane cutter during the harvest season, and almost as much in the months of cultivation. Ebenezer reasoned that if the going got tough, he could always make a living at the nearby citrus groves, which was precisely what he was forced to do from 1958 until his retirement.

As a teenager, Bob Steil frequently accompanied his father to the fields, and there he became acquainted with the levees, collecting canals, and lateral ditches that controlled the water table and soil moisture. Eventually Bob became an apprentice at the refinery, and when the Army drafted him in 1944, he was perfectly capable of decolorizing liquor through a vegetable carbon process.

What he had endured during his tour of duty was anybody's guess. He admitted going to Europe, being under fire, becoming a corporal, and getting an honorable discharge, but nothing else. Among relatives and friends, it was common knowledge that the only way to rouse Bob Steil into a fury was by pressing him to recount his war experiences.

His return to Sebastian coincided with the nation's reconversion to a peacetime economy. Experts predicted massive layoffs, and unions reacted with a wave of strikes in key industries, from General Motors and Allis Chalmers to AT&T and the railroads. Sugar producers froze expansion programs, and the young veteran found that his position had been filled by a lifelong employee too old to be sacked. A friend told him that his former boss in Fellsmere's carbon house, under contract at the Hershey sugar factory and refinery in Santa Cruz del Norte, Cuba, was looking for a skilled and trustworthy operator. Bob wrote to the man, and on June 6, 1946, he stepped out of a battered 1932 Plymouth taxi and stood in awe before the second largest sugar refinery in the world.

Bob Steil liked the place. From the plant's upper floors he could gaze to the north at the exceedingly blue waters of the Atlantic. The view to the west was restricted to the rooftops of bungalows, warehouses, and office buildings. But to the east and south a fairly large valley – sugar cane fields, grazing land, vegetable gardens, a river, and the feathery fronds of hundreds of palms undulating in the soft breeze – looked magnificent. The climate was warmer than Florida's, which suited him fine after experiencing a cruel German winter. Three and a half miles away, Santa Cruz del Norte supplied fine shore and boat fishing, a humble saloon, and three young, comely, and fun-loving whores.

Hershey's management slipped fifty bucks to the local union leader for explaining to his comrades that the young American hadn't signed on as a regular worker. In fact, he was a junior manager on a training program and would become a carbon house foreman as soon as he learned enough Spanish to make himself understood. Having no choice in the matter, the grumbling masses accepted this deception; ten months later, to everyone's surprise, it became a reality.

Intent on an informal, amusing, and fully practical method of learning Spanish, Bob Steil devoted much of his free time to mingling with the natives. He fished, drank, played baseball, and went to parties with his Cuban coworkers. Out of an innate sense of balance, he learned to play golf, went to church, talked politics, and celebrated the Fourth of July with the lower echelons of the small American community. On September 11, at a combination party and vigil held for the Virgen de la Caridad del Cobre, Catholic Cuba's patron saint, Bob met the woman he would marry exactly a year later.

You two looked enraptured in those faded black-and-white photos Mom treasured. You weren't handsome, she wasn't beautiful, yet you appeared to be when flashing those glorious smiles or looking into each other's eyes. Before Natasha, I couldn't imagine what you must have felt. You were stricken. 'How could I live without her?' you'd say. I've been there. Does love die or does it merely change its object? Perhaps it was my birth that altered your love, or that Mom devoted less time to you, or that I used to sob, ask for a glass of water, have nightmares when you were enjoying a romp; maybe I sucked the firmness from her breasts. Were you pissed at me? You certainly didn't seem to lose interest. I'd be the worst creep on Earth if, even now, I voiced the tiniest complaint about my childhood. It was wonderful. I had your devotion every inch of the way, especially in all of those belittled yet vital initiations: fishing, camping, flying a kite, fielding a grounder. I can still see your confused amazement, your repressed amusement, the evening you found me jerking off behind a tool shack. A few weeks later you wiped my tears as I watched the death throes of the first bird I'd shot with the BB air gun Santa left the night before under our Christmas tree. No complaints up to then, Dad.

In 1951 Bob Steil made a sweet deal with both Hershey and Fellsmere: He would spend the crop season – November to March – in Florida. From April to October, he'd decolorize affinated liquor in Cuba. Carmen María de la Caridad García Soto – Carmencita to her parents and friends, Carmen Steil in the United States – arrived at Tampa's international airport on December 5, 1951, carrying a fifteen-month-old baby in her arms. He'd been baptized in Santa Cruz's local Catholic church as Elliot. At the time, Carmen's mastery of the English language could have been mercifully described as elementary, and she spoke and cooed to her child in Spanish. Bob, however, addressed his son in English. At two, Elliot's vocabulary included good morning, *niño lindo*, *mami*, Daddy, *caca*, pee, *papa*, and son of a gun.

Years slipped by. Bob Steil discovered his business acumen at twenty-seven, when he began espying opportunities. Before flying south he would pack two or three suitcases with working clothes bought cheaply at military-surplus stores. Returning to the States, he carried boxes of top-of-the-line hand-rolled cigars and the fine Italian neckties that were regularly smuggled into Cuba. Profits were deposited in a savings account.

Back in Cuba, in early September, 1956, Carmen registered Elliot at Santa Cruz's primary school. By the time the child had mastered the letters *m*, *a*, and *p* in Spanish, he was flown to Florida and enrolled in Sebastian's grade school. Patient guidance helped him adjust, and the boy did reasonably well until mid-April, 1957, when he was shuttled back to Santa Cruz despite the courteous yet firm objection of the principal. Concerned with the child's welfare, the Cuban school's principal refused to readmit him five weeks before the end of the term, and both parents started giving serious consideration to their son's education.

Santa Cruz was home for Carmen. She visited her parents on a daily basis, gossiped as much as she liked with lifelong girlfriends, understood perfectly the plots of radio and TV soap operas, and found exquisite black beans. Bob didn't want to sever his Fellsmere ties, particularly since his kid brother had landed a job in a Tulsa, Oklahoma, jewelry store and claimed to be too busy and prosperous to visit Ebenezer and Edna more than twenty-four hours a year. Carmen and Bob realized the long-term effects their transience would have on Elliot's education, and jointly decided that he would complete his elementary studies in Cuba. The child could learn English in Santa Cruz with Mrs Myers, a native American married to the refinery's power plant second-in-command. Sylvia Myers had been a grade-school teacher in Montgomery, Alabama, and gave private lessons in the afternoon, more to revel in what she called 'the pure joy of teaching' than for the few pesos she made and didn't need. Her tutoring would complement Elliot's education and help prepare him for high school in Florida.

By then the couple had shared ten years together, and of the initial flames of passion, only glowing embers remained. Though still attracted to each other, they were unaware that responsibility, habit, and parenthood had become the essential themes of their marriage. Carmen took for granted that Bob would refrain from womanizing for the same reason she would shun improbable admirers: fidelity, virtue, and love. Bob reckoned he'd occasionally sheathe his whang in rubber and bed a hustler, but if asked, he would have ruled out the possibility of jeopardizing the future of his family for another woman. Both believed they knew everything there was to know about one another, and, looking confidently to the future, they made plans to spend all Christmases and Easter holidays together in Florida. He was thirty, she twenty-seven.

Must've been a broad. You changed. Not towards me, no. In fact you showered me with affection during those short vacations. You took me everywhere from Key West to Bainbridge. You spoiled me with apple pie and thick Howard Johnson's chocolate milk shakes whenever I refused the steaks and salads Mom wanted to gorge me with. Yet you were different towards us; you excluded her. Using me as a buffer you rarely held her hand, put your arm around her waist or over her shoulder. Maybe at night your lovemaking was reduced to the pitiful and hurried mechanics set in motion with women we no longer desire. Maybe that was the last (or the first) inkling she had. She certainly tried to win you back. I recall her repeated attempts: laughing away frictions, hugging you, prettying up at each gas station. I also remember your restrained reactions: embarrassed smiles, exasperation bulging in the muscles of your jaw, fleeting apologetic looks. And when the time came for us to fly to Cuba you looked so relieved. Oh boy, you suddenly looked so happy the ten or fifteen days were over, and you could get back to whatever you desperately wanted to get back to!

Neither Elliot nor his mother had the faintest notion that they were seeing Bob Steil for the last time when they waved goodbye to him on October 14, 1959, after that strange summer. He'd flown to New Orleans on three occasions, claiming vague business demands.

On the morning of December 4, the mailman handed

Carmen a letter from her husband, nine scribbled lines advising her to call off the usual Christmas trip to Sebastian due to urgent matters that he needed to attend to in Louisiana. Remittances arrived punctually, but the 1960 Easter cancellation was further reduced to a two-line Western Union cable in mid-February. Carmen feared total rejection, figured her marriage was on the verge of collapse, and experienced the frequent and rather irrational response of rekindled love. Her increasingly concerned letters remained unanswered, and on the evening that the long-distance operator informed her that Bob's phone line in Sebastian had been disconnected, Carmen called her mother-in-law. Edna excused her son, blaming long working hours seven days a week, yet Carmen sensed a nuance of commiseration in Edna's voice as she groped for explanations and promised to mediate. On April 14, an overjoyed Elliot ran into the living room of his Santa Cruz house waving a letter postmarked Cocoa Beach, Florida. It read:

March 22, 1960

Dear Carmen:

I hope you two are fine. I miss you a lot but won't return before Castro's fall. I won't work for Commies. Chances are somebody will soon arrange a hit on the bastard. Don't worry, I'll keep sending you money. Please don't call Mom again. She got pretty upset and you know about her heart condition. Give Elliot a big kiss. Don't write, Reds read our letters. I'll be in touch with you soon.

Love,
Bob

* * *

Elliot Steil's bowels grumbled and contorted painfully. He discharged spurts of diarrhea. Panic, cold, and rum caused him to urinate excessively, and he woozily pondered the paradox of dehydrating in the middle of the ocean. His throat felt raw from howling and his tongue and palate were dry, but he refrained from drinking seawater. Concluding that he could do nothing to save his life, Steil considered his available options to shorten the agony. Since being ripped up by sharks depended on the beasts, only drowning remained. Yet he couldn't face volition's supreme test. Diving down as far as he could and swallowing as much water as possible was beyond him. This confirmation of his cowardice overwhelmed him, and once again his tears flowed.

I'm so dizzy. Or am I? This is a womb. I'm suspended in silence, ignorance, blackness, and cold. No, wombs are not cold. Can't believe this stillness. It's like a pool. Give me one star, oh God, one fucking sign that other worlds exist. Oh, Mom. Here's your Elliot crying out to heaven. Remember how you hated my supposedly deep-rooted atheism, my restrained exasperation at your blessings and prayers and Hail Marys? Well, here's your Elliot whining to the Almighty. All sudden turnabouts are propelled by fear. Oh, how I hate these fucking spasms. Epilepsy must be like this, except that epileptics don't tremble continuously. Sharks won't get close; they ain't fond of Jell-O, far as I know. Fear made me hate Dad. Fear of loneliness and despair and abandonment and disillusion. Fallen idol or misjudged man? Difficult to pinpoint when you're ten.

The teacher experienced an altered state of hazy memories interspersed with fragments of his endangered present. His mind worked simultaneously on different tracks. Overall consciousness was devoted to fearing for his life; a smaller yet sizable portion of himself registered bodily sensations; a third examined faint memories; like a film loop, a fourth and the tiniest fragment played over and over the past few days, in which he searched for clues leading to his predicament. Freed from inhibitions in the face of death, he mumbled to himself in a hoarse, weak voice.

If only something would pull me down and end this agony! Ha! Words and meanings. A man could live a hundred years and never know agony. I've never seen such thick clouds. Perfect lining for a wet coffin. Gastler told the right stories, moments only Dad and I shared. The lexicographers who define it, the wise scholars who reflect on its definition, the clever teachers who teach its meaning never get close to understanding agony before death. Maybe not even then. Will I see dawn? I wish I could peep for a second at the Academy's dictionary, or Webster's. Torment is different. It's inflicted by someone. Anguish is mental. Agony is . . . fate's last mocking grimace at men, the final misery in a long string of miseries.

By late 1962, Carmen Steil had abandoned hope. She surmised that recent US Treasury regulations, extensively covered in the Cuban press, were the reason Bob had stopped supporting his son. Carmen relinquished her efforts at keeping her husband's image alive in Elliot, answered the boy's frequent inquiries evasively, and tried unsuccessfully to overcome the guilt that would burden her for the rest of her life. She felt certain Elliot would cope in a perfectly normal way with the absence of a father; his devil-may-care attitude was proof.

Carmen was mistaken. The confluence of social upheaval and family disintegration brought about silent twists and turns in the boy's development. In the beginning, Elliot couldn't figure out what had gone wrong. He'd given up trying to understand adult life, especially marriage, but he considered himself as much Cuban as American and rejected any kind of xenophobic behavior. Those who formerly had been affectionately called *americanos*, Yankees, or johnnies were now imperialists preparing to crush Cuba, and even though US residents in Santa Cruz had already fled, hand-painted banners displayed everywhere ordered them to go home.

Elliot would have loved to identify with the revolutionaries, march behind the platoons of ebullient refinery workers toting Garands, M-1s, and weird-looking Czech 9 mm automatic pistols. He wished he could collect money to buy planes and weapons and wear a black beret, but he was looked at contemptuously and snubbed by the same boys and girls who two or three years back had been mesmerized by his Florida stories. His English was no longer revered; now even the public-school English teacher seemed ashamed of his proclivity for the foreign language. The closest father figure available, his maternal grandfather, besides having seven other grandchildren, became a workaholic after being promoted to chief of the refinery's quality-control lab, and frequently expressed thinly veiled criticism of his daughter's choice of an American husband.

All of this was fertile ground for further maladjustment when the turmoil of puberty kicked in, coinciding with his admittance into junior high school. At the age of thirteen, Elliot found himself puzzled by his sudden acne, worried about his sparse pubic hair, and horrified at his erect penis being only five and a quarter inches long. Older boys said that to really satisfy a woman, you needed a solid eight-inch dick.

In his new educational environment, he struggled in vain with physics and chemistry, and was besieged by bullies. Counterrevolutionaries were called worms, and one day Elliot was labeled a Yankee worm. He decided enough was enough, and in a month won the student body's respect with seven fights, of which he was the undisputed loser of five. But swollen lips and bruised limbs didn't unveil the arcane world of uniformly accelerated motion or covalent bindings, and he flunked both sciences. After repeating seventh grade, he barely passed his science courses in the eighth and ninth, although he excelled in English and sailed through Spanish, history, and geography. Teachers and friends unanimously agreed that Elliot's future lay in the humanities, specifically English. The choice of profession for the seventeen-year-old student was obvious when he was drafted.

His Army life consisted of two different phases: six months of basic training, and two and a half years raising cattle. As infantry rookies go, Elliot was fairly decent. He made himself unobtrusive, obeyed orders, showed dexterity in disassembling his weapon, and obtained high marks at the rifle range. But after marching for a couple of hours he complained of intense pain in both his legs. X-rays revealed metatarsal bones that were too short, and he was given a pair of boots with orthopedic corrections before being transferred to an Army cattle farm fifteen miles south of Santa Cruz.

There Elliot lived the gloomiest days of his life. The future he had envisioned as a brilliant and well-connected English professor, interpreter, and translator never seemed more distant than among the Brown Swiss herd he was required to milk, feed, water, vaccinate, and shepherd in the company of nine other recruits and a master sergeant, who had earned his stripes becoming an artificial inseminator.

Because Elliot was an appalling horseman, the sergeant taught him to drive. Having mastered the farm's tractor, he got his driving permit, then graduated to a Russian Gaz jeep, later to a Zil light truck in which, during the last five months of his tour of duty, he drove milk canteens to and from an Army supply depot.

His pleasant memories of the US, conflicting feelings for his father, and love of the English language kept Elliot in a wait-and-see attitude about anti-Americanism. He had embraced the mixture of fierce independence and social egalitarianism at the core of local contemporary politics, yet he never blindly believed the propaganda machine churning out declarations that the United States government existed for the sole purpose of erasing Cuba from the face of the Earth. The Bay of Pigs invaders had been Cubans, and since the truly dangerous October 1962 missile crisis, captured raiders and rebels were as well. It was obvious to the young man who the American government sympathized with, who it assisted, and who it backed, but he was under the impression that Kennedy and Johnson in the past, and Nixon at present, wanted to topple Castro, not destroy his country of birth. Nevertheless, he knew inwardly that he would fight for his homeland should future events prove him wrong.

Unfortunately, inwardly was not enough. Neighbors, friends, and Army buddies noticed the way Elliot repressed yawns at political rallies, applauded only mildly, murmured (instead of screamed) 'DOWN!' when the speaker shouted 'Down with Yankee imperialism!' at the end of a tirade, and in general didn't show the ardor expected of young revolutionaries. Most people shrugged off Elliot's indifference, some shared it, and a few laughed it away, but in every group there was at least one person who expressed concern for the apathy shown by the son of an American citizen. Sometimes a remark had no consequence; on other occasions, it was reported and filed away.

You probably guessed it, Mom. Or maybe someone whispered a word of advice to you. You said we should leave, get lost in a city of a million and a half, keep a low profile, act like public-spirited citizens, and tell snoopers my last name came from my great-grandfather, an American who died at the turn of the century. Gastler never said how he found me. I wonder if Dad knew our Havana address. Never before have I felt so deprived. This is the Void. No light, no sound, no earth, no fire, no hope. Only water and air. You tricked me into it, Mom. No, you were straightforward from the start, and I was so tired of small-town tattle, so frustrated by the impediments of enrolling in a university forty miles away that I readily agreed. In the beginning, things must've been like this: floating, decaying substances, nutrients for new life forms. Not only in the beginning; it has always been like this, always will be.

Because the buying and selling of real estate between private citizens had been banned, Carmen García swapped the spacious two-bedroom house bought by her husband in Santa Cruz for a small Havana apartment. Without telling Elliot, she posted a letter to her mother-in-law notifying her of their change of address, and soon after got a job as a receptionist in an old city hospital. Her son became a mailman, and in October of '71 enrolled in a night course at Havana University's Workers and Farmers Faculty to complete his secondary education.

The still-virgin and sex-starved Elliot Steil was promptly seduced by Daisy Loret, a divorcée who corresponded with a cousin of hers living in Santiago. The sophisticated, attractive thirty-two-year-old cartographer had an eye and a taste for sexually inexperienced young men. At twenty-one, Elliot was beyond her age ceiling, but she perceived a combination of aptitude, eagerness, and latent promise worthy of exploration.

Six months later, a very well-proportioned, bright-eyed, stunningly handsome seventeen-year-old new neighbor provided her with the perfect reason to dump Elliot. For fifteen minutes after their split, the map maker experienced the sadness of a grade-school teacher seeing off her prodigy. Daisy knew she could treat herself to a lot of taller, stronger, and better-looking young men, but she suspected she'd never again find a natural, the kind of guy with an uncanny, innate perception of female sexuality who enormously enjoyed learning the tricks, being tender, dispensing and lingering on pleasure; the uninhibited perfectionist who pulled out all the stops and made his lover vibrate like a pipe organ; the easy-to-love and difficult-to-forget kindhearted pauper; the dangerous enemy clever girls enjoy for a while and then discard at the first sign of dependency, concluded Daisy.

So, it's true. Life is relived at its end. Daisy, an open copy of Kama Sutra. Fancy-free feelings and full physical involvement. The loveless lover. First to fuck me, first to sack me. And then I got the scholarship.

I guess this is the swell, this almost-imperceptible swaying uuuup and doooown. Death cradling me. 'Words, phrases, and clauses that are appositional, or parenthetical, or independent, as nouns of direct address, exclamations, absolute phrases, are set off by a comma or commas,' Mr Reedley would dictate. Next week we'd refute him by brandishing the work of a young or not-so-young American writer. He'd carefully read the text, and his sneer would debase it beyond serious consideration. Uuuup comma doooown. Best years of my life. Books, broads and booze. Discovering Steinbeck, Updike, Dreiser, Capote. Discovering Lidia, Margarita, Ada, the stouthearted but fragile Luz. Stout-hearted or stouthearted? 'Most compound adjectives consisting of two or more words are hyphenated, though in several cases particular adjectives . . .' Uuuup . . .

Physically and emotionally drained, Elliot Steil lost himself in sleep. Nearly an hour later, he opened his eyes to the promise of dawn, a delicate evolution in the bank of clouds, from charcoal-gray to dark silver. For an instant the teacher wondered why he felt so numb, so utterly exhausted. A sudden shove against his right shoulder brought him back to reality. A giant shark ripping out his side flashed in his mind, and his instinctive response was a horrid scream. Frantic arm and leg movements pulled his torso up. His right arm hit something hard, and excruciating pain stormed through his brain. A second scream reverberated in exclamations that bounced away across the calm surface of the sea. A pop-eyed Steil discerned a floating shape manned by blurred ghosts. Then he signed off, and his lax body began to sink.

3

My first reaction after waking up that morning was to marvel at having been able to doze for a while. Dani was still asleep by my side, his head resting on arms crossed over the inner tube, his waist joined to mine by a piece of rope. A pang of remorse made my eyes moist. My watch said 6.11. I turned back and saw Papa and Tito paddling slowly. Mama presented me with one of her comforting smiles, poured a lukewarm cup of espresso from the thermos, and passed it to me. Mario said, of all things, 'Good morning.' I sipped and looked around the empty ocean. We'd been on the raft for close to thirty hours, and fear was drilling holes in my wavering confidence.

My attraction to the unknown had led me to read many newspaper and magazine articles on the Bermuda triangle, so when Papa talked to all family members for the first time about fleeing Cuba, I started recalling stories about ghost ships and disappearing planes. I kept my mouth shut because I wanted to be free more than anything else and felt certain I'd become the laughing stock of the men in my family should I voice my misgivings. For Mama the trip would be jinxed if I said something worrisome. I was returning the empty cup when you appeared.

Know something? I'd never heard anybody holler so loud in my life. You looked like a demon bubbling out from the bottom of the sea to claim us, a magician's assistant cut in half by the handsaw during a mad performance. Having lost everything beneath his waist, this glistening, wizened half-apparition screaming his lungs out would pull us down to hell's underwater chambers. Startled, each of us blurted out some curse like coño or carajo. Papa must have said his only profanity, cojones. Then you collapsed and a few moments went by before we realized you were drowning. We found ourselves gaping at each other in utter bewilderment. As usual Papa recovered first. He crossed a leg over an inner tube and grabbed you by the hair.

Tito moved over to help Papa. As they were hauling you up, you came to, moaning softly. I noticed you were trying to protect your arm, and I screamed out, 'His right arm is busted!' Papa let go of your forearm, and relief spread across your face before you passed out again.

Now that I've seen what some people have sailed out on, I understand what a solid raft Papa had built. But ours had been designed for six people, and you couldn't sit or kneel like us. After much pulling and pushing, we managed to lay you down at the center, where the inner tubes joined and offered some sort of resting place. Your head was between me and Dani, who was now wide awake, your hips between Mama and Mario, your feet dangling onto Papa and Tito's inner tubes.

I watched your face closely. Breathing unevenly, you coughed and spewed up seawater. I washed your lips with fresh water from my plastic bottle, and you came back mumbling something, looked at me, and tried to grab the bottle with your right arm before squeezing your eyes shut and groaning in pain. Eventually I let you guzzle. Dani said, 'Don't move, mister.' You glanced at him, smiled, and passed out.

We engaged in useless guesswork for maybe ten minutes, and then you fixed your big, bloodshot brown eyes on me and stared before asking for a glass of water. A glass, you said. Papa and Tito had resumed paddling. We understood it wasn't the right time for questions. You had sustained an injury, suffered a severe nervous breakdown, no doubt, and you needed time to recover.

After guzzling water and sipping espresso, you slept so soundly that you missed seeing our attempts at nursing you. We all wore wide-brimmed straw hats, long-sleeved shirts, sunglasses, and pants, but had nothing to spare. I covered your face with Papa's undershirt; we immobilized your right arm by tying one end of my bra to your wrist and the other to your neck. Mama and Mario applied homemade sunblock on your scrawny legs and left arm. 'Is he gonna die?' Dani asked. I shook my head and started making breakfast.

You were cast into oblivion pretty quickly. By 7.30 we were all scanning the horizon from east to north to west and back. We knew when somebody had peed, because they filled the plastic bucket with seawater and poured it onto their lap. So far only Dani had defecated: uninhibited childhood. Mama and Mario were paddling, which seemed to keep the raft heading north but didn't move us very much onward. Papa was fishing and Tito smoking a cigarette. We had enough food and water for a week, but ever since his prison experience, Papa has believed that you never have enough food, and he was planning on as many raw fish meals as possible for all the men on board. Time crept agonizingly toward nowhere.

At some point, your free hand retrieved the undershirt from over your face. 'Could you please give me something to eat?' I fed you a poached egg, a cup of green vegetables, three crackers, some more espresso, and a cup of water. Then you were lucid enough to thank us in your most solemn tone of voice. Papa said not to mention it and asked you what had happened. You started to say something but suddenly clammed up. Then you asked where we were headed. 'To Key West,' Papa said. You nodded, or at least tried to from your awkward position, and remained silent, probably considering whether lying to the people who had just saved your life was the proper way to show your gratitude. Obviously you decided that yes, it was the proper way, for at last you fed us the story of the lone escapee on a one-man raft that had sunk after a few hours. Papa being Papa, he wanted to know what had gone wrong, the materials you'd used, if the inner tube had been new, if it had been secured to the planks with rope or steel wire, air pressure, type of valve, the works. In your uncertain replies, your hesitations, it became clear to us that you were lying horrendously, for it was plain as day you didn't know the first thing about building a raft. Papa, Tito, and Mario looked miffed. Mama and I didn't care. From his ten-year-old perspective, Dani concluded that you were a fool.

Probably to regain our confidence, you told us your first name, Havana address, and other details, then tried to engage Dani in conversation and praised Mama's espresso. The men gave you the cold shoulder, and you returned their silence. The sun's glare was subdued *by the clouds, but you covered your face. I noticed your left hand gently feeling your right arm, and I made you swallow two pain killers. Fifteen minutes later you dozed off.*

All the rafters I've met since then agree on one thing: they'd never do it again. Maybe the lucky ones picked up after sailing for only a few hours would be willing to relive the experience if they were sent back to Cuba. I've never met one. Before getting under way you think you know anxiety, despair, and exasperation. You don't. So, as we kept peering at the horizon, I wondered what it would have been like to somehow find yourself floating alone in the middle of the ocean for God knows how long, at night, without food, water, and hope, and tears streamed down my cheeks.

Around noon we saw it. We shouted and waved our hats. Papa took off his white shirt, tied a sleeve to a paddle, then swung it frantically over his head. There are three images stored in my memory that will remain until the last minute of my life: the first moment I laid eyes on my son, the screaming sea demon, and the beautiful eighty-two-foot US Coast Guard boat swiftly approaching our raft.

We were hoisted on board, and a paramedic took over your care. The next time I saw you was going ashore in Key West, when you asked the stretcher bearers to stop by our side, thanked us again, and smiled mirthlessly. There was something dangerous and bewitching in your eyes. Papa was so exultant he either forgot or excused your deception, asked for a piece of paper and a pencil, and scribbled my uncle's phone number. You said you couldn't reciprocate because you had no relatives, but you'd keep in touch. Your second lie.

*   *   *

Elliot Steil closed the 10½" × 8" spiral notebook, set it by his side on the daybed, and stared at the ceiling of the efficiency he had rented three weeks earlier in an old Miami apartment building on the 3500 block of NW 18th Avenue. Before giving him a peck on the cheek and leaving at around 6.30, Fidelia had pulled out the notebook from her handbag and dumped it onto the sleep sofa. 'You storm into my life on page twenty-

one,' she said while unlatching the door. Curiosity got the best
of him. He opened the diary and flipped through it. The sheets
were numbered in the upper right corner, figures encircled by
perfect rings. Few words had been crossed out or substituted.
After so many years of grading papers, Steil had unintentionally
become proficient at identifying gender by handwriting. The
careful longhand was feminine, purposefully formed and predominantly rounded. Her Spanish was both cultivated and
unpretentious. For six minutes he had read with mild surprise.

Now, watching the dim circle of light from the night lamp
on the ceiling, Steil recalled his recent past. Yes, he had
bellowed, flung his arms about, and kicked like a madman,
thus consuming the last sparks of his strength. For the
umpteenth time he wondered what had crashed into his arm.
He hadn't asked Fidelia and had not seen her relatives again.
It must have been a solid wooden platform beneath the six
inner tubes. It didn't matter. The outcome was a fractured
cubitus, and for thirty-two days he had to wear a cast that
extended from his knuckles to an inch below his elbow.

For the first two or three hours, exhaustion had been so
overwhelming that he had been deprived of the energy required
to smile, whisper his immense gratitude, and express concern
about cutting into their food and water reserves. Gonzalo's
words kept flashing in his mind: *'Methinks he hath no drowning
mark upon him; his complexion is perfect gallows.'*

Just after drinking the espresso on the raft, something eerie
had happened. For an indeterminate span of time he couldn't
see the undershirt's fabric or the pale glow of the overcast
sky, couldn't hear the rafters talking, and only vaguely
remembered being looked after. All he could see and hear
was Gastler, his comments, gestures, smiles, and suggestions.
Emotions he'd never experienced, only knew from reading –
blind hate, cold fury, murderous rage – were revealed to him.
They seeped into his marrow, stoking the desire for revenge.
Those few hours in the sea had turned him inside out, trans-

formed him into a different person. Absolutely certain that nothing could prevent their rescue and safe arrival in the US, he had started plotting then and there.

He would walk into the first police precinct and tell his story – his fantastic, unbelievable story. Was the bastard's real name Gastler? He'd only seen a driver's license, a credit card, and a business card, all probably under a false identity to evade hotel and car rental company records in Cuba. The murderer had paid with cash at the Floridita and the Morambón. He'd heard that in order to help US citizens circumvent Treasury regulations, Cuban immigration officials did not stamp American passports, so a false passport cursorily examined was also a possibility.

'Why did the old man try to kill you?' a skeptical detective in a squadroom would ask. 'Did he steal something valuable from you, Mr Steil? Did this stranger owe you money? Do you have any knowledge of the man being involved in drug trafficking, kidnapping, grand larceny, armed robbery, counterfeiting, or any other serious crimes? Wasn't it possible, Mr Steil, having admitted you were drinking, that you fell overboard by accident? Maybe Mr Gastler was so looped himself that he didn't register your fall. Anyway, let's try to find out something about this guy. He claimed to have been sent by your deceased father. What was your father's last place of residence? You don't know? What business was he in? Thirty-four years without news from him? Okay, we'll let you know.'

The detective would fill out some form that he would place into a circular file sixty seconds after Steil had left the place. No police department would devote an hour of their time or spend taxpayers' money tracking down an American charged with pushing a drunk illegal immigrant into international waters.

By the end of the journey, Steil had second thoughts about going to the police. A paramedic commented on the watch strapped to his wrist. With a broad smile, the young Cuban-

American informed Steil in colloquial Spanish that he could live comfortably for an entire year in Miami by selling that watch. Steil grinned and let it pass.

That was proof. Everybody – at least everybody in Florida – would know that no run-of-the-mill Cuban living in his country of birth could afford an expensive watch. The creep had overlooked this; he'd been too busy scheming. What was the damn thing worth? According to the cost-of-living indexes Steil had glimpsed through in American newspapers, and discounting the paramedic's jovial mood and the Cuban propensity for exaggeration, the piece would have to be worth thousands of dollars if it could cover a man's expenses for a full year. Maybe the watch could even be traced. And what if he handed it over as evidence, and it disappeared from a police storeroom the way so many kilos of cocaine and heroin vanish? He didn't know what he was doing, but he would be driven by the most powerful motivation: that of the victim.

Victim, enemy, aggressor – before Dan Gastler these words had been meaningless. There had been people he disliked, even couldn't stand, guys he found disgusting, insufferable, or arrogant, but he had no enemies. Perhaps there had been unknown ill-wishers who did nothing more harmful than give him a mauling behind his back. It surprised him to discover a new side to his personality – the going-after-the-sonafabitch side. *No matter what.* If that was becoming vindictive, okay, he was vindictive, and fixated.

Steil had kept himself very busy since arriving in Miami. With assistance from the Cuban Refugee Emergency Center, he had formalized his legal status. He observed behavioral patterns, listened to people in the streets, did research in libraries, studied a Dade County street map and Greater Miami's phone book, nursed his arm to full recovery, and dried out.

For the past six weeks the teacher had also hauled cardboard boxes, pulled pallet-laden lifting jacks, and stocked shelves at a supermarket. In his free time he was making some high-risk money on the side as a means to an end. Fury, bitterness, and retaliation spurred him on. The notion that he was trying to outfox a killer on his own turf never crossed his mind.

In his opinion, misspelling his name to a Key West nurse had been a brilliant move. E-L-I-O E-S-T-E-I-L, he'd said. In fact, breaking his arm became a blessing. At the hospital he had more than forty hours to plan his moves before the interview with the Immigration and Naturalization Services. Hiding Gastler's watch was the first. The second was misspelling his name. Should the geezer somehow inquire if a Cuban named Elliot Steil had been rescued on the high seas, no alphabetically ordered computer printout would give him away. He moved his date of birth forward five years, five months, and five days; his place of residence, five blocks north and five east. He reported that he'd been an office worker in Cuba with an elementary knowledge of the English language. The only four accurate pieces of personal information that he furnished were his race, sex, nationality, and marital status. The Cuban-American INS employee who conducted the first official interview two days later took him at face value. There was no way to check Steil's veracity, and five adult witnesses and a child had testified to his personal ordeal. He had never been so deceitful, and the hospital stay had provided the perfect venue to begin his transformation into a two-faced, crooked sonafab-itch, traits necessary for tracking down the sleazeball.

The hospital's PR lady, upon hearing that he had no friends or relatives in the US, appealed to the Key West Salvation Army, and Steil was shipped to the Men's Lodge on South River Drive in Miami. He entered the place with mixed feelings, the costly watch in his left pocket. Having cried out to God when death was a distinct possibility, he was ashamed to fear coercion from His soldiers. To Steil's surprise, no religious demands were imposed on him. There were services, prayers, songs, and invitations to repent, but no one said a word to the recovering Cuban, who skipped devotionals and other forms of worship with a moderate feeling of guilt. A casual comment led to free secondhand clothing and a brand-new pair of orthopedic shoes. He was pleased to find an ideological organization that did not make observance compulsory. He would have to patch things up with the Almighty at a later date and without outside help.

Steil had been hypersensitive and anxious at the Key West hospital before identifying these conditions as withdrawal symptoms. Drying up allowed him to reflect on his drinking. He admitted to himself being an addict and decided to kick the habit on his own. The lesson had been too dramatic, and he would never again place himself at that disadvantage before friend or foe.

The lodge's captain told Steil in broken Spanish and sign language that job hunting with an arm in a cast was out of the question. To keep himself busy, the teacher began his groundwork with the three thick volumes of the phone directory. There was no reason to think there was a Steil or a Gastler living in Miami, but he nonetheless looked them up. No Southern Bell customer with either name was listed in the white pages, nor did any private investigator from the yellow pages have the geezer's name. He checked watch dealers, car and boat rental companies, libraries, and marinas.

On his first Miami afternoon, using the fifty-dollar bill he'd been given by a Cuban exile group in Key West, he bought a street map and took a bus to the city's main public library, at 101 West Flagler. A library assistant explained the computerized cataloguing system, and three hours later he found that the Fellsmere sugar factory had been closed in 1958. He'd been considering a trip to Fellsmere to check on his father's resignation or retirement date at the factory, learn if some senior employee could put him on the right track to unravel Bob Steil's past, and attempt to trace his connections with his contemporaries, especially old Army buddies. His paternal grandparents must have died years ago, and it was unlikely that records of a business concern extinct for thirty-six years were still preserved, so he ruled out visiting Sebastian. On his way back to the lodge, the teacher wondered where his father had lived during the winters of 1958 and 1959, when he and his mother believed he was in Fellsmere.

The following morning Steil bought a Marlins baseball cap and cheap plastic sunglasses, and for the next two weeks spent almost every day pacing around marinas and boatyards. He would get up early, eat a hearty breakfast at the lodge, then get under way. In the beginning he would walk to the nearest marinas on Miami River, where he met a Cuban dubbed Hairball, who eventually became essential to his plan. When he moved along the coast to the north and south of Biscayne Bay, bus connections were a must. Finally he visited Key Biscayne and Miami Beach's boating and fishing facilities. Steil admitted to himself that he was betting on chance. He didn't know the name or port of registry of the yacht he was looking for, nor any of its external identification marks. There were thousands of vessels, many like Gastler's, and on the few occasions that he asked permission to hop on board and take a look at the cabin, his request had been curtly denied. By the time the teacher headed back to the lodge, he was starving and dead tired, and his feet hurt like hell, but he always tried to read the *Herald* and watch the news before turning in.

He hadn't exercised so vigorously since his stint as a Havana mailman twenty-five years earlier, and it surprised him at the end of his first month in the US that he had to suck in his gut to button the waist of the jeans he had been handed down. He never asked for second helpings and rarely ate ice cream or other high-calorie foods, but it was as if his brain had ordered all cells to stockpile just in case the weirdo decided to go back to Cuba. Two weeks later, he searched out the lodge's captain and sheepishly pointed at the space between the button and the buttonhole on his slacks. The man smiled and Steil was given a new set of second-hand clothing two sizes larger.

Gradually Steil learned to enjoy the dark, double-edged delight of secrecy. By concealing his knowledge of the country's language, he was able to listen with impunity to the conversations of those who believed him to be unacquainted with their mother tongue. He practiced local cadences in his mind and learned new expressions, like on the day his cast was removed. The teacher was at the lodge, turning the pages of the bilingual phone book one more time, when a gray-haired Anglo wino told a friend, 'Guy's gonna have to put his fucking arm outta the window to get an even tan.' On other occasions, pretending to be inept felt like a burden. Some library assistants, office staff, and store attendants didn't know a word of Spanish, so he was forced to place the tips of his fingers over his temple, squeeze his eyes shut, and say two or three key words in pidgin English, such as coastal community, job-assistance center, and notepad. Sometimes a Spanish-speaking citizen volunteered to be a translator.

From time to time his impressions sidetracked him. Miami was a completely different place from the flat, humble, medium-sized city he remembered from his childhood, and the most outstanding single change was the people. Cubans, Nicaraguans, Salvadorans, Guatemalans, Mexicans, and natives from all over Central and South America abounded. In large sections of the city, Spanish was the predominant language. But Steil also explored downtown, the business and financial district, the banks on South Biscayne Boulevard and Brickell Avenue, the Federal Courts on NE 4th Street. He paced through wealthy neighborhoods and the University of Miami's main campus, visited public libraries in Key Biscayne and Coconut Grove, and in these places rarely heard Spanish. Steil wondered if the supposed Latin takeover was just a much-ballyhooed sham. The centers of real power in federal and state governments, the business community, and higher education appeared to remain firmly in Anglo hands. Once in a while, a

few crumbs were dropped to the best and brightest of first-
and second-generation immigrants. Letting them in was one
thing, relinquishing power another.

Little things also served as distractions. He was amazed that
Howard Johnson's main business was now the hotel trade and
astounded by the impossibility of finding a Royal Castle diner
where he could order a bowl of vegetable soup and saltine
crackers. Sex shops were intriguing to a man who had always
engaged in inventive lovemaking without resorting to sup-
plements. Well-paved streets filled with shiny cars, the diffrac-
tion of sunlight over gushing sprinklers on manicured lawns,
the absence of pigeons in Crandon Park, fifty or sixty high
rises on a coastline that used to have only four or five: Little
things seeped in.

*   *   *

Sunlight filtered in through the room's window, obliterating
the circle of light on the ceiling. Steil freed his hands from
under his head, cracked his knuckles, and stretched, then consulted the cheap Hong Kong watch on his wrist. He sat up
and put on his plastic thongs, turned off the night lamp, and
stood.

Taking three steps across the linoleum floor, the teacher
reached a tiny bathroom. He took off his boxer shorts, urinated,
flushed the toilet, and entered the shower. Three minutes later
he plucked a towel from its hanger and dried off. Facing a
rust-stained sink as the toilet tank hissed, he looked at his
reflection in the medicine-cabinet mirror, shaved, then brushed
his teeth and returned to the room. He opened the dresser's
top drawer and donned a pair of fresh underwear.

From the middle drawer the teacher removed a brand-new
dress shirt, a plain black tie, and a Burdine's shopping bag. As
he took nine pins and a plastic mold out from under the shirt's
collar, Steil clicked his tongue, forced a smile, and shook his
head sadly at the superfluity of consumerism. Only those who

had lived with scarcity could fully appreciate it. The teacher looped the tie into a Windsor knot and turned to the closet for a lightweight charcoal-gray suit. He placed the jacket on the bed and put on trousers that were a little too baggy for his taste. He returned to the closet, removed his only belt from his worn jeans, and snaked it through the new pants' belt loops. After putting on black socks and his well-polished black orthopedic shoes, he slipped into the jacket and pulled out the cuffs a little.

The teacher returned to the night lamp and turned it upside down, removing its bottom with practiced movements by using the room's key. He withdrew Gastler's watch and slid it into his jacket's inner pocket. Steil reassembled the lamp, then picked up an impressive wad of bills, a handkerchief, a small PVC bag, and loose change from the reading table's only drawer. He slipped a tiny notepad and a ball-point pen into his shirt pocket. Before leaving, he grabbed the shopping bag, turned off the bathroom light, and kicked his slippers under the bed.

Steil had two bagels and two cups of coffee at a nondescript cafeteria close to Allapattah Station, then hailed a taxi. The cab dropped him on the corner of Fifth Avenue and 26th Street, where a car rental company advertised that credit cards were not required. The attendant on duty, distrusting a Cuban who had recently been issued a driver's license, forgot everything about civil-action suits and demanded a $500 deposit plus $135 for the twenty-four-hour rental of a vintage white Rolls-Royce. To the man's surprise, the client laid six large ones and a fifty on his desk.

Driving the impressive car with utmost care, the teacher took Miami Avenue, turned right on 36th Street, and cruised along the Julia Tuttle Causeway into Miami Beach, obediently following traffic signs. He abandoned the Arthur Godfrey Road by taking a left onto Collins Avenue, and followed it up to 87th Street, where he handed the Rolls keys to a Surfside Beach Hotel parking valet. Steil traversed the lobby to a phone booth, closed the door, dropped a quarter, and tapped out a number.

'Tourneau Corner. May I help you?' an educated female voice whispered almost immediately.

'Good morning,' Steil said.

'Good morning to you, sir.'

'May I speak to the manager, please?' the teacher requested with a passable British accent.

'Who's calling?'

'My name is Rupert White. I'm Lord Covington's personal secretary.'

'Just a moment, Mr White.'

Steil slid the tip of his tongue over his lips as a muzak version of 'Blue Danube' played, and he felt the palms of his hands become wet. According to the society columns of the local press, a Lord Covington was spending a few days at a rented villa in Miami Beach. He owned a seventy-four-foot Stephens Flybridge, which he sailed in the most prestigious boat races. The teacher had been listening to British English-language tapes at the downtown library for the last four days.

Less than twenty seconds had elapsed when a velvety male voice caressed the ear piece: 'Yes, Mr White. My name is John Warner. May I be of some assistance to His Lordship?'

'I hope so, Mr Warner. I most certainly hope so, to spare me making two hundred phone calls.'

'That many?' He laughed.

'Oh, yes. Milord entertained last night, and when the pool attendant showed up this morning to perform his duties, he found a rather expensive watch lying on the bottom of the pool.'

'Is that so?'

'He handed it over to me. Quite a decent chap, I'd say. Well, Milord has instructed me to return this Breguet to its owner. Imagine, there were close to two hundred men here last night.'

'I see.'

'So, I thought perhaps you could help us. Milord is a devoted Audemars Piguet patron.'

'A fact that confirms His Lordship's fine taste. And how can we be of assistance to you, Mr White?'

'We're sailing to Bermuda this evening and Milord would like to leave the matter settled. Since you also represent Breguet, I was wondering if you could identify the owner for us.'

'An identification is perfectly possible,' Warner said. 'Computer records are kept on all buyers for obvious reasons. But we'd have to see the watch and ask Geneva who bought this particular piece. Of course, the original buyer might have resold it or presented it to someone. Can our messenger pick up this Breguet?'

'That would be troubling you too much. We can send a chauffeur right over to your shop.'

'As you wish. Please give me the phone number where I can reach you as soon as Geneva faxes its reply. It shouldn't take more than a couple of hours.'

'I suppose it's better if I ring you back a little bit later,' Steil said without the slightest hesitation. 'We'll be flying to Isla Morada by helicopter in a little while and won't be back before 5.00. Milord hates cellulars, you know? I'll give you a ring around 3.00. Must you keep the watch or can the chauffeur bring it back after you see it?'

'We just need to look at a number on the dial. Breguets are individually numbered. We'll give it back to your man immediately.'

'Excellent. By the way, how much should he bring to cover your charge?'

'Nothing at all, Mr White. Serving such a distinguished client and helping another one to recover his lost property is a pleasure, not a business transaction.'

'Thank you very much, Mr Warner. Our man will be there in fifteen minutes.'

'You're very welcome, sir. Goodbye.'

'Goodbye.'

Steil replaced the handset and breathed a sigh of relief. He left the booth, entered the almost-deserted men's restroom and, pretending to wash his hands, soaked Gastler's watch, shook off the drops, slid the timepiece into the small PVC bag, and dropped it into his jacket's pocket. He blow-dried his hands, walked back to the hotel entrance, and handed a five-dollar bill and his car ticket to the parking valet.

Three minutes later he was creeping along Collins wearing a charcoal-gray chauffeur's cap that he had taken out of the shopping bag. He parked the Rolls facing the luxurious Tourneau Corner in Bal Harbour Shops, locked the car, and entered the place removing his cap. The shop was empty at that early hour, and a slightly surprised middle-aged salesman immediately approached him.

'May I help you?'

'I come see Mr Warner. Mr White send watch,' Steil said in the worst possible Spanish-accented English.

'Just a minute,' the salesman snapped before directing a meaningful glance at one of the two security guards flanking the swinging plate-glass door, then making an about-face. Not that the guards needed any spurring – both were perfectly aware of their typical clientele and knew that Steil didn't belong. For close to a minute the teacher stood, cap in hand, curiously eyeing one of the places where only the very rich or fatuous shop. Small TV cameras angled down from the ceiling; plush white curtains draped the windows; two-inch thick carpeting covered the floor. In the display windows and glass-encased counters, a glistening couple of million was casually laid over purple lining. The guards' gazes seemed superficial and disinterested, Steil observed, but somehow they managed to count his every wink.

Suddenly he noticed a man with silvery hair parted on the left motioning him to a small counter. As Steil approached the distinguished-looking Warner, he had to admit the man's subtlety. The manager appeared fine in his expensive-looking indigo-blue suit worn with an elegant white shirt and lilac silk tie, but his sartorial display was discreet enough not to outdo a rich client who wished to make the best-dressed men list.

'Mr Warner?' Steil asked rolling his *r*'s.

'Yes. I understand you have a watch for me to inspect.'

'Here it is.'

Steil handed over the PVC bag, and the manager disappeared through a side door. Less than a minute later he came back and returned the piece to the spurious chauffeur.

'Okay, *amigo*. Take it back to Mr White.'

'Yes, sir. Thank you,' Steil said as he slid the watch into his pocket and adjusted the cap on his head. Then he turned around and left the store. For lack of someone else more suspicious to keep an eye on, the guards watched him get into the Rolls and drive away.

The capless teacher spent the rest of the morning cruising around suburbs he had never visited: Golden Beach, Golden Shores, North Miami Beach, Hialeah Gardens. To rein in his impatience, he passed the time by continuously changing scenarios. Heading south through the Florida Turnpike, he reached Sweetwater, Westwood Lakes, Kendall, and Cutler Ridge. Taking the Dixie Highway, he entered the more familiar grounds of Coral Gables. At 1.15, the teacher left the car in a supermarket parking lot, walked two blocks east, and entered a cafeteria on Alcazar Avenue. He had ordered a Cuban sandwich and a red pop when a white man close to forty, dressed in tight designer jeans, an opened, white flamenco-dancer shirt, and cordovan loafers, perched himself on the stool next to Steil. The teacher gave him a sidelong glance, then returned his gaze to the wonderful legs of the Cuban waitress.

'How you doing?' the man asked in Cuban Spanish.

'I'm not complaining,' Steil said.

'Suit and tie; moving up in life,' the man commented. His

79

clean-shaven cheeks and chin were shadowed by dense black hair. The man also had a carefully trimmed mustache and bushy eyebrows. Tufts of hair grew out of his nostrils and ears, and his hands were hairy, too, but the man's crown was bald as a billiard ball. Two heavy gold chains with medals of the Virgen de la Caridad del Cobre and Santa Bárbara showed under his mat of chest hair. Save for family members, almost everybody called him Hairball.

'Moving, not up,' Steil specified.

'Got a sweet deal for you tonight,' Hairball said.

'Four to twelve shift tonight.'

'What do you work for, pardner? You can make all the foolas you want driving for me.'

'Playing that key reminds me,' Steil said. 'I want to renegotiate. A thousand from now on.'

'You kidding?'

'No.'

'Forget it.'

Steil's sandwich and soda arrived, and he took a bite without uttering another word. Hairball ordered a beer before addressing Steil again: 'You can't be serious.'

Steil limited his reply to nodding twice while chewing.

'Know something?' Hairball hissed. 'Ten new rafters arrive in this town every day. Half of them would drive for me for a hundred.'

Steil swallowed, and sipped from his pop. Then he chewed some more. The waitress with the sexy wheels came back with the beer, and for nearly a minute Hairball mused about something between sips. The teacher finished the sandwich, swallowed the last gulp of his soda, and dabbed his lips with a paper napkin. Then he signaled for the waitress and handed her a five-dollar bill.

'Listen, Ball,' Steil said, rotating the stool and looking Hairball right in the eye when the waitress left. 'I was new in town, didn't know my way around. Not anymore. I want a thousand per from now on. You know where to find me.'

'What did I do?' Hairball asked.

The waitress came back with the change. 'Keep it, beauty,' Steil said to her. 'Just looking at you is worth ten times that.'

The teacher wiggled his fingers at Hairball and departed. Back in the Rolls he followed the same route from Miami Avenue to Collins. At 2.50, he left the car with an Eden Roc parking attendant and called Warner from a booth in the lobby, ball-point pen poised over the tiny notepad.

'Yes, Mr White,' the manager said into his extension's mouthpiece.

'Have you learnt anything from Geneva, Mr Warner?'

'Certainly, sir. This particular Breguet was bought at a Sarasota jewelry store ten years ago by the man who owns the place, a Mr Edward Steil.'

Silence reigned for five seconds.

'Hello?' Warner said. 'Mr White? Are you there, Mr White?'

'Yes, yes Mr . . . ah, Warner. I was jotting down the person's name. In Sarasota.'

'The name doesn't ring a bell?'

'Oh, no, no, it doesn't. No, not at all. No.'

'Is there something wrong, Mr White?'

'No, nothing's wrong, no. I want to thank you most kindly for your help.'

'Don't mention it. Please present our respects to His Lordship.'

'I most certainly will. Goodbye.'

'Goodbye, Mr White.'

* * *

Steil remained in the booth for close to two minutes stupidly reading the names of a man and a town over and over. Craving a drink was his first conscious reaction, the thing that pulled him out of his daze. The teacher found his way to the pool, spotted the empty bar, sat on a stool, and ordered a double shot of Bacardi. After filling a four-ouncer to the brim, the barmaid busied herself with the cash register. She had spent enough time in the trade to know when to leave a dude alone.

With elbows on the bartop and fists against his temples, Steil fixed his eyes on the glass for a full minute. The smell of the sea and the far-away murmur of small waves rolling in and breaking against the shore did the trick. He clicked his tongue, shook his head, and looked sideways.

'Get me a Coke, will you?'

September is always like this, the girl reasoned as she pulled the tab. Dead month, few customers, tips were 10 percent of what she made in January and February, and to top it off she had to put up with occasional weirdos, like this reformed soaker in the middle of a crisis.

Steil swilled the soda, paid the check, and left without touching a drop of liquor.

The teacher returned the Rolls, called in sick, and went back to his rented efficiency. He took off his clothes sneering at the vagaries of his life. Wearing his boxer shorts, socks, and shoes, he sat on one of the two director's chairs with bright-yellow canvas that came with the place. He ruled out coincidence. Not a chance in a million. The watch's owner was the paternal uncle he'd never met. Perhaps when he was a baby or a toddler, in those early stages of life when memory lasts only hours, his uncle had visited the Steils' rented apartment in Sebastian, or his grandparents' small house. He did recall from conversations among adults that his father's brother was in the jewelry business in some other state. That the man had returned to Florida and opened a jewelry store was a valid assumption. To figure out why he had sailed to Havana, enticed his nephew into fleeing Cuba, and then pushed him overboard was beyond the teacher's reach. The fact that the assailant was his own flesh and blood spread a thick coat of sadness over his vengefulness. Maybe his father was still alive somewhere, unaware of what had happened. Befuddled and emotionally drained, Steil took a second shower. Donning jeans and a short-sleeved tan sports shirt, he headed out to a pizza parlor on 36th Street. On his way back home he grabbed a copy of the *Herald* from under the plexiglass cover of a rack.

The teacher used the newspaper as a coolant for nearly an hour before addressing his puzzle from a different perspective. A trip to Sarasota was imperative, but what was he supposed to do once he got there? A long probe into the unknown was fruitless. Only after careful consideration could he figure out a plan with reasonable probabilities of success. For that he needed more money. It was the only counterbalance to an environment devoid of relatives, friends, contacts, and acquaintances who could do or repay favors. He'd be forced to do a lot of driving for Hairball before implementing the Judaic precept of an eye for an eye.

At 10.55 Steil killed the night lamp and tried to sleep, but his mind uncontrollably revisited the same recollections, emotions, and speculations. At 11.45 he turned on the night lamp and started reading from Fidelia's notebook, page one.

*　　*　　*

Nineteen days and getting over cultural shock. I walk into a drugstore and find a shelf stocked with ten different brands of toothbrushes, each brand offering ten different models; each model, ten colors; each color, ten toothbrushes dangling from a peg. There are maybe 10,000 toothbrushes on display and shoppers walk by oblivious to the affluence around them; the 10,000 nail polish vials, 10,000 hairpins, 10,000 lipsticks.

Comparisons are inescapable. Most people, like Papa and Mama, react with . . . let's see, simple-minded awe? awesome simple-mindedness? economic naïveté? They shake their heads in wonder and smile and think up the same jokes a million Cubans before us must have thought up. 'Did you bring your ration card and your female-worker ID?' 'Is today your group's buying day?' 'Remember, if you already purchased the deodorant you can't buy the toothbrush.'

And I smile too, a little condescendingly perhaps, and nod while recalling that two blocks away there's another drugstore identically stocked. Then I consider the whole city, the whole state . . . that's as far as I can imagine. Nationwide there must be . . . trillions? of articles in retail stores, quadrillions if you include the stocks of wholesalers and manufacturers. Yes, Communism is crushed under the American Way of what Lenin called 'satisfying the ever-increasing needs of the population'. Even if your personal quest is for freedom, if you're still unemployed and don't want to squander your only twenty-dollar bill, you recall the pitiful Cuban stores and feel, actually feel, the across-the-board failure of a materialism devoid of substance. I ended up buying this notebook.

The first big shock came when I found out that my uncle, who after twenty-two years of hard toil in low-paying jobs, relies on food stamps to support himself and his wife, donates ten dollars every month to the Foundation even though he hates the fat cats who run it. And sensing his embarrassment at explaining why, seeing his eyes move evasively from the floor to the walls and back to the floor of his spotless little house, it dawned on me that he and God knows how many other Cubans in Miami still live under the same oppressive atmosphere that Communism enforces in Cuba — where you must join and pay the dues of the union, the Committee, the Women's Federation, and the militia whether you like it or not. If you don't you become suspect. It seems to me that many people here surreptitiously send money, clothing, and medicine to their destitute relatives because the Foundation opposes it.

'So what?' Tito said five days ago, just before leaving. 'You want a perfect world? Don't you realize somebody's in charge everywhere, and you either bend or get broken?' I could've kicked myself for speaking my mind in his presence. He's an all-environment unsinkable chameleon capable of adapting to Marxism, Fascism, Nazism, democracy, monarchy, oligarchy, even matriarchy or mob rule if he had to. He could change from white supremacist to champion of the anti-apartheid movement within ten seconds. He gladly licks the soles

of the shoes of those at the top and demands identical groveling from others. He uses people like paper towels, then tosses them into the wastebasket.

His disappearance was a mild shock. Of course, I pretended to be alarmed and went through the motions of feigning distress, and wringing my hands I went to the police. No tears came, though. Our week-long neighbors commiserated in the warm, affectionate way we learn from childhood: by bringing a bowl of soup; wiping my forehead with a perfumed handkerchief; holding my hand as if we were in a funeral parlor; and exacting the promise that I won't hesitate to report fresh news on my husband's whereabouts even in the middle of the night (as if he had been abducted). The compassion of the fortyish Cuban-American police sergeant on duty had probably been exhausted by the outcome of so many identical cases. He listened with his elbow resting on the desktop, chin cupped in the palm of his hand, eyes fastened to mine. The solemn, laissez-faire expression on his face seemed to convey that I should let things be, as if fully aware that the husband who hadn't made love to me in over six months had just performed the final willful dissociation. He filled in the blanks of a missing-person form in block letters, and his words of comfort, which made Papa frown in confusion, were the right ones: 'A new life begins for you in this country, ma'am. Make the most of it.'

Mama will never ask for my opinion on what happened to Tito, she's too shy, but eventually Papa will. I'll explain why I hope we'll never see him again, and he'll tell Mama. We've already agreed on telling Dani his father went to New York in search of a nice job and will visit us after a few months. I wonder if I can file for divorce. Maybe this leaves me in limbo. I'll seek some legal aid after a couple of months. Enough for tonight.

I feel like writing about my business-as-unusual daily life. I am . . . no, WE are all doing the things we've never done: reading classified ads; filing immigration, relief, and job application forms; learning English; gleaning information on grade schools, apartments for rent, health services, taxes, buses, the metrorail; and a hundred other things that seem offbeat and keep us permanently aghast at prices. You make five hundred dollars a month in Cuba, you're a millionaire; you make five hundred dollars a month here, you're a beggar: The thing is, I was getting paid three dollars a month in Cuba, and four days ago Papa landed a job with a plumbing contractor that pays thirteen dollars an hour: Talk about the exploitation of man by man. I'm bewildered: Plumbers are kings here, and Papa is a first-class plumber: As a lawyer I'll probably have to settle for a position scrubbling garbage trucks.

Even house chores are full of surprises. 'A machine that washes dishes? No more scouring and drying?' On the second day Dani started voicing the amazement we adults shamefully hid. 'A garbage disposal? A microwave?' I operate household appliances I'd only seen in weekend TV movies, although my uncle and his wife tell us they were bought secondhand and are outdated. A vacuum cleaner. Punching instead of dialing. A sofa that transforms into a double bed for Mama and Papa. Sleeping bags. Frozen foods. Tap water that we can drink without boiling first. One-hundred-page newspapers. My uncle's eight-year-old Chevy would be gawked at in any Cuban town.

The lesson: Hard work can get me this. I don't have to pretend as I did in Cuba and do endless unpaid overtime to cover for the inefficiency of those in charge, and maybe I'll be rewarded in four or five years with a coupon to buy a fridge or a TV set or a truly outdated washing machine. Money is the name of the game, and I can make the money needed to pay for all this. A little house, a used car, appliances, clothing, food. I know I won't get rich. I'll never own a five-bedroom mansion with a three-car garage and a swimming pool at some exclusive suburb, but neither will I have to endure a life embittered by a lack of essentials or stomach the ostracism forced upon those who oppose the system.

Papa looks ten years younger. He gets up at 5.00, sips his usual cup of espresso after washing up, then leaves close to 6.00 for the bus stop, carrying a lunch pail crammed with two thick ham-and-cheese sandwiches wrapped in aluminum foil ('Aluminum foil?' Dani gasps) and a thermos with ice-cold milk. Mama suggests menu changes to no avail. Papa argues he didn't eat ham-and-cheese sandwiches for over thirty years and has a lot of catching-up to do. I'm so glad for him. He suffered so much.

Mama keeps her post as guardian angel. She knows we won't let her get a job mopping floors, which is just about the only position she can hope for here. She feels sure she'll again become the domestic backup once Mario and I find jobs, and suspects that sometime the novelty will wear off and Papa will hanker for a visit to his parents' graves, or Mario will brood over the sweet girl he left behind, or I'll miss the small joys and frustrations of my law practice. She must hear everyone out and give comfort without even hinting that she is longing to visit her own parents' graves, her old church, listen to the gossip of neighbors, to Cachirulo's barking when someone approaches our gate, and once again gaze at the quiet, colorful, perfumed rural surroundings of the old house Grandpa built with his own hands, driving every nail into the rough-hewed wood and positioning every red curved tile on its roof.

I wonder who will be the first stranger to walk on its cement floor, clean away the cobwebs, watch the Brazilian soap opera on the old black-and-white Russian TV set. The relatives of some small-time government bureaucrat? A police or Army captain? A municipal prosecutor or factory manager? Any Party member firmly in the system's lower rungs, what the higher-ups call a cadre. This man and his most likely large family will notice the swing on the porch while still on the sidewalk; will stare at the mahogany rocking chairs and armchairs in the living room, at my parents' squeaking brass-and-iron double bed in the master bedroom, at the kerosene stove in the kitchen, at the cracked mirror on the bathroom's medicine cabinet. Maybe the family will feel a little embarrassed at first, like trespassers, but that will only be fleeting because they'll be overjoyed at the improvement in their living conditions. Later, once the National Housing Institute officials have left the place, after the devoted Marxist-Leninist and his no less revolutionary wife have introduced themselves to the neighbors, they will kneel on the floor and thank God and light a candle to whichever Catholic patron saint or African deity protects homes.

Naturally, their kids won't witness the worshipping, for they are too young to grasp the conflicting demands life imposes on true fidelistas.

Smiling, the teacher closed the notebook and turned off the lamp.

*   *   *

Three days later, in the fading light of a beautiful Miami sunset, Elliot Steil walked onto Flagler and entered the southwest section of the city through 38th Court. The teacher ambled past unpretentious one-story houses with narrow front lawns, aluminum awnings on single hung or sliding windows, short driveways to carports, and walkways to tiny covered porches. Rounding the corner onto 4th Street, he came across similar surroundings, with the exception of three notably large houses, each with two-car garages and TV dishes on their wide, land-scaped lawns. In the driveway of the big, cream-colored house, a catering service was unloading cartons from a van. Steil walked faster, like a man with a destination, until he reached the corner of LeJeune and 4th, where he made a left turn. Two blocks ahead, the teacher entered a small diner, and, sitting in a booth, ordered a well-done steak, French fries, and a salad. Sipping tomato juice and waiting for his supper, he mused upon his criminal career.

Steil had met Hairball while strolling around Dole's Dry Dock and Boat Yard on South River Drive, where the bald Cuban kept a twenty-foot runabout powered by an outboard Yamaha.

Steil didn't know that Hairball, whose real name was Blas Taboada, had begun his career as a car stripper in Little Havana two weeks after Cuban prison officials put him on a Miami-bound yacht during the big boat lift in June of 1980. The Cuban leadership had concluded that President Carter should admit more than just the educated, law-abiding people claimed by their US-based relatives. The American government, they felt, should also get a taste of the scum of socialism – the burglars, rapists, gamblers, pickpockets, and child molesters serving time. The Cuban-Americans who had rented yachts to pick up their kinfolk were told that for each relative on board, 'a person who wants to immigrate to the US and lacks transportation must be taken'. Refusal entailed sailing back empty. That was how Blas Taboada, serving a two-year sentence for stealing a motorcycle in Varadero, embarked on a boat aptly named *Second Chance*.

Fourteen years and two grand-theft auto convictions later, Hairball was one of the best operators in South Florida, a committed family man who in a ten-year period had spent close to $82,000 supporting and eventually bringing his parents, two married uncles, two married aunts, and three cousins with spouses and offspring, a total of twenty-four people, to the US.

Hairball believed in diversification. Through relatives fronting for him, he owned three small businesses: a discreet round-the-clock escort service employing nine women and four men, a five-person catering service, and a muffler-and-brake shop specializing in expensive foreign cars with six employees on its payroll.

Hairball also believed in information. The shop's reputable and skilled mechanics performed grade-A jobs at reasonable rates, while their boss – Hairball's paternal uncle – learned the names and addresses of clients and the particular brand and type of each vehicle's alarm. The cousin running the catering service reported on private parties that would bring together ten or twelve automobiles in a quiet neighborhood at nightfall. Escorts informed Hairball's maternal uncle and manager about their clients, including their driving rituals, car security systems, and drinking habits. Even though he wasn't prone to self-praise, Hairball liked to tell his close friends that he had never engaged in blackmail, although the good Lord knew opportunities hadn't been lacking.

Besides, should someone with the right connections wish to

get rid of a greenback gobbler and collect his auto insurance, Hairball obliged. Many YUCCAs – young, up-and-coming Cuban-Americans – hoped to delude friends and business associates into believing they had Made It. With the instant financing provided by eager dealers, many became owners of Mercedes, Jaguars, Infinitis, or Porsches overnight. But a few months later the financial burden would become unbearable, and one solution was to have their cars stolen.

Hairball was a full-blown, successful, discreet, family-loving crook with a significant shortcoming: compulsive spending. Having covered what he termed operating expenses – among which ranked first the retainer of the criminal defense attorney who had sprung him out of American penitentiaries after serving one-third of each sentence – every month he blew his cash on beautiful women and gambling. In February 1994 he awoke in a Miami Beach hotel with a hangover, a broad, and a lonely portrait of Ulysses Grant in his billfold, probably setting the 1993 world record for spending by men who had pulled in close to three hundred thousand dollars.

The bald man lackadaisically admitted his weaknesses to himself as a mushy ass-chaser and reckless gambler, as well as his inability to reform. Yes, he owned three legitimate enterprises, a two-bedroom house in Hialeah, the boat, and a 1991 Camaro, but there were no secret bank accounts, no cash reserves stashed away. Should he, on one of his bad days, fall into the hands of a desperado demanding a grand, he would have to surrender his beloved medals and chains, almost twelve ounces of pure eighteen-karat gold.

For this reason Hairball had never given a moment of thought to his retirement. His lifestyle required an inexhaustible cash inflow and, as far as he was concerned, only one source could provide it.

Hairball justifiably took great caution with every step, considering the raging national debate on the three-strikes-you're-out judicial reform and the Miami Police Department's frustration after the charge of its Auto Theft Detail was brought against him in 1992, then dismissed for lack of evidence.

Not that he personally stole cars – he'd quit in 1987 to become a ringleader. With the exception of junkies and weirdos, everybody in the trade understood that the truly overexposed and underpaid asshole was the thief, who would face two to five years in the slammer if caught red-handed.

Hairball considered himself the mastermind of an operation executed by a first cousin, the husband of another first cousin, himself, and the unsteady roster of drivers he was forced to find, cajole, and train on a permanent basis. In fact, handling drivers had come to be the most time-consuming part of his profession. Since he shunned drunks, addicts, and nuts, during his many hours as talent scout Hairball screened male immigrants, particularly the abundant supply of penniless Cuban rafters without friends or relatives.

But Elliot Steil ignored all of this, and what he was actually chewing on besides his steak at the small Le Jeune Road diner that evening was the speculation that if he kept driving for Hairball he'd soon be capable of tracking down the geek. Thanks to the $1500 earned by stealing three cars, he'd been able to rent the efficiency and the Rolls, buy some clothing, and carry out his Tourneau Corner inquiry. After some plaintive harping on car prices, Hairball had patched things up with Steil the day before by agreeing to double his cut. The teacher figured that with five or six more thefts he should be able to travel to Sarasota.

By now he had dropped the vague moral qualms, which had troubled him for a couple of days following his first theft: a brand-new Seville left unlocked by an old lady at a mall parking lot. His turnabout from respectable citizen to thief had stirred up only mild amazement in him. He had accepted Hairball's overtures and training without batting an eye. Steil considered whether the low level of risk, so convincingly and soothingly explained by the ringleader, supported the notion that

America's penal system enticed people into crime with the probability of evading punishment. Was it true that tame Cubans under Communism frequently became tough guys in free societies? Or was he too hell-bent on revenge? When he stole his second car, a one-year-old Saab in perfect condition, Steil had stopped wondering.

While sipping espresso, asking for the check, and waiting for his change, the teacher repeatedly consulted his watch. He left the diner at 8.06, crossed the street, and strolled leisurely to a bus stop on the corner of Le Jeune and 5th. Sitting on the bench, Steil rested his ankle on his knee and watched passing cars. At 8.15 Hairball joined him. The reflection of neon signs danced on the man's head. He wore a beige sports jacket with narrow lapels over an unbuttoned purple shirt, crimson slacks, and motorcycle boots. Steil cut short his tongue-clicking, head-shaking reaction, and sighed. Hairball casually laid a yellow 3" × 5" envelope on the bench and glanced around before talking: 'Dark-green, 415.'

Steil marched away tucking the envelope in his shirt pocket. He took a right on 4th and, after crossing 40th Avenue, peered at the big, cream-colored house where, it appeared, a party was underway. Several nice cars were parked on the eight-foot-wide mixture of grit and grass between the blacktop and sidewalk. Without losing his stride, the teacher removed the envelope, ripped it open, and slid a key and a remote-control activator into his left hand. He spotted a dark sedan and noticed as he approached that the last three numbers on its license plate were 232. Like all recent arrivals from Cuba, the teacher couldn't distinguish a Lamborghini from a Volkswagen; to avoid confusion, Hairball only told rookies the car's color and the last three digits of its license plate. The teacher was preparing to steal a BMW.

A moment later, Steil found the German car. It was stationed in the right direction, a good space between the Audi ahead of it and the Seville behind it. He aimed the remote control and pressed a button; the ping from under the hood was barely audible. The teacher unlocked the driver's door, slid behind the wheel, and groped for the ignition where Hairball had taught him to. A few seconds later, he inserted the key and turned it. The deceptively soft whisper of the engine made the teacher smile. He backed up two feet, turned the wheel, shifted gears, and carefully crept forward on the tarmac. At the first corner he took a right onto Bobadilla, and after much fumbling turned on the headlights. On the next block he turned left, eased behind a 1992 Toyota Corolla parked on Salamanca Avenue, killed the lights, and shifted into park.

The Corolla's passenger door was flung open at the same time that Steil alighted from the BMW. The husband of one of Hairball's first cousins walked to the stolen car as the teacher approached the Corolla and plopped himself down on the passenger seat. The BMW's door was shut as Steil pulled his closed, buckled up, and stole a glance at the ringleader, who had his eyes glued to the rearview mirror. The BMW coasted past, turned on its headlights, and took a right on 37th Avenue. Hairball eyed Steil with amusement and smirked as he turned the key in the ignition and slid the gear shift into drive.

'Any problems?' the ringleader asked.

'No.'

'Then why are you charging me a thousand bucks for five minutes of your time?'

The teacher turned a little to his left and stared at Hairball. The bald man roared and repeatedly hit the wheel with his palm before obeying a stop sign. He kept laughing and wiping tears from his eyes while waiting for an opening in the stream of vehicles.

'Just joking, man,' he managed to say at last. 'Take it easy, will ya? Life's short. Here's your dough.'

Steil finished counting the fifty twenty-dollar bills as the ringleader took a left onto 37th. 'When's the next job?' he asked while pocketing the money.

'The way I go about it, can't say for sure,' Hairball replied in a suddenly sober tone. 'Got four in line, but safety comes first. I'll let you know.'

'Okay.'

'Drop you at the same place?'

'Same place,' Steil agreed.

Silence reigned, and once again Steil enjoyed the ebullient sensation that followed danger. He also registered that the weird aftertaste of wrongdoing had dwindled to a whiff. Hairball was an outstanding driver, and the teacher frequently spied his deft movements when he changed lanes, turned corners, and crossed intersections. But suddenly, as they were gliding along Flagler's eastbound left lane, a squad car cruising along the center lane adjusted its speed to the Toyota's. Steil saw the driver throwing looks at him without losing sight of the road. His partner in the passenger seat, wrapped up in shadows, was staring, too.

'Cops are giving us the look,' he said.

Hairball bent forward a little, rolled his neck, and peeked at the police vehicle. 'So what? This car's legit,' he snapped after recovering the proper driving position.

The squad car's flashers were turned on and its spinning rays added ominous hues to the glow of streetlights and neon.

'They're signaling us to pull over,' the teacher mumbled.

Hairball sighed, switched on his right turn indicator, and changed lanes just after the prowl car slowed down and fell behind. 'Motherfucker's gonna give me a speeding ticket. You tell me, was I speeding?'

'No, you weren't,' Steil agreed as a very sad foreboding loomed in his mind.

' 'Course I wasn't. First thing you learn in this trade is to never, under any circumstance, commit traffic violations,' Hairball added while stopping alongside the curb.

The squad car followed suit ten yards behind, and the driver remained at the wheel while his partner got out, slamming his door shut.

Hairball knitted his brow when he noticed in the rearview mirror that the approaching officer kept to the sidewalk, as if headed for his passenger instead of him. A few seconds later Steil found himself blinded by the beam of a five-cell flashlight.

'Well, well, if it ain't my fucking English teacher,' a pleasantly surprised voice said in Cuban Spanish.

4

I'm afraid Dani will find it hard to adapt. He's always been a shy boy who's afraid of being laughed at if he screws up. 'Just like you,' Mama reminds me. I read somewhere that shyness is genetic.

Times change. Bike-riding, roller-skating, and ball-playing seem to be losing ground, at least on this block. Video games, skateboards, and cartoons are fashionable. Some nine-year-old boys play poker. School-age kids speak only English. Spanish is a concession to grownups. But Dani doesn't know a word of English, so he can't mingle and spends close to twelve hours a day watching TV, mostly in Spanish.

Clara says that's common behavior for newly arrived children. She predicts Dani won't suffer an educational setback because elementary school in Cuba has higher standards. I giggled at this and said, 'Sure, our kids are experts in the history of the international Communist movement.' She shook her head and didn't even grin. My uncle's neighbor says around 50 percent of immigrant Cuban children are way ahead of their American schoolmates in basic subjects like math and biology and qualify for a higher grade. Even their reading and writing skills are above average when compared to those of English-speaking kids. But one out of four remains at the same level, and the remaining one is set back a year. If she's right, Dani will start in sixth. He's been a straight-A kid since first grade.

I mentioned the frequent Granma articles on school violence in the US. She nodded soberly. Somehow fifth- and sixth-graders manage to smuggle knives, marijuana, porno magazines, and even guns into schools. A few have died in violent outbreaks in the last couple of years. According to Clara, school violence is one of the worst problems this city faces. When I asked her how this is possible, she sighed, pushed her slipping glasses up, and shrugged her shoulders. Imagine.

Hundreds of shiny patrol cars manned by beefy guys armed to their teeth, and they can't control gunfights in elementary schools. The most dangerous weapon ever found in Dani's classroom in Cuba was a razor blade for sharpening pencils; the heaviest drug, a stinking cigarette butt.

Back when he was a gung-ho revolutionary, Papa used to say that America confuses liberty with libertinism. Maybe he had a point. My homeland and this country face the same fundamental social issue: the limits of control. In Cuba, laws, rules, and regulations govern almost everything a person can do, and you wind up feeling enslaved. In the US, respect for individual rights seems to have turned freedom into a form of anarchy in certain social strata.

I wonder if there is a human settlement on this planet where you can live a normal life. Sweden? Switzerland? Maybe it exists in one of those countries you almost never hear about, like New Zealand, Norway, or Denmark − a place where you can make a decent living, own a little house, and speak your mind without fearing reprisals. It would also be a place where you are properly educated in your youth, decently cared for in the end, and get taxed for it all in between. If you don't pay taxes for what you are given, you become either a parasite or a slave to power-hungry demagogues and faceless bureaucrats.

I get carried away. Clara says private schools have internal security and are practically free of violence. What rules out this option is the tuition, somewhere between three hundred and five hundred dollars a month. 'Look, little daughter, what you have to do is move to the right place.' I'm little daughter or Fidelita to all my women friends and to my neighbors over fifty, just like in Cuba. According to Clara, in the affluent white communities that we can't afford to live in, public school violence is minimal; in the predominantly black poor districts, rents are low but crime is high. So the proper place for new immigrants with school-aged children is one that is moderately safe but affordable.

School begins in three weeks, and Mario and I really need jobs. If we can add a second source of income to Papa's, we'll rent an apartment and buy some furniture and kitchenware on credit. With the three of us working, we'll be fine. The more resumés I type, the more trips I take to employment agencies, the more convinced I become that the way to do it is the Cuban way. Somebody's friend learns that a friend of a friend needs someone. And we must hurry, for a new wave of immigrants will soon flood the job market.

After rioting in Havana yesterday, my namesake authorized Cubans who want to flee to the US to sail unimpeded from the island's north coast. Thousands are building rafts on the streets. TV newscasts show the same police officers who the day before were under orders to arrest rafters for illegal emigration, affably overseeing swarms of people feverishly sawing boards, tying ropes, inflating inner tubes and floats. The weirdest and flimsiest fleet since man discovered the sail is about to be launched.

Miami is terrified. Radio commentators broadcasting to Cuba in Spanish are practically imploring their fellow countrymen not to come. They talk about treacherous currents, immense waves, ferocious sharks, pangs of hunger and thirst, seasickness, and how these hardships affect small children, the elderly, and pregnant women. There may be some truly concerned humanitarians among them, but I suspect most are spokespeople for a community fearing, above all, a new influx of desperate criminals who will resurrect the terror brought about by the marielitos in the early '80s, as well as the new economic pressures this human flood would bring.

I'm exhausted.

* * *

Perched on a stool, sipping 7-Up, and occasionally glancing at a TV set tuned to a Marlins baseball game, Elliot Steil picked his brain one more time for a recollection of the man who a minute earlier had excused himself and disappeared into the men's restroom to piss away the two beers he had guzzled in forty-five minutes. It was only natural that nothing came to his mind, Steil reasoned. He'd taught English for seventeen years to more than three thousand students. The only ones he

98

remembered were the exceptionally gifted — maybe eight or nine in all — two punks who made his life miserable, and six or seven extremely beautiful girls. Besides, the substantial transformations some of his pupils underwent between their adolescence and their late twenties or early thirties sometimes made them appear perfect strangers.

The night before on Flagler, when the backslapping and rejoicing subsided, Tony Soto had vehemently requested Steil's address, and the nonplussed teacher had complied. In an ebullient mood the cop jotted it down on his clipboard and insisted on a noon get-together the following day at Charlie's Lounge, a spacious bar on 27th Avenue. Later Steil had to calm Hairball, who wanted to know why he'd never heard Steil utter a word of English or apply for a job consistent with this highly regarded skill.

The teacher downplayed his expertise as much as possible. He had taught nothing beyond the alphabet, the numbers, and the verbs *to be* and *to do* to first-level students. Not before living in Miami had he really understood his incompetence in the country's language. Only in a Communist country where bright kids learned Russian had it been possible for him to become an English teacher. Hairball mulled this over for a few blocks before suggesting that Steil keep away from the asshole.

Now, after half an hour of sharing memories and telling jokes, and another ten minutes inventing reasons why he had quit drinking, Steil suspected that Tony Soto hadn't been admitted into the force for his proficiency in languages. His grip on conversational Spanish was appropriate, yet heavily sprinkled with Americanisms. His short, perky exchange in English with the barman, obviously an old acquaintance, revealed a vocabulary rich only in pet words and slang, and a barely passable accent. The young man had to be skilled in police officialese, though. Having shunned the Cuban community for nearly four months, Steil wondered if Soto's linguistic deficiencies were present in the majority of immigrants.

So far Tony's story was nothing out of the ordinary. The whole family had immigrated in 1986, four years after filing the proper forms at the US Office of Interests in Havana. Under the patronage of an uncle, the family had settled in Albany, New York, where Tony completed high school. Although his parents managed to secure well-paying jobs, Mrs Soto found snowstorms unbearable, so they moved south, first to Jacksonville, then to Miami. At a karate school in Columbia Shopping Plaza, Tony befriended two young men who eventually applied to the police academy. On an impulse, he jumped on the bandwagon and now was the only one of them remaining in the force. While assigned to the Downtown Mini Station, he married a divorced Cuban woman five years his senior. His first (her second) daughter had been born when he was serving in the Street Crimes Unit of the South District Substation, and their first son was born two days before Tony was transferred to the Biscayne Boulevard Mini Station, Bayside Detail. At twenty-six, the talkative Tony Soto described himself as a happily married man, a proud father, a seasoned police officer, and a confident debtor who, God willing, would settle the home equity loan on his $140,000, three-bedroom Coral Gables house by the year 2012.

Elliot Steil had fed Tony Soto his story, improved to perfection with remarkably few opportunities. The teacher had discerned that the best way to avoid questions about his Cuban past was to mention the ordeal early on in the conversation. After learning his nationality, guys invariably asked, 'When did you leave Cuba?' His standard reply first disclosed the date and followed with the soft understatement, 'I was rescued at sea by six people on a raft. My own had sunk many hours before.' With the exception of Fidelia, the few acquaintances he had made – Lodge residents, coworkers, the apartment building's super, a neighbor, and Hairball – were so fascinated by the trying experience that they showed no interest in the rest of his life story. With Tony he had an additional advantage:

Having met Steil as an English teacher in Havana, the self-centered policeman believed that he knew all there was to know about his guest.

Tony Soto emerged from the washroom zipping up the fly of his bleached jeans. A patron crossing his path faked a few punches at him, and Tony in turn pretended to kick the guy's ass before shaking hands and exchanging a few words. The shirttail of the short-sleeved khaki shirt he wore bulged around the .38 Special Smith & Wesson six-shot revolver on his right hip. He was an inch over six feet and his straight hair, which was combed back, had the same brown hue as his heavily lashed eyes. Beneath his beaked nose, a mustache and a confident chin framed well-formed lips. Although the ample garment concealed his torso, his meaty shoulders, thick neck, and the calluses on his hands were indications of the swollen pectorals and biceps of a man who pumps iron on a regular basis. Tony Soto was handsome in a rugged, menacing way, so long as he didn't smile. When he smiled he looked harmless, and when he laughed he was all charm.

Steil absent-mindedly inspected the premises. Six early birds at a place that could easily accommodate forty were not exactly exhausting the bartender and waiter who conferred in low tones at the far end of the solid, s-shaped mahogany counter. Four customers occupied booths lining the two sides of the lounge – a middle-aged couple to the teacher's left debating something in hushed tones, an old man behind him, and the guy talking to Tony at the rear near the restrooms. Over the sparsely stocked bar shelves, a huge mirror offered visual coverage of the entire place. On the remaining walls hung several amateur oil canvases depicting landscapes. The smell of cigarette smoke and liquor, cooled by the frigid air conditioning, was still faint.

The cop finally returned to the bar and hopped on his stool like a cowboy mounting a horse. He ordered his third beer as Steil took a sip of his second soda.

'You happen to know the guy driving you around last night very well?' Tony Soto suddenly asked, looking at the glass into which he slowly poured his beer.

Steil tensed up and watched the TV screen as if interested in the next play. 'Not really.'

'Know what he does for a living?'

'He once said he owned a garage or a service station. I don't remember.'

'When and where did you meet him?'

Steil moved his gaze from the hefty batter on the TV screen to Tony's face, turned a little to his right, and grinned. His ex-pupil had just let go of the bottle and was closing the fingers of his right hand around the glass. 'Hey, hey, what's the matter?' Steil asked in a light tone. 'I thought this was your day off.'

Tony sipped his beer, placed the glass on the bartop, wiped foam from his mustache with the back of his hand, and smiled back. 'It is,' he confirmed, nodding. 'I just wanna make sure you don't get into a piss-poor deal with your eyes closed, you know?'

'Is he a criminal?' Steil asked, hoping to sound astonished.

'When and where'd you meet him?'

Considering that he was talking to a cop, Steil tried to stay as close to the truth as possible: During his first two weeks at the Salvation Army, the cast on his broken arm had prohibited a job hunt, and after a few days of inactivity he became restless. To kill time, he would stroll along the Miami River bank, where he had met Hairball. The bald man had been friendly and supportive, and they frequently shared a meal or went for a ride.

'He offered you a job?'

As he tilted his head to indicate ambiguity, Steil marveled at his progress in make-believe at the same moment that he yearned for a drink. 'Not in so many words; he's hinted at it.'

Tony Soto nodded, rotating his stool to face Steil. "Okay,

teacher. Now listen to me, 'cause you don't know your way around here. Hairball leads a ring of car thieves. Specializes in foreign cars. Great scam, you know? Take a top-of-the-line Mercedes. Showroom price – sixty G's. Thief who steals it gets paid four. Hairball sells it to the syndicate for twelve or fourteen. The pros alter it beyond recognition, ship it somewhere with perfectly legal papers, and sell it for thirty-five, maybe forty. When something goes wrong, guess who takes the rap?'

'The thief?' Steil guessed acceptably.

'You bet. Hairball recruits people like you – rafters or illegals hard pressed for money. He teaches them how to and gives them chicken feed. Six . . . no, five months back, one of his drivers was gunned down. Somebody fucked up and handed the wrong car key to the poor bastard. He was so desperate, he kept trying to unlock the door, and the owner came from behind and shot him in cold blood.'

Tony Soto paused, took a long drink, and again wiped the foam from his mustache. Surprised at learning that his life had been endangered, and mad at Hairball for having shortchanged him, Steil didn't realize he had dropped his guard. Instead of expressing disbelief, indignation, or gratitude, he stared fixedly at the commercial on the TV screen, though he wasn't seeing it. Tony Soto grasped the situation perfectly.

'My pardner saw you guys last night when you took 37th, and we followed you,' the cop went on. 'Every squad car in town is after Hairball. Brass wants to nail him, DA wants to nail him, insurance companies want to nail him. If everybody is after you, you can't beat the rap. When I saw you in the car with him I couldn't believe my eyes.'

Steil again craved a drink. Mustering the willpower to resist had weakened his acting abilities. His eyes avoided Tony's, and suddenly he clicked his tongue, forced a smile, shook his head sadly, and looked sideways. The body language seemed vaguely familiar to Tony Soto.

'I like you, teacher,' he said. 'Almost everybody in our class liked you. You didn't preach, didn't pretend, worked with us in the fields. So now it's payback time. Cut loose from Hairball. I don't wanna know if you drove for him or not. You can't make ends meet earning four bucks an hour? Wanna make a little on the side? Okay, you're only human. Come to me, I'll give you a hand. No risk, no problem. Just cut loose from Hairball, okay?'

Suspicion seeped in as Steil sipped. Tony's account of Hairball conformed to fact, and he was supposed to show appreciation, but additional 'no risk, no problem' assistance could bring him fresh trouble and divert him from his immediate goal. Hairball had given him the same assurances, with almost the same words. Nonetheless, it was plausible that a former student would remember a teacher fondly and lend him a hand later in life. Then why did he smell a rat? Would Tony suggest snitching to the Miami Police Department?

'Now I see what he was driving at,' the teacher said in a sad tone. 'He used to talk a lot about how easily bright guys make money here. Just baiting the hook, I guess.'

'He offered you a loan or something?'

'Twice,' Steil lied. 'I refused.'

Tony Soto drained his glass, belched, and wiped his lips and mustache with a handkerchief before pulling out a folded, half-inch-thick wad of bills from his shirt pocket. The cop flipped past several hundred-dollar bills, selected a twenty, and placed it on the bartop. 'Hey, Jim!' he shouted.

The fat bartender was talking to the lean waiter and stopped mid-sentence to come over. He picked up the bill and marched to the cash register.

'Hairball's no fool, teacher,' Tony Soto said, looking Steil right in the eye. 'All of a sudden you no longer go out with him, keep giving excuses, he'll work it out. So, I figure it's best if next time you see him you tell him exactly what I just told you. It won't surprise him; he knows we're after him.

But a fresh reminder might make him wise up and lay low for a while. Maybe you should throw in that you don't believe a word of it, thank him for the free meals, and tell him I scared you shitless and you wanna be left alone.'

The bartender came back with the change, and Tony Soto waived it aside. Steil guessed that the tip was bigger than the check. How much did cops make in this town? 'What if he blows his top?' he asked.

'Who, Hairball? Oh no, never,' Tony said, suppressing a laugh. 'Hairball's a cool cocksucker, never blows his top. He'll write you off as a bad investment. Gotta run now, teacher. Promised the wife I'd take the kids to the Miccosukee Indian Village. Can you believe it? A sixty-mile round trip on my day off?'

'It's okay. Listen, Tony, I can't thank you enough for this. I wouldn't have stolen for Hairball anyway, but I didn't know the company I was keeping. Thanks for telling me.'

Tony Soto slid off the stool, and Steil followed. On the way to the door, Tony wrapped things up: 'You have my home number. Wanna make a little extra dough, give me a call. No risk, no problem.'

'Doing what?'

The cop pushed the padded door open, and the heat socked them like a recoiling punching bag. On the way to his Buick, Tony Soto seemed to be at a loss for words, shaking his head in uncertainty, pulling down the corners of his mouth, and staring blankly at the sidewalk. 'Don't know. I'll have to think of something.'

The policeman turned off the car's alarm and fished his keys out of the pocket of his jeans. Steil went around the hood as Tony opened the door for him from the inside. The teacher plopped down on the seat, closed the door, and buckled himself in.

'Drop you at your place?' the cop asked while starting the engine.

'Sure. I'm on the graveyard shift. Gotta lay down for a few hours.'

Looking at the rearview mirror, Tony turned the wheel and cautiously joined the stream of vehicles.

'Know something, Tony? From the standpoint of financial security I lost all the adult years of my life. Most guys my age have a house of their own, a car, a few grand in a savings account. No big deal, but it's something. I got nothing.'

Tony Soto made no comment, and they rode in silence for a couple of blocks.

'My profession, what I'm good at, well . . . you know,' Steil continued. 'There're a thousand jobs I can do to get by, but I guess I'll end up like most geezers all over the city, telling lies to each other, playing dominoes, living on relief.'

'The important thing is you wised up,' Tony Soto said as he turned a corner. 'You risked your life to get your ass over here and succeeded.'

If he only knew, Steil thought. 'Yeah, but keep in mind the Cuban saying: "Born for bedpan, shit falls on you out of the blue." '

Tony Soto chuckled. 'Hadn't heard it.'

'There're variations,' the teacher said. ' "Born for tamale, corn husk falls on you out of the blue." '

'That I'd heard.'

'Same meaning. Destiny is laid out at birth by mysterious forces.'

Tony Soto thought this over for a moment. 'Teacher, with all due respect, let me give you some very Cuban advice: "Don't eat shit." You can be what you wanna be if you ain't too ambitious and are willing to run the necessary risks.'

The policeman stopped the Buick behind a Land Rover at a red light. Steil knew no offense was intended and remained silent. Was there a hidden meaning behind what the man was saying?

'You survived your biggest risk,' Tony said to the windshield. 'Only run the necessary risks from now on.'

Steil thought it wise to probe a little. 'You said no risk, no problem a little while ago.'

'Oh, c'mon, give me a break,' the cop snapped and stared at his passenger. 'It's an expression. Taking a shower is a risk. You might slip and fracture your skull. I've seen it happen in real life, you know?'

A horn tooted. Tony Soto drove on. 'But taking a shower is a necessary risk, stealing cars for a well-known criminal with a yard-long record ain't. You willing to bend the rules a little in your favor? Welcome to the club. It's what everybody does. But look for the right backup, people with friends, the kinda guys can lend a hand if you get in trouble.'

A few seconds elapsed. The teacher finally said, 'I'll give you a call tomorrow or the day after.'

'You do that.'

*　　*　　*

Hairball wiped his lips with a napkin, finished his Pilsen, and pushed the plate to the center of the Formica-topped table before picking up a steaming cup of espresso. He positioned it where the plate had been, ripped open two packets of sugar, poured them into the coffee, and stirred deliberately for close to a minute as he brooded over the news.

The teacher, having devoted three full minutes to recounting the part of his conversation with Tony Soto that concerned Hairball, was still polishing off his supper and speculating that the best Cuban dishes were being cooked in Miami these days. Natasha, his ex-wife, would have loved this meal: loose long white rice, a delicious black bean pottage, tasty fried pork, and deep-fried plantains. A health-food advocate's nightmare prepared with all the necessary ingredients: olive oil, onions, garlic, green pepper, sour orange, and other produce unavailable to 99 percent of Cuba's urban population.

Hairball downed his espresso like a true Cuban – several small sips interspersed with clicks of the tongue and smacks of the lips to savor the flavor – then returned the cup to the saucer. He watched as Steil finished his meal in a silence born out of concern, not politeness. The waitress served the teacher's coffee and returned to the kitchen.

'So?' Steil asked.

'So what?' Hairball countered.

'What are you gonna do?'

The ringleader turned his head to gaze at the street. Steil sweetened his espresso and drank. La Carreta was on the corner of 8th Street and 36th Avenue, three or four feet above street level, and its huge windowpanes allowed a good view of cruising vehicles, illuminated stores, and pedestrians. The restaurant's superb cuisine cut across all class distinctions. Respectable elders reminisced with tears in their eyes, but didn't mix with the drug dealers born and raised on the island. This was a section of the city where Anglos seldom found an English-speaking person fluent enough to give a direction. Homesick Cubans walking along 8th Street liked to believe they were back in Havana.

A patrol car coasting past prompted Hairball: 'I'm sick and tired of this harassment, so first thing I'm gonna do is see my lawyer. I'll sign off for a few days and take some extra precautions, then go right back to business. This is my racket, Elio. Can't quit 'cause a lousy cop throws a scare on me.'

The teacher nodded solemnly, keeping his eyes on Hairball. The ringleader wore a white-on-black, polka-dotted, long-sleeved shirt, thousand-eyes shoes, and baggy white trousers.

'What about you? You want out?'

'Let me put it this way,' Steil murmured in a low tone, though the adjoining booths were empty. 'If you believe for a minute that after learning what I've learned I'm gonna keep putting my hide on the line for the kinda money you're paying me . . .'

'Hey, hey, hey, wait a minute,' Hairball shot back.

'I'm not waiting a second, Hair,' Steil barged in, raising his hand to quell the interruption. 'You're more than entitled to recover expenses and make a nice profit. I don't know how you do it, but you find out the right time and place, furnish the gadgetry, and pay on delivery. It's a great scam; kudos to you. Now, you sell a car like the other night's BMW for sixteen, seventeen thousand . . .'

'Is that what the sonafabitch told you? Listen to this, Holy Santa Bárbara,' Hairball expostulated, lifting his gaze to the ceiling to seek the saint's intercession.

'I won't argue with you,' Steil went on. 'I'm just letting you know I'll keep driving for you only if you're willing to fork over four thousand per. You can't pay my price, no hard feelings. You go your way, I go mine, and thanks for everything.'

Hairball inhaled and peered at the street, shaking his head as if dismayed at human ingratitude or greed or both. 'You leveled with me,' he said, turning his gaze first to the teacher, then to the tablecloth where he swept away a few bread crumbs with the edge of his hand. 'I owe you, so I'll have to break even, or maybe lose a little money . . .'

'Oh, c'mon, Hair, where do you get off giving me this bullshit?'

'No, no, it's true. But it's okay. I trust you, you're good, don't stall the merchandise, so I'll pay you four for high-priced imports, three for American heaps.'

'You got a deal.'

'Fine. Now, I want you to become real chummy with this cop and find out if . . .'

'No.'

'Whaddaya mean, no? We gotta milk the bastard, learn if there's something new on me.'

'No, I won't do it,' the teacher deadpanned. 'This guy's on the level. He could've asked me to snitch on you, but he didn't. Besides, he's given us fair warning and probably won't mention it again.'

Hairball pursed his lips in disapproval, but refrained from

further contention. The silence became uncomfortable, so Steil signaled the waitress to bring him the check.

'After you . . . reopen shop,' Steil continued, 'we shouldn't give ourselves away. I mean, driving around together, or meeting in public places.'

'I get it. This is authorized. You wired?'

Steil frowned before understanding the question, then smiled. 'Are you mad at me? Am I guilty of something?'

Positioning the tips of his fingers on the edge of the table, Hairball sighed deeply, his cheeks ballooning and his eyebrows raised, directing an annoyed look to the street. 'I guess not,' he said at last.

'Great. You agree with me on limiting our public meetings? For your sake and mine?'

'Yeah.'

'Good. Now, can you get me a driver's license from some other state?'

Hairball squinted in suspicion. 'Sure.'

'How much?'

'Five hundred.'

'Okay. Get me one.'

'Any particular state?'

'No.'

'Any particular name?'

'A very American one. Like Richard Nixon, Gerald Ford, Jimmy Carter . . .'

Hairball smiled for the first time that evening.

The bill was $12.75. Steil handed a ten and a five to the woman and told her to keep the change.

'Ready to go?' the teacher asked.

'Let's get the hell outta here,' Hairball snapped.

* * *

My lucky day. Got a job and bumped into Elio.

I was rinsing my hair when I got a call from the law firm of

Robins Weinstein and Bencomo, with offices at 3915 Miami Avenue, suite 515. Sounds impressive? Well, appearances can be deceiving. With Mama helping, I toweled my hair dry in less than ten minutes, brushed it (I must trim it soon), dressed, and applied a little makeup. I put on a dress with a button-down bodice, collar, and short sleeves that Clara gave me; a handout from her daughter-in-law. The pumps kill me, but they are my best pair of shoes, courtesy of Regla, the lady living across the street. The man said he wanted to interview me immediately, so I called a cab. Its black driver didn't know a word of Spanish, and I had to write down the address for him. An $8.75 fare. Unbelievable!

The small, beat-up building had its lobby sectioned off into small areas. The elevators were very old, with sliding grilled doors. The whole place smelled awful: disinfectant, insecticide, stale cigarette smoke, mildew, and perfume. The firm was on the fifth floor. The musty corridor's worn-out carpet led me to a door with a frosted glass panel that had the partners' names painted on it. The term 'suite' is a bit of an exaggeration for a private office and a small waiting room separated by a door. The waiting room had two sofas with overstuffed arms, two leather armchairs, a small desk with a phone, an answering machine, an electric typewriter; and a typing chair where I will sit from nine to five.

Bencomo, a man in his late sixties, led me into his empty office. It was like a set from an American B-movie about a lone peewee shyster, save for the parrot in a cage. When I entered, the bird whistled admiringly, then croaked something that sounded like 'Down with Communism!' Apparently the guy is so used to this, he didn't smile or show any sort of reaction. Come to think of it, I'll probably have to feed it. Bencomo eased himself carefully (like uncle Ramón, who has a bad case of piles) into a leather executive chair at one side of the desk and motioned me to one of the two club chairs used for clients.

The firm is in the injury business. A person gets run over by a car or falls and breaks a leg, and a stranger is blamed for it. Someone is badly treated by a doctor or gets poisoned by a can of sardines, and with my boss's assistance, he or she sues. If the person dies, the closest relatives sue. He gets a percentage of the recovery, the money paid in compensation. In Havana this man would find a hundred clients a week and still live in absolute poverty.

Bencomo is Cuban by birth, but he studied law here and became an American citizen 'many years ago'. He showed me his ad in the phone book. It must have cost a fortune. It takes up three full columns in a four-column page and has a photograph of a smiling Bencomo, twenty years younger, in a nice suit, flanked by two older, well-dressed partners. 'They retired,' he explained.

I'll be his secretary. My English is not a problem since his practice rarely involves Anglos. I was chosen because of my university degree, and he believes I might become his legal clerk if my English improves. In the same breath he instructed me to forget the whole Spanish legal system on which Cuban jurisprudence is founded because 'this is a completely different ball game'. I'm supposed to type documents in both Spanish and English. He'll write the latter in easy-to-read block letters or furnish typed copies of writ applications prepared for past cases where only the names and addresses of plaintiffs and defendants need to be changed. Anyhow, this will slow me down enormously.

There's no fax machine, photocopier, or PC, which is regrettable and a strong indication that this is a stingy business. To confirm my impression, Bencomo offered me four dollars an hour. I know a Cuban woman who's making between eighty and one hundred dollars a day cleaning houses on her own, so I shook my head and asked for six. After we settled on five, Bencomo looked relieved. Since it was Friday, he let me go and asked me to report to work on Monday morning at nine.

Standing on the sidewalk, I unfolded my transit map to figure out how to ride back home on a bus, so I could save money and learn the way. Bus route 6 has a stop two blocks from my uncle's, and I was close to downtown, where I had taken it before. I don't like to ask for directions, especially here, so I looked around to get my bearings and turned south on Miami Avenue. I had covered a few blocks when I spotted a middle-aged, broad-shouldered, serious-looking man coming my way. He looked vaguely familiar, so I stared. Suddenly his eyes found mine, and he gave me an embarrassed smile, which took me milliseconds to recognize.

We kissed on the cheeks and chatted for about fifteen minutes. I was delighted to see him and showed it. I reproached him for not giving us a call, and he said he'd lost my uncle's phone number. Most likely true. Or maybe he wants to be left alone. I think Elio hides something. Perhaps he's on the run for some dark reason, like killing someone in Cuba.

I told him about us, and included Tito's desertion, in a disgusting and shameful attempt to let him know that I'm free. I don't even remember the last time I threw myself at a guy. He's put on twenty or thirty pounds, and is no longer the pitiful scraggy rafter trembling with fear. Tall men look emaciated when they weigh under 150. He mentioned that three days ago he got a job at a Publix supermarket on Biscayne Boulevard and 48th, and was on his way to work.

I wasn't carrying a pencil or paper, and neither was he. I mustered enough courage (or was it a sudden pang of sexual starvation that made me so bold?) to stop a pedestrian and use sign language to ask for a pen. Elio wrote our number on the palm of his hand and promised to call. If he doesn't, I think I'm going to shop at a Publix, which, according to my transit map, is not too far from Bencomo's office. I want this man.

*　　*　　*

'Tony says you're a good teacher,' Ruben Scheindlin said to begin the interview. He spoke English with a strong Slavic accent.

'I certainly tried to be one for many years,' Steil admitted with his best pronunciation. Tony Soto, sitting on an armless swivel chair identical to the one Elliot was perched on, had made it clear that English was a prerequisite for the job.

'Tell me about yourself,' the short old man said with a fixed grin.

As usual, Steil tried to divert attention from his past by

focusing on the lonely rafter tale. There was an unhealthy pallor to the balding hardware-wholesaler's wide face. Something seemed to be wrong with his small brown eyes. Behind the thick bifocals mounted in antiquated plastic frames, his irises lifted every four or five seconds, as if checking something suspended in midair. Scheindlin wore a short-sleeved white shirt over a T-shirt; the rest of him was concealed by the huge metal desk. Steil estimated Scheindlin's height to be around five feet four inches when the old man stood up to shake hands as he and Tony Soto entered his office in the cavernous warehouse on 17th Avenue and 171st Street in North Miami Beach.

The forty-foot-high, three-hundred-foot-long windowless building served as head office for IMLATINEX, a trading company with only two shareholders: Ruben Scheindlin, who owned 80 percent of the shares, and Samuel Plotzher, who owned the rest. The place was sparsely filled with spools of wires and cables, drums on pallets, and many wooden crates of various sizes. Three battery-powered forklifts and an overhead crane could also be seen. The three men sat inside a ceilingless eight-foot-high, glassed-in cubicle. Other than Scheindlin's desk, the room contained assorted office equipment and a safe. Two lamps with four long fluorescent tubes hung from the warehouse ceiling. It was a few minutes past eight.

Ruben Scheindlin expressed mild amazement at the end of Steil's story. 'You were lucky. But tell me about your life in Cuba: How come you speak such good English? And where did you teach?'

Steil made his life story as brief and boring as possible. His father had died when he was ten, his mother twenty-four years later. He had a BA in English Literature from the University of Havana and had taught at a technological institute for the past seventeen years. His childless marriage ended in divorce after five years.

"You served in the army?' Scheindlin wanted to know.

Steil recounted his years as a cattleman. Tony Soto let his amusement show with a broad smile, but the old man held a fixed grin.

'What kind of position are you after, Elio?'

'The money-making kind, Mr Scheindlin.'

'Ruben, please.'

'If you wish.'

'Want to make up for lost time?'

'Very much so.'

'And . . . besides teaching, what skills can you bring to an import-export business?'

For a second Steil feared the interview was not progressing as well as he had hoped. 'Well, I could translate, or move things around here, or drive a truck, or . . .' His voice trailed off.

Scheindlin's grin evaporated. 'But these are not money-making positions,' he observed.

Steil was at a loss for words.

'Okay, Elio, now listen to me,' Scheindlin said, suddenly sitting upright and resting his forearms on the desk. 'Time lost is lost forever. You win the state lottery tomorrow, you can't buy back time, right?' The man paused to let his words sink in.

The teacher thought about clarifying things by saying that all he hoped for was to catch up, but decided against it when he remembered that all the bosses he'd ever known hated being contradicted.

'Now, you're here 'cause this young fellow, this close friend I like and respect, vouches for you, says you're smart. Maybe I'll find something for you. But let's get something straight from the start: In this town, a guy with your job experience can't make money fast teaching or translating or delivering goods.' Scheindlin allowed a few seconds to pass before pointing his left thumb at Tony. 'Since our mutual friend is a police officer, let's put his mind at ease by making clear that I'm not suggesting you should break the law.'

Tony chuckled, and Steil smiled.

'To make money fast, you must do something that' – and Scheindlin lifted his forefinger – 'most people don't know how to do' – the middle digit went up – 'or don't want to do' – the thumb flexed out – 'or are afraid to do 'cause it involves some risk they ain't willing to take. For people like us, who can't sing or hit home runs or play roles in movies, money-making and risk go hand in hand. So, you want a sideline where there's no risk? I'll squeeze you in; I owe it to Tony. But it won't be a money-making position.'

Steil cleared his throat and stared at the linoleum floor for a few seconds. The old man and Tony Soto exchanged swift glances. 'Mr Ruben, I'd very much like a low-risk, money-making position, if you know what I mean. Tony made clear you're a highly principled businessman, so I know you'd never engage in illegal activities, but just to make my point I want to tell you my limit. I wouldn't become a criminal for a number of reasons. For two reasons, in fact: fear and moral scruples. But if in everyday life I have to bend the rules a little to earn good money real fast, I'm willing to do it.'

'Fine, give me your phone number,' the old man demanded, pulling a cheap ball-point pen from the pocket of his shirt.

'I don't have a phone.'

'Maybe you should get one soon. How's your workday at the supermarket?'

Four minutes later the teacher and Tony Soto left the cubicle and crossed the length of the warehouse to reach the huge sliding door where a night watchman let them out. Riding in the cop's Buick, they drove along 167th Street before turning south on 22nd Avenue.

That afternoon on the phone, Steil had accepted Tony's invitation to grab a bite at his place after the meeting. The cop called his wife from his car phone, and it was obvious that she hadn't been informed of this. The speakerphone revealed the impatient, reluctant tone of Mrs Soto's voice as she agreed to heat up two frozen pizzas in the microwave. Steil glanced at the digital clock on the dashboard when Tony broke the connection. 8.32.

'You liked the kike?' Tony wanted to know.

'Tickled the hell out of me.'

'Be serious.'

Steil scratched the tip of his nose for a moment. 'Looks okay. He's got that I-know-all-the-answers attitude that I see in a lot of old men, but he's unpretentious.'

'Un what?'

'Not pretentious. You know, doesn't try to look important or rich or powerful. Way he dresses, his office: all very low key.'

'Typical,' the cop snapped.

'Of who?'

'Kikes. Most of them don't want to look affluent.'

'Our opposite,' the teacher scoffed.

'Yeah,' Tony Soto concurred as he took a right on 136th Street. 'Kikes own this town, you know? Maybe the first who came liked the climate, saw the potential. Old timers say they started grabbing real estate quietly and have been at it for the last fifty years. And, yes, they invented low profile. I know a kike drives a Honda, buys his suits from the rack, has an . . . unpretentious' – the cop stole a look at Steil, and they shared a smile – 'house in West Wood Lakes. You're not in the know, you figure the guy's pulling in forty grand a year. His real worth is anybody's guess. Some say four hundred, some say six.'

'Million?'

'What else?'

Steil remained silent for a few seconds. 'What's Ruben worth?'

Tony Soto looked bewildered for an instant and shrugged

off the question. 'I have no idea. Maybe ten, twenty, thirty. Who knows?'

'He's not a native, not with that accent,' Steil observed.

'Word is he got here after the Second World War. Was born in Poland or Lithuania or some place like that. Nobody really knows.'

The conversation fizzled out at the Le Jeune-Douglas connector. Ten minutes later, Tony Soto parked on Asturia Avenue in front of a modern house with a sandstone facing and windows with slated awnings. A 1986 Ford Taurus was stationed in the driveway. The lawn had been recently mowed. A footwalk led to two steps and a small porch, where a rattan couch covered with pillows appeared dated and out of place. Tony unlocked the front door and waved Steil in.

The demands of raising three children and managing a household seemed to have worn down the short, overweight Lidia Soto. Her thin lips gave Steil a hospitable smile. She had humble brown eyes and shoulder-length dyed black hair. In her sleeveless blouse, culottes, and leather thongs, Lidia looked ten years older than her husband, and Steil guessed that she might be mistaken for his mother before too long.

Tony kissed her affectionately on the cheek, made introductions, and learned that the kids were already in bed. The living room was decorated with three leather love seats surrounding a rectangular brass and glass cocktail table. Near one wall stood a large-screen TV. The teacher glanced around the room at the high-tech sound system, the two floor lamps, and the partially opened miniblinds on the huge window facing the lawn. The wall-to-wall carpeting felt thick under his feet. The air conditioning hummed quietly.

They ambled over to the dining room, and the men sat on the stools at the counter facing a fully equipped kitchen. Lidia served pizzas topped with sausages. She looked puzzled when Steil declined a beer, but quickly poured him a glass of freshly squeezed orange juice.

After the espresso Tony recounted some funny anecdotes from his years as a teenager in Havana. Amused, Steil turned slightly to face his host, and registered the very nice dining room set behind him. It consisted of a pedestal table, four sidechairs, two armchairs, a carved sideboard, and a glass-fronted china cabinet, which were all very clean. Returning his gaze to Lidia, he caught her failed attempt at suppressing a yawn.

'Gotta run, Tony,' he said, glancing at his watch. Then, to Lidia: 'I know it's rude to eat and run, but I gotta punch in at midnight at my supermarket. Still have to go home and change. Could I use your phone to call a cab?'

'No, just a second,' Tony Soto ordered, and slid off the stool. He disappeared into the living room.

'Thanks for the meal, ma'am.' Steil heard a door open and close.

'You're welcome. When did you leave Cuba?'

'Four months ago.'

'How are things over there?'

'Pretty bad.'

'Are people starving?'

Steil saw real concern in her eyes. 'Nobody dies of hunger, but most people look gaunt. I lost forty pounds in four years. When I see guys here dieting and exercising to shed a few pounds, I can't help thinking our government could make a lot of money selling its program to fat tourists. They would just need to move to Cuba and live by the ration card.'

'It's not a new idea,' the plump Lidia Soto said coolly, and in a flash Steil realized he had been rude and that the joke was trite, at least in Miami.

'I guess not,' he said, blushing slightly.

'My mother doesn't want to come,' Lidia complained.

'Why?'

'She fears neighbors may convene for a repudiation meeting, throw eggs at her like they did to us, to me and my first husband, when it became known we wanted to emigrate. She panicked that day and fainted.'

The teacher recalled the shameful days in 1980. People who had asked relatives abroad to send for them had been 'repudiated' by revolutionaries at their workplaces and homes. Screaming mobs bombarded them with eggs and sometimes rocks for the crime of openly admitting their wish to emigrate. They were called worms and were forced to wear hoods with 'I'm Scum' written on them.

'There's always that risk,' Steil said.

Lidia nodded. A door closed somewhere in the house.

The teacher was getting ready to say something else when Tony Soto reappeared. 'C'mon, I wanna show you something.'

'Just a minute, Tony. Let me tell your wife a true story.' Turning to Lidia, he began: 'In my apartment building there lived a young economist. He was twenty-nine in 1980. Party member, married, one kid. His parents had left in the seventies, settled here. He stayed in Cuba, believing things would improve. When the boat lift was announced, his father rented a boat and sailed to Mariel. To this day, I don't know if he made the decision on his own or if his son asked him to. Immigration people came to the building one evening and told the economist that his father was in Mariel with a power cruiser. Did he want to leave Cuba? "You bet," the guy said. While the man and his wife packed a few essentials, some neighbors heard the news. A little mob waited for them on the sidewalk. They were called worms, counter-revolutionaries, traitors, well, you know, the full list of epithets. There was this particularly aggressive woman in her fifties. She threw eggs at them, called him a fag and a son of a whore. Okay. Twelve years later, the economist came back to Cuba to visit relatives. Now he was bald, thirty or forty pounds heavier, wore nice clothes. The woman was seventy-one, living on a small pension, was nothing but skin and bones. Nobody had an egg to eat, much less to throw. The guy went to a dollars-only store and bought thirty eggs. Back then most Cubans weren't allowed in these stores.'

'I remember that,' Lidia said. 'The possession of foreign currency was a crime. A friend of mine served a two-year prison sentence for having a twenty-dollar bill in his wallet.'

'Right. From the store, the guy took a taxi and went to my apartment building, knocked on the old woman's front door, and said, "Lady, I have a present for you." "Who are you, why are you giving this to me?" the old woman asked. The guy said, "Lady, I'm *Fulano de Tal*, don't you remember me? After all the eggs you threw at me twelve years ago? Maybe you need them now, so I'm paying you back."'

Tony's smile became a laugh. His wife covered her mouth with both hands in full amazement.

'She accepted the eggs?' Tony asked.

'She said she threw them away. But the next-door neighbors swear that there were egg shells in her garbage for two weeks. Lidia, it's been a real pleasure.'

Steil shook hands with Lidia and joined Tony at the door. The cop approached the Ford in the driveway. His wife said a final goodbye, a smile on her lips.

'I got this heap real cheap at a police auction two years ago,' Tony explained. 'It had been impounded from some nickle-dime dope dealer, and Lidia needed a car, so a friend bought it for me and resold it to her.'

The teacher had one of his rare sensations of déjà vu. Since sitting alone by his mother's casket ten years before, he hadn't experienced the phenomenon. Now he foresaw what was about to happen.

'Two weeks ago I bought her a station wagon. Perfect for moving three kids around. School, shopping, you know. It's in there.' The cop pointed to the garage door with his thumb. 'Pretty soon you're gonna need wheels, so I guess you could ride this until you're able to stand on your own two feet and then maybe pay me some money for it.'

Steil clicked his tongue, shook his head, and forced a smile. Tony Soto successfully fought off a laugh. 'What's the matter?' he asked.

'Tony, you're a real friend,' the teacher said, thrusting his hands into the pockets of his slacks. 'I really appreciate your offer, but I don't want to get into anything I can't live up to. Maybe I botch it with Ruben, fall sick, lose my job, you'll end up with zilch.'

'Tell you what, teacher,' Tony asserted. 'You take the heap now. If in three months you haven't paid me a grand, I'll have it repossessed.'

'Come again?'

'Ah, ha, ha,' the cop quipped, 'the teacher learns from the student. Repo is when the shark swallows the little fish in credit sales.'

'Got it. Repossession; taking back possession. You figure I'll make a grand in ninety days working for Ruben?'

'You'll probably make that in your first month.'

'You sure?'

'Absolutely,' said a smiling Tony Soto, dangling a key ring in Steil's face.

Two minutes later and ten blocks away, the teacher pulled the Ford over, killed the lights, and cut the engine. He remained deep in thought behind the wheel. What was he getting into? Who was he lining up with? Dan Gastler's image melted with Scheindlin and Tony in his mind. The nice old man risking his freedom to fulfill the death wish of an Army buddy, the young police officer bubbling over with affection for an ex-teacher, the businessman who would hire a perfect stranger out of gratitude to a twenty-six-year-old cop. Suddenly Hairball seemed as innocent as the Archangel Gabriel.

The teacher acknowledged a turning point. Was he willing to go all the way along an unknown and suspiciously foul-smelling road? Was stealing cars a safer way to make money before traveling to Sarasota? Was revenge his sole motive for engaging in shady deals? He didn't have any clear-cut answers, but he arrived at two decisions before turning the key in the ignition: to give it a try, and to buy a handgun and a small tape recorder as soon as possible.

5

Now I think I know who I'm writing this for. Maybe I'm wrong. I've never been good at rating people. Marta always used to say that I overestimate new acquaintances. Perhaps after so many disappointments I've lowered my expectations and you might live up to them.

The first significant evidence is that you're not trying to make an impression; you don't strut your stuff. You aren't embarrassed by silence if it is the only alternative to foolish babble. Finally, you seem resigned to the fact that life is passing you by.

I loathe to be led on, but you're leading me on in such a subtle way it makes me feel pleasurably horny.

Mystery plays a part too. Women are suckers for mysterious men and when it comes to you, I'm 100 percent female. You wouldn't have this effect on me if you flatly refused to talk about your past. It's the way you downplay everything: parents, childhood, education, jobs, beliefs, failures, dreams. Like the other day when that mean drunk said something to us, and you snapped back at him in what sounded to me like perfect English. 'You speak English?' I asked, astounded. 'Just a few sentences,' you said.

I guess we commune well when we make love. What is new to me is the constancy of your tenderness. The men I've known have been insufferably demanding before the act, then disappointingly distant afterwards. You baffle me with your unhurried prologues, surprise me with your languorous epilogues.

You must have experience. It looks promising.

What bothers me is having to keep Dani out of it. Mama wised up early on. When I got home the day we made love for the first time, she just looked at me. She didn't say a word; she didn't have to. Papa is also in the know; he never asks why I arrive home late from work or take off Sunday afternoons. And the puzzling phone calls: 'Can I talk to Fidelia, please?' They both suspect you because I told them about our casual encounter. They were happy to learn you were doing fine, and they want to have you over for supper. So far I've been able to sidestep this by explaining that you work nights, but I wish you'd come out of your shell for a few hours to pay us a visit.

My first reaction after waking up that morning was to marvel at having been able to doze for a while . . .

The teacher thumbed through the pages he'd already read, then closed the notebook.

*   *   *

On weekdays, just before 7.00 a.m., after his two cups of tea with English biscuits, the self-effacing Ruben Scheindlin marched to the library of his Miami Beach home, lit the floor lamp behind a plush brown club chair, and sat down to pore over the *Miami Herald*. On Saturdays and Sundays he read *The Economist*. This required considerable effort and willpower, for Scheindlin suffered a rare, incurable ailment that made his eyes jump every few seconds, repeatedly causing him to lose his place on the page. But one of the wholesaler's secret pleasures was considering himself well-informed.

Scheindlin had never been interested in the planet's ozone layer or its hole over Antarctica until he learned in 1989 about a treaty to ban the production of chlorofluorocarbons – CFCs, in journalistic jargon – on a global scale in the 1990s. The article explained that this was the gas used in domestic refrigerators, air conditioners, and aerosol sprays. According to scientists, CFCs were largely responsible for the depletion of the ozone layer, and its production would be phased out.

Scheindlin was an indoor businessman, not a beach bum, and he wondered if the millions of cooling units in US households would function with substitute gases. What if they wouldn't? Were people supposed to throw away perfectly good units just because the gas was no longer produced? What about cold storage plants, theaters, refrigerated trucks, ice skating rinks? Did they also depend on CFCs?

Since the mildly curious entrepreneur didn't know the first thing about refrigeration, he began gleaning information. He read about R-12 and R-22, HFCs and HCFCs, the probable return to hydrocarbon gases such as propane and butane, existing CFC plants in the US and abroad, standard containers and their transportation and storage requirements, prices for wholesalers, and related topics. By the end of 1992, Ruben had three files on CFCs in his four-drawer filing cabinet at home: one with newspaper and magazine clippings, another with data on companies dealing with the servicing and repair of refrigerators, freezers, and air conditioners in the Greater Miami area, and the third with technical and economic information on the worldwide production and distribution of ozone destroyers.

Research and reflection took time, what with the many other deals Ruben Scheindlin had going on. A year later he reached three conclusions: The existing CFC-based cooling systems couldn't work with ozone-friendly substitutes; in South Florida alone, by reason of its warm climate, there were millions of refrigerators, freezers, and air conditioners that required the soon-to-be-banned chemical; and last but not least, unless human nature had changed behind his back, most owners wouldn't get rid of their units if somebody could supply them with CFCs. Prices would skyrocket due to the demand, and huge profits could be made – it all boiled down to who would grab that dough.

The producers of CFCs and the manufacturers of refrigeration equipment aided and abetted Ruben. In the beginning, both industries had tried to decelerate the ban's implementation, but after finding the right substitutes and assessing market implications, they changed course and cut back on the enemies of ozone even faster than the protocol dictated. Suddenly everybody was overly concerned with protecting mankind from ultraviolet rays. Soon CFCs would no longer be produced in the US or imported there, so Ruben figured that the man who could smuggle CFCs into Miami would make a killing.

The accursed chemical could be bought openly in the Third World countries still producing it. The only risk was the smuggling operation itself. But as Ruben very well knew after many years of wheeling and dealing, there were ways to get around this. The sensible and glitch-proof ways were expensive. On the other hand, the cheap ways were risky; if something went wrong, the merchandise would be confiscated and the people involved sent to prison. But Ruben Scheindlin always experimented first with low-cost options.

Which was why Elliot Steil returned to Charlie's Lounge on the evening of Thursday, November 3, and sat in a booth, where he listened attentively to Tony Soto issue him detailed instructions on his assignments for the next twenty-four hours. The young policeman gave Steil three addresses typed on a slip of paper to be flushed down a toilet later that night, a manila envelope containing shipping documents, and $1700 in cash.

From the bar Steil drove to a dilapidated four-story apartment building on NW 24th Street. In the tiny living room of apartment 34, he attended a two-hour crash course on bills of lading, warehouse receipts, and customs procedures, imparted by an emaciated man who worked from nine to five at a small shipping agency. Steil slid the papers back into the envelope, paid the instructor $200, and left for the second address, in Overtown, where he advanced $500 to a tough-looking black man with a shaved head, telling him what needed to be done.

The following afternoon, the teacher left the port of Miami sitting in the cab of a rented flatbed driven by the black man, with a shipment of twenty drums of cup grease reconsigned in Tampico, México. From Port Boulevard, the driver took Flagler, turned right onto the Palmetto Expressway, and reached the address memorized by Steil, a medium-sized, poorly lit warehouse on 31st Street and 79th Avenue, a few blocks away from the international airport. The place was almost empty, with just some racks and shelves stocking ball bearings, hand tools, and grindstones of all types and sizes. The only men in the warehouse – one driving a forklift and another who maneuvered the cup grease drums like weightless toys – unloaded the truck. Steil and the driver shook hands with the warehouse attendants and left.

At 5.35 p.m., having set the alarm of his wristwatch for 11.00 and prepared for bed, the teacher lifted the handset of his recently installed telephone, tapped out Tony's cellular number, and told the cop he wouldn't be able to attend next Sunday's softball game because of a sprained wrist. Ten minutes later, the officer left the Biscayne Boulevard Mini-Station, grabbed a cup of coffee at a deli, and called Ruben's un-listed number at the North Miami Beach warehouse from a street pay phone. Covering the mouthpiece with his hand, Uri Gold, Scheindlin's secretary, relayed to his boss that the shipment had cleared customs and was stowed at the place they'd agreed upon. The old man nodded approvingly, although he had already heard the news from Samuel Plotzher an hour earlier.

Ruben's partner and close friend was the trading company's muscle. He could do everything in a warehouse, from taking inventory to operating an overhead crane. That afternoon, while Ruben slipped a sealed envelope to a Dodge Island customs inspector, Plotzher had posed as a forklift operator and, by the time the teacher was at his home asleep, was freeing the last twenty-five-liter cylinder of R-12, the gas used for domestic refrigeration, from the protective plastic wrapping covered with cup grease. Plotzher moved the cylinder to the small padlocked room at the back of the ware-house, where the other thirty-nine identical containers were stored.

Ruben Scheindlin had reason to feel complacent. Four other shipments would arrive before the year's end, the perfectly legal documents couldn't be traced to his firm, and Plotzher was the only other person who knew what had been smuggled. He was not aware that the new man on his employee roster had reasons to be generally mistrustful of everyone, and that early the next morning he would rent a safe-deposit box at a West Flagler bank to store a costly wristwatch, two cassettes, and photocopies of the shipping papers he had handled the day before.

*   *   *

Fidelia was not used to seeing men scrub toilets or sinks. She watched Elliot from her canvas chair with a mixture of respect and compassion. She wore jeans, a brown cable-knit sweater over a butterscotch long-sleeved blouse, and sneakers, and looked somewhat impatient holding a steaming mug of coffee. Another mug waited for Steil on the bedside table.

'Your coffee is getting cold,' she said, sipping hers.

'Just a minute.'

Her father had fixed toilet tanks, replaced washers in faucets, and changed drainpipes, but cleaning had always been a female chore performed by her mother and, to a lesser degree, herself since childhood. In her experience, men hated dripping faucets and hissing toilet tanks, but couldn't care less about rust-stained sinks or mildewy tiles. Her lover seemed unperturbed by the permanent gurgling and whistling of his toilet tank, but he kept the bathroom spotless. A different type of guy. She had to fight back the urge to take the mop from his hands and finish the job herself, something she'd never do if asked.

The Cuban Party had instructed the media to represent the cutting edge of feminism. Beginning in her early teens, Fidelia had avidly read newspaper and magazine articles on the subject, and she had watched many TV programs and movies condemning machismo. She tried, to no avail, to convince her father and brother to help with household chores. During her university years, she was sneered at by male students and smiled at condescendingly by her female peers for her extreme views about women's equality. Her first sex partners had tried unsuccessfully to adapt to her views. She had dumped them unceremoniously. Then, when Fidelia fell madly in love with Dani's father, she'd put aside much of her feminism for a number of years, but her beliefs had resurfaced when the marriage began to disintegrate.

Though an eloquent and educated woman, the lawyer had lost faith in words. She had come to believe that one of the greatest tragedies of her time was what she termed 'the loss of meaning'. In Cuba, Fidelia had known people who movingly expressed the loftiest ideals with words, but did in their daily lives the opposite of what they preached. Still, she knew that hypocrisy was not restricted to a country, political party, profession, or layer of social strata. It was a worldwide phenomenon cutting across borders, economic systems, cultures, and even religions. The exception that proved the rule seemed to be pure science: There was no hypocrisy where words were few and numbers and symbols reigned.

Fidelia was extremely sensitive to the loss of the power of words because she loved language. For her, language was the supreme human achievement. But if a self-indulgent, pampered, and dissolute bastard talked or wrote about the benefits of asceticism, she felt that he was damaging some of mankind's jewels. To her this was similar to the destruction almost wreaked by the certified nut who took a swing at Michelangelo's Pietà with a sledge hammer. Fidelia didn't preach virtue or vice, moral excellence or immorality, self-denial or selfishness, celibacy or promiscuity. What she asked of others was to speak their minds, put their money where their mouths were, or remain silent.

And she had met her match, for Elio Esteil didn't talk much and looked like he would act on what little he said.

Elliot returned to the room drying his hands. He sat on the daybed and rested the towel on his knee. He wore light-blue chinos and a denim jacket over a white T-shirt. The teacher dunked the coffee bag up and down for a few seconds, then sipped from the mug. 'Good,' he said.

'Mine's weak.'

'You pull the bag out too soon. Let it sit for a minute and then dunk it several times.'

'It gets cold in this weather.'

Steil shrugged his shoulders and sipped some more. Fidelia ran her hand through her hair, crossed her legs, and watched the man drink.

'It won't be a white Christmas, but it will certainly be a cold one,' she mused after a few moments.

He nodded.

'Will you dine with us tomorrow?'

'I don't know.'

Fidelia uncrossed her legs in annoyance. 'I wish you would make up your mind. Today Mama asked again.'

Steil set the mug on the bedside table, turned a little to his right, shook off his flip flops, and reclined. 'Come over here,' he said, smiling and patting the mattress.

Fidelia finished her coffee, marched to the other side of the bed, took off her sneakers, and lay down. Steil covered their feet with the blanket under which they had made love an hour earlier.

'Let's work this out,' the teacher said. 'I'm not ungrateful. I'm still breathing thanks to you folks . . .'

'Just a minute, Elio!' Fidelia snapped, lifting her right hand. 'Mama and Papa . . . My God! You don't know my parents. You think they are asking you to spend Christmas Eve with us 'cause they want you to . . . to show your gratitude?'

'Will you let me finish?'

Fidelia sighed deeply. 'Sorry.'

'I lost my father when I was nine. I don't know if my

mother then went to bed with a hundred men or if she never made love again. You know why? Because no man ever entered our home. I loved my father very much, I would have hated the guts of anyone trying to take his place.' Steil paused for a moment. 'As I grew up, I became more aware of my mother's tact, or maybe of her sacrifice for me. When I started messing around, I never accepted the invitation of a divorced mother to dine at her place, much less to stay over.'

The teacher picked up his mug and drank some more coffee. Fidelia remained silent, once again amazed by the behavior of this man, her sixth sexual partner. Steil returned the container to the table.

'By your own account, Dani idolizes his father,' Steil went on, 'and we have a relationship that's important to me, that I want to nurture and prolong. In these things precedents shape the future. Tomorrow we have a reason to meet; it's Christmas, Dani was on the raft, too, maybe he'll be pleased to see me. But then you catch a cold in January, and I pay you a visit. In February we pick Dani up after school some afternoon. It'll be some boy's birthday party in March. In April we go together to Butterfly World, and pretty soon he'll catch on, 'cause he's a bright kid. You told him his daddy is in New York, that he'll visit in the future. Dani has no idea he fled, and I don't want your son to doubt you.'

Steil finished his coffee and Fidelia turned on her side, slid her hand under his T-shirt, and stroked the mat of salt-and-pepper hair on his chest.

'So, I believe it's best if we don't set precedents. However, if you want me to dine tomorrow with your folks, I'll do it. But I suggest that when Dani goes to bed we talk things over with your mama and papa, confirm what they probably suspect, and explain why I won't visit until Dani is old enough to learn what his father really did. Okay?'

'Okay.'

A silent minute passed.

'Can I make you some more coffee?'

'Make me some more love,' said Fidelia, smiling.

*   *   *

The teacher stayed awake, pondering Fidelia's role in his trans-formation. After his love for Natasha dissolved with the unbear-able consequences of her infertility, he devoted most of his spare time to casual relationships. Staring death in the face had not only turned him into a vindictive man engaging in criminal exploits; it had also changed him in his attitude toward sex. Before chancing upon Fidelia, he had only contemplated the Miami women who caught his eye. He had wondered if obses-sions prevented testosterone production, or if the downward slope of his virility curve had taken a plunge.

Then she came along: an attractive woman in her mid-thirties, with coal-black eyes that could evolve from the sad sheen of commiseration aboard the raft into radiant dark pools of simmering sexuality inside the efficiency. Fidelia was an intelligent, perceptive person with strong opinions and emo-tions, who was trying to carve a niche for herself in an environ-ment for which she was not even half ready. Together they formed the right combination of disappointments and expec-tations, frustrations and achievements, beliefs and incredulities, years lived and years to come.

Fidelia became the first woman after Natasha whom Steil thought worth caring for. Through her, he was recovering a little faith in humanity. She was straightforward, stubborn, and inflexible, but also kind-hearted, romantic, and sweet. Her feminism seemed extreme, for she blew her top whether dis-cussing wife beating or housecleaning. However, Steil was accustomed to dealing with very independent women, and was fully trained in domestic chores, having lived alone for many years. And he enjoyed opening her up sexually. At first, she'd been primitive and embarrassed, vehemently refusing what in her book was dirty or kinky. But within a month she accepted the innovations, blushingly and with closed eyes. Now she turned off the lamp before assuming the initiative.

Fidelia shivered in her sleep, turned onto her side, and curled up under the blanket. What passes for winter in Miami had come as a complete surprise five weeks earlier, when the first cold front of the season rolled over Florida. Like many recently arrived Cubans, Steil was caught off guard by the sudden drop in temperature. Hearing that Central Americans were even more startled offered little comfort. Suddenly weather forecasts and the Fahrenheit to centigrade conversion – so unabashedly ignored in the summer – became unavoidable, and mental scales had to be formulated. Steil felt awkward shopping for warm clothing when locals and retirees from northern states greeted the cooler temperature wearing baggy cotton shorts, pullovers, and sandals. Born in the tropics, Steil found it a permanent source of embarrassment to see Canadians sunning by the pools on the same days that he wore light winter clothing.

The teacher rose quietly, slipped into his shorts, donned a T-shirt and chinos, slipped on his flip flops, and marched to where a kettle sat on top of a one-plate electric range on a drop-leaf table. He filled the kettle and rinsed the mugs in the sink. As the water warmed, he dropped three sugar cubes and an instant-coffee bag into each mug. He glanced at Fidelia as he waited for the kettle to whistle. She looked childish, her facial features relaxed, lips half-opened. A trickle of saliva had dribbled down her chin onto the pillowcase.

In his new frame of mind, Steil wondered why most heterosexual men, himself at the top of the list, were more seduced by form than by fundamentals when approaching and eventually choosing a sexual partner. What was the influence of culture on this outlook? For how many generations had artists and writers promoted the image of women as beauty queens also blessed with the intellectual and moral qualities most cherished by their contemporaries? The odd combination had become the pursued archetype.

Women like Fidelia and Natasha were pretty, but no raving beauties – sultry in a half-conscious, innocent way; opinionated, clever, decent women passing unobtrusively through life, with an incredible talent for love, but one major drawback, a tendency to suffocate the subject of their affection.

The kettle hissed, and Steil poured the boiling water into the mugs. While dunking both bags, he decided against spoiling the evening by telling Fidelia that soon he would be leaving Miami for an unknown period of time. After stealing three cars for Hairball in the past month, he had enough money to finance his plan. He was ready. In 1995, he would settle the score.

*   *   *

'To have a sparrow' is a popular phrase in Cuba for feeling homesick. Steil first heard the expression during his junior year at the Faculty of Languages, when both staff and students had been sent to the fields for one month of hard toil, cutting sugar-cane stalks. Attracted to a classmate who sat alone by a barbed-wire fence moodily watching the sunset on a Sunday afternoon, young Elliot had ambled over and asked what was the matter. 'I have a sparrow,' she replied.

Eventually, he learned that it was a very popular expression among professionals who had received their degrees at Eastern Bloc universities, officers and soldiers stationed in African nations, and even among diplomats and trade executives living abroad. How such a small, common, and unendangered bird had come to represent homesickness eluded him even on New Year's Day of 1995.

Agreeing, for Dani's sake, not to repeat the Christmas Eve family reunion, Fidelia and Steil spent the last afternoon of 1994, a Saturday, together at his efficiency. After what Hoffman's stepfather in *Little Big Man* probably would have described as disgusting white man copulation, they gobbled twelve grapes each and shared a bottle of Spanish cider a little before 6.00 p.m. Driving back from Fidelia's, the teacher craved a drink. It was the cider that did it, he guessed. On the 24th he had cautiously sipped a beer with his food, and now the low-alcohol apple juice was stirring the beast. *I better watch out*, Steil warned himself. He went to bed early that night.

He woke at 3.15 a.m., showered, and shaved. Then the figurative sparrow flew into his room, just as he finished his mug of coffee while sitting in a canvas chair. A sudden, overwhelming nostalgia filled him. Havana was the old apartment that hadn't seen a coat of paint for as long as he could remember. It was his beloved paperbacks, the obsolete TV set, the bed where he slept soundly, the toilet seat he had grown used to. He missed his building and neighbors; Sobeida in her ample skirts, busily knocking on doors to deliver what 'had arrived' at the store; the block full of screaming kids pretending to be Zorro or whichever character was being shown on Channel 6 at 7.30 p.m.; the Polytechnic Institute with its students and fellow teachers; the ruined school desks; the pieces of chalk that for some mysterious reason were so hard they scratched the decrepit blackboard.

Havana was also a radio tuned to the 2.00 soap opera; wet underwear hanging on a clothesline; the metal ring nailed precariously to a lamppost by basketball players; bikers pedaling uphill; a butt making the round among smokers; an art gallery full of incredible landscapes; a family doctor sipping the meager ration of freshly brewed coffee brought by one of his patients; three guys on the corner making crude remarks to a young woman with a large behind wearing pink Spandex shorts; old people lining up on the sidewalk for the smelly mixture of soybeans and ground beef at Susana Vila's supermarket.

Steil rinsed the mug, returned to the daybed, locked his fingers behind his head, and stared at the ceiling. What personal achievements had he left behind? Why should memories make him feel so miserable? He hadn't raised a family; he'd squandered the free time of his best years reading fiction, drinking, and chasing women. Why? Lack of ambition? After some soul-searching, Steil concluded that he had never felt the urge to stand out, excel, or bask in general approval. He had read somewhere that leaders and leaders-to-be had little interest in sex. Perhaps. He had been a very sex-oriented person and never sought power. Did he seek appreciation for a job well done? Yes. Hope for a promotion because he was the most qualified and had seniority? Sure. Desire to boss people around? No thanks. In a rigidly stratified society, where success hinges on the authority a person wields, opportunity would always pass by those who were indifferent to power. If, in addition to a man's lack of concern for domination, decision makers considered him a political risk, he was cast into oblivion.

Then why should he feel he had lost so much? It was all intangible: the people, the streets, the smells, the quiet nights, the chaotic diversity of an architecture blending a thousand styles, the blaring horns of the oldest cars in the world that still ran, the music, the jokes, the resigned smiles and the knowing looks with which many unjustifiable privations were tolerated.

Steil turned over and stared at the blank wall. Santa Cruz del Norte. Its permanent sea breeze and clean streets and peculiar atmosphere – one-third fishing village, one-third rural town, one-third rum distillery. On its rocky coastline on calm days, the flood tide filled little pools where he watched tiny crabs and fish and abalone thriving under a burning sun. His father beckoned him to take a swim. In the distance, the refinery's chimneys spewed out dense, black smoke. It was back in those years when nobody mentioned pollution and oil was cheap.

Mom, grandpa, grandma, and his cousins and uncles and aunts. Men scraped a living and discussed politics and played dominoes in the evenings. Their wives cooked, scrubbed floors, washed, ironed, gossiped, and listened to soap operas. Kids attended school and played games and wondered about sex. On Sundays they all went to church. Everyone was oblivious to the happiness in which they were immersed. Those were the perfect years every big family lives, when nobody is too old, seriously ill, indigent, in prison, or divorced.

Maybe he was like his mother, sentimental. A person's fundamental nature is difficult to explain, he thought. Two, maybe three years before dying, on a quiet evening in their Havana apartment, Carmen had confessed that she'd never felt at home in Florida. He wanted to know why. Was it the language barrier? English was never a problem; her husband or her mother-in-law interpreted for her. And the whole state was so beautiful, Elliot protested. The weather was similar to Cuba's. Farmers lived in modern houses, not huts made of palm wood and thatched with palm fronds. Most cars were new, and the streets were well paved and clean. Then there were the beaches, stores, movies, popcorn, marshmallows, and Big League baseball. Elliot rambled on, a grown man formulating an opinion based on childhood impressions. His mother just nodded and smiled as he piled up reasons why he disagreed with her. So, why, Mom?

'Florida didn't enter here,' she finally said, pointing to her heart.

An irrefutable argument.

Carmen never confessed that Havana hadn't found its way into her heart, either. She didn't want her son to feel guilty. But as the years passed, Elliot came to realize that they had moved to the Cuban capital for his sake – to broaden his horizons and escape a past tainted by an American father and bad memories. But in doing this, she had lost her moorings. She visited her parents twice a year and sometimes spent a couple of weeks with them. The night before leaving for Santa Cruz del Norte, as she ironed her dresses and packed them in her old rawhide travel bag, she behaved like a different person, with sparkling eyes, swift graceful movements, and a fixed smile. She stepped into the old trolley car to Hershey the following morning, looking as if she were boarding the Concorde for the first leg of a trip around the world.

When he moved in with Natasha after their marriage, Carmen sometimes spent an entire month in Santa Cruz, coming back for a week to clean the apartment and buy their ration-card quotas, then setting off again for her hometown. But after his divorce, she returned to Havana quietly resigned; she was there to take care of her son. For her entire life she had been a lousy cook, but a great housekeeper. As her hypertension worsened, Elliot was forced to do all the housework, and it saddened her to acknowledge that she no longer was useful to the person she most loved.

The teacher shook his head. *Snap out of it*, he ordered himself. He was beginning a new life in the same place he had spent good times. Though it wasn't paradise, Florida had won a corner in his heart. For the first time, he felt like a man with a purpose.

He now knew the meaning of *having a sparrow*. It meant flitting back over the naïve years of your life, when you believed that everyone had nice intentions, the people you loved never died, the good won, the bad were punished, and the lone avenger was a Hollywood ruse.

What a way to begin a year! he thought as he got up to hit the streets and have an early breakfast.

Part Two

Part Two

6

On the evening of January 7, 1995, Elliot Steil left the coffee shop where he had used the bathroom and ordered a glass of milk. He was unlocking the passenger door of a rented 1994 Buick LeSabre with tinted windows when a voice behind him asked, 'Gotta light?'

The teacher pulled out his key from the door and turned around. He was immediately reminded of the young woman who had approached him with the same question six months before, on the evening that forever changed his life. This woman, a light-skinned black, wore a tight miniskirt that was even shorter, and instead of a tank top, she was wearing a white gossamer blouse over beautiful, bare breasts. Like the Cuban prostitute, she wore big earrings, and a cigarette dangled from her full lips. Steil grinned sheepishly and shook his head.

'No light?'

Steil shook his head once more.

'How about buying me a drink?'

The teacher blinked twice. 'I'm driving.'

She leered seductively. 'Wanna have a little fun, baby?'

'Some other time.'

Resignedly, 'Okay. This is my turf. For a great time, ask for Donna.'

'Sure.'

Donna looked around, then opted to turn right and stroll south. Nice figure, Steil thought. He inspected his surroundings. Like city limits everywhere, Sarasota's northern edge was not very impressive. He pulled the door open, sat down in the passenger seat, and found a city map in the glove compartment.

He had left Miami early in the morning in Tony Soto's Ford,

which he had now paid for in full. Around 11.00, to avoid passing through Sarasota in broad daylight, the teacher abandoned Highway 41 a mile after Laurel, by the north access to Route 75. At 2.05 p.m., Steil removed a small suitcase from the trunk and left the Ford in the long-term parking garage of Tampa's international airport. Half an hour later, he drove the rented Buick to the city's old section and had lunch in a small restaurant overlooking the bay. As his gaze moved over the high-rises gleaming under the sun, the teacher sensed that when he had landed there in his mother's arms forty-three years back, the place must have looked pretty different.

In order to reach his final destination by nightfall, he drove south leisurely, enjoying the scenery in the golden late afternoon, his road map on the dashboard. At dusk he turned on the headlights and saw a sign announcing Sarasota County. His brain shifted gradually from contemplation to anticipation. The upper rim of a blood-red sun was dissolving in the waters of the Gulf of México as he entered the coffee shop.

After a few minutes of careful inspection, Steil refolded the map to the town's center and coastline. Cruising along Tamiami Trail, peering at signs, and frequently consulting the map, the teacher found his way to the Selby Library and spent two hours cramming for his scheme. Sarasota's social directory described Edward James Steil as a businessman, yachtsman, and philanthropist, born on January 19, 1930, in Statenville, Georgia, the son of Ebenezer and Edna Steil. He had moved to Sarasota in 1955 and married Marie Joanne Victorson on February 26, 1959. He had no offspring and his wife had passed away on August 14, 1987. He owned Steil's Jewelry Store on St Armands Circle, and was active in community affairs.

At 9.30, Steil returned to the car, feeling the sudden drop in temperature, now probably in the low 60s. He drove into St Armands Key, coasted past its circle looking at the upscale tourist shops, then turned into Lido Key on Benjamin Franklin Road. Street lights and illuminated storefronts revealed an infrastructure quietly evolving from affluence to luxury. At the end of the road he made a U-turn and settled on the Half Moon Beach Club, one of the more unassuming hotels catering to winter birds. The two-story building surrounded a small, amoeba-shaped pool in a patio with sun decks and wrought-iron furniture painted white. Three wings of rooms protruded into landscaped gardens. The place smelled clean and green. He filled out the registration card presented by a flaxen-haired young woman, marched unaccompanied to room 108, locked the door, and looked around. It was there on the night stand.

Leaving the suitcase and hotel key on the closest of the two single beds, the teacher grabbed the Sarasota phone book, moved to a round white plastic table in the corner, sat down in a plastic chair, and started flipping the pages. A *Steil, E.* lived at 4205 Augustine Avenue. He withdrew the city map from the inner breast pocket of his navy-blue sports coat and located the address using the street index and grid. There was just a single block between Wilkinson Road and Maiden Lane. The area was residential, sprinkled with schools, churches, and shopping centers. The teacher leaned back in the chair, interlaced his fingers, and rested both hands on the top of his head. Looking at a canvas on the cream-colored, windowless wall, he tasted the thrill of the big-game hunter approaching the wild beast's lair. The difference, he reasoned, was that, as a rule, the prey had never harmed its stalking hunter.

*   *   *

At 8.35 the following morning, Edward Steil knitted his brow as he exited his garage; the ascending door revealed a dark green Buick LeSabre with tinted windows blocking his driveway. He tapped the gas pedal of his 1995 Lexus, but stopped the car before reaching the sidewalk, and tooted the horn as the garage door closed automatically. Nothing happened. A longer toot produced no results. With muscles bulging at the base of his jaw, the jeweler shifted the stick into park, jerked his car door open, and stepped out. He wore a pearl-gray sports coat over a purple shirt, dark brown slacks, and loafers.

Approaching the passenger door of the offending vehicle, Edward Steil cupped his palms over his eyes to form a visor and peered inside. A man was reclining against the driver's door with his feet resting on the passenger seat. A baseball cap covered his face. He looked fast asleep, drunk, or drugged, oblivious to the inconvenience he was causing. Edward Steil walked around the trunk, noted the license plate indicating that the car was a rental, and surmised that this dozing asshole was a tourist. He moved angrily toward the driver's door, when it was suddenly flung open.

'Hold it right there, Pop,' the teacher said with an assumed husky voice as he uncoiled himself from the seat. He wore a pair of surgeon's gloves. The Marlins cap covered his hair, and dark sunglasses hid most of his features. A shopping bag hung from his left hand, and his right was hidden inside a paper bag pointed at the jeweler.

'There's a gun in this paper bag,' Elliot Steil continued, flexing his wrist slightly. 'I just wanna clean up your place, so don't play hero or I'll blow your fucking head off. Insurance claim or graveyard: Take your pick.'

Edward Steil had all the signs of a nonplussed man, but he didn't act terrified. He thought things through for a couple of seconds. 'You horsed out?' he asked. He heard the click of a hammer being cocked. 'Okay, what do you want me to do?'

'Go back to your car and hand me the keys. Then go straight to the porch, tap the alarm's code, and open up. I'll be right behind you.'

Edward Steil followed the instructions perfectly. After closing the front door, the teacher shook off the paper bag and revealed a .357 Magnum Colt King Cobra. The one-story, two-bedroom house was the appropriate size for a wealthy, childless couple. Expensively furnished and decorated, it smelled nice and was very clean. Elliot inspected every room to be sure that no mistress or cleaning lady would suddenly appear, then ordered Ed to lie prone on the tiled dining room floor. He tied the prisoner's ankles and wrists with pieces of cord, which he removed from the plastic shopping bag as he questioned him about how the garage door worked. Using an expensive-looking ashtray as a doorstop, the teacher propped the front door open. He pocketed the gun, returned the Lexus to the garage, stripped off the rubber gloves, and moved the Buick around the corner onto Wilkinson Road. As he walked back to his uncle's home, he saw a '94 Seville pulling out of the driveway of a house on the other side of the street. The elderly couple in the car were well-dressed and looked as if they were on their way to church. They seemed unfazed by the tall pedestrian.

Back in the dining room, Elliot Steil gloved his hands and pushed record on the recorder hidden in the shopping bag. Then he turned the prisoner on his back and with much pushing and shoving managed to seat him precariously on a solid wooden chair. Elliot sat in a matching chair facing his uncle.

'Your store opens at ten on Sundays,' the teacher said in his normal tone.

A frown. 'Right.'

'So we have close to an hour before someone starts wondering where you are.'

'Probably.'

Elliot took his time removing the cap and sunglasses, enjoying himself immensely. A wide-eyed Edward Steil paled visibly. The teacher fished into the pocket of his denim jacket and shook the Breguet in front of his uncle's eyes. Edward's gaze moved past the watch to the floor tiles.

'Uncle Ed, give your nephew a sound piece of advice. What should I do with you?'

The jeweler kept his eyes fixed on the floor.

'Wanna know what I'd love to do?' the teacher fumed, anger boiling inside him. 'I'd love to rent a boat and dump you fifty miles off shore, right in the middle of that Gulf of Mexico you've been sailing on. But that's impossible. There's no way to do it and get away with it. So, should I put a bullet through your head? Strangle you maybe? Pour a gallon of gas over your fat old body and burn you to death? C'mon, Uncle Ed, give your nephew a sound piece of advice.'

Half a minute passed. Both men sat paralyzed, breathing heavily. At last Edward Steil grimaced, still looking at the tiles. 'It wasn't personal,' he said.

The teacher stared blankly at his uncle before chuckling. 'For Chrissake, Ed, can't you come up with something more original?'

The old man suddenly looked resigned to his fate. He shrugged and forced a smile. 'No,' he said.

Elliot nodded repeatedly before standing up. He switched the Breguet to his left hand and recovered the gun from the dining room table. Moving behind the jeweler, he spoke: 'I can't figure you out, 'cause I presume you ain't crazy. Of course it wasn't personal. I never laid eyes on you as far as I can remember, and you'd probably never seen me before we met in Havana. So I'm curious. It's only natural. I want to know why, and telling me might, just might, save your life. I'm not promising anything. Maybe you tell me why, and I blow your head off anyway, but at least I'm giving you a slim chance, something you didn't give me. I learned to hate this watch. Look at the second hand. I'll give you a full minute. You don't start telling the whole truth in sixty seconds, I swear on my mother's grave I'll shoot you in the back of your fucking head.'

As the hand started sweeping the dial, the teacher almost wished his uncle wouldn't say a word. He wanted to close this chapter of his life and move on to whatever lay in store for him. His yearning for revenge was so consuming that he felt sure he wouldn't have qualms about snuffing the only person he had ever truly hated.

Edward Steil realized he was one step away from death

around second twenty-five, when he noticed that the Breguet hanging from his nephew's hand was as stationary as if it had been nailed to the wall. Like sprinklers being activated, the pores on his forehead started gushing sweat. He ran the tip of his tongue over his parched lips.

'I didn't have the guts,' he croaked.

'For what?'

'To shoot you. I had a gun in the cockpit.'

'That makes you a saint. You got ten seconds.'

'I was paid to do it.'

'By whom?'

Edward Steil sighed. 'I don't know.'

The teacher uttered a growl that frightened his uncle. 'Two guys came here,' the old man added rapidly. 'City slickers, big limo. The names they gave were phony for sure: Mr Bergen and Mr Jones. They'd done their homework, knew I'd have to file soon for chapter eleven.'

'What's that?'

'Bankruptcy.'

'Go on.'

'They said you had to be taken care of.'

'Why?'

Edward Steil let out another sigh when the watch was removed from before his eyes. 'Story they fed me you ain't gonna believe.'

'Let me be the judge of that.'

'Bergen said Bobby . . . I mean Bob, your father . . . had been working for US intelligence since he was a young man. The president had nominated him for a top position, but a political rival had threatened Bob with exposing that a son of his lived in a Communist country. The scandal would force Congress to deny his confirmation and discredit the president.'

The teacher reflected on this as fast as he could. 'My father worked for the CIA?'

Edward Steil shrugged. 'I don't know, they didn't say. CIA,

NSA, FBI, what's the difference? Maybe Bob was with Army intelligence during the war and was asked to do some under-cover work when he became a civilian again. He never said a word to me. I had him figured as a sugar man. You know, Fellsmere, Cuba, Louisiana. Then these two guys came over and swore me to secrecy before . . .'

Edward's voice trailed off. His nephew's anger fizzled out as his astonishment grew. 'Go ahead,' he demanded.

'They said I was the right guy for the job. I'd save my brother from disgrace, and my business would make a comeback with a hundred grand from Bob.'

The teacher was speechless for a few seconds, then his anger returned to its previous level. 'My father paid you to kill me?'

'No, no,' Ed Steil said, shaking his head firmly. 'He didn't know what was going on, about terminating you, I mean. Bergen said he hadn't been consulted because everybody assumed he'd be against it. He never got over deserting you and your mama. Jones implied they were acting under orders from some intelligence bigwigs. The dough would be routed through one of Bob's bank accounts to make it look like a brother-to-brother unsecured loan. It has to do with money laundering. These days you can't walk into a bank with a hundred grand in a briefcase and make a deposit.'

Elliot realized he was missing any clues surfacing in his uncle's eyes and returned to the chair to glare at the prisoner. His suntanned face was a little ashen. Sweat trickled down the deep wrinkles in Edward's face, drenching the front of his shirt and collar. The teacher noted that he should have removed the old man's jacket before tying him up, but sneered at himself in the same breath for commiserating.

'Where's my father?'

A forced smile. 'He's dead, Elliot.'

'Listen, you stupid asshole, you better start making sense real fast or I'll kill you. The president was going to nominate a dead man?'

'He was alive then.'

'When did he die?'

'June 11.'

'June 11?'

Edward Steil nodded resignedly.

'One week after you pushed me overboard?'

'Right.'

The teacher took a deep breath. 'How did he die?'

'Massive cardiac arrest.'

'Where?'

'His place in New Iberia.'

'Where's that?'

'Louisiana.'

The teacher's anger and frustration climbed steadily. Sympathy for the helpless uncle plummeted.

'Did you collect?'

Edward Steil nodded, his eyes returning to the tiled floor.

'If you believe,' the teacher grumbled, 'I'm gonna swallow this hook, line, and sinker for the second time, you're pretty naive, uncle. You know I can't check any of this. Bergen and Jones are ghosts; my father is dead. I'm inclined to believe you're making all of this up.'

The jeweler remained silent, breathing hard, though some color had returned to his face. Once again he moistened his lips with the tip of his tongue.

The teacher continued: 'My father may have had a wife, a son or daughter, maybe business associates. Your life depends on verification. You have his address and phone number?'

The prisoner considered something for a moment, then lifted his head. 'Open the top drawer of the writing desk in the den. You'll find an indexed notebook. Look under *B*.'

* * *

Returning the watch to his jacket pocket, the teacher marched to the den, coming back a few moments later with the notebook, a Sarasota phone book, and a cordless phone he'd found on the desk. Ed Steil had squeezed his eyes shut, and his brow was knitted as if in anger or pain. Elliot flipped through the pages of the notebook and found an area code followed by seven digits next to the name *Bob*. Having checked in the phone book that 504 was in fact a Louisiana area code, he sat in silence, trying to craft a plan. Disconcerted by the absence of sound, Ed Steil fixed his eyes on the teacher. His nephew was staring at the tabletop as if it could unravel the mystery.

Close to three minutes elapsed before Elliot completed his design, picked up the phone, and punched out the number. The old man watched anxiously.

'Hello.'

'Is this 504—555—9809?'

'Yeah.'

'This is Sergeant Martínez from the Tampa Police Department.'

'Yes, sir.'

'Are you the phone line's legal customer?'

'No, sir. I'm the maid.'

'Is the legal customer on the premises?'

'Where?'

'At home.'

'I guess so. I'll take a look. You said you were . . . ?'

The teacher again gave his false identity, and his gaze roved to his uncle. Their eyes locked. Elliot wished he could drill into the brain behind the blue eyes and discover the truth. The old man looked a little surprised and expectant. Over a minute passed before a smooth, educated woman's voice spoke: 'Yes, Sergeant Martínez, what can I do for you?'

'Sorry to bother you. Are you an adult?'

'I am, yes.'

'And your full name, please?'

'Mrs Shelley Steil.'

'Could you please spell your last name?'

'S-T-E-I-L.'

'Thank you, ma'am. Is this phone line in your place of residence?'

'Yes. Could we get to the point, Sergeant?'

'Certainly. Are you related to a Mr Edward Steil?'

Her slight gasp and second of hesitation were revealing, Elliot thought. Ed Steil was again sweating profusely, his eyes fixed on the younger man absorbed in improvisation.

'A man in his sixties? Lives in Sarasota?'

'That's him, ma'am.'

'Oh, well, I'm the widow of his brother, Sergeant. But we are not close. I've only seen my brother-in-law on two, maybe three occasions. Is he . . . uhh . . . in some sort of trouble?'

'A squad car found him this morning in very bad shape on the sidewalk of a mean street here in Tampa. He seemed to be suffering a nervous breakdown and was taken to a hospital. We found two hundred and twenty-seven dollars, a driver's license, and a couple of credit cards in his wallet. He still had his car and home keys, so we know he wasn't mugged. But he's incoherent and keeps mumbling strange things. Nobody answers the phone at his place. You happen to know if he lives alone?'

'I understand he lost his wife eight or ten years ago. What kind of strange . . . ?'

'That figures. Well, apparently no crime has been committed and we are trying to notify his closest relative. Does Mr Steil have a son or daughter we could get in touch with?'

'Not that I know of.'

'A nephew maybe?'

'Nephew? Well . . . ahh, my son . . . but they've never met. What kinds of strange things is he saying?'

'Oh, he's talking nonsense, ma'am. Jumps from one thing to the other. Mentions his brother, your late husband, I presume, some sort of confirmation hearings, repeats two dates, let me check, yes, June 4 and June 11. Mentions a drowned nephew. Two men named Bergen and Jones. Very confusing, if you ask me.'

'Listen, Lieutenant Mar . . .'

'Martínez, but I'm a sergeant ma'am.'

'Of course, Sergeant, sorry.' An urgency had crept into the woman's voice. 'Listen, my late husband loved his brother very much, and I'm sure he'd do everything in his power to help Ed if he was still alive. As his widow, I should do what he would've done. I'm not without means, and I can send the required health-care specialists to assist Ed. Could you please tell me the name of the hospital he was admitted to?'

The teacher felt as if a bucket of ice water had been poured over his head. 'Just a moment,' he muttered. Covering the mouthpiece, he stared at the wall for inspiration. 'Tampa General,' he managed to blurt out an instant later.

'Thank you, Sergeant. Give me your number, in case I need to get in touch with you.'

'Sure.'

A few seconds slipped by. 'Well?' the woman demanded.

'Oh, you ready?' The teacher made up a number and an extension.

'Got it. I'll see what I can do. Thanks, Sergeant. By the way, how'd you find my number?'

Big smile. 'His wallet. "In case of accident notify."'

'Really? That's odd. Well, I'll see what I can do. Thanks again.'

'My pleasure, ma'am. Bye.'

'Bye, bye.'

Elliot hung up, placed the cordless on the table, and once again stared at Edward Steil, this time with considerably less animosity in his eyes. The teacher wondered if among the rivulets of bodily fluids streaming down his uncle's face one or two were tears. He stood up, moved to the kitchen, drank two glasses of water, and brought one back to the old man.

Carefully pouring the liquid into his uncle's mouth, Elliot knew he wouldn't kill the man. For reasons not clear to him, his hate had abated below the critical point.

'Thanks,' the prisoner said.

The teacher nodded, returned to his seat, and placed the empty glass by the phone. 'As we say in Cuba, Uncle Ed, today you were reborn. I'll let you live.'

Edward Steil closed his eyes and let his head hang.

'You leveled with me, up to a point. But I can't figure everything out. Too many holes. I guess I'll dig around a little. Maybe go to New Iberia, have a talk with Mrs Steil.'

The old man lifted his head, a fresh worry reflected on his face. 'Listen, Elliot, I know this is gonna sound pretty stupid, I mean, me offering a piece of advice to you, but . . . let it lay. Don't mess with the wrong people.'

'You mean the spooks?'

The jeweler nodded. 'They can track you down in twenty-four hours, Elliot. No matter how you cover your tracks, these people can find you and have you killed in no time. They can access records, have informers everywhere. This is a very embarrassing story and they'd hate to see it aired. So, get lost, change your name, move to Canada, return to Cuba if you feel like it, but don't mess with these people.' Ed Steil sounded convincing, and Elliot gave him his undivided attention. 'Let me loose. I won't lift a finger against you,' the old man continued. 'You have every reason in the world to do what you've done today. I understand. Listen, I can't press charges against you, because you'd tell your side of the story and get me in a real mess. We're . . . well, not even, but this whole episode can end right here and now if you wish.'

Elliot absent-mindedly drummed his fingers on the tabletop. 'She sounded worried when I mentioned the hearings, the dates, and a drowned nephew.'

'You bet.'

'She was in?'

'I can't say for sure. But my old man used to say she was the power behind the throne.'

'What throne?'

'The sugar refinery.'

'My father owned a sugar refinery?'

'He was the majority stockholder in a public company.'

'He was . . . rich?'

'I'd say he was very well off.'

The teacher shook his head before voicing his thoughts: 'Maybe she was influential in business matters, but concerning government secrets, you think my father would've . . . ?'

'How should I know? He probably told her about you. She might have learned about the threat to expose that part of Bob's life. And she might've suggested something to someone.'

Elliot nodded in approval.

'But that's water under the bridge. Forget it. I mean it, Elliot. Don't mess with these people.'

The teacher crossed his legs, closed his eyes, and massaged his forehead. He felt drained, utterly exhausted, as if he had worked in a Cuban potato field for twelve hours straight. He forced his eyelids open. 'There's no way you can hide from her the fact that something strange happened to you today. In a little while this will ring' – he patted the phone – 'right after she finds out there's no Tampa General Hospital, or if there is one, that you ain't a patient there. When she realizes Sergeant Martínez took her for a ride, she'll call, maybe even send someone here.'

Looking befuddled, the old man again hung his head. 'You should have believed me.'

'Oh, yeah. Just like in Havana.'

The jeweler let it pass, and Elliot glanced at his watch. 9.54 a.m. 'I'm leaving,' he said. 'Don't try to find me. If you do and succeed, finish me off 'cause I'll kill you if I ever lay my eyes on you again. Is that clear?'

The old man nodded, smiling sadly.

'The police will come for you in a few hours,' the teacher went on. 'You were burglarized. Wanna wait sitting right there or lying on the floor?'

'You aren't gonna let me loose?'

Elliot smirked. 'In Havana I was an asshole. Not any more.'

Edward Steil chose to lay prone on the floor. The teacher donned his cap and sunglasses, turned off the tape recorder, and dropped the gun into the plastic shopping bag. After jotting the phone numbers on his notepad for Shelley Steil and the Sarasota police, he started for the front door.

'Who rescued you?' Ed Steil asked.

'Human beings,' his nephew said over his shoulder.

In the living room, Elliot picked up the paper bag, crunched it into a ball, and stuffed it into his back pocket. The window overlooking the street showed no pedestrians. Keeping the door ajar with the tip of his sneaker, Elliot wiped off the doorknob. He was pulling off his gloves when the cordless phone rang. Smiling, the teacher pocketed the gloves, exited, and pulled the door shut, covering his fingers with his hand-kerchief.

Cruising up Tamiami Trail in the Buick, Elliot spotted the coffee shop where he'd had a glass of milk the night before. He hadn't eaten since then, but ignored his hunger pangs. Donna was probably sleeping, the teacher speculated as he searched for her. In less than sixteen hours he had pulled off what he'd estimated would require a week. What incredible luck!

At 12.16 he returned the rented Buick to the Tampa airport, and just past 1.00, he was gobbling down two cheeseburgers and a soda at a McDonald's. Before filling up his Ford at a gas station, he called the Sarasota police department from a public phone to report that Edward Steil had been burglarized and was tied up at his Augustine Avenue residence. It was a long drive back to Miami.

7

On Sunday night the teacher went to bed after a brief telephone conversation with Fidelia. Around 1.00 in the morning,
his full bladder woke him. In the bathroom, he relieved himself
with his eyes closed, then went back to bed and was asleep
within a few seconds. His watch alarm beeped at 7.00, but he
did not rise until his bladder once again forced him out of bed
just past 8.00. In a haze, he recalled a dream. He had stolen
all of the watches from a jewelry store and was running stark
naked along a Miami street. On the sidewalk, Natasha and
Fidelia stood holding hands, laughing uproariously as he tried
to cover his privates with the briefcase that held the loot.

He took a long shower, shaved, brushed his teeth, and made
a cup of coffee. As he sipped it, he reconsidered the findings
he had been sifting through on his return trip.

Before closing down in 1958, the Fellsmere Sugar Producers'
Association could have experienced financial difficulties dating
back to '57, maybe '56, which might have forced Bob Steil to
search for a new seasonal job in the US. His father had mentioned Louisiana and New Orleans several times before leaving
Cuba for the last time. After his mother's death, Elliot had
found a batch of letters, including three from 1958 and 1959,
which offhandedly referred to Louisiana. Ed Steil had said that
his brother was the majority shareholder in a refinery. Had his
father worked his way up from operator to owner? Was Louisiana really a sugar-producing state? Where was New Iberia?
The teacher dressed and left for the public library on Flagler.

By lunch time, Steil had learned the essential facts about the
eighteenth state. He devoted an extra fifteen minutes – three
phone calls – to discover that Sarasota had no daily newspaper

and that the *Tampa Tribune* could be found at a North Miami Beach newsstand.

Still on the graveyard shift, he drove to the newsstand on a cold and gray Tuesday morning and bought the Monday edition of the Tampa daily. Back in the car, he scanned the front page, but couldn't find what he was looking for, so he headed south to the Allapattah Station cafeteria where he had become a regular. The teacher returned home after breakfast. He washed up, then sat on a canvas chair to pore over the newspaper.

It was on page 7B: The sole proprietor of a Sarasota jewelry store had been burglarized on Sunday morning. Police found the victim tied up and lying on the floor of his home at 1.30 p.m., twenty-four minutes after an anonymous phone call traced to a Tampa public phone reported the theft. Edward Steil had been taken to the hospital and was treated for hypertension and circulatory problems caused by the ropes that had bound his hands and feet.

Mr Steil had reported a theft of $700 in cash and $53,000 in family jewels that he had kept in his home safe, including a diamond necklace he had presented to his late wife on a wedding anniversary and a costly watch of his own. The teacher threw back his head and laughed. He could see Uncle Ed claiming the insurance money for something he must have hidden, pawned, sold, or given away heaven knows when. He had probably planned to do this while waiting to be rescued. What a cool scam artist! Elliot thought, and resumed his reading.

The burglar had acted swiftly, the paper said, and the victim opened the safe under duress. The jeweler had remained tied up on his dining room floor for over three hours. Four neighbors had seen a dark green sedan blocking the entrance to Mr Steil's driveway early that morning, but none of them had jotted down its plate number. The victim affirmed that the illegally parked vehicle had been a ruse to get him out of his own car when leaving home close to 10.00. Police were following several leads.

The teacher glanced at the night table drawer storing the watch that he had inadvertently taken back to Miami in the pocket of his denim jacket. He should have wiped off his fingerprints and left it on the sonafabitch's dining room table as a reminder, which would also have reduced the insurance claim. He would throw it away soon. Would he? Should he throw away several thousand dollars? Wasn't it wiser to find out if Hairball knew a fence who'd give him a couple of thousand for it? No, it wasn't. The watch was hot now. He should get rid of it.

The phone rang. It was Fidelia, wanting to know if she could drop by after work.

*　　*　　*

Ruben Scheindlin shook hands and smiled perfunctorily before easing himself into his swivel chair. He seemed to be wearing the same clothes that he had on their first meeting, and Elliot wondered if the man bought white short-sleeved shirts and T-shirts by the dozen. His mind flashed back to the seventies in Cuba, when practically every man went to work in the gray khaki shirts and pants the government distributed free of charge.

Elliot had been summoned to the warehouse by the boss himself two hours earlier, around 7.00 p.m. It was their second exchange of their five-month-long association, and Scheindlin had personally phoned him. The night watchman fifty feet away appeared to be the only other person in the warehouse. The suspicion that Tony Soto had been deliberately excluded sprang to Elliot's mind.

'You getting used to Miami?' Scheindlin asked, interlacing his fingers and resting both hands on his belly.

'Sure. And how are you doing, sir?'

'I'm not complaining. Let's get down to brass tacks.'

Steil tilted his head, giving him a faint smile.

Scheindlin grinned openly. 'Yeah, I keep using outdated expressions, like old people everywhere. Okay. You've been with me for a few months now, Elio. Didn't make much money, but you were on trial. Now you can move up one step in this organization. You want to?'

'Very much so.'

'All right, listen.' The trader pushed up his glasses, which had slipped down his nose. 'I'll give you some money for the down payment of a cargo van. Lease it in your name. I'll cover the monthly installments, too. You'll deliver gas cylinders to companies dealing in the servicing and repair of refrigeration equipment. I'll tell you where to go, the number of cylinders to deliver, and the money you must collect from each client. You get to a place, ask for the guy on your list, and tell him you got the merchandise in the van and wanna see the cash before unloading. Guy's not in, you don't talk to anyone else; guy says he'll pay you the next morning or tries to give you a check, you turn around and leave. Guy says he wants an invoice, a receipt, you turn around and leave. It's very important to never lose your temper.'

'I won't.'

'Fine. Guy says he wants more freon, you make a note and tell me. Don't mention names, you know nothing, you just drive, unload, and collect. Don't negotiate prices, quantities, or delivery dates; that's my turf. You'll take the van to the 31st Street warehouse in the mornings. Somebody from my staff will hand you a clipboard with the names, addresses, and quantities to deliver to each place. The charge will be there, too. At the end of the day you leave the van at your place, get in your car, drive over here, and hand the cash to Uri, my secretary. You understand?'

'I do, Mr Scheindlin.'

'Ruben. You drive carefully. I mean *carefully*. Always fasten your seat belt, check that your brake and backup lights work properly every morning, don't double park, don't fly through yellow lights. Forget about speeding. We don't want the police snooping around. You still working nights?'

'Yeah.'

'It's up to you if you want to keep that job. First coupla weeks you'll probably make deliveries one or two days a week, to maybe three or four customers a day. By noon you'll be free to bunk down. But in a month or two you'll either become a zombie or quit the supermarket.'

'How much will I make doing deliveries for you, sir?' Steil asked, having difficulty calling Scheindlin by his first name.

'I'll start you off with a hundred a day.'

'Count me in.'

'I already had. Maybe you should consider moving to a quieter, more respectable neighborhood. Rent an apartment in some building with parking space for the van.'

There was a pause. To Scheindlin's left, a thermal-paper fax machine started spewing out a message. Both men stole glances at it, then locked eyes again. 'You got any questions?' the wholesaler asked.

'No, sir.'

Scheindlin tilted his head and scratched his right temple. 'How would you deal with the unexpected?'

Steil shrugged. 'I'd improvise.'

'Okay. Suppose a cop orders you to pull over, asks for your driver's license, vehicle registration. You give it to him. He wants to know who you work for. What's your answer?'

The teacher took a deep breath, lifted his head, and stared at the empty space beyond the glassed-in cubicle. The fax machine beeped and stopped. Steil mulled things over for close to a minute before returning his gaze to Scheindlin. 'I'd tell him I'm self-employed. I deliver merchandise all over the city.'

The wholesaler nodded. 'Now the cop wants to know where you loaded the gas cylinders in the back of your van.'

Enjoying the game, Steil smiled. He moved his eyes to a

filing cabinet. 'I got a call around seven in the morning. Guy asked me to go to . . . well, some place where truckers usually go, like eateries on US 1 or the Florida Turnpike – I'd have to look that up – go to this place and pick up cylinders from a huge trailer. I tell the cop that a trucker gave me the clipboard. I show it to him. It has a list of names and addresses, and the money I should collect from each. I tell him that after completing the route, I'm supposed to drive back to the trailer, give the trucker his dough, and get paid three hundred bucks. Cop wants me to go with him to make a positive identification of the truck and trucker, I say sure. We get there, there's no truck, no trucker; I can't believe this is happening to me. Cop asks if I got the truck's plates. I ask him, Why should I have? I was collecting money for the guy. Why should I be distrustful? Cop asks for a description, I make one up. How did I do?'

Ruben Scheindlin observed the amusement on Steil's face until his eyes sprang up. He forced them down to focus on the teacher. 'I can't think of anything more dangerous. Now your alibi is almost ready. You shouldn't have to spend time making one up like you just did. You get busted, don't worry. As long as you stick to that story, you'll get the best legal assistance money can buy in this city and be back on the street in no time.'

Elliot nodded, and the old man opened a drawer in his desk and took out a wad of hundred-dollar bills. He dropped it on the desktop. 'Count it,' he said.

The teacher counted fifty notes. 'Five thousand.'

Scheindlin produced a ball-point pen and a sheet of legal-sized bond paper from the same drawer. 'Write down what I dictate,' he ordered, then he paused. 'Mr Ruben Scheindlin lent me five thousand dollars to start a delivery business of my own. The loan is interest-free and will be repaid at my convenience.'

'Is that all?'

'Sign and date it.'

The teacher did as he was told and returned the pen and paper to Scheindlin.

'Open a checking account at some bank early tomorrow morning. Then lease the van. It'll cost you around two thousand, including taxes, registration fee, and the first monthly payment. Pay all expenses from this fund: gas, tune-ups, tires, everything. Save the receipts. When you need more money, let me know.'

The old man rested an elbow on the desktop and cupped his chin in his palm as he mentally checked for loose ends. Steil remained silent.

'Maybe you should place an ad in the *Herald*. Professional services section. Something like "Deliveries everywhere. Fast and dependable", along with your phone number. It's cheap, around ten dollars a week, and gives you a cover. Run it for a few months. And if somebody calls and you can accommodate him, do it. It won't hurt.'

'Perfect.'

The wholesaler leaned back in his chair and gripped the edge of the desk. Steil pocketed the money. 'Anything else . . . uh . . . Ruben?'

'I'm a man of few words, Elio,' Scheindlin said as he stood. 'Let me put it this way: You got a future in this company.'

'Thank you, Mr Scheindlin.'

They shook hands. 'Ruben,' was Scheindlin's parting shot.

*   *   *

On Saturday morning, a few minutes before 9.00, Elliot Steil opened the front door of his 18th Avenue efficiency to let Fidelia in. He was in his underwear, fresh out of the shower, shaving cream around his lips and on his cheeks, a disposable razor in his hand. The lawyer entered, pulling a copy of the *Miami Herald* out from under her arm. She playfully threatened to hit Steil in the groin with it. He fled to the bathroom and locked himself in. She dropped the paper and her handbag on the bed and moved over to the drop-leaf table. She wore a calf-length, cream-colored skirt, pumps, and the brown cable-knit sweater over her blouse. She had to make a formal promise of non-aggression before the teacher agreed to open the door to let her fill the kettle in the bathroom sink to make coffee.

Steil finished shaving, and they kissed for a while on the bed. As he dressed, they discussed the weather. He slipped on brown woolen socks and his orthopedic shoes, then grabbed the newspaper. In his canvas chair, he flipped through the pages and scanned the headlines.

The name *Sarasota* drew his attention to a two-column article in the Florida section:

SARASOTA JEWELER SLAIN

Four days after being robbed of jewels worth $53,000, a man was tortured and murdered in his own home.

The body of Edward J. Steil, sixty-six, sole proprietor of a fashionable jewelry store in the golf course capital of the world, was found Thursday morning by his cleaning lady. The coroner's report said the cause of death was a .32 caliber gunshot fired point blank between the victim's eyes. The partially naked corpse had round, third-degree burns on the chest and testicles, possibly inflicted by a lighted cigar.

The victim's hands and feet had been bound with duct tape to the legs and arms of an armchair. Marks on the face indicate the victim was gagged at some point during the ordeal, presumably to prevent neighbors from hearing his screams.

Last Sunday a thief had forced Mr Steil to open the safe in his Augustine Avenue residence and tied him up before fleeing. Sarasota police freed the victim three hours later, and a local hospital treated him for hypertension and minor bruises.

Permanent residents of the wealthy resort town are baffled, not knowing if the two crimes are related.

But consensus is building that the two incidents are not connected. A local homicide detective said that whereas the Sunday morning thief reported his action to spare unnecessary suffering to the victim, the

Wednesday night murderer apparently left without taking any valuables.

'What's the matter?' Fidelia asked, two steaming mugs of coffee in her hands.

Unable to hide his bewilderment, the teacher stared vacantly at Fidelia as he forced himself to change mental gears. 'Uh?' he managed to say.

'You're paper-white. You weren't even listening.'

Steil reached over for a mug and sipped from it. 'I'm sorry, Fidelia. Now, listen to me. I just remembered something very important. Give me a few minutes to think it over. Take a seat, drink your coffee, read the . . . sorry, I forgot you don't read English, but please give me a few minutes to myself, okay?'

The teacher folded the newspaper and dropped it on the floor. The lawyer, poorly hiding her annoyance, plopped down on the other canvas chair and drank her coffee in silence.

His eyes fixed on the window's stained shade, Steil recalled his uncle's warning: 'Don't mess with the wrong people.' He could picture Ed, drenched in sweat, telling Bergen or Jones or somebody else that his nephew had somehow survived, that he had reached American shores and managed to track him down. Perhaps his uncle had mentioned the watch and the cocked gun at the back of his head. He must have sworn that he hadn't disclosed the real reason for trying to snuff out Bob's son. Then how come the guy phoned Shelley? the interrogators probably wanted to know. The jeweler might have pleaded that his crazy relative had demanded some confirmation and that he was forced to give him Shelley's number. Surely he tried to con his way but had failed, and somebody lit a cigar.

Shelley Steil held the key to Ed Steil's murder. She probably realized that she had been duped, and reported what had happened to someone, maybe in good faith, unaware of the implications.

The teacher realized he was losing time in speculation. The killer would try to find him. It wouldn't be easy. He had rented the Tampa car and registered at the motel under the name on the North Carolina driver's license Hairball had sold to him: Timothy Blackburn. He didn't leave fingerprints; he had wiped the room and car clean. It wouldn't be easy but neither would it be impossible, particularly for somebody who could make use of the federal government's investigative powers.

The new position in Scheindlin's company provided the perfect excuse for severing all ties with present acquaintances. He would split. Never again would he visit the barber shop where a young black man sold guns and bullets like ice cream cones. He'd never return to the coffee shops, restaurants, movie theaters, libraries, and pizza parlors he had frequented. He would immediately quit the Publix job – first thing Monday morning. Trade in his car. Rent a new safe-deposit box at a different bank. What about Fidelia? No, he couldn't dump the best person who had crossed his path in the last ten or twelve years. Should he write down everything he had found out and stash it away somewhere?

The teacher turned toward Fidelia and stared at her. She pretended not to notice and shifted her gaze about the room, sipping coffee.

'I love you,' Steil said.

She was caught off guard. Smiling, she shook her head and fidgeted, looking confused. 'You know I love you, too,' she whispered.

'Okay, let's read the classifieds and circle the apartments that look promising, then pack my things. I'm moving out right now.'

'Right now?'

'Why not? The decision is made, all my things fit in that Salvation Army suitcase, and we'll find something nice today. Why come back here?'

Fidelia looked around. 'What about the range?'

'Leave it here.'

'Are you nuts? In perfect working condition? I have a shopping bag in my purse. Cuban ways die hard. We'll take the range with us.'

Around 4.00 they returned to a place they had seen on Virginia Street at noon, a nicely furnished, one-bedroom apartment with an eat-in kitchen, central air conditioning, and heating. It was on the fifth floor of a Coconut Grove building erected in 1965. The place had round-the-clock security, private parking, a high-tech gate, and could be had for $695 a month. Virginia Street was four blocks from the coastline, neither rich nor poor, architecturally modern, quiet and bright, absolutely middle class.

Fidelia had enjoyed the day enormously, and the teacher managed to temporarily put his tribulations aside. Each secretly hoped to spend most of their free time together at the new dwelling. Steil decided that only if Fidelia's choice turned out to be definitively contrary to his own tastes would he object. Consequently, when she wrinkled up her nose at two South Dade condos, he mentally crossed them off the list; her disapproving looks in response to three other places led him to the same decision.

Over lunch they discussed the two places she favored. First, Fidelia tongue-lashed the Virginia Street landlord for charging almost $700 for what she thought didn't merit $500, and in the same breath, she pointed out all of its perks: the well-equipped kitchen, the queen-size bed, the modern bathroom, the love seat and lamps in the cozy living room, the incredible ocean view. Steil therefore knew which place he would finally rent as they drove to her second favorite selection, a condo on Keys Gate that she insisted on revisiting when they left the Kendall Diner.

After Steil signed the Coconut Grove lease and wrote a

check for $1390, they stocked up on essentials, from linen to toiletries, at a downtown Burdines. House-hunting and feelings of self-fulfillment had spurred a sexual urge in the couple that had to be released.

Fidelia called her mother from a public phone.

'I'll spend the night out, Mama. Will you tell Dani I'll be late? . . . Just *late*, I'll be back around eight, before he wakes up. Can you get him into bed before ten? . . . I know, Mama, I know. Ask him to, as a favor to me . . . Yes, he's right beside me . . . Mama, please . . . Oh, c'mon . . . Okay, okay, I'll tell him . . . Thanks, Mama. Bye . . . You too, bye bye.'

She behaved aggressively in bed that night, passionately demanding and initiating their lovemaking. At a quarter to one, with her elbow on the pillow and her head propped on her hand, she watched Steil yawn prodigiously.

'Elio?'

'Uh?'

'This morning, something you read in the paper shocked you. I don't know what. Now, I hate to sound possessive, and I know I should mind my own business, but please take care of yourself.'

'Okay.'

'You fall in love with someone else, I won't stand in your way. But don't get mixed up in things that might jeopardize your life or your freedom. Protecting yourself is protecting me. Okay?'

'This is a different world, Fidelia.'

'I know, I know, just take care. Good night.'

'Good night,' Steil said before swiftly falling asleep.

8

Driving the Dodge cargo van all over Dade County with a street map close at hand, the teacher got to know those big city gray spaces that tourists and transients never see: commercial stretches devoid of decorated windows, shoppers, and neon signs where basic trade takes place. From Cutler Ridge to Norland, between Miami Beach and Hialeah, Steil discovered miles of streets without residential homes, landscaped gardens, and playgrounds. Lots were surrounded by Cyclone fences, to protect unattractive buildings with windows covered in metallic grillwork. They were the huge, medium-sized, and small warehouses of importers, exporters, wholesalers, and retailers; the repair and service shops; the tiny, no-frills coffee shops, cafeterias, and bars catering to the clerks, repairmen, drivers, salespeople, and office staff making a living in the circuit.

Steil couldn't figure out why the perfectly innocuous delivery of freon cylinders to businesses dealing in the service and repair of air conditioners, refrigerators, and freezers was shady. For the first two days on the job, he was tense and overly cautious, but by the end of the week his self-confidence had grown. Most clients greeted him with friendly comments. Hands were shaken, nobody asked for a discount, new orders were placed. During the second week, Steil's most pressing concern was the three or four thousand dollars stashed in a metal cash box under the driver's seat at the end of the day.

For this reason, he called Tony Soto and arranged a meeting at Charlie's Lounge. The policeman heard Steil out with the slightly disinterested look of a bad actor pretending to ignore what he already knew. Tony studiously made circles on the bartop with the mist sweated out of the glass, inserting comments like, 'What'd I tell you?' 'I knew you'd make it,' and 'Great.' After six minutes of bringing Tony up to date, the teacher voiced his concern about the cash. The policeman nodded condescendingly, drank some beer, and wiped the foam off his mustache before he spoke.

'They'd have to be stoned punks, Elio. No self-respecting professional would plan a job with a three- or four-thousand-dollar payoff. That kinda money ain't worth the risk. Just to play it safe, I'll sell you a throwaway. Some kids try to clean you out, you show it to them. They'll run like hell.'

Steil sipped his 7-Up. 'Suppose they don't. Suppose they come after me with guns drawn, ready to shoot.'

Tony Soto arched his eyebrows, then fixed his gaze on the bartop. 'Well, that's something you should think over well in advance, Elio. I mean, what you're gonna do, how you're gonna react. You let them grab the dough, you're out of a job. You wanna keep the job, you gotta run a risk. Pistol-whip the motherfuckers . . . or shoot them. You don't have to kill them. Go for their balls. That way you either make them eunuchs for life or hit them in the legs, which is what usually happens.'

'Then what?'

The cop laughed, throwing his head back. 'You really need to have it spelled out for you, huh? Okay. Then you run, man. You get into your fucking van and get the hell out as fast as you can. I don't mean speeding. But you leave fast. Wipe the gun clean and get rid of it. You hear me? Get rid of it immediately.'

The teacher frowned at the notion, but remained silent. He had a little more than eight thousand dollars remaining from his car-stealing days. If he was held up, maybe it would be wiser to surrender the cash, conceal the robbery from everyone, and cover the loss with his own money. Getting convicted for murder or manslaughter was not in his plans.

Tony Soto spied his ex-teacher's expression out of the corner of his eye. 'If worse comes to worst, self-defense is a pretty strong legal defense in this country,' the cop said. 'Your lawyer proves there was imminent danger to your life, or that you ran the risk of getting the living shit kicked out of you, you walk. But if you get busted, button up. Call Scheindlin's office and tell them where they have you. Don't sign anything before you talk to a lawyer. Just say, "I fired in self-defense." And you bought the gun from a stranger in the streets for self-protection. You don't know the guy's name, never seen him before, never seen him again. Understand?'

'Yeah.'

'Fine. Now let's find you a piece.'

Tony Soto liked the 1991 Chevy that Steil had acquired by trading in the Ford. He sped away in his own car. Steil followed the taillights while mulling things over. The policeman pulled in behind his wife's car, went into his house, and returned after three minutes. Sitting on the Chevy's passenger seat, Tony Soto produced a .38 caliber Colt Cobra.

'You saw *The Godfather?*' he asked.

'Sure.'

'Remember the piece Al Pacino used to gun down Sterling Hayden? Its stock and trigger guard were covered with insulating tape. Do that to this one. Makes fingerprint lifting more difficult.'

'Got it. How much?'

'Five hundred dollars.'

'I don't have that much on me now.'

'C'mon, teacher. We're Cubans, we're friends. You pay me when you can.'

On St Valentine's Day, the teacher delivered the last three twenty-five-liter cylinders of the day to a small air conditioner repair shop on 803 NW 12th Street, Homestead. It was the most distant location Steil had yet served, and he braced himself for the long drive back. His watch said 4.39. He was taking

Fidelia out for dinner that night and had to shower, then drive his car to the warehouse to hand over the day's collection before picking up his date at 8.00. Steil opened the van door, slid behind the wheel, and stowed the cash in the metal box. He returned it to its usual place, lowered the window, inserted the key in the ignition, and started the engine.

As he shifted into drive, Steil noticed a dark Lincoln sedan parked on the other side of the street, facing the van. He pulled away from the curb and turned on the tape deck to continue listening to Isaac Delgado sing Cuban salsa. The sedan moved. It looked as if its driver wanted to make a U-turn, although the road didn't appear to be wide enough. Steil braked. The car stopped, too, blocking the street. The teacher frowned.

The Lincoln's passenger door was flung open, and a tall white man in his thirties wearing mirror shades got out. Leaving the door open, he walked briskly toward the van. When he was about thirty feet away, his swinging right hand disappeared momentarily under his tan jacket and came back out holding a mean-looking automatic weapon.

The teacher froze. His mind went blank for an instant before mysterious forces changed the design he had developed after much consideration. He had mapped out a non-violent response. He would raise his hands and say, 'Don't shoot. I'll give you the money.' But instead, he surprised himself by bending forward and groping for the Colt under the seat. He found it, straightened up, and held it in his left hand. Ten feet away the stranger was lifting his gun. Steil thrust his arm out the window and opened fire.

Three, maybe four seconds later, Steil realized the hammer was clicking on empty shells. The white man was out of his line of vision. Breathing hard, the teacher dropped the Colt on the passenger seat, shifted into gear, and turned the wheel to the right. Stepping on the gas pedal he invaded the sidewalk. The van was ten feet away from the Lincoln's hood when a second white man emerged from the driver door, gun in hand. The teacher ducked. The van hopped like a mad goat past the sedan, from the sidewalk to the curb to the street, then back from the street to the curb to the sidewalk. Partially deafened by the blast of his gun, Steil heard the muffled sounds of rounds being fired at him. He eased up on the gas and veered left to return to the street.

At the corner, frightened and indecisive, he looked both ways before lifting his gaze to the rearview mirror. The Lincoln remained angled in the middle of the street, its doors wide open. The teacher opted for a left turn and sped west for two blocks before he realized that he should slow down and get his bearings. At the next side street, he peeked at the rearview before turning right and pulling over by the curb. He studied the map for ten seconds. His legs felt rubbery. In a syrupy voice, the crestfallen Isaac Delgado lamented being duped by a luscious Havana chick, who had given him a false phone number.

Steil decided to drive straight for a few more blocks, then turn right. Far away, a siren wailed. Nothing behind him. Steil silenced the crooner and headed north at thirty miles per hour until he reached Avocado Drive, a wide avenue with light traffic. He rolled around the corner, and a minute later joined the heavy flow of traffic on US 1.

Steil's fear gradually became replaced by anger as he sped north. Hitting the wheel with both hands, he let out a cascade of Cuban profanities. When he noticed a woman gaping at him from the passenger seat of a Lexus, he shut up. His mind got back on track. *Control yourself. Think.* Tony had insisted on getting rid of the gun fast. Steil took an off-ramp at Auburn Avenue, stopped the van, got out, and dropped the Colt into Black Creek Canal. Returning to the vehicle, he spotted five bullet holes on its left side, one on the door. Circling the van, he found three exit holes on the other side. Steil wondered if the Lexus woman had been more surprised by the perforations than by his soliloquy. What if a curious patrolman in a squad car ordered him to pull over? Should he tell the truth, including his firing back? He would try to reach the warehouse discreetly in the increasingly dense late-afternoon traffic. He would call Fidelia and cancel their evening plans. Then he'd explain to Scheindlin what had happened.

It was not until that precise moment, almost ten minutes after the attempt on his life, that uncoupled elements in the teacher's brain became interlocked. Everything became crystal clear. They had found him; they wanted him dead. The teacher bit his lower lip and nodded in full comprehension. Then he opened the door and sat still behind the wheel.

*   *   *

Three and a half hours later Steil was retelling his ordeal to Tony Soto inside the glassed-in cubicle of the North Miami Beach warehouse. They spoke English in deference to Ruben Scheindlin and Samuel Plotzher, who sat behind their desks. Both Cubans were perched on the armless swivel chairs used during office hours by the secretary and the man in charge of the computer.

Samuel Plotzher observed the teacher with a steady gaze. Nearing sixty, Plotzher had a mane of permanently disheveled white hair and a ruddy face with charcoal-black eyes that seemed like ponds of vitality. He generally favored overalls and long-sleeved checkered shirts with the cuffs rolled back to his elbows, but on this occasion he had been urgently summoned to the warehouse just after taking a shower, and wore a bone-white sports coat over a deep-green shirt, black slacks, and loafers. Ruben Scheindlin leaned back in his chair, his hands gripping its arms, listening attentively for the third time. Between jumps, his eyes moved from Steil to Tony to his partner.

At the back of the warehouse, in the central drive-in passage for forklifts, a three-man team had finished repairing the van's

175

damaged bodywork and was getting ready to repaint it in the same shade of gray. At the other end of the building, the night watchman oversaw the team's progress with arms folded over his chest and his back turned to the closed sliding door.

Tony Soto had interrupted Steil five times. When the teacher finished his story, the cop rotated his seat to face Scheindlin. Pulling down the corners of his mouth and holding up the palms of his hands, Tony gave a look of incomprehension.

'It ain't right, Ruben,' he said. 'Two white guys in their thirties in broad daylight and for that kinda payoff. It ain't right.'

Scheindlin nodded. Plotzher cleared his throat before speaking. 'Now, Elio, don't get me wrong. But maybe you've been talking to someone about this job, the money you move every day, your pay . . .' The teacher shook his head vigorously, but Plotzher kept talking. 'Maybe to some guy worked with you at the supermarket, maybe to some broad . . .' Plotzher's voice trailed off in uncertainty.

'Mr Plotzher, my circle of friends is very small, and I've only mentioned what I do to Tony,' Steil said. 'The only other people who know how I make a living are clients.'

A portable air compressor coughed into life, breaking the ensuing silence. It seemed to inspire a fresh idea, and the teacher moved his eyes to Scheindlin. 'Isn't it possible a competitor is trying to elbow you out, sir?'

The old man scratched the back of his head. 'It's not what they usually do, but it's possible. We should look into it. And there's also the possibility this attack was against you, not against me.'

'Against me? An attack against me? I'm new in town; I don't have any enemies. Why would anyone try to kill me?' Steil hoped he sounded sincere.

Scheindlin shrugged his shoulders. 'How would I know? Maybe you messed with someone in Cuba who lives here now. He saw you somewhere and wants to finish you off.'

Steil spoke in a patient tone. 'Mr Scheindlin, in Cuba I was an English professor. Tony knew me in that position. I never held a government post, never managed a business. During my Army years I was a private raising cattle and driving a truck. I never harmed anyone. Some people liked me, some people didn't, but enemies?' The teacher completed the idea by shaking his head in denial.

'Maybe a student who flunked out, the husband of a broad you screwed,' the wholesaler theorized. 'I admit it's unlikely, but you should think about it and watch out. Now, let's discuss the future. You wanna keep working for me?'

Steil had been considering Fidelia's runaway husband and paused for a second before nodding.

'Good,' Scheindlin said, then looked at Tony Soto. 'From where you stand, Tony, how should we deal with this?'

The smell of fresh paint reached the cubicle. Scheindlin sneezed. Plotzher said something in Yiddish. The policeman crossed his legs and looked at the floor for a moment, then lifted his gaze to Scheindlin. 'I gotta pal with the Homestead police, Joel García. I'll ask him about the shooting, see what they got, and report back to you. But that may take a day or two. I see you're having the van fixed when gunpowder is still in the air, and on my street that means you ain't gonna budge.'

Plotzher smiled and looked at Scheindlin, who was also slightly amused. Tony Soto continued: 'I'm one hundred percent for it, but I'd recommend you hire a security guard to ride with Elio the next few weeks. Guy with a shotgun and a big Mag in plain view. That sends the right message. The motherfucker's a competitor, he knows you're standing your ground. He's Elio's personal enemy, he'll learn it'll be harder next time.'

Steil experienced a wave of gratitude. The cop had finished talking and turned his head to flash his charming smile at his ex-teacher. Scheindlin asked Plotzher something in Yiddish, and the junior partner shook his head.

'Okay,' Scheindlin said, straightening up in his chair. 'I guess we should call it a day. Elio, you'll keep making deliveries the next two, three weeks, just to show whoever did this that we don't scare easy. Then somebody will replace you so you can move ahead in the company. You've earned it. Be here tomorrow at seven. The guy in charge back there says the paint will be dry by then. A security guard will be waiting for you; Sam will see to it in a little while. Make deliveries like any other day.'

Scheindlin turned to the cop. 'Tony, please find out what you can with this Homestead cop. I'd appreciate it. Think you can get Elio a new gun?'

'Sure,' the policeman said with a grin.

'Perfect. I'll pay for it. Could you drop him at his place?'

'Of course. Let's go, teacher,' Tony Soto said, realizing they were being dismissed.

'Yeah. Thanks for your support, Mr Scheindlin.'

'Ruben,' said the old man, smiling broadly.

'I just can't, sir.'

'No problem. Sleep well.'

*   *   *

Steil phoned Fidelia from his apartment. He was back from the 'urgent delivery' to West Palm Beach that he'd told her about at 6.00. He said he was sorry but that he'd been unable to turn it down. Most Cuban women would be suspicious if their boyfriend or husband vanished on Valentine's Day, and Fidelia didn't fall into the carefree minority. She pretended to be unconcerned and forgiving, but cut the conversation short. Steil smiled for the first time in hours at her fit of jealousy.

Feeling beat, he took a shower, drank a glass of milk, and plopped into bed, hoping to sleep like a log. At 3.30 he got up to relieve himself, but couldn't get back to sleep. Sipping coffee on the living room loveseat, he reviewed his options.

His foray into Sarasota, then Ed Steil's murder, had kept

him from going to the authorities. He couldn't prove what Ed had done to him six months back; the watch had been declared stolen, and he'd dropped it into a sewer. He'd reported that his raft had sunk. He had flimflammed the INS and the state of Florida, and had deceived employers, landlords, and banks with a false identity. Even if he successfully concealed his work for Hairball, he would still spend the rest of his life in prison convicted of armed robbery, assault and battery, maybe even murder. The alleged relationship between his deceased father and the intelligence community might make him fresh meat for the national press. No, going to the police with his story was out of the question.

What alternatives remained? Running away seemed to be the only one. Where to? He could board a northbound plane, bus, or train, backtrack a few hundred miles, then head east or west to some big city and become one more ant in the anthill. Except that ants didn't have to present Social Security cards to secure a job. For guaranteed anonymity, he would have to mug people, push drugs, or beg for the rest of his life. He would lose Fidelia. What about México? As far as he knew the Mexican government, so upright and disapproving when some of its own illegals in the US were deported, unceremoniously rejected almost all Cuban rafters reaching its shores before they could say 'Viva México.'

Cuba? He imagined himself facing an immigration official at Havana's airport. 'I have no passport,' might be his opening admission. 'You what?' the guy would snap back. They'd hear him out, check what could be verified internally of his incredible story, and maybe send him to prison for a year or two. His apartment and furniture had almost certainly been reassigned to someone else. He would never be reinstated to his teaching position and would probably end his days sweeping the streets, lowering coffins, or cutting sugarcane stalks in the fields.

Should he enter the lion's den? Drive the Chevy all the way to New Iberia, knock on Mrs Steil's front door, and see what would happen? Her conscience might be lily-white, but on the phone she had sounded cautious, guarded. Steil toyed with the notion for half an hour. Calling Miami his home turf was an overstatement, but at least he was getting to know the city. He had some credit with Scheindlin, and maybe Tony and Hairball would lend him a hand with something that involved minimal risk.

The teacher concluded that there was no way out. With this thought, he experienced a very strange physical reaction: His body relaxed, his brow unfurled, and he felt at ease, resigned to his fate, a little philosophical. The only option was to live in a constant state of alarm and fight back if attacked. Maybe he would be safe with an armed guard. But at night, on the weekends, in the streets, right here, he'd be on his own. Maybe he had wounded or killed the man in the mirror shades. He would stay away from Fidelia until he was sure the hunt was over. He would see her one more time. What story could he concoct that she might swallow?

She was right: Life had passed him by. In Cuba, as a young man, he'd been too assertive and self-confident to blend into a stifling system in which beliefs and outlooks were expected to be subordinated to political goals. Just as he'd been in 1981, when he was asked to volunteer to teach in Nicaragua. Natasha was at the bottom of a deep depression, brought on by the scientific confirmation of her infertility. Deserting her then would've been cruel and dangerous. A month before all Cuban teachers were summoned to come forward, he awoke in the middle of the night to find his wife by the medicine cabinet, swallowing a handful of tranquilizers. They kept it quiet – only her psychiatrist was informed – and Steil refused to offer his services to the mission abroad. Truth be told, he would've loved to teach Nicaraguan kids, especially after two Cuban teachers were murdered by the Contras. But when his superiors wanted to know why he wouldn't go, he refused to betray his wife's privacy. If Comrade Steil was a healthy, childless young man and thousands of female teachers – including hundreds of mothers – were volunteering, why had he declined? Why, Comrade? Personal reasons, he had said. Ba-a-a-d move.

Had he given his real reasons for not volunteering, perhaps he would not have been blackballed. Whether or not you were a Party member, you were supposed to inform the secretary of the Party cell at the Institute of such a decision. The Party was supposed to care for every citizen and wanted to provide assistance and guidance to anyone in need of it. The Party wanted to know why he wouldn't embrace such a noble cause. The Party wanted to know if it was because you had hemor-rhoids, if you were afraid your wife would be unfaithful, if the roof of your home was about to cave in and kill your loved ones. The Party couldn't heal your ass, convince your wife that she shouldn't play the field, or rebuild your house. But it had to know why you wouldn't volunteer. Because if you didn't have any grounds for refusing, the Party concluded that you didn't approve of the mission, which automatically labeled you a potential enemy of the people, a scum, a worm. Was this typical of how so-called internationalist missions were arranged? Maybe not. Or maybe there was always a certain measure of behind-the-scenes arm-twisting at the core of some of the praiseworthy social tasks carried out abroad by Cubans.

Steil had decided at the time that he should yield, and strove to become just one more actor on the stage.

Then there was the school's mandatory month of agricultural work. Far removed from the intricacies of economics, he none-theless realized that from a cost/benefit perspective it was a total loss. And from an ethical standpoint, the commendable goal of teaching kids the value of work was lost through intimi-dation, mismanagement, and the wrong role models. Most teachers marched the boys and girls out into the scorching fields, then moved beneath the nearest shady tree and sat down to pontificate to the sneering pupils about how planting, weeding, or picking a crop advanced the cause of socialism.

After the first few days, the principal, both assistant principals, and the Party secretary were invariably prevented from taking part in any physical exertion by some unpostponable meeting. But when the students returned to the barracks for lunch and supper, the camp's leaders were found reading the paper, listening to the radio, chatting leisurely, or playing dominoes. Only a black Army captain in charge of military training, a female chemistry teacher, and Steil toiled all day alongside their pupils.

Ba-a-ad move. The captain and the chemistry teacher were Party members. Steil wasn't. In their private conversations, the principal and his cronies wondered who the worm thought he was fooling. The man was obviously trying to win the kids' respect to further counte-revolutionary ideology under the cover of teaching English, the language of the enemy. Everybody was aware that when the worm read certain passages aloud from the textbook – '*I have a friend in the US. His name is Ken. Ken is an anti-imperialist fighter. He is against exploitation, racial discrimination, and Yankee intervention in political matters of other countries*' – his tone sounded disdainful. It was insulting.

Steil joined the Territorial Troops that same year. The non-professional army had been hatched by the Santa Fe program, born the day Ronald Reagan won the American presidency, and feverishly staffed with volunteers from all walks of life when Alexander Haig threatened to 'go to the source'.

Steil explained the problem with his feet and was given a desk job. At his block's Committee for the Defense of the Revolution, he stood watch one night each month, and donated blood once a year. He never missed Teacher's Union meetings; he recycled paper, plastic, and bottles, especially rum bottles, and never spread the side-splitting political jokes he heard. But all of this was to no avail. Everybody could see that his heart wasn't in it, that he lacked the minimum ability as an actor and would never be anything other than one of the many extras on the set.

After his divorce, his former father-in-law finally opened up to him. Gustavo Cano never thought much of Steil before his daughter's emotional breakdown. He had hoped that Natasha would wed a prestigious professional or a well-known scholar, not a lowly English teacher. His affection for Steil developed during Natasha's long treatment, when he saw his ex-son-in-law faithfully visit her three or four times a month, escorting her to medical appointments when neither parent could, locating and buying hard-to-find prescriptions for her, undaunted by the failed marriage, displaying a rare kind of asexual love.

Steil knew that both Gustavo and Josefina came from well-to-do families and had become devoted Communists and Russophiles during their university years in the mid-1950s. When their daughter was born in November 1961, the couple considered two names for the child: Maria Alexandrovna, to honor Lenin's mother, and Nadezha, after the revolutionary's wife. Ultimately they settled on Natasha, the nickname for Natalias, less prestigious but easier to pronounce in Spanish and still a popular Russian name.

Natasha's four grandparents didn't see the light and fled Cuba. Gustavo and Josefina remained staunch revolutionaries until Gustavo lost his position as undersecretary in the Ministry of Internal Commerce, along with his Party membership, in 1973, when it was discovered that he had been secretly corresponding with his mother, a widow in Tallahassee, Florida. The teacher learned this ten years later, on a rainy afternoon at the couple's pleasant Santos Suárez home, while a heavily sedated Natasha slept in her room and Josefina stood in line at the butcher's shop a block away. 'I couldn't believe it,' Gustavo had said. 'Bureaucratism and inefficiency were rampant. Other people cheated and stole and dispensed favors to friends with impunity, and I was sacked for writing to my mother. I never imagined things would turn out this way. This was not my idea of socialism.'

At present, Steil owed his life to yet another disillusioned

Communist. On Christmas Eve, the teacher had found out that in 1989, Luciano Orozco began serving a two-year prison term for publicly cursing the man after whom he had named his daughter. Now Luciano lived comfortably in the nation he had lambasted in his youth, awestruck by its affluence, astonished at the apparent opportunities, bewitched by the mirage.

Steil wondered why his own reaction to America was so temperate. Setting aside past and present emotional issues, he loathed its cult of money. Most Americans knelt and prayed at the altar of the almighty dollar. Social status was determined by monetary worth. Money was the key to everything, including the criminal justice system if, as seemed increasingly likely, OJ would get away with it. Even charities were linked to tax exemptions, something that made him skeptical. Ruben Scheindlin's respect for Steil had soared when it seemed the teacher had risked his life to safeguard company money.

Steil's brain paused, and he experienced a second strange reaction: He felt himself frown and tense up. Bucks, not faith, moved mountains. If he had enough greenbacks to unearth the truth about his father – hire private investigators, buy information, retain lawyers – in a week he would learn the essential facts, in a month he would know everything he wanted to know except government secrets. Great. And how could he possibly get his hands on that kind of money? What bank, loan shark, or regular citizen would fund a desperado living a hand-to-mouth existence under false pretenses?

Steil clicked his tongue, shook his head, smiled sideways, and peered at his watch. It was 5.15. He took his time shaving, still trying to come up with a solution, then slipped into the same jeans and denim jacket he had worn the day before. While snacking on a cheese sandwich in the kitchen, he reflected that it could take Tony Soto a day or two to find him a new gun. He wouldn't drive around unarmed, guard or no guard. After drinking a glass of milk, he marched to the closet and took the revolver he had used in Sarasota out of a suitcase. He wrapped it in a rag, then tuned the television to the Channel 10 morning news. The absence of a report on the Homestead shoot-out meant that he probably hadn't even wounded the man in the mirror shades. Later, he would skim the *Herald* for a report of the incident.

At 6.32 a.m., he stepped out of his apartment and braced himself for a new day of delivering freon and dodging bullets.

9

The following Friday, at a little before 3.00 in the afternoon, Steil was cruising down Collins in the cargo van. He had delivered two cylinders to a 71st Street air conditioning contractor and was headed for another company on Purdy Avenue. The sun shone in a cloudless blue sky, the temperature was in the high 70s, and the teacher was enjoying every minute of it, having heard on the radio that a cold front was expected to sweep over the city around midnight. Collins brought childhood memories back to Steil. He found it incredible that the small beachfront hotels of the thirties and forties were still thriving. Facing them were the new forty- and fifty-floor condominiums built on what used to be yellowish sand and coconut trees. Seniors strolled in the benign climate in strange head gear. Most of the old men wore Bermuda shorts, while the old women sported sleeveless blouses and shorts. Middle-agers were scarce. Young people – almost naked in their scanty swimwear – looked offensively carefree and feline next to the retirees.

'I like it here,' said Max Meisler. 'Grew up close by, you know?'

'Really?'

'Yeah. Moved over here in '49. My folks were sick and tired of Chicago.'

'Where're they now?'

'Where do you think? Dead. I'm fifty-nine.'

'You don't look it.'

'Well, I sure feel it. When me and my sister went out on our own they moved to Israel. Their pensions went a long way there, you know?'

'Really?'

Steil was suddenly annoyed with himself. Max wasn't much of a talker, but when he felt like shooting the breeze, he inserted 'you know' in his speech every fifteen or twenty words. For some reason the teacher considered it impolite to remain silent. 'Really?' was almost all he could come up with as a response. He thought of Cuban kids and their buzzwords.

'Sure. Cost of living was cheaper there in the sixties. The government also provided nice health care for senior Jews, you know?'

'No, I didn't.'

'Didn't what?'

Steil stole a look at Max. 'Didn't know the Israeli government did that.'

Max nodded and let his gaze sweep over the street. 'Twenty years back this section deteriorated. You could find a room for fifty bucks a week. Rich people moved to Bal Harbour, you know?'

Steil remained silent.

'Then some dudes started building those condos and renovating the little hotels and things began to catch up. Like the Bowery, you know?'

'The Bowery?'

'Up in New York City. Place was totally run down, full of winos sitting on the sidewalk nursing the bottle. Then real estate smart alecks began pumping money into it, and it became fashionable. Yuppies invaded the place, you know?'

The teacher seemed inattentive, and his bodyguard lit a Pall Mall.

Meisler was swarthy, heavyset, three inches over six feet, and not too bright. His uniform consisted of brown shoes and pants, a tan shirt with an embroidered shield on the left sleeve identifying him as a Greater Miami Security Services guard, and a chocolate-colored cap. He was bald and mean-looking. From his waist hung a revolver in a clamshell holster, spare ammo, handcuffs, and a gas canister. For extra firepower, Meisler cradled a slide-action, twelve-gauge, double-aught shotgun with a pistol grip. The dissuasion routine calmed Steil's working-hour fears but also embarrassed him. Toting the shotgun, Meisler got out of the van first, gave nearby vehicles and pedestrians a once-over, then nodded to Elio. He never returned to the passenger seat before a delivery was completed and Steil had the engine running.

'How many places left?' Max asked after a minute.

'This one on Purdy and one more on Lenox.'

Meisler took a deep drag on his cigarette and crushed the butt in the overflowing ashtray. 'Weekend,' he said with anticipation.

Steil nodded. 'Probably a cold, drizzling one.'

'Doesn't matter. Just to move around the house in pajamas and slippers is great. Twenty pounds less on my waist and in my hands makes me feel like a fucking angel hovering around the place. Heaviest thing I hold during weekends is a drink, you know?'

'Really?'

'You bet. Only problem is the old lady goes, "Liquor is bad for you, Max." And I go, "What else is new?" And she goes, "You smoke too much when you drink." And I go, "Don't worry, my pension plan will carry you through."'

Both men chuckled.

Max had been kept in the dark for more than just the obvious reasons. The man who hired him and the one he was protecting hadn't learned a thing about the man in the mirror shades. Tony Soto's source in Homestead confirmed the predictable: Nobody had seen a thing. Although this served Steil's own interests in a certain way, he was flabbergasted. In the self-proclaimed beacon of democracy, in the land where freedom of speech was a constitutional right, in the country with the world's biggest and most expensive witness-protection program, nobody, *ever*, came forward when organized crime was supposedly involved. The repair shop owner and his two mechanics swore they had kissed the floor and closed their eyes when they heard the first gunshot. No, no client or supplier had been at his place when the shooting began. Area residents stated that they had ducked behind walls and furniture. The eighty-year-old retired Air Force colonel who called the police was half-blind. From tire marks on the sidewalk and lawn, police knew that a van had been involved; spent .357 cartridges proved that an automatic had been fired. Not a single drop of blood was found. End of inquiry.

The teacher realized that normal people may or may not squeal on the infidelities of a politician, turn in their videotape of a police beating, or reveal that they had seen a movie star sniffing a line. But normal people were fully aware that you never, under any circumstance, squeal on or videotape or in any other way interfere with organized crime. The six people who saw what happened suspected a feud between opposing factions in the drug trade and kept their mouths closed. For this reason, and to seek unimpeachable corroboration, Scheindlin sent Samuel Plotzher to Homestead. The minority shareholder thanked the shop owner for his discretion, presented him with four freon cylinders free of charge, and offered his apologies. The man told Plotzher that he really appreciated the gift but, no, he had not seen the Lincoln's plates. His decision to change gas smugglers at the first opportunity remained unspoken.

Returning to the warehouse close to 4.00, Steil remembered the heated and heartbreaking exchange with Fidelia from the previous evening. As agreed, he had picked her up a little after 5.00 by the curb at the Miami Avenue building where she worked. When he drove into a motel parking lot without warning, she became incensed and refused to get out of the car. He apologized and in his most solemn tone explained that his life was in danger and begged her for the chance to explain why they shouldn't go to his place or, for that matter, see each other at all for weeks, maybe months. Off balance and slightly mollified, she jerked open the passenger door.

'I don't know, Elio,' were her last words when he dropped her off two hours later at the old two-bedroom house on NW 12th Street that her father had rented a week before. She didn't know if she would wait for him, if she believed the unsubstantiated threat on his life, if the presumption was correct that keeping her in the dark guaranteed her safety. Hurt and confused, she hadn't felt like making love. As he left the MacArthur Causeway, the teacher was once more searching for a way to end his ordeal.

Having made his daily report and deposited the cash with Uri, Scheindlin's secretary, Steil felt exhausted and helpless. Just like the two previous afternoons, after Max Meisler had ensured that the money made it into the safe, he departed in his white 1992 Chrysler. On Wednesday, Scheindlin had considered it best to leave the van in the warehouse at nights and on weekends, so when Steil sat behind the wheel of his own car a little before 5.00, he really understood the term 'sitting duck'. It was useless to keep glancing in the rearview mirror, to look both ways as he waited for a green light on his way home, to have the new .32 Taurus Model 73 revolver supplied by Tony Soto close at hand. It dawned on him why world leaders got killed. The bodyguards, the precautions, don't guarantee a thing. A single well-informed person with guts and the right hardware could take out anyone. And he wasn't even a block leader. He was a lonely asshole turning paranoid. He clicked his tongue, shook his head, and started the engine.

At 5.17, Steil extended his left arm out the window and inserted his resident card into the slot. The barred gate slid noiselessly behind a ten-foot wall and he maneuvered the Chevy into its designated space in the building's parking lot. He got out, seized the gun from beside the stick shift, and inserted it under his belt at the small of his back. Certain notions about the inefficacy of alarms had made him dispense with one. As he walked back toward the gate, heading for the covered porch in front of the building's main entrance, the teacher remembered his past contempt for security measures. Now he loved the closed-circuit TV cameras, the bank of monitors overseen by a guard in the lobby with a hand radio unit, the gate, the wall, the works.

Car keys dangling from his hand, he lifted his gaze to the closed gate. On the sidewalk, twenty feet away, a guy in tan shorts, a green polo shirt, sandals, and a flat cap was removing a club from a golf bag. Why would . . . ? The teacher hit the ground the instant the man straightened up as he manipulated something. Steil rolled over to a line of parked cars. He felt his gun biting into his flesh with every turn. The golfer thrust the barrel of an Iver Johnson Enforcer between two steel bars, took aim, and opened fire.

Crouching between a passenger van and a classic '57 Thunderbird, Steil sought protection behind the van's rear tire and closed his eyes. The quick succession of gunshots blended with the beeping and honking and howling of car alarms, creating an earsplitting roar. Debris showered down on him, and the fumes of oil, gas, and brake fluid reached him in a gush of hot, rubber-scented air. Gun reports ceased as the golfer changed clips. The teacher looked around. The tire was flat. He was covered with shards of glass, and something seemed to be trickling down the bridge of his nose. He was groping for his revolver when a new hail of bullets erupted. Pieces of asphalt jumped around him like black grasshoppers. He shut his eyes and covered the top of his head with both hands. The van shook as slugs drilled its body and smashed against the solid-steel chassis, hubs, shaft, gears, and axle. The second clip ran out. Steil opened his eyes to blood-soaked hands. Amid the alarms' fanfare, a screech of brakes was heard, a revved-up engine, wailing tires.

The teacher wanted to stand, but his legs didn't respond.

He sat back, turned to grab the T-Bird's handle, then pulled himself up. The first thing that came to his mind was that the '57 classic looked like it was straight out of Chechnya. The van had been turned into a sieve. A security guard stalking the parking lot, gun in hand, spotted Steil and hurried toward him. He grabbed the bleeding resident by the arm and said something. The teacher shook himself free. 'I'm okay,' he heard himself saying. *Get a hold of yourself*, he thought.

'Can you walk?' the guard asked, close to the teacher's left ear. Steil nodded.

'Let's get inside. You're bleeding.' Steil nodded again.

*   *   *

Stripped to the waist, jeans and boxers down, Steil looked out of the corner of his eye into the medicine-cabinet mirror, trying to see if all of the scratches the gun had left at the small of his back were covered with iodine. It seemed they were. The teacher jerked up his shorts and jeans, then turned around. A pile of blood-stained clothing lay by the toilet.

Four and a half hours earlier, sitting in the lobby as the security guard punched 911 on his cellular, Steil had discreetly dropped the Taurus into a huge clay flowerpot holding an artificial shrub. He was relieved not to have to explain to anyone why he was carrying it. He asked for the guard's cellular and tapped out Tony's home number. Lidia told him that her husband was on duty. Steil punched the mini-station number just as the ambulance arrived. While a paramedic inspected his head, the teacher rattled off into the phone in Spanish.

'Somebody just fired at me, Tony.'

'What?'

Patiently, 'Tony, somebody fired at me two minutes ago. I'm being taken to a hospital.'

'You wounded?'

'My head's bleeding. It hurts, but I guess it's not serious. I'm thinking clearly.'

'Where are you?'

'My place. The lobby.'

One, two, three, four seconds of silence ensued.

'Mistaken identity,' Tony said.

'What?'

'Somebody mistook you for somebody else.'

A blip flashed on Steil's mental screen. 'Of course.'

'You . . . you . . .' Tony was groping for words, trying to phrase something innocuously, '. . . what did you do?'

'I ducked and prayed.'

'Good. You know what else you should do.'

'I already did it.'

'Where are they taking you?'

Steil asked the paramedic. 'Jackson Memorial,' he repeated to Tony.

'I'll be right over.'

Steil inspected himself in the mirror one last time. Only three stitches in his scalp, but the bandage made it look like brain surgery. He had been under the impression that shatterproof glass didn't cut. Wrong. The teacher returned the iodine vial to the medicine cabinet, shook out two caplets from a plastic Tylenol bottle, then marched to the kitchen. Guzzling a beer in the loveseat, Tony Soto watched him pass. To quell his frustration with Steil, he had bought a six-pack at a convenience store before coming over. Steil swallowed the analgesic, entered the bedroom to don a T-shirt, then ambled over to the living room, where he eased himself into the armchair. Cold-front drizzle had misted over the windowpanes overlooking the sea.

The teacher felt exhausted, lonesome, and helpless. He shifted his gaze to the cop. Tony wasn't buying his I-don't-know-what-the-fuck-happened story; feeling excluded made him mad. The cop now felt certain that the first shoot-out hadn't been an attempted robbery. Driving back from the hospital, he had angrily questioned Steil. Didn't he realize somebody wanted him dead? There had to be a reason. Steil had sheepishly mumbled something about gas deliveries. Tony Soto blew a fuse. Gas wholesalers didn't hire professional killers to gun down the competition, goddammit! Had he messed around with drug dealers? Maybe pushed some coke and kept the money? Was Steil fucking somebody's broad? Did the teacher think Tony would always be available to tell him what to say, talk to others officers, go flowerpot fishing, pull strings, cover up for him?

A little after 9.00, Tony broke the news to Scheindlin by phone from Steil's apartment. The wholesaler jotted down Steil's address and said he'd drop by around 11.00. But ten minutes before the designated hour, as the teacher dozed on the armchair and Tony Soto finished his third beer, the lobby guard called to announce the visitor. Steil liked his employer's offhanded approach to being supportive. No fuss, no excitement. He squinted at the bandage as if the teacher had accidentally bumped his head on a cylinder. Did it hurt much? Steil offered the armchair to his boss out of deference and sat beside Tony on the loveseat. The old man didn't want a beer. And no tea or coffee either, thanks. Would Elio please tell him what had happened? The teacher complied. Would Tony explain how he reacted? The cop told about his coaching, how he had coaxed the investigating officer into not complicating an otherwise straightforward case of mistaken identity. Scheindlin interlaced his fingers and rested his hands on his lap.

'Tony, my good friend,' he said, 'I wanna thank you most kindly for keeping the company outta this mess. Once again I owe you. Now I'd like a word in private with Elio. Would you mind?'

The policeman shook his head with a slightly annoyed expression, then rose. Steil embraced him warmly and whispered in Spanish, 'Thank you, brother.' Scheindlin shook hands with Tony and nodded in appreciation. The cop left immediately.

The guest and the host returned to their seats. Scheindlin stared at Steil for the few seconds that his eyes allowed him to. The teacher crossed his legs.

'I like you, Elio,' Scheindlin began. 'You're hard working, always on time, miss few things, keep your mouth shut. Tony's streetwise, you're intelligent. There's a difference. You change environments – country, job, culture – you adapt fast. Tony quits the police, moves to some other country, it would take him years to adapt. Probably wouldn't get ahead in life. You're more educated, older. I'd like to keep you in the company. I really would. But I can't keep a man who gets shot at every coupla weeks. It's bad for business.' Grinning, Scheindlin paused.

Steil clicked his tongue, shook his head, and forced a smile, looking at the three empty beer cans on the chrome-and-glass coffee table.

'Now we both know the Homestead shooting had nothing to do with freon,' Scheindlin went on. 'For some reason somebody is after you. Maybe you know who and why. Maybe you can guess. Maybe you really don't know. The third possibility is hard to believe, and the worst one. A true case of mistaken identity – you can't go to the police, can't finger someone, can't imagine who's trying to kill you. If that's the case, I feel sorry for you.'

Scheindlin stopped speaking to let his words sink in. Steil's gaze was glued to the front door.

'But if you know or can make an educated guess as to who is after you, and you don't report it to the police, then it means there's something weird going on. You're new in this country, have few friends, probably none of them has the means or the connections to give you a hand. Many years ago, I was new in this country, too. But our community stands up for itself, and I had a head start. I repaid my debt helping others out, but I think it would be sound business practice to maybe get you off the hook. That way, you can devote all your energies to working for me.'

Five seconds slipped by. Steil inhaled deeply.

'Now, Elio, I'll ask you one simple question. If your answer is no, I'll give you back the receipt you signed a few weeks back. There should be around twenty-five hundred left from the five thousand. You keep it as severance pay, and I wish you the best of luck. If your answer is yes, you'll have to come clean with me, and I'll see if I can do something for you. Question is: Do you know or can you guess who's after you?'

Steil felt the truth ascending inside of him like the lava in a volcano about to erupt. 'Yes,' he said simply.

Scheindlin leaned forward on the armchair. 'Do you want to tell me about it?'

'Yes.'

'Are you aware that I might not be able to help you even if I want to?'

'Yes.'

'Okay. You have my word I won't tell others unless you approve. Now I want a cup of tea. Could you brew some?'

*　　*　　*

It took Steil over an hour. He left out childhood memories, feelings, moral and political considerations, and personal beliefs, little of it bearing any relationship to the present circumstance. Sticking to the facts, and after some indispensable background information on his parents and past, he told the story chronologically, beginning with the late afternoon in Havana when a man named Dan Gastler had tracked him down.

When the teacher got to the part where Gastler pushed him overboard, Scheindlin was hooked. He lifted an eyebrow as the Tourneau Corner inquiry unfolded, leaned forward in the armchair at the beginning of the trip to Sarasota, knit his brow when he learned about the possibility of a connection with US intelligence, and from then on hung on Steil's every word. When the teacher had finished, he leaned back and slapped his thighs.

'Well,' he said, 'your mess is a lot worse than I figured.'

Steil nodded.

Supporting his left elbow on the arm of the seat, Scheindlin rested his chin on the palm of his hand and looked at the windowpane, thinking things over for nearly two minutes. The teacher watched him fixedly.

'You a movie fan?' the old man asked at last.

The question caught Steil off guard. 'What?'

'Simple question. Do you like movies?'

'What's that got to do with it?'

'Depends on your answer.'

Impatiently: 'Yes, I like movies.'

'Thrillers, private-eye movies?'

'Yeah, the good ones.'

Scheindlin nodded and smiled openly. The teacher was becoming annoyed.

'So far, you've tried to deal with a very serious situation like some handsome movie actor in a thriller,' Scheindlin said. 'You ain't an actor; life isn't a movie set.' He paused, then scoffed, 'You ain't even handsome.'

Steil stared, teeth clenched.

'You got a temper, too,' the old man went on. 'That's bad. Cancels out intelligence, your greatest asset. I admit you had very good reasons to seek revenge, to distrust the authorities. I also admit that lacking friends and relatives, you couldn't trust anybody here. That's all valid. But stealing cars was absolutely stupid.'

The teacher's jaw fell. He hadn't mentioned Hairball.

'Yeah, I know. Tony's pretty sure you stole cars for this Cuban. You needed money and needed it fast. Going to Sarasota was dumb, too. Now, we gotta think this over carefully, Elio . . . I mean, Elliot. First of all your personal safety. Take you outta the streets, hide you somewhere 'til we know what's going on. Then we hire professional investigators. Find out about the Steils, your father, your uncle. Is your father dead? Alive? This New Iberia story, is it true? Then we gotta seek legal assistance. Learn what steps must be taken to prove you're Bob Steil's son if it needs to be proven. If your father died rich, like your sonafabitch uncle said, you probably got some money coming your way. How can you prove your story in a court of law? Maybe with your birth certificate, your parents' marriage certificate. I don't know. Nowadays DNA tests have made this kind of parenthood proof simpler. But what's really tricky is, who's trying to kill you? Back in the sixties, I'd have thought a CIA hit team was after you. Not today. How can we find out if this spook story is true? Don't know. I do know one thing: You can't tell anybody about your trip to Sarasota. Not a lawyer, not anyone. I guess the best option is to forget about your uncle altogether. Stick to the story you gave the INS. You were sick and tired of Communism and built a raft to flee Cuba. It sunk, you were rescued by other rafters; there're witnesses to this. So forget this uncle. The man never existed or . . . maybe you read about him in the *Herald*, that he had been murdered. Why you changed the spelling of your name? You'll have to think out a credible reason for that. Those are my suggestions for the moment.'

Steil was seeing another person scrutinize what he, and only he, had examined a thousand times – figuring the angles, probing, examining alternatives. Just hearing out Scheindlin made him feel better.

'All this is gonna cost, Elio.'

The teacher shrugged his shoulders.

'Tell you what. I'll spend a little money on this, a few thousand you may be able to pay back working for me if your father is alive or if he died poor. Should you inherit a nice figure, you invest some of it in company stock, become a partner, okay?'

'Mr Scheindlin, there's nothing I'd like more,' Steil said vehemently. 'But if no money is coming my way, I give you my word I'll work for you as long as it takes to pay back what you spend on this.'

'Good enough. Well . . .' Scheindlin glanced at his watch, pushed his glasses up, and stood. The teacher rose as well. 'Don't leave this apartment before I tell you to. Tony said he recovered the last gun, the one I paid for. You still have the one you bought from that black guy at the barber shop?'

'Yeah.'

'Keep them close at hand. Anybody tries to break in, you shoot them. After what happened this afternoon you'll walk.'

Steil nodded. It was the only piece of advice he didn't need. Scheindlin took a cell phone from his jacket pocket, extended its antenna, and tapped out a number.

'Everything okay?' he said into the receiver. 'Good. I'm going down now.' He broke the connection and, smiling at Steil, forced the antenna down and slipped the phone back into his pocket. 'Max Meisler's doing a little overtime for me,' he said to Steil. 'When you mix with people who get shot every other day, you gotta take some precautions. Sleep well, Elio; I mean, Elliot.'

'Thank you, Mr Scheindlin. Thank you very much.'

'Ruben, please.'

Part Three

Part Three

10

The bleak Saturday morning weather didn't dampen Steil's soaring spirit. Expectant and optimistic, he drank his morning coffee standing before the window, looking out at the sky and sea. Later he downed two painkillers, took a shower, and applied fresh iodine to the scratches on his back.

A little before 10.00 Scheindlin phoned and suggested that he pack a suitcase. The teacher complied with anticipation, and at noon Max Meisler knocked on his front door. The guard squinted at the head bandage, clicked his tongue repeatedly, and asked if they could get going. It wasn't in his nature to be so unconcerned, and Steil guessed that the man had been told not to ask questions. While waiting for the elevator, he noticed that Meisler wore civvies and didn't look unhappy to be making extra money packing only his Colt under a parka.

It was drizzling outside. Two pedestrians stared at the mummy in the gray suit and black tie. Steil got into the back seat of Scheindlin's car, a deep-blue Volvo with tinted windows, as a black chauffeur stored the suitcase in the trunk. Meisler pulled the passenger door shut, the driver moved behind the wheel, and the car slid north along South Bayshore Drive. The teacher felt like complimenting Scheindlin on his light-blue dress shirt.

'We're going to a place where I hope you'll patiently spend the next few days,' the wholesaler said in a Spanish no less Slavic-accented than his English.

The teacher was too surprised to do anything other than shake his head and look sideways at the wet asphalt. When he looked up, the trader was tittering, his paunch bouncing spasmodically. Steil smiled openly, and Scheindlin forced himself back to business.

'Been dealing with Latin America for many years now. Had to learn the language. And certain things we should keep to ourselves,' the old man explained as he shot glances at Meisler and the chauffeur. In a flash, Steil suspected that Scheindlin was having a great time with his predicament. Reliving dangerous years?

'I'm taking you to a safe house,' the old man continued in colloquial South American Spanish as the squelching car sped past the glass-and-steel high-rises on Brikell Avenue, crossed the Miami River, and turned onto Flagler heading west. 'From the outside it looks like a nice, standard residence. But it has state-of-the-art electronics, bulletproof glass in its windows, extra-thick walls, and the doors have a one-inch-thick aluminum core wrapped in steel sheathing. You would practically have to bring a light cannon or a bazooka to force your way in. And then you'd have to deal with two guys like Meisler, only younger, who know their way around M-16s.'

Hearing his name mentioned in a strange language, the guard turned to his left and rolled his neck to look at Scheindlin. The boss shook his head, and Max reversed his movements.

'It's mostly used by poker high rollers who shun regular joints 'cause they don't want the bad publicity or are afraid some punk may be tempted to hit them for the sixty or eighty thousand each carries. Owner charges a grand a day.'

The driver turned left on 87th Avenue.

'The place has three . . . well, units, for live-in guests,' Scheindlin went on. 'Actually tiny apartments with a den, a bedroom, and a bath. Room and board costs five hundred dollars a day. You're not supposed to leave your unit before telling the man in charge. There's a TV, phone, books, magazines, CD player, a deck with videocassettes. You can even ask for a portable PC if you feel like it, but anyway, it's like going to prison on your own free will. Difference is you can leave whenever you want, go to the movies, visit a lady, whatever. But I suggest you remain holed up 'til you hear from me. These people are accountable as long as you're inside their place. You go out, it's your neck. It shouldn't be more than a week.'

Scheindlin had a policy about giving information: Never exceed the vital minimum. He had kept it to himself that the safe house also had meeting rooms where some wheeling and dealing took place. Local politicians discussed secret funding arrangements, lawyers and judges debated fees, foreign government officials took bribes from American companies, and on three occasions, drug cartel bosses had ironed out differences there. Meeting-room clients were usually people who knew they were finished if somebody got them on tape. The owner was no saint, but he delivered what patrons wanted: security and 100 percent unbugged premises.

Scheindlin let his jumping eyes wander over the wet expanses of South Miami, and the teacher figured that his boss had nothing else to say. For two minutes they rode in silence along the Don Shula Expressway, then turned left on 120th. As the car entered Rockdale, Steil wondered why the driver had not taken a shorter route. An instant later he realized the man may have been trying to detect a tail.

'It doesn't matter if we're being followed,' Scheindlin said as if to himself, but in Spanish. The teacher fleetingly speculated that the old man might be able to read minds. 'The guys after you are locals; they'll know they can't get at you when they see where we're going. If they come from somewhere else and know their trade, they'll catch on.' And reverting to English: 'Notice anything, Walter?'

'No, Mr Scheindlin,' the driver answered in a deep bass.

Two blocks before reaching the Palmetto golf course, the Volvo turned left into a car entrance and stopped before a closed gate. A tall, wrought-iron fence extended for close to thirty yards in both directions, with the gilded heads of simulated spears threatening the sky. Behind it a driveway meandered toward the colonnaded entrance of a white, two-story mansion. The gate slid open, and the car slowly approached the residence. At the porch, Walter and Meisler got out. Steil followed. The chauffeur opened Scheindlin's door and retrieved the suitcase from the trunk, then the teacher took it from him. The guard and the driver returned to their seats just as the front door was opened by a silver-haired, very British-looking butler, minus the coattails. The man smiled, waved both men in, and said, 'What a pleasure to see you again, Mr Scheindlin.' Steil had no way of knowing that he had just begun the most physically inactive time of his days in Miami.

*   *   *

Scheindlin introduced him as Mr John, and the butler marched them to a one-bedroom unit on the second floor. The teacher was kept busy for almost half an hour duly logging all relevant information on the Steils for his boss, beginning with his grandparents and the Fruitland railroad station where his father had been born, and concluding with Shelley Steil's phone number in New Iberia.

The first day sped along greased by novelty. The food was good, the view of the landscaped garden and quiet surroundings soothed Steil's spirit, and the feeling that things were finally brightening up made him happy. He unpacked, watched a little TV, read magazines, and listened to a Sinatra CD. At around 7.00 in the evening, a male nurse unbandaged his head, put some cool liquid on the stitches, and covered the wound with fresh gauze. Later, in bed, Steil relished feeling safe and cared for.

He hadn't been locked up since his cattleman years in the Cuban Army. In 1969, Cuba was living the second of its three Volstead Act years. A dozen distilleries were in full swing, churning out huge vats of alcohol from sugarcane molasses, but most of it was exported, and hard liquor was unobtainable. Although no law had been enacted, bars, liquor stores, and nightclubs were closed. The word on the streets was that some Party bigwigs had decided that liquor consumption – like doing business, throwing parties, and celebrating Christmas – was a human frailty that the New Man could dispense with. After sniffing the air, some top-level economic experts brandished US statistics proving that drinking lowered productivity and induced labor-related accidents. The black market boomed. A four-peso bottle of rum climbed to forty pesos. People who rarely drank suddenly wanted to end the day knocking back a short one.

But in Santa Cruz del Norte rum was not difficult to get. The town had an ancient distillery on its coastline, on the opposite bank of a small river emptying into the sea, which consumed molasses from the nearby Hershey refinery. The overwhelming majority of its workers lived in Santa Cruz.

Al Capone was to blame for setting the wrong precedent. During the Prohibition years, he had sent rumrunners to load up at the recently inaugurated installation. And thirty-odd years later, during the socialist dry period, rum was freely smuggled out when it became public knowledge that some Ministry of Sugar officials – who seldom visited the old distillery under their tutelage before the hard-liquor shortage – made frequent inspections and left the place with three or four gallons of 90-proof alcohol in the trunks of their cars.

Nineteen years old at the time, Elliot went on a drinking binge with former schoolmates at a farewell party on the seventh day of a one-week leave of absence. Pretty loaded, and having refused the invitation of his three friends to strip and swim at the mouth of the river, Elliot sat atop a seawall under a full moon to contemplate the calm waters and sing at the top of his lungs the double entendres of a popular song involving Christopher Columbus, the Pinzón brothers, and an Indian tribe. Angry neighbors called the police.

Elliot explained to the prowl-car officers that he was one of the brave soldiers defending the Motherland from imperialist plots, and his refusal to enter the vehicle was in line with his commanding officer's order never to surrender, under any circumstance. And besides, how could he be sure they weren't CIA agents? The cops exchanged patient glances. The company's political commissar had told him that the CIA had all the money in the world – it could send enemy agents disguised as Cuban police comrades to abduct soldiers of the Revolution. Then Elliot's stark-naked and equally intoxicated civilian friends climbed the seawall to stand by their pal. That did it.

The next morning the company's political commissar – dubbed Stalin by the soldiers for his extreme left-wing views – drove to the Santa Cruz police station to pick up Elliot. The 7.00 a.m. to 3.00 p.m. desk sergeant on duty – who had heard the story at roll call – split his sides after learning that the soldier of the Revolution was in fact a stable boy. The following day Elliot was indicted by a military court for being drunk and disorderly, conduct unbecoming of a soldier. Alarmed by the legal mumbo-jumbo, fearing a two-year prison sentence, and following the advice of the same political commissar, who also acted as defense counsel, Elliot admitted his guilt at the arraignment and begged for mercy.

Familiar with such incidents, the prosecutor and the judge managed to keep straight faces when the commissar said his defendant deserved a long penalty not only for disturbing the peace of a socialist community of workers and fishermen who toiled all day long, but also for consuming black-market rum, thus depriving the people of much-needed foreign currency. But above all, the defendant's most significant offense was of a moral nature, for he had indulged in a weakness that, though understandable in older people who under capitalism became alcohol-dependent as the only way to escape exploitation, was unforgivable in a member of the new generation entrusted with building socialism. Elliot had to use all of his self-control not to strangle the son of a bitch right before the eyes of the sneering judge, who was eyeing him amusedly.

But, the commissar went on, the Revolution was full of understanding, the Revolution was generous, the Revolution was forgiving. The comrade judge and the comrade prosecutor had heard Private Steil admit his guilt, which was undoubtedly the first step toward rehabilitation. Private Steil had carried out his military duties with diligence for over two years, and this was his first crime. Accordingly, and despite the fact that the defense was fully aware of the soldier's grave offenses, it begged the comrade captain judge to be lenient.

Steil was sentenced to a month in jail and sent back to the farm. Since there was no cell, the sergeant in charge confined him to a stable. For thirty days he had to eat his meals, sleep, and do nothing in the company of nineteen cows. But the worst part of it came when the political commissar made surprise visits to verify that Private Steil was serving his time properly. The man indulged in long tirades about the Russian Revolution, Marx, Engels, and Mao, then read passages of an Alexander Beck novel, *The Men of Panfilov*, to the exasperated prisoner. Around ten years later, Steil learned from another ex-soldier that the commissar ultimately went off the deep end, was given an honorable discharge, and spent six months in a mental hospital before being sent home to live out the rest of his life on a pension.

Now, having holed up in the safe house for five days, Steil was getting restless. The air didn't smell of cows, the political commissar had been replaced by TV personalities, and compared to army chow, the meals were epicurean. Twenty-six years after his first imprisonment, the teacher was beginning to reach the same conclusion: Second to air, water, and food, freedom is man's most pressing need. Ambivalence set in. Scheindlin phoned daily to confirm that things were moving along and results were expected within a few days. Just for argument's sake, the teacher thought about having to spend the rest of his life in hiding. Would it be worth living? He couldn't make up his mind. His near-death experiences – first at sea and then getting shot at – had taught him the difference between conceptualizations and brutal reality. Did he have the balls to call the whole thing off? He didn't. That night he went to bed consoled that he was still alive.

On the sixth and seventh days, he began longing for Fidelia. Only by reading was he able to distract himself from thinking about her. He wanted to call her but refrained, fearing an argument over his unexplained disappearance. The wound had healed, and hair was beginning to shade the bald spot clipped away at the hospital. That evening he was resignedly gazing out of the window when a car was admitted to the illuminated driveway. It looked like a deep-blue Volvo. During his usual mid-morning call, Scheindlin hadn't intimated that he might visit, but the teacher's pulse started beating faster nonetheless.

Two minutes later, there was a knock at his door. Steil made a dash for it, and a different, American-looking butler told him that Mr Scheindlin was expecting Mr John in conference room number two. Would Mr John be kind enough to follow him?

* * *

The teacher had to restrain himself from embracing his boss. He gripped Scheindlin's right hand with both of his and pumped it repeatedly before sitting beside the old man. The windowless room was of Spartan simplicity. It had a glass-topped, chrome conference table surrounded by six leather executive chairs. The floor was made of bare granite, and there was an overhead light fixture with four long, fluorescent tubes. The absence of paintings, drapes, mirrors, and vases gave it a cold, futuristic look. Scheindlin sat in a chair on the side of the table furthest from the door, facing the entrance. When Steil eased himself into a seat, the wholesaler rolled back to face him, then smiled.

'I must admit your life story is pretty far-fetched, Elliot,' he said in English, resting an ankle on his knee.

Steil gave him a wide smile. 'You telling me?'

Scheindlin grinned. 'Almost as far-fetched as mine. And you're a lucky sonafabitch, too. Unlike myself.'

It was the first time Steil had heard the old man complain. He reined in his impatience.

'Okay, let's see,' Scheindlin said, keeping his eyes on the ceiling for a few seconds. 'Your father died when your uncle said, June something, last year.'

'June 11.'

'Right. He owned forty percent of the Southern Star Sugar Company, which made him majority stockholder, president, and CEO. SSSC owns an old, not-too-efficient refinery worth around seventeen, eighteen million dollars. Besides the stock, your old man owned a big house, some land, and a hardware store. The total worth of his estate may be around nine, ten million.'

Steil held his breath in awe.

'He probably never worked for US intelligence or the FBI. Presidential nominations get wide press coverage in this country, so I ordered a search beginning with the present administration. Your father wasn't nominated for any government position from January 20, 1993, to the day he died. That was a lie your uncle made up or the story somebody fed him to hide the real reason for trying to finish you off. I tend to think the latter is true. Tell you why in a little while.

'He married Shelley Steil in 1960 and, unless he divorced your mother behind your back, became a bigamist. A boy was born in 1961. This man, Donald Steil, now thirty-four, is with the Bureau.'

Totally unaware of his reactions, the teacher bent forward in his chair, hanging on Scheindlin's every word. 'The Bureau?' he asked.

'FBI.'

Some implications stirred in Steil's mind. 'I see.'

'I bet you do. Let's move on. Your father died under circumstances that would lead anyone who hears your side of the story to suspect foul play. Massive cardiac arrest, like your uncle said. At home.' Scheindlin paused dramatically. 'When the ambulance got there, they found a corpse. No autopsy was performed, and the body was cremated. The family is highly respected and influential in New Iberia; nobody there even dreams he may have been murdered.'

With all of his powers of concentration at full strength, Steil stared at the trader's face.

'He left a will naming four beneficiaries: his first and second wives, and his two sons.'

The teacher stood and retreated to a corner. Hyperventilating, he turned around and stared at his boss. 'Go on.'

'Lawyers frequently have opposing views on the interpretation of the law, so don't consider what ours says to be final. But according to him, the probate court demands that the first wife and son be informed before the will can be executed. That means notifying the Cuban government and/or the US Office of Interests in Havana, and asking them to contact you. If a properly signed-and-sealed death certificate issued by Cuban authorities proves that Robert Steil's first wife is dead, then the estate is divided among the three surviving beneficiaries. And if Cuban authorities also certify that the first son died or disappeared . . . well, I don't have to spell it out for you, do I?'

With parted lips, the teacher blinked in stupefaction.

'So, and now I'm guessing,' Scheindlin went on as he uncrossed his legs, 'if the two beneficiaries living in the US learned about this will when it was drafted, and if they wanted to deprive the first wife and son of Robert Steil of their rights, they might have hired someone to go to Cuba, find out about you and your mother, and somehow convince the two of you, or only you if your mother had died, to flee Cuba and . . .' Scheindlin stopped in mid-sentence. It was needless to state the obvious.

Steil returned to his seat and plopped down on it. He rotated the chair to face the table, suddenly looking exhausted. He placed his elbows on the thick glass top and held his head with both hands.

'You okay?'

The teacher nodded, contemplating the tips of his shoes.

'You sure?'

Softly, 'I'm okay, Mr Scheindlin.'

'To be perfectly honest with you, I figure that's why your uncle sailed to Cuba. And the fact that your father died one week after Ed came back and reported both you and your mother were dead makes me suspect your old man might have been murdered by his wife, your half-brother, or someone they hired. They are the two people with the best possible motives. And, unless I'm very mistaken, their lawyers must be moving pretty fast to get official Cuban papers proving that your mother is dead and you have disappeared. Maybe they don't have them yet. The will's execution is still in the preliminary stage.'

Befuddled, Steil was no longer paying attention, and Scheindlin noticed.

'Now, Elliot, listen to me. I want your full attention. Are you with me?'

The teacher sighed before lifting his head and turning to face the old man. 'I'm with you, sir, I'm with you.'

'Good. According to our lawyer, there're two states in this country whose legal systems are not derived from common law: One is Louisiana, the other is Puerto Rico. In these two places, descendants are protected against disinheritance by what experts call indefeasible shares. And this means that even if your father hadn't named you in his will, you'd still have a right to a share by proving you're his son. That's why I believe you're a pretty lucky guy.'

'I won't argue with you.'

'Thank you. Now, first thing you should do is go back to Cuba and get notarized copies of every scrap of paper proving –'

'Just a second, Mr Scheindlin,' the teacher interrupted, raising his hand. 'Now *I* want to ask a few questions, okay? But let me first say that I can't go back to Cuba – I'd probably be charged with illegal emigration and sent to prison. And there's no need to. Cubans in Miami file forms, send them to the Cuban Office of Interests in Washington, pay a fee, and after a few weeks they get all kinds of papers – birth, marriage, passport, divorce, anything. We don't have to worry about that, okay?'

'Okay.'

The teacher paused to calm his brainstorm. 'Question number one is, how can I prove, or . . . Just a second, let me rephrase that, how can I petition for a forensic . . .' At a loss for words, Steil hesitated. '. . . forensic something . . . I mean, they could've given him a cup of cocoa laced with cyanide. Could've made him swallow a sleeping pill and then held a pillow over his head for a minute or two . . .'

Scheindlin shook his head. 'You can't. He was cremated. Listen, I assumed you were going to react like you just did. Now, I don't want to argue with you, but I suggest you go step by step, 'cause you're walking on a minefield. You gotta be very careful with your next moves and map out every inch of the way. Want a little piece of advice?'

'By all means.'

'I'll be totally frank with you. Probate proceedings in this country are lengthy, and in this case they will be even more so by reason of your having to prove your identity. It might take months, a year maybe, possibly two. It depends on the widow and the other son. They may well contest your right to a share. You should keep what I've just told you to yourself, put your emotions aside, and become a cunning bastard. The lawyer has an idea, he wants to explain it to you.'

Steil squinted while digesting Scheindlin's advice. 'C'mon, Mr Scheindlin, you think I can –'

'You got to. You have no alternative.'

The teacher ruminated on this for a few seconds. 'I don't know. Maybe. Now, question number two is something you probably don't know. I want you to help me figure it out. How did these people find me? I've told you I was very careful in Sarasota, rented the car under a false name, didn't leave my fingerprints. You think this FBI swine pulled some strings?'

Scheindlin heaved a sigh. 'Well, my friend, I've read estimates that ninety percent of Cubans in the United States live here in Florida. When they found out you were alive and kicking, next obvious step was to find where you lived. So, the first place comes to mind when you wanna locate one of you people . . .'

'But I changed my name!'

Scheindlin lifted a hand. 'No, Elliot, you altered your name. And if somebody runs a computer search and the right name doesn't pop up, they may assume there was a spelling error and start thinking of possibilities, first among them vowels at the beginning of your last name, like Asteil, Esteil, Isteil . . . Suddenly an Elio Esteil surfaces. From then on its child's play . . .'

Looking embarrassed, the teacher clicked his tongue, shook his head, and glanced sideways.

Scheindlin continued: 'Anyway, no John Doe comes off the street into INS offices in Miami and says, "I want you to look up this guy for me." There has to be an official request from some department or . . . someone repaid a favor or was bribed. And of all the actors in this play, no one is more well-connected for this kind of thing than your half-brother.

'Besides, people dealing in intelligence and counterintelligence, without exception, are affected with the secrecy syndrome. It's a mental condition. Everything that can't be explained in logical terms is a secret. And this stupid story about your father being nominated for a position in the intelligence community seems like it was cooked up by a guy who thinks in those terms, someone who can't come up with anything more original.'

The teacher suddenly perked up. 'And he's a fucking murderer! He's hired people to get me killed! Are you implying I gotta keep hiding here for the next couple years 'til this . . . this probate shit ends, and I can charge him with attempted murder?'

Scheindlin remained calm and patient. 'Elliot, cool off. Don't jump to conclusions. The first attempt on your life wasn't reported; after the second, you and Tony claimed it was a case of mistaken identity. For this kind of accusation, you need proof. And you can't get the proof you need if you go wild.'

The teacher hung his head for a few moments. When he lifted it, he ran his hands over his hair and inhaled deeply. 'Mr Scheindlin, no man, ever, has done anything for me that remotely compares to what you're doing. If I live to be a hundred, I'll never forget you. But this costs five hundred dollars a day. You said it might take a year, two maybe. Even if I don't go mad locked up in my room, I'd have to transfer all the dough I inherit to the owner of this place. And if I don't get any money, if this probate court says I got no right . . .'

Steil cut his tirade short as the businessman lifted his right hand for the second time. 'Elliot, take it easy, will ya? I told you our lawyer has an idea. You won't stay here forever. Maybe next Monday you'll be back on the street.'

The teacher gaped at Scheindlin. 'Really?'

'I think so. Now, I suggest you calm down. Go to your room, sleep off your pain, and I'll phone you first thing Monday morning. Okay?'

'I won't even be able to nap for fifteen minutes tonight. I know myself. I'll start endlessly processing this conversation, trying to foresee what's gonna happen . . .'

'Take a pill,' Scheindlin suggested with a grin.

'I never take pills.'

Scheindlin shrugged, then stood. 'Well, Elliot, I'm tired, I need to go to bed early tonight. I sincerely believe things are moving in the right direction. Don't worry. I'll phone you Monday morning. Good night.'

And shuffling tiredly, Ruben Scheindlin left the conference room.

11

David Sadow looked funny and cheap.

The five foot two, fifty-two-year-old man sported a comical goatee, suspenders, and a Mickey Mouse watch. The patch of disheveled graying hair on his bald head gave him a clownish appearance, an impression enhanced by his minuscule ears, which curled forward as if to compensate for their size. He wore a well-tailored, charcoal-gray suit which somehow looked off the rack on him, and was chewing an unlit Cohiba Espléndido to pieces, something that would have enraged the most novice cigar aficionado. But as Elliot Steil would realize, this lawyer who specialized in contested wills wasn't at all laughable and was far from cheap.

Sadow was a senior partner with Shapiro Appleton Rosen Weinberg and Sadow, a law firm occupying the fourteenth floor of a modern building on 705 Brickell Avenue. His office looked posh as well as a little kitsch with its glass-topped chrome and crushed velvet. Drapes concealed a floor-to-ceiling picture window with a splendid view. To Sadow's left hung four avant-garde paintings. Behind his high-backed executive chair, atop a credenza, stood a solid-silver frame with a photograph of a beautiful middle-aged woman, three huge, leather-bound books, an intercom, and an ultramodern cordless telephone. Having seen hundreds of movies in which over-flowing bookcases lined the walls of legal offices, Steil felt the absence of this effect in Sadow's. Maybe the age of PC – characterized by the minimalism of a computer terminal and keyboard on an eight-foot-long, glass-topped desk – had changed things, the Cuban speculated. It was 10.09 a.m. on February 27, a Monday.

Scheindlin completed the introduction, Steil and Sadow shook hands, then the lawyer motioned the visitors to the comfortable client armchairs facing his desk. Refreshments were offered and declined before Sadow eased himself into his seat.

'Mr Steil, you certainly have a story to tell,' Sadow said with a smile that revealed long, tobacco-stained teeth.

'I guess I do.'

'It is my understanding you left Cuba on a raft eight months ago. You were rescued on the high seas by other rafters, then made it safely to Key West. Were you officially admitted into the US?'

'I was.'

'May I see your Social Security card?'

The teacher pulled out his wallet and handed the ID to Sadow. Clenching the cigar between his teeth, Sadow examined it closely, returned it to the teacher, and mumbled, 'Why the wrong spelling?'

Steil heaved a sigh and let his eyes wander across the desk. 'Well, Mr Sadow, maybe this is difficult to understand. Mr Scheindlin has told you about my father. As a kid I loved him very much, but after he deserted us I developed sort of . . . a deep resentment towards him. I was filled with anger, maybe even hate. This feeling abated over the years as I understood life better, as I matured, but when I got here, I suddenly realized I had the opportunity to sever all ties with my past, start from scratch, if you know what I mean. I had no Cuban ID, and I even considered that giving my real name might make INS people wonder who this guy with an American name might be, maybe even try to locate my father to confirm my story. I didn't want that to happen, didn't want him to vouch for me if he were still alive, so I misspelled my name and changed my date of birth on all the application forms.'

Sadow withdrew the cigar from his crushing incisors. 'I see. But you should realize this complicates your case. Probate court will examine all the documents related to your true identity with great care. In your childhood, did you attend some American school?'

'I was in grade school for a few months back in . . . oh, maybe '56, '57.'

'Where?'

'Sebastian. A small town on Florida's east coast. My father and grandfather worked at a sugar refinery in Fellsmere, a few miles from Sebastian.'

The lawyer nodded. 'We'll try to see if those records are still kept. Fat chance. Let's move on. Your last name isn't common, but anyway there must be hundreds of Steils in the US. What persuaded you that the slain Sarasota jeweler in the *Herald* piece was your uncle?'

The teacher relaxed and crossed his legs. Sadow returned the cigar to his mouth to rotate, suck, and crush it a little more. 'I knew I had an uncle from my father and grandparents. But I don't think I ever met the man, at least I don't remember meeting him. When I was seven or eight, I somehow learned he had moved to Sarasota. That made an impression 'cause I remembered Sarasota from a vacation with my parents. I never forgot the Ringling Brothers circus. So, close to forty years later, the headline caught my attention and everything came back to me.'

The cigar was plucked out. 'Your memory is remarkable. When your parents took you to Sarasota, do you recall staying at a private home? Your uncle's maybe?'

The teacher made his first reevaluation of Sadow as he pretended to sift through his recollections. 'No, I don't. He probably moved there after our trip.'

'Probably. What did you feel after realizing the man who was murdered was your uncle?'

Steil tilted his head and acted as though he were recalling. 'I felt . . . maybe a little compassion. I wondered if my father was still alive, if he'd go to the funeral.'

Holding the chomped cigar in his left hand, Sadow tilted back on his chair and stole a glance at Scheindlin. 'Okay. Now tell me how you reached the conclusion that the attempts on your life were linked to your father.'

The teacher scratched his temple and looked at the ceiling for a moment. 'Well, the first time I thought they were after Mr Scheindlin's money, but the Saturday before last it was obvious his money wasn't the motive. So I tried to work out what was going on, and the only motive that came to my mind was that someone was trying to snuff family members, first my uncle and then me. Why? Not even in my wildest dreams could I think of a reason. And the big question was how had anyone found out I was a Steil? Then Mr Scheindlin offered to help. I told him my real name and life story, and only now, after his findings, do I suspect this second wife or her lawyers sent someone to Cuba to investigate. This person learned that my mother had died and I'd disappeared. Disappearing Cubans are not the victims of death squads; they usually surface in Miami. Figuring out where to look for me didn't require a high IQ. Plus, they had the right contacts, especially this half-brother with the Bureau, but, of course, you know all that.'

Sadow seemed satisfied. He dropped the cigar into a wastebasket, and Steil noticed that there were no ashtrays on the desk. The teacher thought that any man who buys twenty-five-dollar cigars for chewing only has to be an absolute ding-a-ling. 'Well, Mr Steil, I think you stand a very good chance of inheriting some money.'

The lawyer spent close to ten minutes explaining US probate law wills, succession, primogeniture and ultimogeniture, invalidity, executors, petitions for the admission of the instrument to probate, and similar legal jargon with rapid-fire fluency, which the teacher later discerned was only intended to soften him up for what was to come.

'*But,*' Sadow said at last, and the teacher sniffed the proximity of the heart of the matter, 'we must be in full agreement on three very important issues before I take your case. Ruben has told me you'd like to investigate the possibility that your father was murdered. I strongly disapprove. Your father is dead; nothing will bring him back. If you file charges against other beneficiaries of your father's will, it may take ten years to reach a final verdict. Such action on your part would preclude *inter-vivos* trusts and joint tenancies, which means that an officer of the court would be appointed as executor, and we wouldn't see a penny of your money before the full criminal process ended, including appeals. You might have read in the press that it sometimes takes ten years to execute a convicted murderer in this country, even with a confession, due to the appeals process. So I will represent you only if you sign an agreement, including a clause not to take any steps in that direction before probate in the solemn form is concluded.'

Sadow paused, his eyes fixed on the teacher. Seconds slipped by. Steil nodded.

'Does that nod mean you agree to clause number one?'

'It does.'

'Fine. Clause number two closely resembles the first. You shall not press charges against any other beneficiary of the will involved in criminal acts against you, even if you uncover indisputable proof. Same reason. It'd take years to untangle the will, and it's already pretty complicated. You agree?'

'No, I don't.' Steil knew he was losing his cool, but plowed ahead anyway. 'You're right about my father; nothing can bring him back. But I'm pretty much alive, and I see only two ways to remain so: One is to live in total seclusion until this probate thing is over, which I can't afford, financially or psychologically. The other is to do something, go to the police, press charges, I don't know, but I have to do something. If I agree to this clause, I won't last a week on the streets.'

'There's a third way,' Sadow said softly.

The teacher stared at him for a few moments. 'Which is?'

'A face-to-face meeting with the other beneficiaries and their lawyers.'

The teacher kept staring.

Sadow spoke patiently: 'I call their lawyers. Explain you're my client. Ask for a friendly meeting to come up with an amicable agreement and resolve any dispute. I tell them I'm trying to persuade you not to press charges against the other beneficiaries. They'll ask, "What fucking charges?" My reply will be, "Ask your clients," which they will. And in less than a week we'll have Mrs Steil and your half-brother sitting in my conference room, right behind that wall, tame as lambs. What do you say?'

Steil kept his eyes on the lawyer. He was considering that if the Louisiana Steils could be threatened with exposure, he was also open to criminal charges regarding his Sarasota expedition. 'What will you say to them?'

Sadow bared his teeth with a smirk. 'When you're sick and go to a doctor, you don't ask him what surgical procedure he'll use or why he'll prescribe a certain drug. Please, trust me on this. When you deal with a professional, trust is essential. I want you to sign a will I'll draft, naming the federal government of the United States as your sole beneficiary. You can have it annulled when this is over. In a sealed annex to it you'll write down everything that has happened to you in Miami and explain why you suspect that Mrs Steil and her son are behind the murder of your uncle, the attempts on your life, and possibly the murder of your father. At the end, you ask the proper authorities to conduct an investigation if you die a violent death. That will and deposition are our weapons. And with these weapons, I have reasons to believe you'll live to be one hundred and five, like the song says.'

The teacher liked it. He moved his gaze to Scheindlin. The old man nodded. 'Okay,' Steil agreed.

'Very good. Clause number three stipulates that my fee is fifty percent of your share, before all federal and state inheritance taxes are deducted.'

Smiling openly, Steil shook his head in amazement and looked sideways at Scheindlin. His boss shrugged, pulled down the corners of his mouth, and lifted his eyebrows in what the amused teacher interpreted to be a take-it-or-leave-it expression. Sadow had taken out a fresh Espléndido from a leather cigar case that he carried in the inner breast pocket of his jacket. Holding it poised over the desk, he looked a little off balance.

'Have you been able to estimate how much my share'll be?'

'With a wide margin of error, yes,' Sadow said, deftly rolling the cigar back and forth between his fingers. 'It depends on many variables, and time is essential. A share that today is worth ten dollars might rise to twelve or drop to eight six months later. I'm told the future of refined sugar consumption in this country isn't rosy. The refinery needs to modernize now, more so in the future. Being bearish – which is always the best way to plan – if the estate is split three ways, each may collect between two and three million dollars. A bull may say between three and four.'

'What do you mean by *bearish* and *bull*?'

Sadow took a couple of minutes to explain.

Steil knew he had no alternative, but remained silent. Sadow continued: 'If you think I'm stealing you blind, let me clear things up for you. For starters, this will is going to be executed in Louisiana, a jurisdiction that, as Mr Scheindlin probably told you, has a peculiar legal system, unlike any other in the continental US. That means we have to retain a very knowledgeable New Orleans firm specializing in probate law to advise me, do all the paperwork, comply with all statutory formalities, and so on. In fact, this firm has already started working on your case, made the preliminary inquiries. They are the best, and like the best everywhere, they are not cheap. Their price is twenty-five percent. Trips will have to be made, and that means plane tickets, hotel rooms, meals, car rentals. My firm will cover all charges, including what's needed to obtain the legal documents in Cuba, which prove your true identity, and then we'll make an appeal to the US immigration court to correct your present identity. This involves retaining the best local law firm specializing in immigration and naturalization. We'll be working for you for the next six months, minimum, maybe a year, so from our twenty-five percent, after all expenses are deducted, we may end up with fifteen percent of what you get.'

'Please,' Steil said, a smile on his lips, 'let's sign this agreement right now, before you raise your percentage to sixty.'

'A sense of humor. Wonderful,' said Sadow, then took his first bite into the fresh cigar.

An unattractive, fiftyish woman in a blue suit slipped into the office without knocking and closed the door behind her. Sadow lifted his gaze, knitting his brow. Scheindlin and Steil turned in their seats. 'Yes, Martha?' the lawyer mumbled.

'There's an urgent call for Mr Scheindlin on line three,' the secretary said before making an about-face and exiting discreetly.

Sadow rotated his seat, grabbed the cordless, punched a key on it, and handed the set to Scheindlin, now sitting on the edge of the armchair. The old man said something in Yiddish and listened for a full minute as the blood gradually drained from his face. What little control he had over his eyes was lost, and the irises hopped madly behind his thick bifocals. Scheindlin leaned back on the seat as if searching for stability. The teacher and Sadow bent forward. The old man managed to utter what sounded like two questions, listened to the other party, then spoke for nearly thirty seconds as his face began to recover its natural color. He extended his hand to return the set. Noticing that the lawyer was out of reach, Steil served as intermediary. Sadow pressed a key and rested the phone on the desk. Time seemed to have stopped in the ensuing silence.

Scheindlin lifted his head to the ceiling and inhaled deeply before he spoke. 'It seems somebody mailed a letter bomb to my office. It blew up when my secretary slit it open, and he's seriously injured. Please excuse me. I must leave now.'

*   *   *

Scheindlin refused Steil's vehement requests to ride with him to the North Miami Beach warehouse, insisting that the teacher stay behind and do what Sadow had suggested. He left the office shuffling, looking ten years older. The teacher squinted at Sadow and started to ask, 'I wonder if . . .' but left unsaid what was looming large in his mind. The lawyer nodded abstractedly for a few seconds, his gaze lost in the folds of the drapes, before rattling off instructions into the intercom.

Ten minutes later, as a legal clerk began drafting Elliot Steil's will on a PC, an assistant arranged a conference call for 12.00 sharp. Sadow's secretary took down in shorthand the agreement that her boss was dictating, while the shaken teacher sat alone in a small conference room to write in longhand the partly spurious story he had concocted to incriminate others without inculpating himself. He struggled to force the bombing incident out of his mind, but his gut instinct told him that it was unequivocally linked to his predicament.

The first three-page draft was completed by 11.25 a.m. Sadow placed the agreement before him several minutes later, and the teacher interrupted his rewriting of page two of his deposition to read the document. For a legal text it was plain enough and conformed to what had been discussed, so Steil signed it, and Sadow followed suit. The lawyer reentered the room fifteen minutes later with the prepared will and two witnesses Steil had never seen before. After confirming that the Federal Government of the United States of America was the only beneficiary of his estate, Steil clicked his tongue, smiled sadly, shook his head sideways, and signed. Having performed their task, the witnesses left, and Sadow took a seat in order to start carefully revising the teacher's account. Steil noticed that the man read like a semiliterate person, word by word, his mind searching for hidden effects or derivations. He was on the first lines of the second page when the secretary entered the room with a cordless in her hand. It was precisely noon.

'Both parties are on the line, Dave,' she said.

Grabbing the phone, Sadow pulled out a folded A4 bond sheet from the pocket of his jacket, then thanked the woman and leaned back on the chrome-and-leather office chair. She stood by his side like a well-trained Doberman.

'Hello?' he said. 'Do I have Mrs Shelley Steil and Mr Anthony Gaylord on the line?' He waited for a reply. 'Thank you most kindly,' he began, looking Steil right in the eye, 'for giving me a few minutes of your very valuable time. I'm David Sadow, a Florida bar certified attorney and senior partner with Shapiro Appleton Rosen Weinberg and Sadow, a Miami law firm.' He lowered his eyes to the sheet. 'I hope that I'll soon have the pleasure of meeting you, Mrs Steil, your son, Donald, who unfortunately is not available today, and of course, you as well, Mr Gaylord. My attention has been called to the well-earned prestige of the New Orleans law firm of Gaylord Copeland and Edmonds, which your father founded almost sixty years ago.' He took a deep breath. 'The purpose of this call is to inform you that I represent Mr Elliot Steil, son of the testator Robert Steil and one of the beneficiaries of the will made by the late Mr Steil with the New Iberia attorney Alain Truffaut on May 5, 1993.' He paused, but no one spoke on the other end. 'It is my understanding that you, Mr Gaylord, petitioned for the admission of the instrument to probate, and on August 19, 1994, the Court officially requested that the State Department contact Cuban authorities and ask them to locate a woman named Carmen María Steil, née García, and her son, Elliot Steil García, in the town of Santa Cruz del Norte, Cuba.

'My client has told me his mother died in 1984, something that we will prove in court with her death certificate, but Elliot Steil has been residing in Miami since June of last year, and he intends to claim his share of the will.

'However, for reasons which he has not disclosed to me, my client has drafted his will today, and it has only one beneficiary, the United States Federal Government. Annexed to this will there's a sealed envelope to be opened only after my client passes away, and only if he is murdered or dies in an accident. My client tells me this envelope contains a three-page deposition in his own handwriting, addressed to the FBI, listing the reasons he has to suspect, and now I'll quote my client's exact words, "that people living in the United States have conspired and engaged in criminal acts with the purpose of depriving me of my father's legacy". End of quote.

'As you may realize –' Sadow stopped in mid-sentence, and a malevolent smile distended his lips. 'Did Mrs Steil hang up, Mr Gaylord?' The lawyer nodded after registering a brief comment from the other end. 'Well, let's not jump to conclusions; maybe she suddenly became ill. I assure you, sir, that my client wishes to find a mutually satisfactory compromise for all surviving beneficiaries, which will facilitate a speedy legal process. We would be overjoyed if you and your clients would meet with my client and myself next Monday, March 6, here in my office, to examine the matter.'

Now Sadow listened for a full minute, his eyes again on the teacher, while he held his smile. 'I fully understand, counselor. But please keep in mind that I have devoted no less than three hours of my time to convince my client that we might all lose if he files charges. For reasons that he refuses to divulge, he's pretty certain of having been victimized and claims to be sure of who is behind these unpleasant experiences. Mr Steil has spent, and is still spending, substantial amounts of money on security and . . .'

An interruption made Sadow pause for ten seconds.

'No, he's not paranoid, sir. Certain incidents shouldn't be discussed over the phone, but if you hear him out like I have, perhaps you'll agree that the man has reasons to take every precaution. I'm sure you'll examine this new development with your clients as soon as possible. There may be family problems we don't know about, rivalries, who knows. This might get out of hand, which would be detrimental to our convenience – yours and mine, I mean.' Sadow listened attentively to the attorney's response. 'With great pleasure. I look forward to it. Thank you very much. Goodbye.'

He broke the connection and returned the cordless to the secretary, who nodded at Steil then left the room.

'She gasped and hung up,' Sadow said simply. 'Now let's go back to this.' Then he resumed the careful reading of page two of the teacher's deposition.

*   *   *

'What the fuck's going on, Elio?' Tony Soto exclaimed, as he and his former teacher rushed along Brickell Avenue toward Tony's car. 'The kike told me to pack. He wanted me to pick you up and give you protection. He's never asked me to do that before. What the fuck's going on?'

'It's a long story, Tony. In today's chapter, somebody sent a letter bomb to the warehouse. Uri is badly injured.'

'What?'

'Right now I want you to concentrate on getting me to Scheindlin's, fast.'

'Uri? Injured? Holy shit! Hey, wait a minute. Scheindlin said to take you to an address in Rockdale.'

'No, take me to the warehouse. From there we'll go to your place, I'll let you in on what's going on, and then maybe I'll return to Rockdale.' Something in Steil's voice dissuaded Tony from questioning him further. The cop sensed that the nature of their association was rapidly changing. He was being sidelined, becoming a follower.

Driving north on Biscayne Boulevard, the teacher looked over at Tony as though he had just noticed that the cop was not wearing his uniform. 'Night shift?' he asked.

'Yeah.'

'What time'd Scheindlin call you?'

'A little after twelve.'

'What did he say?'

'Just to pick you up and take you to this place. For Chrissake, the man talked like nothing had happened! Same politeness.' Tony mimicked Scheindlin's strong accent: '"Would it be possible for you to pick Elio up at a certain address and take him to another place?" Before hanging up, almost like an afterthought, he suggested carrying. Jesus! The man's made of ice. One of his lifelong friends gets blown to pieces, and he talks like nothing happened. Gives me the creeps.'

Some people hide their grief, Steil reflected, others cry and moan. Maybe the latter get it off their chests more quickly.

They soon reached the warehouse. Steil had imagined the kind of wreckage from blasted places he'd seen on TV newscasts. But from the central drive-in passage where he and Tony stood, everything looked relatively unperturbed. The glassed-in cubicle had lost only two panes. Scheindlin was inside talking to a man wearing a chocolate-colored suit. Samuel Plotzher relayed to the two Cubans what he had learned from two bomb squad experts in the past hour. The firm's second-in-command explained that non-human damage is minimal when a letter bomb explodes, because the victim shields the objects around him, and the charge is slim enough to avoid arousing suspicion in the addressee.

Sam had been at the far end of the warehouse at approximately 10.15, when it went off. Unconscious and breathing laboredly, Uri had lived through the paramedics' first-aid procedures, but died on the way to the hospital. Plotzher, usually a subdued, steady man, seemed shaken. Tony was carrying out his own interrogation. Did somebody offer protection that Scheindlin declined? Was it possible Arab extremists were behind this? Had the company refused to do business with the Russian Mafia? Plotzher kept shaking his head, and Steil elbowed the cop into silence.

'Who's the guy in the cheap suit with Ruben?' Tony asked as his final question. It was the kind of comment that Steil resented. The kind of comment that could scale down a friendship.

'A sergeant from the North Miami PD,' answered Plotzher. 'Investigations, I think he said.'

'They don't know how to deal with this!'

'Take it easy, Tony. It's their turf. Besides, two Miami bomb-squad officers left a few minutes before you got here. They're focusing on Uri's corpse.'

The guy in the chocolate-brown suit shook hands with Scheindlin, and both men emerged from the cubicle. Plotzher approached them and warmly thanked the sergeant as he held the man's right hand between his own two. The sergeant was polite enough to nod at Tony and Steil before he left. The Cubans and Plotzher turned to Scheindlin.

'You're not supposed to be here,' the older man said to Steil.

'Could I have a word with you?'

Scheindlin nodded, and Tony glared at his former teacher. What was the matter with Elio? Who had introduced him to Scheindlin, found him a good job, sold him a nice car with no down payment, put his hide on the line when the man had been shot at? And now the guy had become Mr Mystery, acting superior, ordering him around, making him feel excluded. What the fuck was the matter with Elio?

Scheindlin turned to reenter the cubicle, then did a double take. 'We shouldn't go in there. Police are coming back later to gather more evidence. Sam, please ask Gold to take care of the funeral service. I'd like to go home and rest a coupla hours.'

'Sure, Ruben.'

'Tony, please, give me a few minutes with Elliot.'

'No problem.'

Standing next to a huge crate, Scheindlin listened to Steil's six-minute report with occasional nods. Finally the teacher voiced his misgivings: 'Sir, I can't dispel the notion that this bomb . . .'

Scheindlin chortled, and Steil was taken aback. ' "Can't dispel the notion." I think the last time I heard that was in *Gone With the Wind* or some other classic. You teachers! I know what notion you can't dispel. You're probably right. But you need proof, not a notion. Maybe the police will find a clue; maybe a snitch will learn something. But I don't have much hope. I'm depressed, Elliot. Uri was a friend, a sixteen-year friend.'

The teacher felt the burden of guilt on his back. 'I don't know what to say, Mr Scheindlin.'

'There's nothing to be said. It's just the way things turned out. They were after me, no doubt about it. Probably followed us when I took you to the safe house, guessed I was backing you up, and decided I should be removed. Well, they removed the wrong man. We're going all the way.'

'I can't believe this is happening. Killers roaming the streets firing guns and planting bombs. We know who they are, or who pays them — which is more or less the same — and can't do a thing about it. It's unbelievable.'

'Okay, let's not weep over spilled milk. I think we have reason to feel less vulnerable now. With Sadow on our side, this woman and her son will realize they are one step away from disaster and probably call off their hired guns. But anyway, I suggest you spend a few more days at the safe house. Tony will drive you over.'

'Tony wants to know what's going on, Mr Scheindlin. He's mad at me. I should at least give him an expurgated version.'

The wholesaler considered this for a moment. 'Okay. Ask him to button up. Sadow will keep us posted. Let's call it a day, okay?'

*   *   *

Tony Soto was bent forward on the edge of one of his living room love seats, shaking his head in wonder, forearms resting on his knees. Steil felt frazzled. His former pupil had interrupted him at least twenty times; the discrepancies between the truth and the castrated story forced him to think too much. The cop's curiosity grew as he swilled one beer after another. When Soto's wife had left to pick up the kids at school, he suggested that she take them somewhere – he had important things to discuss with Steil and didn't want the snotty devils interrupting. Now it was close to 4.00, and Tony seemed to be finished questioning Steil. The teacher was voraciously munching on a tuna sandwich that Lidia had prepared. For over an hour, he had been eyeing it on the cocktail table, but Tony hadn't been polite enough to rein in his impatience and let him eat.

'Remember the Cuban saying "Lady Luck is crazy and will walk arm-in-arm with anyone"?' Tony asked.

'Uh-huh.'

'Well, suppose I hadn't spotted you that night with Hairball. You never would've met Scheindlin, never gotten his protection. All that would be left of you by now would be your silhouette in white chalk somewhere.'

'Uh-huh.'

'When the Lady walks with you, she walks with you.'

'Uh-huh.'

'Want some more orange juice?'

'Unh, unh.'

'Okay, I wanna ask one final question. You mind?'

'Unh, unh.'

'What's the kike's cut?'

Steil swallowed. 'What do you mean?'

'What's his percentage? How much is he gonna make when you collect?'

'Nothing. I'll pay him back what he has spent on investigations and protection.'

233

Tony Soto leaned back on the love seat and grinned broadly. 'Are you kidding?'

The teacher frowned in surprise. 'He hasn't said he wants a cut. He did say he wanted me to become a partner, buy some company stock if I collect. But that's not a payment, it's an investment.'

Tony's grin evaporated. 'He's a genius! He takes a cut from the lawyer's fee, and then makes you a partner, which means he gets to manage your dough. The man takes you to the cleaners, and you're grateful for all he's done for you. He's a fucking genius.'

The teacher looked confused. 'Tony, you said the man's rich, that he's worth millions. You think he's after more money? At his age?'

Tony smiled condescendingly. He rolled his eyes and slapped his thighs before staring back at the teacher. 'Elio, you know something? Cubans who lived under Communism for many years are money-simple. I've seen a hundred cases. You've all been brainwashed. You think about money in terms of a job to buy groceries, pay the rent, the HMO. I had you figured wrong. You're so . . . so naive, so . . . gullible. Nobody in the whole world, ever, thinks he has enough money. The more they have, the more they want. And there's nothing wrong with that. Ruben is a good man. Maybe he donates ten thousand dollars every year to his favorite charity, maybe he gives ten bucks to some bum holding a Will Work For Food sign at an intersection. But you know why you're working for him? Okay, I'll tell you why.'

Tony Soto then explained the freon business.

'He spotted an opportunity and went for it, see? He's seventy-five if he's a day. He's a millionaire, and he's trying to make money like he expects to live forever. And you know why I could let you in on this scam? No, you don't, and I'm not telling. Let's say Ruben and I help each other. Of course, it ain't only business. You deal with a guy for a coupla years, some kind of friendship develops. Yeah, he speaks highly of you, says you're efficient. Maybe in the beginning he was willing to spend some dough to help you out, but when he learned you were gonna get a bundle of money, oh boy, oh boy!'

The teacher thought Tony Soto was probably right. So what? He just wanted to live a normal life, something that was only possible if he resolved the will dispute.

'I admit you may be right,' Steil said. 'And it's okay with me. He's entitled to it.'

'Did I say he wasn't?'

'No. But you made it sound like I had an alternative. "Taken to the cleaners," you said. And maybe I'm a fool, if that's what grateful people are. If a new sponsor comes to me now and says he won't charge me a penny, won't ask me to invest my money in his business, swears he'll find me a new lawyer who charges only ten percent, I'd still stick with Scheindlin because he stood by me when none of us knew there might be some money coming my way.'

'Brainwashed,' was Tony's diagnosis.

'Maybe. Listen, can I use your phone?'

'Sure.'

Steil tapped out Fidelia's office number with apprehension, as Tony ambled to the kitchen with the empty beer cans, then placed the sandwich plate in the sink for Lidia to wash.

The lawyer answered in Spanish after the first ring: 'Robins Weinstein and Bencomo, good afternoon.'

'Hi. It's Elio.'

'Elio?' she said with surprise after a brief pause.

Light-heartedly and smiling: 'Am I already forgotten?'

Venomously: 'Should you be remembered?'

'Can you talk now?'

'Sure. Bencomo left an hour ago.'

'Okay, listen to me good. Like they say here, I got some good news and some bad news. The bad news is, I won't be able to see you for the next two or three days.'

'Who says that's bad news?' she replied, oozing with sarcasm.

'I do.'

'That's your problem.'

'What's yours?'

'It doesn't concern you.'

'Okay, I get the message. You're mad at me. I didn't give you a full explanation the last time we met 'cause I couldn't. For two reasons. The first I told you then: I wanted to protect you from knowing too much. Second, I didn't know why certain things were happening to me. Now I know. When we talk face-to-face, you'll change your mind. But we must wait two or three more days. I ask you to be patient, I beg you to be patient. Please, Fidelia.'

Seconds slowly flowed by as Steil waited for her to speak.

'Won't you give me an answer?'

'I'll wait three more days.'

'I love you. Now tell me how you've been. How's Dani, your parents?'

'Oh, Elio,' said Fidelia in a choked voice.

'What's the matter?'

'Papa is ill, Elio, he's seriously ill,' Fidelia blubbered.

She unsuccessfully tried to contain her sobs and explained that her father had begun to lose weight rapidly at the end of January. Everyone had made jokes for the first two weeks. But on the evening of February 15, her father said he felt extremely tired, even though he hadn't worked very hard that day. He was running a temperature. Papa continued at his job for another week as his smoker's cough worsened and phlegm built up in his lungs. He had finally stopped working, and since last Saturday had only left his bed to use the bathroom. He had shed forty-five pounds in two months. An X-ray revealed a shadow on his right lung – the doctor feared an advanced stage of cancer. New tests would be conducted this week.

'I don't know what to say,' Steil mumbled as he recalled

236

the man paddling the raft, celebrating after the rescue, and nodding in understanding on Christmas Eve when he learned that his daughter and the teacher were going steady.

'I need you, *coño*!' Fidelia snapped.

'Soon, very soon. This is an emergency. Please hold on for a few more days.'

'Okay.'

'I miss you terribly.'

'So do I. I have a call on the other line. Be careful.'

'I will.'

'Bye now.'

'Bye, bye.'

As Steil placed the handset into its cradle, an idea exploded in his brain for no discernible reason. He stood very still, his eyes fixed to the floor. Was it viable? Certainly. Was it wise? Not in the least. He suddenly wanted to get back to the safe house as soon as possible, shut himself in his room, and start figuring out all the angles.

Tony Soto returned to the living room. 'I can drive you to Rockdale now if you feel like it, Mr Money.'

'Cut the crap, Tony. Let's get moving.'

12

Shelley Broussonet was having a great time. The place was called Joie de Vivre, a somewhat pretentious name for a white-washed, one-story wooden structure doubling as a dance hall and restaurant in the tiny town of Erath, Louisiana. The band included a fiddle, a triangle, an accordion, a guitar, and an upright bass. A man sang in Cajun French, loud enough to drown out the sounds of dancing feet. She'd filled up on boudin and beer, and her much older dancing partner was easy to handle. For the past few hours she had been able to forget Chad Broussard.

Bob Steil and two coworkers had been headed to the bigger and much livelier Avery Island, when their car broke down on Erath's Main Street. Their efforts at mechanics proved fruitless. A twelve-mile round-trip taxi fare would claim most of their cash, which had been earmarked for spending the night with the broads they had met two weeks earlier. After angrily wiping their hands on rags from the trunk, the three men noticed the small blinking neon sign in the distance and heard a faraway tune wafting toward them. They exchanged glances, shrugged their shoulders, rolled down their sleeves, and without a word, the sugarmen ambled over to the joint to soak their disappointment in beer.

Bob's eyes fell on Shelley as he swilled a Budweiser. The tall, sinewy, twenty-year-old woman looked wild and exhilarated as she danced. She wore no makeup, and tiny drops of perspiration glistened on her wide forehead, rosy cheeks, lean upturned nose, and pointed chin. She had large, liquid light-brown eyes under long eyebrows, and a wide mouth with thin lips. Long dark hair swayed wildly over her back. She wore a cotton dress with a flared skirt made out of two identical Purina Chicken Chow bags. Her shoes – a comfortable pair of high-top childrens' Keds – proclaimed either rock-bottom poverty or total disregard for what was considered proper.

Shelley coolly appraised the thirty-two-year-old stranger who seemed intent on picking her up. He wasn't making an impression. The guy was polite and had a nice smile, but looked like a poorly educated ranch hand in his checkered shirt and dungarees. There was grease under his fingernails, a whiff of gasoline emanating from his clothing, and a gold wedding band on his left hand. But what the heck? Shelley reasoned, no hunk would ever stop in Erath for a beer, and the stranger was a cut above the lanky bachelor in his forties whom she had danced with twice that evening.

It was February 15, 1958, a Saturday.

For the same evasive reasons that had mystified humans since feelings were acknowledged, Bob Steil fell for Shelley Broussonet like a million tons of bricks. The following Saturday night they made love for the first time, and he realized that he was willing to desert his wife and son for her, a certainty that made him miserable for nearly three years. By the summer of 1958, he was unable to sleep with any other woman, including Carmen Steil, but he became insatiable whenever Shelley allowed him to, which was five or six nights a week at the outset. It was a weird, irrational combination of love, passion, adoration, friendship, devotion, admiration, lust, and romance that turned him into a mono-vaginal man for the rest of his life. She played him like the greatest violinists play Strads.

When they met, Bob had already spent a month working at a small sugar mill close to Lafayette, the unofficial Cajun capital of Western Louisiana. To lighten the payroll and keep older and less mobile workers afloat, Fellsmere's management had urged its youngest family providers to find greener pastures until the refinery made the turnaround everybody hoped for. Already respected in sugarmen circles, Elliot Steil's father had no problem finding a new position that winter in Louisiana.

In the beginning, Shelley came very close to falling in love with Bob. Her previous sexual experiences included a cousin four years her senior, who supposedly dumped her for a Bourbon Street stripper, and three other young men. Since she was generally shunned by neighbors and relatives for her extremely independent views on almost everything, finding a man willing to spend every minute by her side, one who laughed away her unusual opinions, indulged her every whim, and could sustain the intensity of his endearment after countless hours of sex, was a new experience for Shelley. Submissiveness and poor education were his major shortcomings, she felt.

Shelley had very humble origins. Hank Broussonet had been a sharecropper on nearby lands, where he farmed with a mule, occasionally assisted by his two sons; in the off-season, they eked out a living trapping nutria and muskrat. In the rude shack where they lived, Shelley and her mother cooked and washed without running water.

All of that changed in 1950, when an oil and gas boom created new jobs, and road-construction crews ended rural isolation. Shelley's father started to make the kind of money he had never dreamed of making. The income with which a single man in New York City or Chicago was unable to make ends meet became the fulfillment of the rags-to-riches ambition of a Cajun family bred in the lowest stratum of American poverty.

A reluctant Shelley was enrolled in Abbeville's high school that same year. To her teachers' amazement, the rebellious girl who barely took notes and let her attention wander most of the time was a brilliant student. She became a voracious reader who shunned her peers and turned down all school honors, including that of class valedictorian. She was an enigma to her classmates. Adults, too, never quite understood her. But Shelley didn't give a damn. All she wanted from life were books and the love of Chad Broussard, the cousin who had seduced her three days before her fifteenth birthday.

Bob had to summon all of his willpower to spend the summers of '58 and '59 with his family in Santa Cruz del Norte. In August 1959, Shelley took a bus to New Orleans and, with tears in her eyes, pleaded with Chad to take her back. She'd do anything for him – beg in the streets, dance naked, rob a bank, kill the fucking whore who had bewitched him. On her way back to Erath, a bruised and black-eyed Shelley began to realize that Bob Steil was probably the best companion life would present.

In November of that same year, Elliot's father embarked on his third Louisiana season. Blessed with an inquisitive, good-natured personality, he had tried to adapt. Sugar factories were the same everywhere; the tiny, nearby communities where seasonal workers boarded and permanent staff and their relatives lived differed in form, but not in substance.

Meals were not a problem. Rice was both a Cuban and a Cajun staple; spicy dishes abounding in pepper, onions, and celery were also shared by both cultures. Bob had acquired a taste for shrimp in Santa Cruz del Norte. From typical Cajun cuisine he relished boudin, liked jambalaya and gumbo, accepted crawfish if the alternative entailed being impolite, and refused alligator with a smile.

He had attended the sugar cane festivals that took place before the harvest began, and was familiar with the Cajun music Shelley enjoyed. Driving around he had seen levee lands, coastal marshes, inland swamps, and the prairies where farmers cultivated rice and soybeans or raised cattle. But he realized he hadn't even scratched the surface of Cajun life and asked Shelley to become his cicerone.

She was defiantly proud of her origins and in love with her birthplace. Shelley first took him to her abandoned childhood shack, and something happened that she hadn't foreseen: she talked for three and a half hours straight, pausing only to sip on her Coke or take a bite from her Aioli sandwich. Memories she had never shared surfaced: the ever-forgetful Santa Claus, the smell of recently hatched chicks, raindrops pelting a flooded rice field. Bob Steil sensed the importance of what was happening and listened in somber silence. When she finished speaking, she led him by the hand into the shack and furiously rode him twice.

A couple of weeks later, they went to Mardi Gras in Mamou and watched revelers in multicolored hoods and frocks coax the farmers they entertained for gumbo ingredients. That same evening, observing the public dance from a distance, Shelley told Bob about Chad Broussard, without revealing his name, in a vain attempt to exorcise the loved one from her mind. Bob listened in silent anger as jealousy bubbled inside him. Intuition told her that she had made a mistake; so, a few minutes after midnight, at the start of Lent, in the moonlit grass of a recently harvested field, she dispensed pleasure to the first man she'd felt safe with.

Having discovered a first-class rival and suspecting that Shelley would leave him if this man so much as snapped his fingers, Bob told her on their next date that he wanted to discuss a very serious matter. After meeting Shelley, he had lost the feeling which had led him to marry another woman. He loved his son Elliot very much, but it would be unfair to apply for his custody and separate the boy from his mother. He couldn't go back to them and live the rest of his life longing for Shelley. He felt that he'd been born to be her lifelong companion, and wanted to prove that no one would love her as he did. He would consider himself the luckiest man on Earth if Shelley agreed to be his lawful wedded wife.

Shelley remained silent in the passenger seat. The car was parked on a country road close to Leeville, and her gaze was lost in the sunlight filtering through a dark cloud bank. At sea level, rippling water surrounded patches of Mississippi silt where coastal vegetation thrived.

She had seen it coming and had been wondering what to do for almost two years. Breaking a marriage was inconsequen-

tial to her; instead, she was held back by two other considerations. The first was her belief that women who married for
security or money were no different than the whores she'd
seen strutting along Canal Street. Would she betray one of
her own deep-seated convictions? Should she always be so
uncompromising? The second consideration was that she didn't
love Bob and never would. Why? It was hard to tell. She loathed
how he confused love with servitude and that his intellect was
so beneath her own. What were the alternatives? Keep hoping
that Chad would come back to her? Remain rootless, friendless,
barely tolerated by relatives and neighbors? Keep working the
drugstore counter for the rest of her life? Change sex partners
every couple of months and become Erath's unpaid prostitute?

'Revocable at my pleasure?' she asked.

'What?'

Shelley sighed. 'You know, I'm kinda weird. It might not
work. If I wanna cut loose, you won't object?'

'I won't.'

'Okay, hon. Let's give it a try.'

Bob Steil so feared a retraction that he told Shelley he would
spend a week in Vegas to get a quick divorce, but instead made
a trip to Sebastian to see his parents – the possibility that it
might take too long kept him from formally severing his marriage. He would have to return to Cuba and possibly spend
months in limbo now that the revolution had turned the already
inefficient Cuban bureaucracy upside down.

It was the only lie he ever told Shelley. An uninquisitive
Texan justice of the peace conducted the ceremony, and, for
lack of guests, Shelley pinned the customary dollar bills to her
husband's white shirt and tie.

*　　*　　*

Living together transformed the couple, which came as a big
surprise to Shelley. Slowed down by pregnancy and childbirth,
she gradually came to realize, to her utter amazement, that

243

Bob had a sharp business sense. Eager to provide for his second family without depriving Carmen and Elliot, and foreseeing wild swings in sugar prices as a consequence of the looming schism between Cuba and the US, he complemented his personal concern for the Caribbean nation with observations about the evolution of the world sugar market. With beginners' luck, he'd sank his modest life savings into six- and nine-month futures nine days before the US government slashed the Cuban quota, and made a killing.

Bob judiciously invested the $7000 profit in less risky business affairs. He bought and resold wholesale a wide assortment of goods, from oilmen boots to impounded cars to Japanese portable radios. He was set back $1900 in '62 when 60 percent of a three-thousand-broiler flock died on him overnight. A sudden drop in the price of alligator skins cost him $3100 one year later. But on the whole, Bob Steil started making more money on the side than what he earned at his regular job as a carbon-house foreman. His Lafayette bank manager noticed the ever-increasing balance of the couple's savings account and readily approved the $50,000 loan Bob applied for in May 1964, to buy a foreclosed hardware store. Steil was airborne and climbing fast.

Chad Broussard receded from Shelley's consciousness little by little as Donald Steil became the joy of her life, the repository for all of her hopes and aspirations. She was proud of his looks, wit, and initiative. She found him charming and irresistible. She treasured and pampered her son. Donald became an insufferable prick.

By 1972, Bob was an ebullient entrepreneur and a mildly happy family man. His wife's esteem and respect for him, if not her love, had grown perceptibly, and he was worth a cool quarter of a million. The only major marital drawback, Bob felt, was that Shelley limited their lovemaking to five or six nights a month.

During the widespread social upheaval that rocked the United States at the time, neither he nor his wife smoked reefer, dropped acid, snorted cocaine, or marched against the war in Vietnam. They had moved to a two-bedroom house on a shady, upscale New Iberia street with manicured lawns and shiny cars. The town seemed to preserve the traditional values of the forties and fifties in which Bob believed. Mellowed by years of an affluent lifestyle, Shelley had agreed to the move. Sadness only clouded Bob's eyes when news about Cuba was shown on television, or when his second son, performing decently in school, flatly turned down his overtures to play touch football or baseball in the backyard.

One of the calculated moves he made to gain status in the new community was to invest $10,000 in Southern Star common shares. At his first shareholders' meeting, he became acquainted with sugar's bleak future. He learned of the adverse factors nationwide. Per capita consumption was declining because of health considerations. Dangerous sugar cane diseases had reappeared; soda pop plants were switching to isoglucose; inflation-fueled price increases did not compensate for the rise in operating costs. Bob also found out about Southern Star's particular troubles. To improve industrial efficiency, new equipment was imperative, but capital was scarce, and layoffs were unavoidable. He volunteered as an unpaid consultant.

Shelley became very active in cultural affairs. She sponsored literary workshops, donated books to New Iberia's libraries, crusaded for a greater appreciation of Cajun culture, and drove to Baton Rouge and New Orleans on occasion to attend significant literary or artistic events.

One evening in 1975, leaving a house on Esplanade Avenue where she had been a dinner guest, Shelley thought that the bearded wino staggering along the sidewalk looked familiar. She stared, clutching the taxi's door handle. It was Chad Broussard. In sixty seconds, her former lover explained that the days of the strip clubs had passed and the dancer he had been living with had eloped. He was now making a living pushing low-grade pot.

The man clung to Shelley like a tick on a cow. He returned to his hometown, became a janitor in New Iberia's high school on his teenage sweetheart's recommendation, and, as cousin Chad, frequently dropped by the Steils' house before taking the late-afternoon bus back to Erath. Having conquered the only thing that she had lacked, Mrs Steil came to be a stunningly beautiful woman in her late thirties who walked through life full of joy and confidence. She had no way of knowing that her lover was bisexual, that the stripper for whom she had been dumped had been named Joe Trent before undergoing a sex change. Nor did she know that during Chad's frequent visits, he had also managed to provide her son with his first homosexual experience.

She found them together in 1978, when Donald was seventeen and she had just turned forty. 'Least you could do is shut the fuck up,' the half-naked Donald had defiantly said to her as Chad slipped on his jeans. 'I know he's been screwing your brains out since day one.' A tripartite agreement on hush-hushing the whole thing was reached in a matter of minutes. In her internal turmoil during the next few days, Shelley found herself choking with indignation, cursing her stupidity, hating her lover. She felt simultaneously ashamed and jealous of Donald. To the dismay of three other teenaged boys, Chad resigned his janitorial position at the high school and returned to New Orleans with a $5000 roll of bills in the pocket of his denim jacket.

Over supper a month later, Donald asked for his father's permission to spend a weekend in New Orleans with three schoolmates. Bob acquiesced and slipped him a hundred, attributing his wife's blush to the advent of menopause that she had been recently complaining about. Donald came home on Sunday evening and sneered at his mother before kissing Bob. The following Tuesday, Shelley called her husband at his office and told him that she was on her way to Baton Rouge for an Ibsen play and a late dinner. She would spend the night at a friend's house and drive back on Wednesday morning. It was her standard behavior, so nobody linked her to the discovery of Chad Broussard's corpse in the port of New Orleans five days after she had returned – nobody except Donald Steil.

In an icy tone she'd never before used, Shelley told her son, 'I want you so deep in the closet that people think you're wallpaper.' That same day she started hitting the bottle in earnest.

Bob Steil managed to turn Southern Star's ill fortunes around and became its majority stockholder and CEO in 1985. Dabbling in real estate, he came to possess one of New Iberia's mansions, fully renovated before the family moved in. But success in business ventures seemed to be inversely proportional to the happiness of his private life. Still attracted to Shelley and sexually active in his sixties, he was only able to make love with his plastered wife five or six times a year. Two half-hearted attempts with whores during business trips had been total fiascoes.

During the late eighties, his mind somehow turned to memories of Carmen Steil and Elliot. Guilt had forced him to stop writing to them in 1960. The financial link was broken when remittances were suspended by the US government. Back in '69, a few months before passing away, his mother had mailed him the new Havana address of his ex-wife and first son, but Shelley had stolen the letter from his desk. Bob assumed that he had lost it. In 1990, he became aware that he was fast approaching the final years of his life. He felt too tired to face the impending problems that threatened Southern Star. Life at home was soured by an alcoholic wife and by a son who only paid attention to him when pressed for money. He decided to compensate Carmen and Elliot in the only way he could.

Donald didn't want to leave Louisiana after high school, so he moved to Baton Rouge and took up law at LSU. For fear of being found out by his right-wing friends and to protect himself from AIDS, he carried on a safe, surreptitious, and stable relationship with a chemistry major, all the while sharing brief trysts with a few women for the sake of appearances. Looking for a stepping stone from which to launch into a political career, Donald set his sights on the FBI. It offered the predominantly male environment that he loved to be immersed in, and the unconfirmed news reports charging that the FBI's founder had been a lifelong fruit made it seem all the more alluring. In his senior year he asked for an interview with campus recruiters, passed all tests with flying colors, and joined the Bureau.

Bob Steil had a heart attack on October 23, 1992. He was sixty-six and frightened. In his hospital bed, with tears streaming down his cheeks, he reassured Shelley that she was the love of his life and made her promise that, when he died, she would do everything in her power to find Carmen and Elliot Steil, and let them know that he had bequeathed half of his assets to them in atonement for his desertion. Shelley was stunned. The will was the only important matter her husband had kept from her since their marriage.

Under the combined forces of willpower and greed, Shelley Steil quit drinking overnight. Bob recovered. The following March she sought the legal advice of Anthony Gaylord in New Orleans, and learned about the difficulty of proving that a testator had been mentally incompetent when a will was drafted if his medical record contained no prior history of psychiatric disorder. And how could it be proven that her husband had acted under coercion or fraud when he hadn't even seen his first wife and son for over thirty years? Courts demand solid evidence, Gaylord cautioned.

A poised Mrs Steil spent the spring, summer, and fall of 1993 thinking things over. Strictly following doctor's orders, Bob was doing fine. Shelley invited Donald over for Christmas, but her son couldn't make it. She reached him by phone in January of 1994.

'Listen, and listen good, Don,' Shelley said. 'If the President of the United States orders you to spend next Monday morning at the White House, tell him you can't. Tell him next Monday morning you have to discuss urgent family business with your mother. Tell him that in ten years you may be begging in the streets while he's living on his fat pension. Get here a little after nine. We should spare your daddy from unpleasant matters.'

*　　*　　*

Fourteen months later, on March 3, 1995, a Friday, another mother and son meeting had taken place in the living room of the New Iberia mansion. Donald made a full report on his Miami findings and actions; a last-resort plan had been agreed upon.

The sun was still out while Donald once again mulled over his mother's sense of drama. Shelley sat in her favorite club chair. Behind it, a sweeping staircase led to the top floor. On its landing, a stained-glass window faced west. It showed a very simple escutcheon with a silver strip at its top, a navy-blue field, and, at its center, a golden lion standing on its back paws threatening an unseen prey with its front claws. The motto read *In Hoc Signo Vincis*. Years earlier, Donald had consulted a Latin–English dictionary out of curiosity and had translated it roughly into *With This Sign You Shall Be Victorious*. As far back as he could remember, his mother had always sat on the same chair in the living room. Between noon and sunset, visitors on the leather sofa would register how the gleaming lion seemed to float protectively above her. The blue halo surrounding the host's rinsed black hair added another mystical touch.

Donald occasionally envied his mother. He was certain that his genes were encoded with her feminine poise and charm, and he felt proud of this. He admitted to himself that he lacked her brains and courage, which would have been extremely useful in his line of work. On the other hand, Donald considered it a blessing that his artistic sensibility was but a small fraction of hers; artists got carried away too frequently.

Shelley wore sky-blue and ivory-striped slacks, a black cardigan over a white turtleneck, and sneakers. To a casual acquaintance his mother would appear to be her usual self, but since his arrival fifty minutes earlier, Donald had perceived repressed disgust in the corners of her mouth, anxiety in her slightly knitted brow. The contempt that gleamed permanently in her eyes whenever she talked with her son seemed to have magnified.

'Okay, I guess that's all,' Shelley said. 'Rooms at the Eden Roc.'

'No objection.'

'There's one more small detail I'd like to discuss.'

Donald had slid to the edge of the sofa to crush a cigarette on a Bohemian glass ashtray. His mother's words made him stop midway. 'Which is?'

A smile waltzed on her lips as she spoke. 'All this bullshit about Louisiana inheritance law, added to your present frustration and ambition and the passage of time, might lead you to consider doing to me what you were unable to do in Miami.'

Donald grinned. He snuffed out his cigarette, slid back, and crossed his legs before lifting his eyes to Shelley. 'Which is what you so efficiently did to Dad, Chad Broussard, and God knows how many others.'

She sipped from a glass of apple juice and ran the tip of her tongue across her lips. 'Single-handedly. Not with a bugger in tow.'

Donald's grin froze. 'To be perfectly honest, the idea has crossed my mind,' he said, only half-mockingly.

'Absolutely,' Shelley said, returning the glass to a side table. 'But you should know I've taken the necessary precautions.'

Donald tilted his head and squinted at his mother before speaking. 'Hey, just a minute. Maybe you've developed a taste for it. Maybe it's the other way around. Are you planning to do me in?'

'No. You're out of my reach, and we live in different worlds.

Then there's the rather minor matter that I still can't get over the fact that I carried you in here.' Shelley patted her belly. 'But I'm not asking you to spare my life. Just be aware you wouldn't get a penny if you did. What you'd get would be a nice lethal injection if, like you just said in your pitiful slang, you did me in.'

Donald Steil stood and buttoned his tweed jacket. 'See you at the airport Monday morning, dear mother.'

'Have a nice weekend, my beloved son.'

'Of a bitch,' Donald replied.

13

The teacher left the safe house at noon on March 2 after Scheindlin told him that the meeting with Shelley Steil, her son Donald, and their lawyer had been scheduled for 11.00 a.m. the following Monday. He spent the next thirty-six hours at Fidelia's. She hadn't missed a day at the office, had stayed up late most nights, and was utterly exhausted, so Steil gave her an abridged version of his ordeal, leaving out Ed Steil's murder, something he considered too gruesome to share with her. Initially Fidelia was speechless. Then, for half an hour, she forgot her personal tragedy and launched a very legal, detailed interrogation. Steil was explaining Scheindlin's fundamental role when Papa vomited.

Fidelia slept soundly on Thursday and Friday nights, having finally learned the reasons for Elliot's strange behavior. Her mother cared for her ailing husband all of Friday, while Steil cleaned the house and cooked. Cuban neighbors drove Dani to school. Back from his 7.00 to 3.00 job as a kitchen hand in a nursing home, Mario sat with Papa until 9.00 that evening, then had supper and hit the sack. In the small hours of the morning, the teacher dozed on a rocking chair by the sick man's bed. On Saturday morning, sexually aroused and realizing that it was neither the time nor the place, the teacher masturbated in the shower. After breakfast, he took a taxi to his apartment, where he changed into fresh clothes before picking up his car in the parking lot.

Considering the day of the week, Steil first drove to Dole's Boat Yard and hit the jackpot on his first try – the man he was looking for was getting ready to go fishing. For once he looked conventional, wearing khaki shorts, a sweatshirt, and a

San Diego Padres baseball cap. He took off his sunglasses and peered at Steil from his runabout. Unsure of what the teacher wanted, the man filed away the smile he had been ready to flash. Steil approached the boat.

'Hi, Hair.'

'Hi, brother. Thought you had rowed back to Cuba.'

'How're you doing?'

'You came here just to know how I'm doing?'

Steil grinned and let his gaze roam. 'You mad at me, Hair?'

Hairball shook his head. 'No. But I thought we had an understanding, we were doing business. Then you vanish into thin air. And I mean *vanish*. You moved, quit your job, never went to the places you used to. That's not the Cuban way.'

Steil felt the sun on his face. 'Something came up,' he said.

'Maybe you're a Castro agent.'

The teacher roared with laughter, and the ice was broken. Hairball put his sunglasses back on and invited Steil to jump in. 'Wanna beer?'

'No, thanks.'

'I forgot, yeah. Okay, what's the deal?'

Steil scratched the tip of his nose. Boarding a boat – even if it was moored – made him a little nervous.

'I wanna tail.'

'A what?'

'I wanna guy who's not a private dick, but knows how to follow people. To tag someone for a few hours and report where the person goes. There's nothing to it. I'll pay cash and don't need receipts, records, or any written reports. He doesn't need to know my name; I'll forget his. Know someone who can do this for me?'

Hairball stared at Steil. 'You a fucking Castro agent?'

Steil smiled broadly. 'C'mon, Hair.'

Hairball fixed his gaze on his deck shoes for a few moments. 'I know a dozen people could do this for you, maybe two dozen. Need a man or a woman?'

'I need a tight-lipped person with a lousy memory.'

Hairball tapped out a number on his cellular. He told the other party that a client named Mr Blue Jacket and Aquamarine Polo Shirt wanted to see him. The connection was broken, and Hairball gave Steil the address of an 8th Street greasy spoon and the meeting time he had arranged. The tail would be wearing a tie with diagonal stripes in different shades of blue. The teacher shook hands with Hairball and thanked him before disembarking. The ringleader watched him leave with a little sadness. Good driver, he thought.

From the boatyard, Steil drove to a supermarket and filled the trunk of his car with groceries to replenish Mama's dwindling reserves. He made small talk with Fidelia while she ironed, then ate a sandwich with a red soda and left a few minutes later.

A little after 1.oo, across a Formica-topped table, Steil faced a dignified-looking Cuban senior citizen. The man had seen better days. His black suit was old, the shirt's collar was frayed, and the wide, striped tie was a relic from the seventies; however, each article was spotless. The clean-shaven old man's gray hair had been combed straight back; deep furrows lined his forehead.

'You mind if I get straight to the point?' Steil asked.

'Not at all, mister.' The man's long white fingers played with an after-lunch cigar. His gray-green eyes held the boredom of those who have seen too much.

'Okay. Monday morning, by phone, I tell you the address of a building. A few minutes before eleven, three people will go in, take an elevator to the fourteenth floor, attend a meeting, and then leave. I don't know how long the meeting will last – an hour, two, three, nobody really knows. When they leave I want you to follow them and tell me where they went. That's all.'

'This has to do with Cuban politics?'

'No.'

'Fine. 'Cause if it did, I wouldn't touch it. Descriptions, please.'

'There will be two men and a woman. I don't know the woman's age, she might be . . . anywhere between her early forties and late sixties. One of the men is in his mid-thirties, the other . . . is probably over forty, maybe older.'

'You've never seen them?'

'Nope.'

The old man brought the cigar to his lips, puffed on it, and stared at it as if he'd never seen one before. 'Is this place a hotel, an apartment building, or an office building?'

'Office building.'

'So, on Monday morning hundreds will probably be going in and out.'

'Probably.'

'And you're asking me to identify these people based on what you've just said?'

Steil nodded.

'The building has a lobby people can sit in and wait and read papers?'

'It does.'

'Suppose they split up when they come out. Who should I follow?'

'The lady,' Steil responded without the slightest hesitation.

Thirty seconds later, the teacher concluded that it was either the man's first cigar or the most beautiful one he had ever seen. Finally the tail moved his gaze to the client. 'Three yards if I get the job done. One if I don't. A hundred now. Two more when I tell you where they went.'

Steil produced two fifty-dollar bills from his wallet, placed them on the table, and locked eyes with the old man. 'Do your best. Here's the phone number where you can reach me at two that same day,' he said, pulling out his ball-point. 'To collect the other two C's, you gotta return this napkin to me.'

The old man smiled and again stared at his cigar. The teacher got up and left.

Sunday morning, Papa was admitted to the Jackson Memorial Hospital suffering great pain. Relief spread across his face after the first shot of morphine. Fidelia and her mother, assisted by Steil, spent nearly an hour filling out forms. After completing the paperwork, the grieving Mama sat on a waiting room chair, and her daughter and Steil distanced themselves a few yards. Leaning against the hallway wall, arms crossed over her chest and looking at the floor, Fidelia reflexively shook her head.

The teacher searched for her eyes, gently lifting her chin. 'What's the matter?'

'I've typed claims. It's how Bencomo makes a living,' she said. 'But it's worse than I thought. The primary concern here is to make sure the hospital can't be sued if a patient falls from a stretcher. It's scary. In Cuba, when Mama's gall bladder was removed, we didn't sign a thing.'

'And you didn't pay a cent. But if something went wrong, you wouldn't have been able to sue the doctor or the hospital.'

'But you said Papa's care wouldn't cost us anything.'

'The lady said so. I just translated.'

'How come we could sue for malpractice even if we don't pay?'

Two orderlies passed and Steil smiled at them.

'Because the federal government pays for Papa's care. This is the county hospital. Doctors here take what the lady called assignments. She said the government has a price list for each test or medication your father gets and foots the bill. It's a privilege for exiled Cubans who got here before last September. If we were from some other country, I don't know who would pay for all this. Since the hospital gets paid, you could sue if your father doesn't get adequate care.'

Fidelia shook her head in exasperation. 'It's unbelievable. Everything here is so money-oriented.'

Steil caressed her with his eyes.

'Tell me again what she said about sending him home.'

The teacher let out a sigh and raised his eyebrows. 'He will probably be sent home in a couple of days, after tests. You'll have to bring him once or twice a week for treatment, maybe chemotherapy, I don't know.'

'Elio, the first doctor said it was terminal.'

'I know, but I guess they treat him anyway. I mean . . . something has to be done.'

Fidelia stared at the floor. 'I don't want to prolong his suffering. I hope they just keep him sedated. Would he . . . die at home?'

'I don't think so. When he's in his deathbed, they'll bring him here or take him to a hospice.'

She lifted her gaze to Steil and stared. 'I knew this day would eventually come, and I tried to anticipate my reaction. I guess everybody does. But I'm not prepared for this.'

'I understand. My mother died when I was about your age. She had been suffering from severe hypertension for years, and I knew one day she'd . . . just go. When it happened, I still wasn't prepared.'

Fidelia's eyes softened. 'Yes, I know. Let's go back to Mama. She's falling to pieces.'

*   *   *

Over the years, the once-unpredictable Shelley Broussonet had learned to rein in her emotions. Nobody noticed her bewilderment when, at 11.07 on the morning of March 6, she, her son, and their lawyer entered the beautiful meeting room that David Sadow and his partners reserved for wealthy clients. With a polite smile, Shelley shook hands all around, graciously sat on a comfortable chair pulled out by Anthony Gaylord, then took a second look.

The lawyers' courteous preliminary phrases were devoid of meaning, but allowed the opposing factions to furtively study each other. Shelley decided not to ask for a glass of water. The color of his eyes was wrong, and he was slightly taller. But these were the only differences that she could detect. Same hair, forehead, and chin. Identical eyebrows, ears, and Adam's apple. On closer inspection, she noted that his nose was straight instead of upturned, his lips fuller. The resemblance was so striking that, for an instant, she was jolted out of her senses. Following her lawyer's advice, she'd brought an 8" × 10" photo of Bob Steil, taken when he was forty-two. The plan was to show it to everyone in the room if the resemblance was minimal or nonexistent – use it to sow doubts in David Sadow's mind. Now she knew it was useless; in fact, she felt like ripping it up as soon as possible. The adopted code was that she would ask for a glass of water before the meeting was under way if the third beneficiary bore little or no resemblance to her late husband. Ironically, at that moment Shelley's mouth was dry and she craved a sip.

However, she reasoned after recovering, something about this man who was whispering to his lawyer made him look completely unlike his father. Bob Steil — at least the Bob she had known — was a born negotiator, always trying to avoid confrontation and make a deal. The guy on the other side of the table had an adversarial aura. His fixed smile was belied by the hostility lurking in his eyes. The widow also noticed that his fingers, resting interlaced on the tabletop, had turned white at the knuckles, as if he were restraining the urge to lunge at her throat.

Give the devil his due: The spic had reasons to be in that kind of mood. He looked cheap in the slopwork he wore. He was probably a Commie rat who desperately wanted to jump ship the minute it started sinking, but she suspected he was clever and dangerous. The bastard had hunted down Ed Steil, forced him to tell what he knew, and found the trail to New Iberia. He had fired back at Donald in Homestead. He'd survived her inept son's second try, too. This was Sergeant Martínez from the Tampa police. The guy who had somehow been able to learn what not even his uncle had known, that he had a share in Bob's estate. The astute son of a Cuban whore, who went with his story to a fucking Jew, enlisted him into his cause for a big percentage, then signed a deposition that could create a lot of trouble for both her and her son. He had retained the Miami clown and the fat New Orleans sonafabitch introduced as Eastlake, for God's sake!

The words of the disgusting man chomping a cigar suddenly started to sink in: '. . . and seeing no future for himself in Cuba, Mr Steil built a raft and sailed all the way to Key West. He had no idea where his father was, didn't plan to contact him. My client just wanted to start a new life in the United States. He was lucky and made it . . .'

Donald Steil and his mother were unable to keep their impulses in check. Their heads turned simultaneously, seeking eye contact. What do you know, Shelley thought, amazed, the slimeball is hiding Ed's role to steer away from his Sarasota foray! You've got to give it to him!

The teacher didn't suspect it was going to be this bad. As soon as Donald Steil entered the conference room, he recognized the man who had tried to kill him in Homestead. Same height, build, and stride. Only the mirror shades were missing. He leaned over to Sadow and relayed the news. The lawyer nodded briefly. Then Elliot Steil concentrated on the brains behind the operation.

The slut must have been a stunning woman in her youth. Tall, shapely, seductive. So different from his plain-looking mother! Her sure-footed march into the conference room, the way she held her head, the firmness of her handshake, the defiance in her eyes – all bespoke a person pursuing her goals to whatever costs. The fine suit she wore was an unnecessary complement; she would have made the same impression in a bathrobe, Elliot thought. Presumably the South Georgia country boy was no match for this prowling puma. The teacher had met a few of her kind in Cuba: women who fall for scumbags and eat nice guys for breakfast. The sort of female who, for convoluted reasons, loves to be rejected and rejects true love. Elliot Steil realized he was facing the person largely responsible for his childhood traumas; the resigned misery of his mother; the murders of his father, uncle, and Uri; the attempts on his life. He felt his face flush. The veins in his temples throbbed wildly. He lowered his gaze to the glossy tabletop and took a deep breath. The urgent emotions he had experienced after being rescued were driving him again, but reason told him that he would be the first suspect if he avenged his father. What was the question the bitch's lawyer had asked that Sadow was beginning to answer?

'Mr Steil had a neighbor in Cuba who's a very good friend of his,' the lawyer said. 'He called him to let him know he had arrived safely. Gave him his phone number. After a few months, this friend called my client and told him Cuban police had been trying to locate him. Mr Steil thought it had to do with his disappearance and didn't think anything of it. Two or three weeks later, this neighbor called Mr Steil again and reported that a US Office of Interests vice-consul had been trying to contact my client in connection with a will. There was only one person in this whole country who might have willed something to him. That's how he found out.'

'I see,' Gaylord said, nodding. He was feeling his way. In fact, the sixty-two-year-old New Orleans lawyer was the best-dressed and least-informed person in the room. Experience told him that something was wrong. He had tactfully asked his clients if there were any other issues that he should be aware of, obliquely indicating that coming clean with their lawyer would serve their best interests, and clearly suggested finding another firm if for some reason he didn't inspire their full confidence. All that he had gotten for his troubles were innocent looks and pat denials. Anthony Gaylord was getting sick and tired of this case.

'I suppose State was acting on the Court's request,' Sadow added.

'I'm sure it was. The absence of news about Mr Steil's whereabouts and the Cuban government's certification declaring him missing have retarded the whole process.'

'Well,' Sadow beamed and opened his arms in a gesture of shared harmony. 'Now we can move on.'

'By all means,' Gaylord agreed. 'My clients respect but ignore the reasons Mr Steil has for suspecting that there's a conspiracy to deprive him of his father's legacy. We can prove we've done everything in our power to inform Mr Steil and his mother that they were beneficiaries of Mr Robert Steil's will. We also wish for a speedy process as soon as Mr Steil's identity is authenticated.'

Sadow resorted to the story that the teacher had concocted to explain his use of the name Elio Esteil, with almost the same words. Shelley Steil kept a straight face, but her son couldn't suppress a smile and covered his lips with his hand in an effort to look serious and reflective. Anthony Gaylord was taken aback. Proper identification of the beneficiaries was the first step in probate proceedings, and when Shelley suggested raising the matter on the plane, he had presumed that she was merely ignorant of the statutory formalities prescribed for executing wills.

'Well, this is a surprise,' he said, his brow knit, as he turned to his clients. Donald Steil gave him a wide-eyed, innocent look and made a passable pantomime by shrugging his shoulders and pulling down the corners of his mouth to express incomprehension. Shelley's arched left eyebrow and knowing look seemed to say, 'I told you so.'

'We're working on it at top speed,' Sadow volunteered. 'All the required documents are on their way, and we hope to have the matter settled soon.'

Gaylord knew this was his golden opportunity, the turning point. 'I sincerely hope you do. Because we shall petition the court to examine Mr Steil's identity with utmost care. In the meantime . . .' He presented a file to Sadow with photocopies of documents related to the case. The Miami lawyer underscored the liaison that Mr Eastlake from the New Orleans law firm of Smith and Parry would provide in the successful completion of probate proceedings.

Inconsequential chatter preceded the meeting's conclusion, and hypocrisy flowed as it only does in lawyers' offices. The widow and the teacher locked eyes for an instant. She forced a smile and a nod, wondering how to deal with him. He remained impassive, considering that fucking money can make mortal enemies out of people who have never met. Ed Steil had been right. It was nothing personal.

Everybody started getting up.

14

From Sadow's office, Elliot drove to the North Miami Beach warehouse. He made a full report on the meeting, and Scheindlin told him that an expert from the same security service as Max Meisler had been inspecting the company's incoming mail every morning since the day after the letter bomb. Steil asked if the police had turned up any evidence concerning Uri's death. Scheindlin shook his head emphatically. The teacher returned to his apartment for the tail's call nursing the weird feeling that something he hadn't been told about was going on.

He forced down a mouthful and started for the phone when it rang. The bite stuck somewhere between his throat and larynx. He ran back to the kitchen counter, left the half-eaten salami sandwich on it, grabbed the tomato juice carton, and gulped some down. Second ring. It felt as if he were swallowing a giant mango. Tears flowed down his cheeks. Third ring. He pounded on his chest and sipped more juice. The lump reached his esophagus, and the teacher pulled out a handkerchief. Fourth ring. He wiped his tears, blew his nose as he approached the night table, then picked up on the fifth ring.

'Hello.'

'Blue Jacket?'

'Yeah.'

'Subject in her early fifties, around five feet eight, had on a light gray suit, dark hair, fancy gold earrings?'

'That's her.'

'She's at the Eden Roc, room 1509. Took a cab from Brickell. Other two guys stayed on the sidewalk, probably trying to hail a cab, too. It looked like ladies first.'

'Good job. I'm buying a paper napkin for two hundred.'

'I'm selling one.'

'Got a deal. Same place at five?'

'I'll be there.'

Somewhere a handset went back to its place of rest, and Elliot replicated the action before reviewing his options. He had considered two possibilities: The enemy would fly back on the same day, or they would spend the night in Miami. If the tail reported that all three had returned to the airport, his plan would collapse. If they stayed, he would move ahead. He was betting on separate rooms in the same hotel. He now knew where Shelley was staying. Where had the other two gone? A different hotel? Not likely. Well, the brain was within reach. He would have to make some adjustments.

The teacher was deep in thought, slowly flossing his teeth, when the phone rang again. He rinsed his mouth, hoping that it wasn't Fidelia with bad news. Second ring. He wouldn't be able to comfort her if Papa had passed away. Not now, not today. Third ring. He paused after turning off the faucet. Maybe he shouldn't answer. Fourth ring. What was the matter with him? Becoming a sonafabitch, too? She'd understand. He plucked a towel from the towel bar and returned to the night table wiping his chin.

'Hello.'

'Elliot?'

'Yes?'

'This is Shelley Steil.'

The teacher was dumbfounded. But Shelley had surmised he would be and pressed on.

'I'm staying overnight for only one reason: I hope to have a word with you in private. Would you mind?'

Fully on the defensive, the teacher didn't know what to say. 'How'd you find my number?'

'There are ways.'

'Of course. How stupid of me. Where are you staying?'

'Fontainebleau.'

The lying cunt! 'Lady, you think I'm gonna meet you there?'

Short silence. 'No. My suggestion is we agree on some neutral ground, a place where neither of us can suspect there are hidden cameras or microphones . . . or eavesdropping strangers. I've been thinking this over for a few days, and the only way we can feel safe is probably by meeting in a public place. Big crowd, you know? Then we flip a coin or by some other random way agree on a bar or restaurant or hotel lobby where we can talk things over.'

Light was breaking as fast as dawn on the tropics in Steil's brain. 'There's three of you,' he observed.

'Donald and Gaylord must be flying back to New Orleans by now. Their flight was scheduled for two thirty-five.'

Steil let a second slip by. 'What's in it for me?' Their kind of language.

'That's precisely what I want to discuss with you.'

'Okay. I could meet you . . . let's say . . . uh . . . there's a hotel at Collins and 12th, small one. The bar's in . . . sort of an upper level behind the lobby, has big columns. I could be there around nine.'

'Collins and 12th, you said?'

'Right.'

'Here in Miami Beach?'

'That's right.'

'You don't know the name of this hotel?'

'Can't remember.'

'Okay. I'll meet you there. Then we'll agree on some place where we can talk in private. I'll come empty-handed, maybe bring a purse you can check to see that there's nothing in it. I'd appreciate it if you'd do the same.'

'I will. See you at nine,' said Elliot before hanging up.

The teacher sat on the bed and stared at the floor for nearly five minutes. Then he slipped on his blue jacket, dropped the tiny recorder into his pocket, inserted the Colt at the small of his back, and left the apartment.

*   *   *

Steil's first move was to visit an escort service on NW 21st Street. He opted for the least attractive of the twenty-one videotaped girls, paid for one full night, and told the man in charge that he would pick her up at 6.30. He called the Eden Roc from a pay phone and reserved a room under the name on his North Carolina driver's license, Timothy Blackburn. He bought a Stetson and sunglasses at the Northside Shopping Center, drove to the greasy spoon on 8th, paid the tail, and recovered the napkin. Back in his building's parking lot, he locked the Chevy, distanced himself a few blocks, and hailed a cab.

The escort, a brunette, said that her name was Cristina. She looked plain enough in her black outfit: leather jacket over tight turtleneck pullover, leather miniskirt, and high heels. A gold chain hanging across her chest with a medal on it and the red earrings dangling from her ears provided the contrast. Her accent suggested that she was Latin – most likely Mexican, Steil judged by her features. She was trying to be nice without appearing servile, and Steil liked her offhanded approach.

Cristina attempted a quick study of her client, trying to predict what he might ask of her. She had come across very plain-looking dudes who had turned out to be frightful creeps. In the back seat of the taxi, cruising along the Venetian Causeway, Blackburn patted her hand as dusk settled. 'Okay, baby, we're gonna have a great time. We'll stay at the Eden Roc. You like the Eden?'

'It's cool,' was Cristina's enlightening observation.

'Best hotel in town, you ask me. But I'm doing a little business on the side, you know?' Steil suddenly chuckled, acknowledging Meisler's influence.

Cristina smiled politely.

'Right now I'm figuring all the angles, you know, trying to beat the competition, so I'm not gonna be much fun before closing this deal. Then we'll see the show, dance a little, have some fun, okay?'

'Cool.'

'So maybe you'll have to wait for me for a coupla hours in our room. Watch TV, eat supper, have a drink if you feel like it. You mind?'

'No, I don't mind.'

'That's my baby.'

Steil tensed as he entered the hotel lobby. If Shelley happened to be around for some reason and spotted him, the whole scheme would fall apart. He had opted against the sunglasses, fearing that too much camouflage might backfire. He pulled the brim of his hat slightly over his eyes and tried to appear confident as he approached the desk.

With a conspiratorial wink to the clerk, the teacher requested and was granted a room on the sixteenth floor. He paid in advance, tipped the man, then guided Cristina to the elevator bank. The call girl wondered why her client looked so relieved when he entered the metal cage.

In the room, Steil flushed the napkin down the toilet, closed the bathroom door, and took a long shower to kill time and review his plan again. Cristina knitted her brow when he came out fully dressed at 7.55. She had shed her jacket and was watching TV, reclining on an armchair. With the back of her right knee resting on her left kneecap, her legs looked tempting. Bedroom tempting.

'Okay, honey, can I order you something to eat?'

She thought this over for a moment. 'You planning a late dinner?'

'Sure thing.'

'Then just a sandwich and a Coke.'

After calling room service, Steil sat down at the writing

table. He jotted something in block letters on hotel stationery and turned to Cristina, beaming. 'Listen, baby, this is a private joke. I'm gonna punch a number and you read this question to the person who answers the phone. She'll say no, then you read the line at the bottom of the page, this one, see? "Sorry to have bothered you, ma'am," then hang up. It's just a joke. Would you do this little favor for me?'

It was evident that Cristina was not overjoyed by the idea. The client who asked her to rub the handset against her pussy as he masturbated came to her mind. This guy was acting a little strange, and she was afraid of men who didn't jump right to it. Forcing a smile, she uncrossed her legs, stood up, approached the writing table, and read the text. A very private joke, she thought. 'Okay,' she agreed.

Steil muted the volume of the TV with the remote control, stood before the phone to block the girl's view, and punched 1509. He passed the handset to Cristina and put his left arm around her waist, his ear close to hers, pretending to be amused. The woman turned the earpiece out for him. She smelled nice, he thought. Five rings later a woman answered.

'Hello?'

'I beg your pardon, ma'am,' read Cristina, and Steil thought her accent added credibility – the percentage of Latins in the Miami Beach hotel trade was high. 'There's been a mix-up in room service, and I just wanna check if you ordered a sandwich and a Coke.'

'I have not.'

'Sorry to have bothered you, ma'am.'

'No problem.'

Smiling, Steil hung up the phone, rubbed his hands in fake delight, then glanced at his watch. 8.01. He folded the sheet of paper and slipped it into his jacket pocket. Cristina was looking confused, and he took her by the arms, pulling her close.

'I like that perfume.'

Coquettishly: 'You do?'

'Aha. Have some more in your purse?'

'You bet.'

'Will you let me spread a tiny drop in your crotch? To keep smelling it as I kiss and lick your ultimate pleasure spot?'

Cristina was taken aback. Ultimate pleasure spot? For Chrissake! 'Now?' she asked, mischievously raising her left eyebrow.

'No, after I close this fucking deal that's keeping me from having fun with you.'

'Okay.'

'You don't mind?'

'On the contrary, I'd love it.'

'I thought so.'

Steil didn't feel like getting stoked up. Suspense, stress, and the need to improvise conspired against being in the mood, but the abstinence imposed on him over the past several weeks had left him vulnerable. The woman felt his hard-on pressing against her and sighed in relief. An over-educated regular Joe, for Chrissake! She kissed him softly at first, almost gratefully, then put her arms around his neck. Her tongue darted over his gums and front teeth.

Cristina had warm, full lips, and the teacher let himself go for a minute. He sucked and breathed and exhaled and got carried away, then abruptly broke away, smiling. 'Oh, baby, I wish so much I didn't have to leave you now!'

'No hurry. We have the whole night.'

'You bet.'

The teacher pulled a twenty out of his wallet. 'Here. Pay for your snack. I'll wipe off the lipstick and get going.'

At 8.09 Steil took the staircase to the fifteenth floor. He guessed that Shelley wouldn't leave her room before 8.30, but what if she did? Having to choose between losing her and drawing the attention of guests or hotel staff, he opted for the latter. The teacher turned the handle and inspected the hallway. It was empty. He made sure that the layout was the same as the floor above, and verified that room 1509 was where he thought it would be. Shelley had to walk by the staircase door to reach the elevators. The teacher looked for hidden cameras back at the staircase and found none. He folded the sheet of paper to make a doorstop and, through a half-inch crack, watched the first guest amble past.

By 8.35, nine people had crossed Steil's line of vision, and he was growing restless. The voices of two approaching couples gave him fair warning, but the hallway's carpet drowned out footsteps, and lone guests became an unrecognizable blur. Then he had to pull the door open a few inches to make sure that his prey wasn't leaving. The teacher was sweating. He was consulting his watch, fearing that someone from security or maintenance might suddenly open the door, when a figure dressed in gray blinked by the crack. It was Shelley Steil. He pulled out the tape recorder, pushed the record key, and returned it to the same pocket.

The teacher entered the hallway. A well-dressed young couple were waiting for the elevator, whispering and trying unsuccessfully to suppress laughter. Shelley was ten yards away from them. Steil hot-footed. He firmly grabbed the widow's elbow and turned her around. The wide-eyed Shelley was rendered speechless.

'I forgot something, let's go back,' Steil said loudly enough for the couple to hear as he pressed the barrel of the Colt into Shelley's belly.

Had the young couple looked closely, been interested in their surroundings, they would have noticed that the middle-aged woman was being half-dragged by her escort. They would have seen her gaping profile as she stared at the man as if he were an apparition. They might have even heard him saying, 'This ain't the Fontainebleau, honey.' But the young couple planning the third night of their honeymoon could not care less.

The teacher stopped before room 1509 and let Shelley loose. 'Open up,' he ordered. She held the key card in her right hand, a tiny purse in her left. Her face was chalk-white.

'How'd you find out?' she asked.

'There are ways. Open up.'

'Listen, take it easy. Let's talk it over.'

Steil shifted the gun to his left hand and snatched the card away from her.

'Keep cool!' she said, and the teacher thought it was a strange comment under the circumstances. *She* should stay cool.

Cutting her off with his body, Steil inserted the card, operated the handle, and pushed Shelley in. He slipped the card into his pants pocket, then returned the gun to his right hand. As in his own room, the bathroom door was to the right of a ten-foot-long hallway opening into the bedroom. He could see a drawer, an armchair, and drapes. Elliot relaxed. The worst part was over. Perhaps he would find out what he wanted to know, maybe get it on tape.

As Elliot stepped inside, Donald Steil emerged from the bedroom section which the teacher couldn't see. The coatless Donald frowned in confusion at his mother before taking in the teacher. For an instant he froze, then went for the gun in his shoulder holster. With his free arm, Steil put a stranglehold on Shelley and retraced a step while lifting his own revolver. His back pushed the door closed. His hat fell to the floor.

'NOOO!' Shelley screamed at the top of her lungs.

Donald hesitated.

'KEEP COOL. THINK.'

Steil cocked the Colt.

An anguished woman's voice cried, '*Ay, mi madre*,' and the teacher thought he was hearing things.

'Either of you fires a shot, we lose everything, go to jail!'

Shelley exclaimed. 'Think, goddammit, think. Let's work this out!'

'*Ay, mi madre.*'

It sounded too familiar. 'Fidelia?' he called

A second slipped by. 'Elio?'

15

The teacher positioned the barrel on Shelley's temple, propelled her forward, then moved to the end of the tiny anteroom. Fidelia lay on a twin bed, feet bound together with duct tape, arms free. A room-service cart with the remains of a meal stood on the other side of the bed.

'Elio!'

'Don't move!' he barked at her in Spanish.

'Elio!'

'Shut up!'

In a fraction of a second the teacher deduced what had transpired. A kidnapping. They wanted to force him to renounce his share. The slimeball had seen them together, staked them out.

'You filthy sonafabitch,' Steil hissed to Donald as the revolver left Shelley's temple and centered on her son.

'Cool off,' Shelley ordered.

'Shut your fucking mouth, you cheap slut,' he commanded, panting.

'No, I won't. You have to hear me out.' The widow's voice sounded half-choked. She had dropped the purse and was grabbing Steil's left arm with both hands, pulling on it to relieve the pressure. 'We weren't gonna hurt her. She's just . . . We wanted to . . . make a trade.'

'For my share.'

'No. For this paper you wrote implicating us.'

The teacher kept his eyes on Donald. 'Put your gun on the floor.'

'No,' Donald said.

'Goddamit, put your gun on the floor, or I'll kill her.'

'Make my day.'

Shelley, half-aphasic, choked up, 'Let me breathe.'

'For God's sake, Elio,' Fidelia shrieked in Spanish, 'you're strangling her!'

Steil eased the pressure.

Donald kept his weapon pointed at the struggling pair, both hands gripping the butt, arms outstretched, fractionally correcting his aim as their feet shifted.

Shelley swallowed and took a deep breath. 'Listen, you two, listen to me,' she gasped and rattled. 'If one of you fires a shot, we lose everything, go to jail. Shoot him, Donald, his will and deposition will get us indicted. You'll spend the rest of your life in prison. You kill one of us, Elliot, both of us, you'll be charged with murder. You should've called the police, not come on your own. There's no way you can walk. Not with so many people knowing what's between us. Think.'

Staring at each other, both men considered her words.

'Nothing has happened to her, Elliot,' Shelley went on. 'Force was not used. She came of her own free will, believing that her boss needed her here to do a job. Donald, you told me she doesn't understand a word of English, so she can't be a witness to this conversation. This is between the three of us.'

'Shut up,' Steil snapped, wanting to disagree but finding it difficult.

'No, I won't,' Shelley insisted, and the half-brothers silently acknowledged that she had their full attention. 'We needed her to make you see that we can't live the rest of our lives fearing you will die in an accident and we will get charged with murder. Okay, it was a mistake. Okay, I apologize. Donald apologizes.'

'Fuck you, Mother.'

The intensity of the antagonism surprised Steil.

'Listen, Elliot. From now on, no more dirty tricks, I promise. We'll split the money and . . .'

Shelley gasped as she was forced toward the beds. She managed to sidestep awkwardly.

'Free her,' Steil ordered, hyperventilating, not letting Donald out of his sight or loosening his hold.

'I can't.'

Steil unwound his arm and seized the collar of her suit. Shelley was able to bend over to Fidelia's ankles. The teacher crouched behind his human shield. For a few moments, the sound of ripping duct tape was the only noise.

'Done,' said the widow, and straightened up. Steil did the same.

'It was your idea!' Donald croaked at his mother. Fidelia started to rise.

'Get behind me,' the teacher said in Spanish.

The lawyer did as she was told. Steil felt her trembling hands on his back.

'Now, you listen to me. Both of you,' the teacher said. 'I'm pretty certain you killed my father.'

'She did,' contributed a sneering Donald, now aiming his gun squarely at Shelley's chest.

Steil's peripheral vision included the back of the widow's head. She stood completely still.

'Maybe she did,' the teacher continued. 'Maybe both of you were in on it. But killing you won't bring him back, and killing you . . . ain't worth a day in jail. You're right, Shelley. This is a no-win situation. So, we're leaving now. I'm taking you with me, Shelley. You'll see us off at the lobby. Stay here, Donald. Don't try anything.'

Side-stepping and walking backward, the threesome reached the main door.

Steil kicked the Stetson out of his way. Addressing Fidelia in Spanish, he said, 'Open the door, go out, and tell me if there are people in the hallway.'

She complied. 'No one.'

Steil exited, grabbing Shelley before closing the door and

pocketing the gun. He guided the women back to the staircase door, opened it, and forced Shelley to go up. Fidelia was right behind him. The teacher felt his legs get more rubbery with each step. On the sixteenth floor he pushed the elevators' down button, eyes on the staircase door, gripping the gun in his pocket. Shelley rearranged her hair, took a deep breath, and, holding her head high, stared at the sliding metal door. Fidelia, still stunned, shifted her gaze from Steil to the widow.

'How'd you find out we had her?' Shelley asked coolly, in control once again.

Steil smirked. 'Lady, that's something you'll never know.'

Shelley nodded as if confirming a suspicion. 'No watch to guide you this time.'

'A little bird,' Steil said, simmering down. He felt like guffawing. If she only knew.

Ten seconds of silence passed. 'You resemble him,' Shelley said.

Something inside of Steil snapped, and he swallowed hard. 'Shut the fuck up.'

Shelley nodded reflexively. 'I know you'll come after us. Maybe a year from now, maybe in five years, but you'll come after us. To settle the score.'

Steil pondered this for a second and knew she was wrong. If he hadn't shot them tonight, he never would. Not in cold blood. But he kept it to himself. One of the two elevator indicators behind them lit up and dinged. Two seconds later the elevator door slid open.

Traversing the lobby, close to the exit, Steil took hold of Fidelia's elbow and ordered Shelley to stop. He searched in his pocket for the recorder and showed it to Shelley without a word. The woman closed her eyes for a second and breathed deeply. Feeling protected, Fidelia was giving her the eye.

The teacher let out the parting shot he had prepared: 'I hope you die after six months of agony – some rotten cancer eating away at you, while you pee and shit in bed, completely paralyzed, depending on uncaring orderlies who treat you like a sack of potatoes. And that son of yours will throw the party of his life when he learns you're kicking the bucket.' He showed her the card key to her room.

The widow lifted an eyebrow and snatched the key. 'The resemblance is only external. Believe me, that's a compliment.'

Shelley then turned and sauntered toward the bank of elevators.

*　　*　　*

On their way back to Miami in a cab, heads pressed together, they listened to the tape. Ninety percent of the five-minute uproar was intelligible. When it ended, Fidelia, speaking in a low tone to prevent the driver from hearing, explained how the stranger had waved a badge at her. He smiled a lot and read to her from a piece of paper: *'Bencomo necesita usted urgente por media hora'* — 'Bencomo needs you urgently for half an hour.' His accent was lousy. He had approached Fidelia on the sidewalk at a few minutes after 5.00, in an impressive limousine. Her boss always left around 4.00 and never said where he was going, so the message seemed credible. He had never asked her to work overtime, but it was only for half an hour, maybe a little more. She was being summoned by an officer of the law. What could she do? Risk her job? Get a citation for disobedience? When she noticed that they were headed for Miami Beach, she realized it was going to take longer. What the heck is Bencomo doing in this hotel? she had thought as they entered the Eden Roc. In the room, she looked around before asking about him. The attractive woman who opened the door tried to explain something to her in English. She didn't understand a word, and suspected something weird was going on, so she made a start for the door. The sonafabitch blocked her way and grabbed her. She struggled and screamed for help. The guy's hand was removed from her lips only a fraction of a second before a strip of tape prepared by the

277

woman sealed them. She was thrown on the bed, where they bound her hands and feet.

After a while, trying to figure out what was happening, she realized that the strangers could be the widow and half-brother trying to snuff Elio. They appeared to be the right ages. FBI people carried badges like the man who had approached her, and in addition, the other two beneficiaries were supposed to fly over that same morning. Were these people crazy? Why her? To pressure Elio, of course. She would go to the police when this was all over. The limousine driver was a witness, if he hadn't been an accomplice. And then it came to her: She wouldn't be able to accuse anyone from her grave. She couldn't describe to Elio how scared she was, like never before in her life, not even on the raft.

Her captors didn't talk much among themselves, but when they did, their words snapped in mutual contempt, and their glances reflected scorn. At one point the phone rang, and it startled them both. The lady answered it, uttered a couple of words, and hung up. She said something to the man, and he looked relieved. The waiter who brought supper was not allowed into the room. After some threatening signs, they removed Fidelia's strips of tape, twenty or twenty-five minutes before Elio crashed in. She forced down a few bites of the food they offered. When she went to the toilet, the door was left open so that Shelley could monitor her. She managed to convince them through gestures that she would keep quiet, and this time only her feet were bound. 'Nada le pasará' – 'Nothing will happen to you' – the woman said to her as she was getting ready to leave. Fidelia wanted to believe her, yet knew she shouldn't.

At Fidelia's place, after a worn-out Mama gratefully accepted the suggestion that she sleep on the couch for a few hours, the couple conversed while keeping a dozing Papa company. Steil made it clear that he hadn't known she had been kidnapped. He just wanted to pounce on the slut and threaten her a little to get her reaction on tape. The rescue had been an act of blind luck. Fidelia wanted to know how he had found out where they were. The teacher told her about the tail and Shelley's call. Tilting her head, she examined Steil as if he were a different person, something new shining in her eyes.

Why couldn't they go to the police? she asked. She had been abducted! She wasn't inheriting a penny. The audio tape was proof. From what she understood, a tape was inadmissible as evidence in a court of law if recorded by a private person, but maybe she was wrong. Elio should consult this hotshot lawyer of his and find out if she could charge these people with kidnapping.

The teacher sighed and revealed the part of the story that she didn't know: Ed Steil's murder. Fidelia covered her mouth in astonishment. The widow and son would find a way to let the police know that he had assaulted his uncle, Steil continued; perhaps they would suggest that he'd shot Ed a few days later. Supermarket records could prove that he was in Miami on the night of the murder, but a librarian and a hotel clerk could place him in Sarasota on the evening of January 7. Ed Steil had declared $53,000 in jewels stolen, and he would be charged with robbery, too. Like Shelley and Donald Steil, he'd go to prison.

In a nutshell, everybody was guilty of something. What his uncle had done to him in Havana couldn't be proven. He had told the INS that he had sailed from Cuba of his own free will, on a raft that had sunk on the high seas. Now a member of the family that rescued him was claiming that she had been abducted by an FBI agent trying to blackmail her lover? And the white knight in shining armor had rescued her? The whole story was too bizarre.

This was why they had acted so boldly, Steil argued. A last desperate attempt, short of murder, which was the only crime they couldn't get away with for fear that the deposition annexed to his will might prompt federal authorities to open an investigation. They knew he couldn't go to the police. The slut had admitted that the purpose of kidnapping Fidelia was to force him to destroy the deposition. Well, they had failed. It was over. Or so he hoped.

Physically and emotionally drained, they sat in silence by Papa, registering the deep grumbling from somewhere in his chest every time he inhaled. It was the first person Steil had watched die since his mother, and he felt sorry for the man. He agreed with Fidelia: Mankind would gradually reach a consensus on sparing human beings this torment.

'Go to bed, Fidelia. It's late. I'll stay here the rest of the night.'

When he felt certain that he was the only person awake in the rented house, he looked up the Eden Roc's number, tapped it out, and asked for room 1611 in a low tone.

'Hello?'

'Cristina?' he whispered.

'Yes?'

'Honey, I'm sorry. I can't make it. You may leave if you want to.'

'What?'

'Something came up.'

'Why are you whispering?'

'Can't raise my voice now.'

'What time is it?'

'Five minutes to one.'

'Holy shit. I fell asleep.'

'You can leave now. Return the key to the desk. Or you can stay the night if you like.'

'I think I'll stay. This is nice.'

'Enjoy. Thank you, baby.'

'Some other time?'

'Sure. Bye now.'

'Bye, bye.'

16

After escorting Fidelia to Bencomo's office the next morning, Steil went to his apartment, washed and changed clothes, then drove to the North Miami Beach warehouse. Scheindlin was busy with some clients, and the teacher had to wait a full hour standing in the central drive-in passage before the visitors left and the old man waved him in. Since two members of the staff shared the same office space and privacy was a must, Steil shook his head. Scheindlin left the cubicle and joined him.

'What's new?' he asked.

Steil gave him a ten-minute summary.

At the end of the story, Scheindlin chuckled and looked up at the ceiling as if asking for some heavenly intercession. He scratched the top of his head.

'. . . and my question is, should I tell Sadow all this?'

Scheindlin shook his head. 'You agreed with him not to press charges against these people. So what's the logic in telling him you got a split personality, Elliot Steil by day and Rambo by night? That you can't keep your word and worked out a plan to sneak into this woman's hotel room and scare the living shit out of her?'

'Sir, they kidnapped my fiancée.'

'Oh, yeah? And you knew they were gonna kidnap her?'

'If I hadn't . . .'

Scheindlin raised his hand. When the teacher fell silent, he stared at him for as long as his eyes permitted him to. Steil realized that his boss was fuming, albeit in a very controlled way.

'Listen,' Scheindlin said, 'the fact that you were able to

thwart this stupid kidnapping doesn't excuse your childish behavior. Had you rescued your fiancée after you learned she had been kidnapped, I wouldn't be tongue-lashing you. You managed to pull a favorable outcome from a legal disaster. Suppose you had been caught. Suppose a shot had been fired. Sadow would have pulled out of the case. Who were you going to turn to for legal and financial support? Not to me, you can be sure of that.'

The teacher brooded, looking at the toe caps of his shoes. Scheindlin turned to his right and marched along the passage, holding his hands behind his back, eyes on the floor. A surprised Steil followed him.

'I'm backing you 'cause I feel you deserve it,' Scheindlin continued. 'But don't overstep, Elliot.'

The old man kept moving. He looked like an undersized bull charging ahead. At the end of the warehouse, he stopped and faced the teacher. 'Okay. I'll get somebody to keep an eye on those two stupid assholes. Report where they go, what they do, who they see. You stay out of their way. Do you understand what I'm saying to you, Elliot Steil?'

'Yes, sir.'

'Next time Rambo possesses you, you're on your own, okay?'

'Okay.'

'And when those two leave Miami, get rid of your guns.'

'I will.'

'Okay.'

Scheindlin turned and started retracing his steps. The teacher followed suit.

'You said Eden Roc?'

'Yes, sir.'

'I forgot the room number.'

'1509.'

'Okay.'

*

That same afternoon, a little before 4.00, just as Steil was getting ready to pick up Fidelia at Bencomo's, his phone rang. It was Scheindlin.

'Our friends left at one fifteen, Delta flight to New Orleans.'

'Well, that's . . . ahhh, fine. Thank you, sir.'

'You still want to work for me?'

'You try to fire me, and Rambo will come after you.' Steil thought he heard Scheindlin emit a repressed chuckle.

'Be here tomorrow at eight,' Scheindlin said.

*　　*　　*

One week later, a very tired Donald Steil tossed his mail on the writing desk near the portable PC and printer in the living room of the one-bedroom Baton Rouge apartment he had rented in 1993. The envelopes fanned out. One revealing the NRA's logo caught his eye.

The FBI agent marched to the bedroom, tripped the light switch, took off his coat, and loosened his tie before removing his gun from its shoulder holster and placing it on a bedside table. He emptied his pockets, undressed, and headed to the bathroom to take a shower. While shaving, he remembered that he was running low on his preferred lubricant. He should shoplift some before next weekend. He never bought such a product.

The agent slapped water on his face, toweled it dry, and took two steps back. Turning to his right and rolling his neck to face the medicine-cabinet mirror, he admired his buttocks for two or three seconds, then nodded approvingly. A hundred squats every morning did wonders, he concluded.

Wearing only furry slippers, Donald strode to the kitchen, where he poured himself a glass of orange juice. Standing by the sink, as he slowly sipped, he recalled the previous weekend: he and Burt in the wilderness, trekking, fishing, and bird-watching, feeling as if they were the only two free souls in the world. Not having to fear hidden cameras or mikes, they could behave like the loving couple they were. He had managed to put the Miami fiasco, his half-brother, and his demanding mother behind him. At night, inside the tent, they delayed what they both wanted for as long as they could, cooing to each other, caressing, massaging, kissing, sucking, until their urges became irrepressible. He prepared himself, then Burt filled him so wide and deep that he thought he might rip open. Thank heaven for lubricants, he thought.

Donald shivered with excitement, finished his juice, and returned to the living room. He pulled out the chair to his writing desk, sat, and produced a letter opener from a drawer. After turning on the lamp, he began inspecting his correspondence. The first three envelopes were easily identifiable junk mail, and he dropped them unopened into the wastebasket. The fourth was the letter with the NRA logo. As an active member, Donald received four newsletters a year, generally a few printed pages with fresh information on the local chapter. He raised the envelope to the lamp's light out of habit and glimpsed at it.

A bomb went off when he slit it open.

The blast threw him back, and his head smashed against the floor. He regained consciousness a few seconds later. The chair was by his side. The lamp was nowhere to be seen, but lights burning in the other rooms provided enough illumination to survey the damage. The PC and printer were on the floor, the desk slightly angled. Agonizing pain coursed through his body when he rose on his hands and knees, causing him to convulse. His head hanging, he looked down at himself. Blood gushed from his torso. Something dangled just below his sternum. He collapsed onto the soaked floor in panic, turned over slowly, and realized that he was going to die. Nobody bleeding so heavily could last more than a few minutes. And the stench, for Chrissake, what smelled so revolting? He grimaced and forced air out from his nostrils. The stink reminded him of putrid meat. Suddenly it came to him. Pathologists become accustomed to it. He had smelled it at morgues. Coming from him? Coming from the same body that had given him so much pleasure? Would he lose the great orgasms that he lived for, the feeling of being one of the chosen few, the money that was coming his way, everything? Tears began to flow. The pain eased considerably. He thought he should dial 911 and tried to move. He couldn't. Not a single muscle worked, but his brain functioned with amazing clarity as he gazed at the white ceiling.

His own mother? No, she wouldn't. Or would she? No, no, she wouldn't. Greg? Maybe. Greg had threatened him. But Greg didn't know the first thing about bombs and didn't have the money to hire an expert. The Unabomber? Michigan militia? National Alliance? A Silent Brotherhood or Davidian survivor? He had been working the ultra-right and the fundamentalists since 1985. Maybe the fucking Miami hebe? Donald coughed, and something seeped out of his wounds. Intestine? He didn't want to know. His mouth filled with something, and he spat it out. Orange juice? Orange juice didn't taste salty. When would this agony end?

It ended half a minute later.

*　　*　　*

Papa went quietly the following morning, Wednesday, March 15. His condition had started to deteriorate rapidly forty hours earlier, and he was taken to Jackson Memorial in critical condition. Resigned to the impending outcome, his relatives were not shocked when they were informed that he had passed away. Mama seemed lost in grief; Fidelia and her brother felt relieved. All three abandoned themselves to quiet mourning beneath thick coats of sadness. Coming from a country where funeral services were provided free of charge, they felt their depression magnified by the financial side of Papa's death. The teacher forked out $2000, and the rest was covered by a $3400 loan from the Funeral Lending Company.

On their way to the funeral home after signing the required papers, Fidelia turned in the passenger seat and addressed Elliot: 'What happens when a lone wolf dies? When there's no one to pick up the tab?'

Steil shrugged. 'I don't know. Probably gets cremated at some municipal facility. No casket, no flowers, no funeral car.'

'Maybe they ship the ashes somewhere to be used as fertilizer,' Fidelia said sarcastically, 'or to make soap or something, recover the cost of the gas or wood or whatever they burn the corpse with.' She paused for a few seconds. 'This country is sick.'

'The world is sick,' the teacher observed, waiting for a green light. 'Some diseases are common to all societies, others need specific environments to thrive.'

'Right,' Fidelia concurred.

Papa was buried at Woodland the following morning. Bencomo had instructed Fidelia to take the rest of the week off, and Steil dropped family members at home before driving to the warehouse.

As Uri's replacement, he had come to realize how the boss's secretary can become the firm's Number Two – in fact, if not in appearances. Plotzher moved around carrying out Scheindlin's directives most of the time, so unless the minority stockholder and Number One were having private meetings, Uri must have known a lot more about IMLATINEX than the second in command. With the exception of documents and conversations in Yiddish, Steil had access to all company information. The teacher felt certain that if he paid attention, within a few years he'd know everything there was to know about this specific trading company and a lot about trading in general.

After 6.00, he and Scheindlin were alone in the office. Steil finished preparing the next day's bank deposit and was about to put the cash in the safe when the old man spoke.

'How was the funeral?'

The corners of Steil's mouth pulled down, and he raised

both eyebrows. 'Like all funerals, I guess. Grieving, silent people saying goodbye to a loved one.'

Scheindlin nodded. 'Someone else you know also went to his final resting place today.'

'Really? Who?' a mildy interested Steil asked.

'Mr Donald Steil.'

The teacher stared blankly at Scheindlin for a few seconds. 'Donald Steil?' he managed to ask.

'Your half-brother.'

Elliot reclined on the chair, rested his eyes on the desktop, ran both hands over his hair, and interlaced his fingers behind his head. When he lifted his gaze to Scheindlin, he was smiling widely. 'How did he die?'

'Somebody sent a letter bomb to his Baton Rouge apartment.'

The smile froze as implications surfaced; connections were swiftly made. He remembered Scheindlin's words: *We're going all the way*. Both hands came to rest on his lap. He swallowed the question that hung in his mouth. 'Who told you?' the teacher asked instead.

'Sadow called this morning, when you were at the funeral. The New Orleans lawyer handling the will issue for you called him.'

Steil noticed that Scheindlin was spying his reactions, and he tried to look unconcerned. 'It seems terrorist attacks are back,' he said. 'Are there any leads as to who . . . ?'

'The press speculates it may be linked to some case he was working on a few years back. He was one of the agents in the Branch Davidians affair.'

'Davidians?'

Scheindlin briefly outlined the 1993 Waco, Texas, catastrophe. By the time he finished, Steil had full control of himself. ' "God moves in mysterious ways, His wonders to perform," ' he quoted.

'You religious?'

'No. I picked that up from a hymn book at the Salvation Army Lodge. But I'll convert right now if the Lord punished this particular sinner.'

Scheindlin leaned back in his swivel chair. 'It's a risky profession. Agents make a lot of enemies, dangerous enemies, I'd say. Okay, Elliot, put the money in the safe, and go to your woman. She needs you. I'll stay a little longer.'

A minute later, the teacher was ready to leave. He approached Scheindlin's desk and waited for him to lift his eyes from some quotation.

'Yes?' the old man said.

'Sir, I want you to know that my current aspiration is to become as useful to you as Uri was.'

'Thank you.'

'Goodnight.'

The teacher left thinking how deceptive appearances can be.

*　　*　　*

Fidelia was anticipating short-term problems. She had mentioned Mama's unpredictable response to widowhood, the sharp reduction in family income, and Dani's increasing curiosity about his father. Bencomo seemed resigned to a dwindling practice, and she feared losing her job. She explained how her boss just sat at the office reading the paper, gazing out the window, visiting the restroom every two hours. Not a single new client had entered the office in February, and only nine phone calls had been received on Monday and Tuesday; she suspected they were from creditors. Their impatient tones snapped at her over the phone. Bencomo, she fretted, might retire any day, or suddenly die.

They now sat on the second-hand couch in the small living room, after cheese sandwiches and camomile tea. Mama was in bed in her room, two sleeping pills flowing through her bloodstream. Her son Mario, who usually slept on the couch they were sitting on, lay by Mama's side to keep her company.

Dani was sound asleep on his bed in Fidelia's room. The teacher hadn't mentioned Donald Steil.

'I can lend a hand,' he said. 'Give you something every month 'til you guys set it right.'

Fidelia shifted and stared at him, visibly annoyed. 'Listen, Elio, Mama is not a girl anymore. If what we just went through happens again soon, I'll ask for your help. If Dani or my brother become seriously ill, I'll holler loud for you, too. I have no one else to turn to. My uncle lives on a pension and food stamps. But for assistance with everyday life, no thank you. Sex almost always penalizes the man with a monetary obligation, which for me is as disgusting as penalizing the woman with silence and obedience. Let's be different. Let's act like loving friends, not like husband and wife. Let's be supportive of each other. I'm telling you about my financial worries to share with you what I can't share with anyone else. It was great that we started going out when I didn't know you were going to inherit a single dollar. What I want from you is understanding, not money. Not more money, to be precise. Do you follow me?'

The teacher clicked his tongue, shook his head sadly, and looked sideways. Fidelia took his hand.

'I guess it would be difficult to meet under more dramatic circumstances,' Steil said as if to himself, looking at the floor. 'When two people live the kind of experience we lived on that raft, something happens. A special, weird, difficult-to-explain bond develops. You don't forget. Even if you never see those people again, the scene and its players are forever etched in your memory. But we met after a few months, and we've shared some truly unforgettable moments. Your kidnapping and the death of your father have been the only unpleasant ones. The rest have all been wonderful.'

Fidelia remained silent while Elliot paused.

'But extreme views have pernicious effects, Fidelia. They lead to arrogance and intolerance. You're a proud person;

that's a plus. If I have to choose between a proud or a humble person, I'll take the proud one. You're also an ardent feminist, and I have nothing against that. Any woman who reads a little and lives a little should strive for a balanced relationship of the sexes.

'But don't go to extremes, don't become arrogant, for the worst dictators, the worst tycoons, the worst scientists and politicians and artists and sons of bitches are incredibly arrogant and intolerant. A common trait they share is not being able to stand criticism. Your feminism shouldn't lead you to underrate all men, to debase the love a man feels for you, to see subjugation every time he lends you a hand or gives you a present or opens a door for you.'

Pause. Silence. They both stared at the floor.

'I won't give you money if you don't ask for it. I won't ask you to marry me if you feel that would make us lose our . . . spontaneity. You want money, ask me for it. You want to marry me, ask me to. And if one day I conclude that you've become an extremist, you go your way and I'll go mine. Now, after speaking my mind, am I jilted?'

'No, you're not.'

Driving home a few minutes later, Elliot Steil wondered if he had made himself clear.

*   *   *

On Friday, March 17, after depositing IMLATINEX's cash and checks, Steil stopped by the Capital Bank office on Main Highway and retrieved some money, papers, and audiotapes from his safe-deposit box. The Eden Roc tape and $2000 remained.

A little before 7.00 p.m. that same day, he marched into the Kmart on Coral Way and spent close to $700 on shirts, pants, and underwear in different sizes. He also bought two pairs of shoes for $75 each. Around 8.30, he left everything in the hands of the grateful Salvation Army captain who ran the Men's Lodge.

From there the teacher drove to a house in Northwest Miami, where Señora Mercedes lived.

The Guatemalan mother of two kids had the misfortune of being married to a lazy, good-for-nothing Cuban who seemed allergic to work. She was also one of the first 'mules' taking dollars to Cuba after the government had authorized its citizens a few months earlier to possess, spend (at state stores only), or exchange the coveted greenbacks printed by its enemy. US Treasury regulations forbade remittances to the island, and a few Central and South Americans living in Miami were making a killing.

Blessed with third-country passports that made them immune from prosecution, mules flew to Havana from Cancún or Nassau on Fridays, delivered money, clothing, and pharmaceuticals on Saturdays, and returned to Miami on Sundays, in order to be back at their jobs on Mondays. The established rate was $15 for every $100 in cash or pound of pharmaceuticals, clothing, or shoes. Big mules landed twice a month at Havana's international airport, each with several hundred pounds of baggage and anything from $5000 to $10,000 in cash. So, a $4000 profit per trip was not uncommon. Netting about $500 per trip, Señora Mercedes was still a small mule, but her husband was finding customers for her at a rate that could make him a millionaire if the embargo lasted another ten years.

Steil told her that he had been recommended by Mario, Fidelia's brother, and that he wanted to send money to two friends. Mercedes looked upright and trustworthy sitting at her dining room table, as she carefully took down the names, addresses, and phone numbers of the Havana recipients. In the living room, her husband smoked, swilled beer, and watched TV. Mercedes explained that she would ask the beneficiaries to sign a receipt that she would show to the teacher as soon as she got back. If someone couldn't be found, the money would be returned to him, but she'd keep her 15 percent commission.

The teacher handed her $700 – $500 for Natasha, $100 for Sobeida, and $100 to cover Señora Mercedes' fee. She jotted down the bills' serial numbers and explained that she would give those same notes to Señor Elio's friends. He stood, shook hands with her, and left.

Before taking a shower that night, Steil burned in his kitchen sink the photocopies of the shipping papers and the audiotapes with the compromising information on Tony Soto and Ruben Scheindlin. He also destroyed the Sarasota tape. After scrubbing the sink clean and letting the water run for a minute, he dried his hands and lit one last match.

'Happy birthday to you,' he sang softly before blowing the match out.

He was now forty-five.